THE
SOLDIER
AND THE SLAVE

Andrew J. Luther

www.vanishing-goblin.com

The Soldier and the Slave

© 2016 by Andrew J. Luther

All rights reserved.

The cover of this novel is an original oil painting by Storn A. Cook. You can see more of Storn's artwork at www.stornart.com

ISBN: 978-09936502-3-9

Vanishing Goblin Inc.
www.vanishing-goblin.com

For Nathan

All the worlds are for you.

By Andrew J. Luther

Tales of the Undying Empire

Undying Empire: Rebellion

Acknowledgements: As always, I want to thank my wife, Pam, for her support.

Thanks to Bev once again for her valuable feedback.

And thanks to Storn A. Cook for a fantastic cover painting.

Chapter One

S WEAT ROLLED DOWN THE BACK OF KIED'S NECK AS HE shuffled forward, a dull clinking noise coming from the chains between the heavy manacles around his ankles as he moved. The sun was cooking him alive, searing the bare skin on his neck, torso, arms, and legs, and he could feel his strength draining out of him as he walked. Stopping to rest, even for a moment, would bring nothing but more pain.

To his left, a burly guard rode his horse at an easy pace, keeping an eye on the half-dozen prisoners heading for the looming gates. The guard's name was Gutter, as Kied had heard from the other men escorting the prisoners. The mounted man's short sword rested easily in his belt, and he carried the reins in one hand and a water skin in the other. Between the weapon and the water, the guard was an avatar of both life and death. To the slaves shuffling toward their fate, the man was a god, with the power to give succor with one hand, and inflict terrible pain with the other.

Kied knew there was no mercy coming from this "god." More than one slave had died along this march, and not a finger had been lifted to save any of them. Their bodies had been let loose from the chains and left at the side of the trail to bake in the sun until nightfall, when the few animals living in this desolate landscape would come out to fight over the remains.

Kied raised his head and squinted up the hill at the entrance to the prison. The walls were timber, cut logs tied together to make a simple palisade. A deep trench hugged the base of the walls, though this was less for defense than it was to make escape more difficult, if not impossible. He expected to find a similar trench on the inside of the palisade as well.

Gutter took a long swig from the waterskin and wiped his hand across his eyes. He saw Kied staring at the looming gate and snorted.

"Think you'll find some shade in there, eh?"

Gutter's words startled Kied. He looked up at the man, all muscle and menace, and then lowered his eyes to the ground once more.

"No, just looking."

"Oh, you'll get shade all right," the guard continued as if Kied hadn't answered. "You'll get so much shade you'll be begging us for a glimpse of daylight before you know it."

Kied kept his eyes on the ground and continued to move, concentrating on getting to the destination alive. Once the march was over there would be new threats to deal with, but he was focused on surviving one ordeal at a time. But the guard wasn't through with him yet.

"You ignoring me?" asked Gutter, and his booted foot shot out and slammed into Kied's cheek, knocking him off balance. He tried to spread his arms to recover, but his wrists were chained together in front of him and he couldn't compensate. He went sprawling in the dirt, and his sideways movement tripped up the slaves both in front and behind.

The prisoner ahead went down on his knees, while the one behind tripped over Kied's legs and also fell. Gutter bellowed a laugh at the hapless prisoners and took another swig of water from the skin.

Kied waited for the slave sprawled across his legs to move before he tried to stand. But the second guard must have figured he was trying to get some rest. The man dismounted, and Kied saw the boot coming for his chest an instant before it connected. He desperately tried to roll with the blow.

The guard's foot caught him in the ribs and nearly shattered bones with the force of the kick. Pain blossomed in his chest, but he knew he couldn't let it slow him down any further. He dragged his feet out from under the other slave and pulled himself upright as quickly as he was able. The other man wasn't nearly so fast.

Gutter dropped the waterskin into the dust as he slid off his horse—Kied watched a thin trickle of water pour out and immediately soak into the parched ground—and grabbed the prisoner by the hair. The slave screeched as he was yanked to his feet. The other prisoners tried to pull away as much as the chains would allow in a vain attempt to avoid the guards' attention. But Gutter had lost all his humor with the interruption of the march so close to their destination.

He punched and kicked each of the prisoners as they hurried past, his anger at the wasted water at his feet focused on the slaves under his control.

"Bunch of bastards, the lot of you! Look what you made me do!" he shouted at them.

The sound of hooves brought Kied's eyes back up from the ground. Four soldiers had emerged from the gate and rode their horses toward the group. They eyed the slaves as they approached, and one reined up in front of Gutter, who had finished his abuse of the prisoners and was now retrieving his waterskin.

"We'll take over from here," the new arrival said to Gutter, who was now climbing back up into his own saddle. Gutter grimaced and spat into the dirt.

"I'm responsible for this sorry lot until they cross the gates. So I'll make sure they get across if I have to drag them by their balls."

The soldier watched calmly as the slaves started trudging once more toward the opening in the palisade.

"Have it your way," he replied. "I figured you might want to ride ahead and get out of the sun."

Gutter snorted again.

"You're bein' mighty considerate of my comfort," he said. "What're you up to?"

The other guard frowned and shifted in his saddle. Kied thought he looked like a hard man, but not cruel. He was obviously more soldier than Gutter would ever be.

"We'll work them hard enough once they're inside," he answered. "They're not much use to us if you bring them in damaged, are they?"

Kied lowered his head and followed the other prisoners through the gates. A quick glance to one side told him he had guessed correctly—another trench hugged the inside of the walls. As the last of the prisoners filed past the gate into the main grounds of the prison, he heard Gutter gallop past them, swearing loudly. He raised his eyes to see the guard stop in front of the barracks and dismount. Gutter gave a last look at the line of prisoners, swore again, and stomped inside.

Kied lowered his head again, but not before getting a feel for the general layout of the prison buildings. He had also noted the generally professional quality of the soldiers stationed here. This could be both a boon and a problem. Professional soldiers were usually less capricious and cruel for the sake of cruelty. But they were also harder to manipulate, to cut deals with, to fool. Escaping from this place was not going to be easy.

The prisoners were marched into a low building made of rough stone blocks, each half the height of a man. Iron-bound doors lined the walls, small metal grates set into their center at head-height giving the guards a view into each cell. A staircase was carved out of the rock and led to another level below ground. At the bottom of the steps, Kied looked down a long corridor, crossed at regular intervals by other passages.

Countless cell doors lined these walls as well, and he knew this was where the bulk of the slaves lived their now-shortened lives. A small group of grizzled veterans unchained the line of prisoners and took them to individual cells.

Kied was led to a cell farther down the row from the rest of those who had arrived with him. The guard opened the door and pushed him firmly but without malice into the cell. In the darkness, he was unable to see any details while his eyes adjusted from the blazing brightness up above. He felt a manacle lock around his ankle, and then the guard unchained his wrists before stepping out of the cell.

"You got the luck of the draw," he said, grinning through a handful of rotten teeth. "Don't do nothin' to piss him off, now. I've got coins that say you'll survive to the end o' the week."

The man slammed the cell door and Kied heard the lock click.

He stood in the darkness for a moment until his eyes had adjusted enough to see another figure sprawled out on the floor at his feet. The other man was huge, and his head was covered by a mane of grey hair that completely obscured his face. The figure let out a loud snore, but didn't move a muscle.

Kied sat on the floor with his back to one wall. As he lowered himself, his eyes followed the chain attached to the manacle around his left ankle and discovered that it connected him to the manacle around his cellmate's right ankle.

Great, he thought to himself. *If the guard was saying what I think he was saying, I just got chained to a madman.*

*　　　*　　　*

THE CELL WAS SLIGHTLY LONGER THAN HE HAD EXPECTED, ENOUGH for his large cellmate to stretch out on the floor, though the man's feet and head touched opposite walls. It was just wide enough for the two men to sit or lie side-by-side. A rotting wooden bucket for their waste sat in a corner, the faint smell of feces occasionally breaking through the odor of unwashed bodies filling the small room. Flickering light from a torch in the corridor crept into the cell through the small crack at the base of the door.

Kied sighed and rubbed at his wrists where the manacles he had worn throughout the long journey to the prison had chafed his skin. The flesh of his head and back was tight and hot from overexposure to the sun. He gingerly touched his cheek to make sure the skin was unbroken—an infection here could be the death of him. He would have quite the bruise, but otherwise he seemed to be okay.

He was more concerned about his ribs. He ran his fingers over his chest, prodding gently to make sure nothing was broken. He knew his survival depended on his ability to work in the mines, and broken ribs would effectively put an end to that.

Sleep was also necessary, though he wasn't quite ready to fall unconscious regardless of how exhausted he was. His mind raced from thought to thought, memory to memory. By all rights, he should already be dead, like the rest of his command squad. Instead he was here, a punishment that would inevitably lead to his demise after all, but not before enduring a great deal of suffering.

This had been his father's "mercy."

He silently cursed his father. But he also knew the greater part of the guilt rested solely on his own shoulders. If not for him and his stubborn refusal to obey orders, his subordinates would still be alive. They were his responsibility, and he had failed them.

As much as his instincts were honed to identify the weaknesses here and exploit them in order to save his own life, Kied almost welcomed the punishment. Maybe the pain he would experience here might repay in some small way the debt he owed to his own men and women. Perhaps his own torture would assuage the guilt he felt.

He sat in the darkness, his eyes open and fixed on the sliver of light at the bottom of the cell door. As tired as he was, he felt like standing and pacing the small room. He knew, though, such movement would wake his cellmate, and that might have dire consequences. So he forced himself to sit and rest.

Even if sleep didn't come, at least his body could have the time it needed to rest and repair itself.

Why *couldn't* he have just followed orders? It wouldn't have been the first time he had ordered his soldiers to do something distasteful in the name of the Emperor. He had overseen the destruction of primitive villages when the barbarian tribes tried to fight back against the Empire's expansion. He had ambushed and slaughtered "enemy" soldiers who were doing nothing worse than defending their homeland from an aggressive invader.

But this had been different. These were Imperial citizens. They were people Kied had tried to believe he was protecting. And his command squad had expressed their own concerns ….

No, this time the Emperor was in the wrong. It was a treasonous thought, though hardly the first that had entered his mind. They had all agreed, the eight commanders coming to the same conclusion. They *couldn't* execute orders like these. It was wrong, not least because it was so very unnecessary.

The Emperor, of course, didn't see it that way. And the machinery of the Empire did not have room for dissension in the ranks. Such aberration must be cut out quickly and efficiently in case the infection spread and caused a wave of treasonous action across the breadth of the continent and into the colonies.

And who was Kied to question the decisions of the Emperor, an immortal being of vast power who had founded the Empire in a time of horrific death and destruction? He was nothing, really. Just a man who had found himself unable to take any more innocent lives.

Now, he was less than nothing, a prisoner and slave in the mines far to the north of Ythis, which was the heart of the very Empire he had betrayed with his refusal to follow the orders of his Legion.

But he also believed—aside from the guilt and anguish over his role in the deaths of his own people—that he had still been right. They had all been right to refuse those orders. There came a time when a person reached a line they could not bring themselves to cross. That line was different for every individual, but Kied and his command squad had reached theirs all at the same moment.

It had all been for nothing, of course. The rest were dead, he was now a slave, and the people they had refused to slaughter would die anyway. The army was still going to move into the area. Another commander would execute the orders Kied had rejected.

The innocent lives would still be destroyed.

So what value was his rebellion, really? What had it accomplished? What had he managed to really change?

Nothing, was the answer.

And yet, he was still alive. He was in a terrible position, surely, and his prospects were bleak, at best. But he hadn't lost his ability to think, to watch, and to plan. Perhaps he was deluding himself and his part in history was already over, but he wouldn't simply roll over and let himself waste away in this place.

It wasn't his pain that would pay the debt to his people. It was his life, and what he did with whatever was left to him. The Empire had tried to crush them, but as long as Kied lived, so did his rebellion.

He took a deep breath, his teeth gritted against the ache in his ribs.

This isn't the end, he promised them silently. *I swear to you I will not give up. I will escape this prison, and I will take the fight back to the Empire that turned its back on us. I will avenge you all, though I don't yet know how. But this I swear, your deaths will not have been in vain.*

An insidious thought crept into his mind, that he might not be making much of an oath. His own life hung by a thread. He was surrounded by threats, most likely chained to the largest danger to his long-term survival. His promise might be all for naught.

But Kied wasn't the kind of man to give up in the face of adversity. His own grief, his own guilt, could either destroy him or give him the strength he needed to face whatever might come his way in this terrible place. It was up to him to focus and use that strength to escape.

And then, once he was free, he could plant the seeds of a greater rebellion. He could nourish it and help it grow until it became a real threat to the twisted nightmare the Empire had become. Like a vine that grew in the cracks of a wall, slowly weakening the structure until it fell under its own weight, Kied would exploit the cracks that already existed in the structure of the Empire.

One way or another, he would survive. He had a new purpose, and beware to anyone who stood in his way.

Chapter Two

KIED AWOKE AS THE MANACLE BIT INTO HIS ANKLE AND HE was dragged backward, his belly scraping on the rough stones of the cellblock floor. He twisted over onto his back to stop his slide across the floor, but the pull of the chain was too strong, and the sudden awakening had thrown his mind into a panic.

He must have dozed off in the cell while sitting upright against the wall. He tried to focus on his surroundings and saw the huge form of the person who was dragging him along the corridor. He looked up to see the mane of grey hair, the chain gripped in the giant's huge fist.

His cellmate must have woken and been let out of the cell. Instead of waking Kied, the other man had simply grabbed the chain and walked out of the cell, dragging Kied behind.

He could hear a couple of voices laughing and realized a few of the guards were taking amusement at his predicament. He gritted his teeth and felt his blood boil.

The giant reached the steps leading up to ground level. As he began to ascend, taking the steps two at a time, Kied rolled to his side and grabbed the edge of the wall beside the staircase. He let the chain go slack for an instant, and then yanked his knee up, pulling on the chain with all his strength.

He knew he might pull the giant off balance and cause the other man to fall backwards down the stone steps, but Kied no longer cared if he injured the other man.

But the chain snapped taught—the manacle biting into the skin of Kied's leg—and the large man pulled up short but didn't fall or so much as take a single step backward. A collective gasp sounded from the slaves behind the men.

The giant let the chain slip from his grasp onto the steps and turned around.

The man's face seemed younger than his grey hair would indicate. Partially covered by a beard darker than the rest of his hair, the skin of his face was bronzed as if he regularly saw the sun—putting lie to Gutter's claims on the road yesterday—and his eyes were dark.

He wore no expression that Kied could read. As Kied slowly stood, the other man merely looked him up and down, moving only his eyes.

"What in the Abyss is wrong with you?" Kied snarled at him, his anger getting the better of his judgement. "You think it's funny to nearly wrench my leg from its socket? I don't care how big you are, try something like that again and you won't live long enough to regret it."

He heard one of the guards mutter "shit" and the clink of coins. He had been awake for less than a minute and already he was going to have what might be the last fight of his life. He focused on the big man and he readied himself for an attack.

His only asset might be their respective positions on the stairs. The giant was above him, but Kied had been trained to fight in unusual situations. As his head was below the level of the big man's waist, the most likely attack would be a kick. But as large as the giant was, Kied knew that once his foot left the stair, there would be a perfect opportunity to put the other man on his back.

But the giant didn't move. He just stared down at Kied. The strangest feeling came over Kied, as if the other man was looking not only at him, but *into* him. He felt the giant's gaze as an almost physical thing that opened him up and exposed his muscles, his skeleton, his heart, and his mind.

And then the huge man blinked, and the feeling disappeared. Without a word, he turned and started walking up the stairs, the chain no longer carried in his fist. Kied followed him before he could be yanked off his own feet again.

He reached the top of the stairs and expected the giant to turn and swing at him. But the man just walked toward the door that led outside. The two guards standing at the top of the stairs stared open-mouthed at the big man, and one grabbed a couple of coins out of the other's hand as Kied passed them, miraculously still alive.

They emerged into the night and he saw the sky above, full of stars with the moon Isri only a crescent above the horizon in the east and Shurrus high and half-full to the southwest. A chill hit him as he walked through the door and a shiver ran through his body.

A half-dozen soldiers stood outside, one holding a torch above his head. As the prisoners filed out of the building, the soldier turned and led them toward the side of the huge hill. The entrance to the mine was a shadowy maw, logs bracing the opening. A faint flicker of light came from within the mine, and Kied felt his chest tighten as he prepared to take his first steps into the hole that broke so many men.

They moved into the entrance to find a large cave holding racks of crude iron implements—mostly shovels and picks. Another handful of soldiers stood here, one handing out tools to the prisoners while the others watched for any sign of rebellion. But the slaves gathered their equipment without incident and were led further into the tunnel.

As they marched, one soldier began to order small groups to head into side tunnels spaced every few dozen paces. Eventually, there were perhaps ten slaves left in the main group. They reached the end of the larger tunnel where a stack of logs sat on the floor.

"Get to it," the guard muttered, and the giant walked over and picked up one end of a log and dragged it into place. As the big man lifted it into position to stand against the wall, Kied stepped in and hammered an iron spike into it to pin it to the rock. The giant said nothing, but eyed the spike and, apparently satisfied that Kied had done it correctly, walked back to grab another log.

At the same time, the other men began to attack the back wall with their picks. The stone was fairly brittle and came off in big chunks. Within minutes, as Kied and the giant put up the second wooden post, they had pushed the tunnel another few feet forward.

Kied wasn't sure how they were going to lift the log that ran as a cross-brace between the tops of the two posts, but the giant dragged it over into position and then knelt down beside it, working his hands underneath the bottom. With a low growl, the man slowly straightened, lifting the log up with no help from anyone else.

When he was fully upright, the giant gave a grunt and shoved the log up against the ceiling. Kied quickly stepped in and hammered two spikes into each end of the bracing log, and the giant stepped back and looked it over again. He glanced down at Kied, and then went back to work.

Kied continued to work beside the giant, the other man saying nothing. He didn't make any effort to start a conversation, needing to conserve every breath. Pushing the mine tunnel into the hill was back-breaking work. Finally, what seemed like many hours later, the guard came back and ordered everyone back to the entrance for their meal.

As they walked back along their path, Kied noticed a discoloration in the wood of one of the posts he was about to pass. He was just opening his mouth to point it out when the post suddenly shuddered and split into shards of flying wood. Two slaves who were right beside the post when it split flinched away from the flying splinters.

A great crack sounded as the cross-brace—no longer supported by the posts— started to pull away from the ceiling. Kied saw it would land on the heads of the two prisoners, and without thinking he dove forward and tackled the men from behind.

But as he hit the other men and knocked them out of the way of the falling beam, Kied reached the end of the chain that still bound him to the giant. He lost his footing, falling on his belly as the wooden brace plummeted down. A deafening crash sounded as the heavy wooden beam hit the floor of the tunnel.

Kied looked back and saw the beam had landed a finger's width away from his own foot, stretched out toward the giant on the other side of the collapse. Luckily for Kied, the rock ceiling did not also come down. He sneezed from the billowing dust in his face.

The giant stepped up and looked down at him, his leg pinned to the ground by the log lying across the chain that connected the two men. Faced by the big man he had threatened some hours ago, Kied now found himself completely helpless at the man's feet.

*   *   *

THE GIANT STOOD THERE, HIS LONG HAIR OBSCURING HIS EYES. Kied said nothing, waiting for the man to make the first move. He knew, though, that if the larger man attacked, there would be little he could do to defend himself.

The other man gave the slightest shake of his head, and bent down to grab the wooden beam. Grunting with the effort, he lifted the log off the chain and pushed it to one side. Kied pulled himself to his feet and faced his cellmate.

"Thank you," he said. "I wouldn't have been able to do that myself."

The giant pushed past Kied and marched up the tunnel, forcing Kied to follow. He looked over at the two men whose lives he had saved, but they did not meet his gaze. Apparently, there was no gratitude coming his way from them. Nor from the guards, who merely watched their prisoners walk up the tunnel.

After some water and a small amount of gruel, the prisoners were led back down to work. More hours passed as Kied and the giant worked side-by-side in silence. The main tunnel was extended deeper under the hill, and other teams of prisoners dug out side channels looking for undiscovered veins of precious silver.

By the time the guards called a halt to the work, Kied could barely lift his pick. His arms were numb, his back ached, and he was starving. But he forced himself to follow his large cellmate—he figured if he collapsed, he would simply be dragged back to the cell by the other man.

More than once, Kied stumbled and nearly fell, but managed to keep to his feet. The group of prisoners reached the main cave and Kied was dismayed to see the sun was already setting. After the countless hours in the dusky tunnels, he had been looking forward to a couple of minutes of sunlight.

Gutter's words came back to him.

You'll get so much shade you'll be begging us for a glimpse of daylight before you know it, he had said. Kied realized now it probably hadn't been an idle threat. By his estimation, they had worked more than two-thirds of a day.

It was likely the prisoners were only going to get a few hours of rest before coming back down into the mine. For the first time, Kied thought he might not be able to do it. By the time his next "shift" came around, he would be so sore and stiff that moving would be pure agony.

But he also knew he didn't have any choice in the matter.

As soon as they stepped into the cell, Kied lowered himself to the floor with a groan. There was no way he was going to have trouble sleeping this time. He would also have to make sure he didn't fall asleep sitting up again.

These thoughts tumbled around in his weary brain as he slowly became aware that the giant had not sat down. Kied looked up to see the other man staring down at him.

Oh, shit, he thought. *He hasn't forgotten about this morning.*

A fight in this cell would be short and bloody. While Kied was well-trained in close-combat techniques, he knew he was completely overmatched against this huge opponent. He tensed, ready for the first strike. Kied considered trying to stand, but it would likely be a wasted effort and precipitate the other man's attack.

Kied was prepared to turn that first attack—most likely a kick—into an opportunity to take his opponent off balance and gain the upper hand, even if only for a moment.

"They're not your men," the giant said in a rough voice, barely more than a whisper.

"W-what?" Kied asked, dumbstruck. These were the first words he had heard the man utter.

"You're not a commander here, and they're not your men. You risk your life for nothing."

Kied blinked up at the other man. "I wasn't about to just watch them die."

"You'll get used to it," the giant replied.

"Have you?"

The big man stood there in silence, staring down at Kied. Finally, he turned away and lowered himself to the floor without answering.

Of course he has, Kied thought to himself. *He's killed some of his cellmates himself.*

"Listen," he said to his cellmate. "I forgot about the chain linking us. I'll be more careful next time. I'm not here to get myself killed."

"If you're smart, there won't be a next time," the giant responded, his back to Kied. "We're not a squad, not a team. It's not "us" and "them." It is each prisoner for himself, here. You survive as best you can, as long as you can, and then you die, and they toss your body on the bonfire and that's the end of it."

"How long have you been here?"

"Long enough."

"So why are you telling me this? Aren't you helping me out by sharing this information?"

The other man lay there, silent. Kied heard the guards approach, and then the door was pulled open and two wooden bowls of gruel were unceremoniously placed on the ground by another slave. The door slammed shut and was relocked by the guards.

Kied picked up his bowl and tipped it up to his mouth. The gruel was barely warm, and thin, but it seemed like a feast to Kied at that moment. His cellmate sat up and picked up the other bowl. Kied noted the portion wasn't any bigger for the other man. He wondered how hungry his cellmate must usually be.

The other man slurped up the gruel in a few large gulps and tossed the bowl back on the floor in front of the door before lying back down. This time, he lay on his back and stared up at the ceiling.

"You work hard and keep your mouth shut," he said to Kied in the same low voice. At first, Kied thought the man was giving an order.

"That's why I'm telling you this," he continued. "I'm stuck with you until you die. You picked up what to do down there right away, and you didn't talk at me all night. There's some value in that. So I'm giving you this advice, but it's the only help you'll get, from me or anyone else."

"Okay," Kied said. "So if I'm going to survive, I just have to work myself into exhaustion, stay quiet, and help no one. Sounds great."

He paused, and the other man said nothing.

"Well, since this is probably the last words we'll say to each other, my name is Kied. In case you decide to kill me in my sleep for annoying you at some point, at least you'll know who you murdered."

He sat there for a full minute, but the giant had closed his eyes and said nothing else. Just as Kied was sure the other man was asleep, he uttered one last word.

"Rotos."

Seconds later, the big man started snoring. Kied could only assume the giant had said his own name.

Now that introductions were made, Kied felt the smallest bit safer. Rotos' attitude, however, didn't fill Kied with any confidence. He knew escape was going to be difficult, but if this place could break a man so badly, what chance did Kied really have?

The question was, would Kied be so exhausted each day that he'd be unable to take any opportunity he found to get out of this place? There was no one coming to rescue him—he had to do it entirely by himself.

He sighed and settled down to get what sleep he could.

Chapter Three

KIED USED THE METAL CHAIN TO SCRATCH ANOTHER GROOVE in the wall on his side of the cell. Another day gone, to add to the nineteen already past. Rotos was already snoring beside him—the big man could fall asleep almost instantly. Kied envied that ability, as he never felt he had enough rest.

He spent too much time thinking up ways to escape.

But now, after twenty days in his prison, he was no closer to getting out than he had been on day one. And the lack of decent food was slowly sapping his strength, taking away the few assets he still had in here.

Rotos rarely spoke to him, though he had turned out to be a decent enough cellmate. Kied occasionally wondered when he'd see the man's temper, something that apparently frightened the guards and the other slaves. Although, at this point, Kied believed Rotos approved of him enough that he was mostly safe from any violent outbursts.

Kied stretched out on the floor of the cell and closed his eyes. He tried to calm his thoughts so that he could drift off, but he couldn't stop thinking about the newest line on the wall.

Day number twenty.

Kied heard the door to the cell open, and he tried to open his eyes, but he couldn't seem to pry his eyelids apart. Someone stepped into the cell, but didn't say anything. Kied wondered if he was dreaming, though everything seemed so real and his thoughts were still clear.

"Rotos," a voice whispered. It was a man's voice, someone Kied had not heard before. The giant didn't respond.

"I know you're awake," the voice continued, slightly louder, in a mocking tone. "You've never been able to fool me, brother."

Brother? Kied tried to lift an arm, but his body didn't respond. *What in the Abyss is happening?*

"What do you want?" Rotos said in a low voice.

"I want the same thing I always want," the other voice answered. "I want to see if you're finally ready to leave this dump and come have adventures with me."

Kied heard Rotos push himself up into a sitting position.

"You're interrupting my sleep," he said.

"Yes, well, when you're awake, you're in that dreadful hole in the ground. I could get myself in and out easily enough, but sneaking *you* out would be a bit of a challenge."

"I'm not leaving," Rotos said.

Kied couldn't believe his ears. The man's brother had managed to sneak into the prison and was here to free Rotos, and the giant was refusing to leave. It didn't make any sense.

"Haven't you done your penance yet?" the other voice asked. "It seems to me you've been in here since the Fall."

That didn't seem right to Kied. It was spring now in the north. Could Rotos have only been here half a year? He acted as if he had been here forever.

"Even if I had, it wouldn't be nearly long enough," Rotos replied. "We've been over this before, Yarrian. I'm here because I choose to be here. I'll leave when I'm ready, not before. And I won't need your help to get out of here, either."

The other man's name is Yarrian, thought Kied. *He's the brother of Rotos.*

Kied repeated the name to himself a couple of times to cement it in his memory. He was sure he was not dreaming, but had no control over his body. This had never happened to him before. Perhaps Yarrian had drugged the food so that he could easily sneak in and out of the prison.

But if that was the case, why was Rotos apparently unaffected?

"Yes, but your method leaves death and destruction in its wake, brother. Which I thought was the whole point of ... this."

"The point of this is that I get to choose my punishment, not you."

Kied could hear anger in Rotos' voice, and something else … sorrow, perhaps.

"You disappoint me, brother. I had hoped you would come with me this time. Things are happening, there is change on the wind, and I would honestly love to share it all with you."

"I know you would," Rotos said, and there was genuine sadness in his voice. "I miss our … travels together. We'll have more of it again, but not yet. I'm not ready yet."

After what Rotos had said to Kied earlier, he was surprised to hear the other man making plans for the future. Kied had thought Rotos had been completely broken by being in this prison.

"You don't belong here, Rotos," Yarrian said seriously. "This is not the place for you. I worry that you're sinking into a pit you won't be able to crawl out of. What happens when we need you? When the time comes, will you push me away then, too?"

Rotos sighed.

"When you need me, I will be there. But the time *hasn't* come—it may never come. Besides, as long as I'm here, you know exactly how to find me."

"Well that's cold comfort," Yarrian replied. He paused, saying nothing for a moment. Finally, he took a deep breath.

"I think I've found her."

"What?" Rotos almost shouted.

"Keep it down!" hissed Yarrian. "Wake the guards and I'll have to leave. Even I can't keep them down if you start shouting."

"All right," Rotos said in his low voice again. "But talk fast."

"She called forth her power again," explained Yarrian. "This time I was close enough to really feel it. Didn't you?"

"No, but I spend most of my time down in the damned mine. I think the rock and … other things … down there block me from it."

"It came from the southeast, brother. I'm betting it was Ythis."

Rotos muttered something in a language Kied didn't recognize. The sound hurt his ears, as if he had suddenly dived into very deep water.

"Yes, well, if they've found her, then we're too late," Yarrian replied. "I'm keeping up hope that she's still free. But it's been years since she opened herself to her birthright. Who knows how long it'll be before she does it again?"

Rotos said nothing.

"Come with me, brother!" Yarrian very nearly begged. "We'll go to Ythis and find her together. Can you imagine it, the three of us together again?"

"Just like that, eh? We'll just walk into Ythis and find her and walk right out again? You don't think we'll attract any attention, the two of us being together?"

"So we just give her up to them?"

"Of course not!" Rotos growled. "But I'm also not going to get her killed. *She doesn't remember*, Yarrian. We can't march into the city and start a war with those two. We'll all end up in their hands, or dead. For real, this time."

Yarrian and Rotos were both silent. Kied waited, listening intently. He didn't understand any of this, but he desperately wanted to remember it.

"So what do I do, brother?"

"Go to Ythis. Do it your way, the quiet way. You'll get in there without them knowing, and if she's in that damned city, you find her. Bring her out and come back here."

"And then you'll join us?" Yarrian asked, excitement in his voice.

"I'll join you. She's my responsibility, after all."

"That makes me glad, my brother. I will find her, and then return."

"Good. Now get out and let me sleep. And don't play any tricks on the guards this time—it's us slaves who get punished when something happens."

"Just one more thing, brother. I see you have a new cellmate."

If Kied had been in control of his body, he might have tensed up at the way Yarrian said those words. There was something in the way he spoke, not mocking this time. Kied heard an implied threat somewhere in the man's tone.

"What about him?" Rotos asked.

"He's awake. He's been listening to us."

Rotos snorted. "I wouldn't think that was possible."

"Neither would I. But apparently it is. And he has. I don't think he can move, but he's aware. How long has he been here with you?"

"Less than a month."

"Shame," said Yarrian. "Well, at least he won't destroy himself in the mines before he dies."

Kied heard the scrape of a blade on a sheath and Yarrian stepped over to him.

"Leave him," Rotos growled.

"Brother, he can *hear* us. He has to die."

"I told you to leave him, and I meant it. He'll die soon enough, but it'll be by his own actions, not yours."

"Brother—"

"He doesn't know what he's heard, and he's chained to me. If he proves to be a threat, I'll kill him myself. But for now, he lives."

Kied wanted to scream out, to alert the guards, but he was completely helpless. One thrust with that blade, and it would all be over.

But Yarrian stepped back to the door.

"I'll never understand why you protect them. But I respect you too much to go against your wishes."

"That's because you know better than to cross me again. I still remember, Yarrian."

There was silence for a moment, and then Yarrian whispered one last time.

"Farewell, brother. I will return soon enough."

Kied heard the door close and lock. His fingertips began to tingle. He heard Rotos sit up and lean over toward him.

"When you get the feeling back in your limbs, don't wake me up and ask any questions. Just forget everything you heard here tonight if you want to survive another day."

Rotos lay back down and was soon snoring softly. A few minutes later, Kied's eyes opened, and he found himself able to sluggishly move his arms and legs.

But as much as he had burning questions for Rotos, he heeded the large man's advice. And, exhausted as he was, sleep overtook him moments later once more.

*   *   *

TIATH SHIFTED HIS SCABBARD AND EYED THE DOCKS, SEEKING THE man who had been sent to meet them. The deck continued to roll under his feet, the small ship dancing on the river that was over-flowing from the spring runoff up in the mountains. He glanced at his comrades, all packed and ready to disembark as soon as the ship was docked.

It took some time for the sailors to get the ship into position and catch the mooring posts with their ropes. The crew was barely ad-equate, Tiath noted. But then, the Captain of this vessel wasn't ex-actly known for his great success, and he would have to take what-ever crew he could get.

More important to Tiath, the man who owned and operated this ship knew how to keep his mouth shut. A few extra coins in his palm, and he'd forget all about Tiath and his people.

With a final bump that wasn't as gentle as the Captain probably would have preferred, the ship came to rest beside a dock and was lashed to the posts with something approaching speed. One sail-or pulled the wooden pin, and the gangplank dropped to hit the deck with a crash. Tiath grimaced, but then realized such a sound wouldn't be unusual here.

Theirs was now the only ship at berth, the other two docks being empty. The town, Chinare, wasn't large, despite being the last point at which travelers in the north could find a ship able to take them down-river toward the coast. Still, there were enough Imperial citi-zens passing through here on a regular basis that his own arrival was hardly noteworthy.

Tiath gestured to his companions and they followed him down the gangplank to the dock. He was glad to be back on solid ground—he hated traveling by boat. At least he hadn't gotten sick this time.

Without needing to be told, his comrades spread out into a loose formation that kept them far enough apart to appear to be separate travelers, but close enough that they could all quickly come to each other's assistance if trouble appeared. A low whistle sounded to Tiath's left and he glanced sideways to see Azam flick his head toward an alley mouth on the other side of the wide street that ran parallel to the docks.

Tiath looked and saw a man peering out of the alley, a rough-looking thug dressed in tattered clothes. The man looked at Tiath and made a gesture with his fingers, the signal that he was Tiath's contact in Chinare.

Tiath nodded once and crossed the street, followed by Azam. The others appeared to hang back, though Tiath knew both Pasill and Deylista were now making their way around the block toward the other end of this alley. It paid to be prepared for any eventuality.

The man stepped back into the alley as Tiath approached, and he followed his contact into the shadows.

"What's your name?" the man asked. He was shifting from foot-to-foot and glancing out at the docks every few seconds.

"You know who I am," Tiath replied. "Are you expecting some-one else?"

His question caught the contact off guard. The man shook his head and wiped the sweat off his brow with one forearm.

"No, I just … I never did this before."

Great, Tiath thought. *They must have put someone brand new here since the message was sent to me.*

This was going to make things more difficult. He couldn't trust this man to remain discreet once Tiath was out of Chinare.

"Where is it?"

"Where is what?" the man asked. Tiath blinked at him and barely kept himself from exploding at this bumbling, incompetent fool.

"The map," he snarled. "Do you have an up-to-date map for me or not?"

The man nodded and reached into his vest and pulled out a tat-tered piece of parchment. It had obviously been exposed to some rain recently, and the edges were torn and ragged.

Tiath took the parchment and unfolded it to reveal a map of the mountainous terrain northwest of Chinare. A series of lines were drawn on the map, with letter and number combinations written at each end in neat strokes. Tiath understood the coded message and folded the parchment before tucking it into his own clothing.

"How many days since you got this?"

The other man thought for a moment and then said "Six?" as if he was asking a question.

Or guessing.

Tiath kept his hands from balling up into fists and took a deep breath.

"It's been some time since I was last here. I need a rundown of Chinare. Where is the best place for me and my team to stay? We need somewhere the proprietor won't ask too many questions or make note of our comings and goings. We've got to get some supplies, and horses, and then we'll head out."

"I can get what you need for you," the contact offered.

"No, I've got a different job for you. Tell me about Chinare."

The other man recounted what he knew of the town, which included a lot of detail that held no interest for Tiath. But he let the man ramble until he got the information he needed.

"Is there anything I need to know about the horse trader?"

The contact shook his head.

"I don't think so. I don't really know him."

Tiath nodded and cleared his throat, coughing three times.

"So what job do you have for me to do?" the man asked.

"The only thing you're good for," Tiath replied. "Bleeding out in an alley."

The man looked at Tiath, dumbfounded, and then he realized the threat and reached for a knife hidden in his clothes. But Tiath merely stepped back away from him as Deylista came out of the shadows behind the contact and wrapped an arm around his jaw.

A glint of steel in her fist led to a bright splash of red on one wall as the contact's throat was opened from ear to ear.

The man dropped to his knees, grabbing at the wound in his throat as if he could hold it closed with his own fingers. But Deylista took a fistful of his hair in one hand, and with the other drove the point of her blade into the back of his neck. The man's eyes rolled up into his head and she let him fall on his face on the alley floor.

"You and Pasill go to the horse trader and get mounts for us. We'll round up the supplies and meet you at the northeast corner of the city at dusk."

"We can hide the body," Deylista suggested.

"It's not that. I was hoping we had made up some time on the river, but it appears we're still late. I need to get some miles under us before I can rest."

She nodded once and turned away to head back up the alley to the next street. Tiath stepped out into the sunlight and spoke to Azam in a low voice.

"I don't like this. The contact was incompetent, as if no one has operated up here in years."

"You think we're being set up?" Azam asked.

"No, not that. But this has the feeling of someone meddling in our affairs. But how can they do that when no one knows we exist?"

Azam said nothing, staring out at the bustle on the dock as the ship's contents were unloaded. He had been with Tiath long enough to know when the other man was asking a rhetorical question.

"Come on," Tiath said finally. "It's time to do some shopping."

Chapter Four

KIED PUT HIS WOODEN BOWL DOWN AND GLANCED OVER at Rotos. The giant was eating slowly tonight, his mind somewhere else entirely. This was the third time this had happened since the visitor had come into the cell seven nights ago.

Rotos blinked and seemed to come back to himself. He looked down into his bowl and then tipped it up and began to eat the runny stew in earnest.

"Rotos," Kied said in a low voice. Rotos continued to slurp up his dinner until he was done, and then he lowered the bowl and looked Kied in the eyes.

"No," he said.

"No, what?" Kied asked.

"I already know what you will say. So hold back. I warned you once, and that's more than most would get."

"This is ridiculous," Kied answered. "Yes, you threatened me. And I've kept quiet about it. But I can't do that anymore. I need some answers."

"No."

"By the Abyss, Rotos, that man was your brother! And he just walked right in here as if he had a key and all the guards were off sleeping in their barracks. Just who *are* you?"

Rotos shook his head and grabbed the chain that linked them.

"You think this gives you the right to know anything about me? You should have been asleep along with everyone else. But you had to fight it off and listen to us. Maybe I should have just let him kill you."

"Maybe you're right," Kied snapped back at him. "It probably would have saved all of us a bunch of trouble. But you didn't let him kill me. And don't tell me you didn't know I wouldn't be able to just forget about what happened. You may not want to get out of this place, but I bloody well do."

Rotos barked out a laugh.

"You think he might help you escape? You're better off in here than owing any favors to that one."

"Really? Why is that? How about you tell me something of the man who wanted me dead simply because I overheard your conversation."

Rotos lowered his eyes to the floor. When he spoke, his voice was even lower than usual.

"I can't. His story is his own to tell."

Kied wanted to scream in frustration. Every day that passed, he felt any chance of him ever escaping this place become more remote. His freedom was getting farther and farther away, and soon only his death would release him from this prison.

But the brother of Rotos—Yarrian—represented a way out for him. He was curious about the man, as well as *this* man to whom he was chained, but ultimately none of that was important compared to the chance they could help him escape.

"I have to get out of here, Rotos."

Rotos raised his eyes to Kied's face once more.

"They all do."

"But not you, right? You're here by choice."

Kied wasn't sure what happened, but suddenly the cell got smaller. Rotos didn't move, but his *presence* expanded until Kied felt as if he was being pushed back against the wall of the cell.

"You are trying my patience, Kied. My choices are mine. They do not concern you, or Yarrian, or anyone else. I will not be questioned by a mor—"

Rotos choked off, and snapped his mouth closed. He continued to glare at Kied, anger radiating from him in waves. Kied's skin felt hot, as if he was sitting too close to a blacksmith's furnace. He could feel himself getting dizzy, and stars began to flash in front of his eyes.

And just as suddenly as it had appeared, the strange feeling drained away, and it was just Rotos sitting in the cell across from him. Kied gasped for breath and leaned back against the wall.

Rotos had been saying something, but Kied couldn't focus on it now. He wondered if there had been something wrong with the stew, as he felt weak and feverish.

"I ... I don't feel well," he mumbled.

"Get some sleep," Rotos answered. "It will pass."

Rotos turned and moved to lie down, but something nagged at the back of Kied's mind. They had been discussing something important, and it was right on the tip of his tongue ....

"No," he said, shaking his head. "We were ... talking about something."

Rotos froze and turned to look at Kied. The expression on the giant's face jogged loose a memory, of Rotos being angry about ... something.

"We were talking about ... we were talking about ... you."

And with a rush, it all came back. Kied gagged as his stomach heaved. He felt as if he had been spun around in circles a dozen times. He latched onto the thought of Rotos and ... *Yarrian*.

"What did you ... do to me?"

Rotos sat back up.

"Who are you?" the giant asked Kied.

"Answer my ... question first."

"I didn't do anything to you, not on purpose. You made me angry. It's not healthy for you."

The thought spun in Kied's head. He still couldn't remember the last thing Rotos had said to him before this feeling hit, but he thought he now remembered everything else.

"You should be asleep," Rotos said, not unkindly.

"So I can let another day pass me by? I'm getting weaker, Rotos. I'm getting weaker, and I haven't figured out how to escape yet."

"You're stronger than you think. But it doesn't matter—you're not going to escape," the giant responded. "No one escapes from here."

"I swore an oath, Rotos. I swore an oath to the people who trusted me to keep them safe. I failed them once and I can't fail them again. I need your help. I can't do it alone, but you have a way to get out of here. Please, just help me."

Kied was pretty sure Rotos wasn't angry anymore. Instead, he seemed deeply saddened by Kied's words. He took a deep breath and let it out slowly.

And then he looked Kied directly in the eyes.

"I can't," he said.

Kied felt despair well up in his chest. He was having trouble getting a full breath.

"Why?" he gasped at Rotos. "It'll cost you nothing. Why won't you help me?"

Rotos lowered his gaze, and his shoulders fell. The giant seemed to deflate in front of Kied. His white hair hung limp around his face, making a cave out of which only his eyes were visible.

"I've taken an oath as well," he said. "We have each failed to do what needed to be done. And this is our punishment. Yours is fleeting and will be over soon enough. Mine will go on much, much longer."

Kied stared at his cellmate, fighting the urge to strike out at the man. He held no illusions about how well he'd do in such a battle. But he wouldn't just roll over and die.

"Keep your secrets, then, you bastard," he snarled at the other man. Rotos looked at Kied and raised his eyebrows.

"Or maybe I've got it wrong," he continued, pushing further. "Maybe you're *afraid* to get out of here."

Kied knew that if he crossed a line, Rotos might well murder him right here in this cell. But his self-control was gone, and now anger was all that was keeping him going. He knew he was making a mistake before his next words came out of his mouth, but he was beyond caution.

"Maybe you're a coward," he spit.

Despite his certainty that Rotos would react poorly to such an insult, the big man was a blur as he moved, and all Kied had time to register was a mighty fist flying toward his face. There was a flash of pain as he lost consciousness.

The Soldier and the Slave

*　　　*　　　*

LAITA NASCHECT REINED IN HER HORSE AND WAITED FOR THE TWO soldiers on patrol to draw near. Rather than stopping just inside shouting distance, they rode right up to Laita and her escort.

Sloppy, she thought to herself. *I'll need to bring some discipline back into this unit.*

"Halt and identify yourself," one of the soldiers demanded. He was a young man, his short beard sparse and his armor ill-fitting. If she had wanted, Laita could easily have put a thrown blade into his throat at this distance.

"I am Commander Laita Naschect," she said in a clear voice. "I've been assigned to take command of this operation."

The two soldiers looked at each other, and the younger one urged his horse to within arm's reach of Laita.

"I'll need to see your papers, ma'am."

Laita pulled her identification from the leather pouch at her side and handed them to the soldier. He looked at them carefully and then handed them back.

"Welcome, commander. I can escort you to the camp if you'd like."

Laita turned to Namal, seated casually on his horse at her left side. He had been with Laita since the beginning, refusing all promotions and offers of transfer. Not that she wanted to be rid of him—she knew the value of having a veteran at your back.

"I can make my own way from here," she said to him. "Take these two and give them five lashes for lack of discipline, and then send them back to their sergeant. You and Saeda ride the perimeter of the camp and see how secure we are."

The two soldiers who had ridden to greet her started to sputter as Laita turned to her other two companions. She had been allowed to split up a squad and take four hand-picked soldiers with her. Namal, Saeda, Bor and Ellend had come with her across half the Empire, and she trusted them as much as she trusted herself.

"You'll stay and assume these men's duties until I can send someone to relieve you," she said to Bor and Ellend, who nodded and dismounted, Ellend pulling a long leather strap out of her saddlebag.

The howls of the two soldiers followed Laita as she rode on toward the camp. She was challenged only once more, by a sentry who understood his duty and called to her at an appropriate distance. Though she told him she could find the way, he ordered another soldier to escort her to the command tent.

That one is sergeant material, she thought to herself. It never hurt to plan ahead for the inevitable desertions, deaths, and demotions that would happen during a campaign.

The command tent was situated on a low hill, providing a good view of the overall encampment. Laita rode up the hill and dismounted in front of the main tent's entrance. Two legionnaires stood at attention in front of the opening, their burnished breastplates gleaming in the sunlight.

Handing the reins to a young slave, she stepped up to the soldiers.

"Commander Naschect, here to see acting-Commander Adai." One of the soldiers nodded, and then turned and stepped into the tent. The other soldier did not step out of her way so that she could follow. Despite her initial impression, it appeared that all discipline had not dissolved since the removal of—.

Laita swore under her breath. The last thing she needed was to think about *him* right now. Deep down she was sure her assignment to this post was some sort of huge mistake, considering her history. But if that was the case, no one had caught it and she was here now.

The legionnaire came out of the tent and saluted Laita smartly. His twin responded instantly, stepping aside and saluting as well. She returned their salute and walked forward into the tent.

The interior was dim and Laita's eyes were still dazzled by the bright sunshine outside. She heard the rapid shuffling of feet as the tent's inhabitants stood at attention at her arrival, though she could not immediately make out anything more than shadows.

Laita returned the salute once more and then muttered "at ease" as she willed her eyes to hurry up and adjust. She silently berated herself for not thinking of this as she stood there. First impressions were important, and Laita abhorred the idea of appearing helpless to her subordinates on their initial meeting.

A man stepped up to her and she could make out the smile on his face, though the details were still obscured.

"Commander, welcome to the Twelfth. I hope your journey wasn't too difficult."

The man's voice was smooth and his bearing friendly, though perhaps a bit too relaxed. Laita pegged him as a noble who had gotten an easy commission. She doubted that voice had ever screamed orders at raw recruits or called for reinforcements to avoid being overrun by a barbarian horde from the mountains in the northwest.

"My apologies for the dimness," he continued. "We're in the middle of an unexpected heatwave, so we're avoiding lighting the braziers unless we must."

"Why have you not raised some of the wall flaps?" she asked.

"The wind around here is too gusty for that," he responded. "Our papers take flight as soon as we try to air it out."

Laita nodded and looked around the tent, now that her eyesight had adjusted enough to see the rest of the inhabitants. Four men and two women sat on folding camp chairs around a table covered with maps and other parchments. They appeared to be in conference but Laita could tell they were eavesdropping on her and acting-Commander Adai.

"Listen, commander—"

"Please call me Chalaj," he said, interrupting her. "We tend not to be that formal when it's just the command squad in here."

Laita mentally counted to five before responding. He was pushing her, deliberately, so that he and the others could get their measure of her. Considering how most of them had come into their current positions, Laita felt like she had stepped into a nest of vipers.

She wasn't a fresh-faced recruit, however. Laita knew better than to play his game.

"You're relieved," she said. He blinked at her, unsure what she meant.

"Your pardon, I'm—"

"You're relieved," she repeated, interrupting him just as he had done to her. "There's no reason to prolong it. I'm used to getting up to speed quickly, and you will stick around for a couple of days until

I no longer need you."

She saw his eyes narrow slightly, and she realized he had taken offense at her comment. That was bound to happen sooner or later, and now she had controlled the manner in which it occurred. It almost made her smile.

"Commander," he said, putting on an ingratiating smile. "Surely you wish to meet with Ambassador Seaphon before you assume responsibility. As you have no doubt heard, this is a delicate mission, of utmost importance to—"

"All the more reason to clarify the command structure as soon as possible," she said, interrupting him a second time. "I am aware of what happened here, Commander Adai. There's been enough confusion, enough dissention, and enough temporary measures. It's time for stability."

Chalaj opened his mouth once more, but this time she cut him off before he could utter a sound.

"Your objections have been noted, acting-Commander Adai. As I said, you're relieved. You may stay to contribute to the briefing, or if you feel you need time to clear your things from my quarters, you can do that now."

She could see the venom in his eyes as he realized she had just kicked him out of the command tent—he would need to make arrangements to sleep somewhere else now. Laita knew she had taken the full measure of him. This one wouldn't fight directly. No, he would try to undermine her behind her back.

As she stepped around Chalaj and turned to the others seated around the table, she silently thanked the gods for the four she had brought with her. Laita was definitely going to need trustworthy allies with *this* group at her back.

Chapter Five

K IED KNEW IT WAS COMING. THE GUARDS IN THIS PLACE—
like in most remote prison outposts—were just corrupt
enough that the boundary between solider and slave had
become blurred in certain areas. The guards had come to an understanding with some of their prisoners, and favors were exchanged
that benefited both sides. And once that balance of power shifted,
became more even, nearly anything could happen.

The slave with the blonde hair and dark eyes had been watching
Kied for the last week or so. At first, Kied had thought it was because of the large bruise on his face where Rotos had punched him,
knocking him unconscious. But then he had seen the slave whispering to others while they worked, and now there were at least half a
dozen who eyed him constantly.

As an experienced soldier himself, Kied understood what was
happening. One or more of the other slaves had taken a dislike to
him. Perhaps they had wagered with the guards about how long
Kied would last chained to Rotos, or perhaps they were jealous
of how well the two men worked together. Ultimately, the reason
didn't matter.

What mattered was that they were working themselves up to the
point where they would attack him. By the time Kied realized what
was happening, he had also come to understand that the guards
would be no protection for him. At some point, favors would be exchanged, and the guards would disappear from the tunnel in which
Kied was working so that the other slaves could gang up on him.

Kied held no illusions that Rotos would come to his aid. The man had not said a word to him since the night he had struck Kied in the face. If he was being honest with himself, he understood he was lucky Rotos had only punched him. The huge man could have done a lot worse.

Despite that small mercy, however, Rotos refused to engage further with Kied. Whatever his secrets were, he was going to keep them to himself.

In the last week, Kied had tried to make overtures towards the guards in the hope that establishing any kind of trade of favors with them might present him with an opportunity he could use to escape. But whenever he tried to talk to any guard, the man would nervously eye Rotos and then brusquely order Kied back to work.

Apparently, as long as he was chained to his cellmate no one was going to deal with him.

And now Kied was facing an imminent attack by other slaves, for some transgression for which he was completely unaware. And tonight, slightly more than a week after Kied's last confrontation with Rotos, and thirty-four days after he had entered this prison, he found himself facing a group of angry slaves.

He and Rotos had been expanding the tunnels again, a job to which they were often assigned. They had developed a routine that didn't require any talk—a good thing since Rotos would not speak to Kied anymore—and they had driven deep under the hill to find two new veins of silver. From the look of things, it was unlikely Kied would be around long enough to find a third.

He had just finished hammering in a spike to brace one of the uprights when he noticed that the two guards who usually watched this work crew had vanished. The slave with the blonde hair was watching Kied, a look of pure malice on his face. As soon as Kied locked eyes with him, the other slave straightened up and spoke.

"What do you think you're staring at?" he demanded. The other slaves, about a half-dozen in all, stopped what they were doing to face Kied.

"I could ask the same thing of you," Kied replied. "You've been watching me for a solid week. Am I that interesting to you?"

The slaved hefted his pick and took a step forward. The others began to cluster closer together, as if they needed the reassurance of being in a pack to go through with this. Rotos turned and sat down on the floor of the tunnel, his back to the wall, and closed his eyes.

Kied cursed under his breath. The big man wasn't going to help out at all.

"I know who you are," the slave snarled at Kied. "You're a soldier, a legionnaire. I saw you at Orm'tai."

Suddenly, it all made sense. The province of Orm'tai had always been an uneasy subject of the Empire, and the people there were restless. A leader had arisen from the common people and preached freedom from the Emperor's rule. It had been a futile gesture—the province was surrounded on all sides by Imperial-controlled lands and there was no way the people would have been able to establish and maintain their independence.

But the leader was eloquent and fired the imaginations of the populace. An uprising had occurred, and the legions were brought in to pacify the citizenry. Kied's contingent was responsible for taking the leader's stronghold and capturing the man who had caused all the trouble. Kied's legionnaires were efficient, overwhelming, and completely without mercy. Ultimately, three-quarters of the men and women inside the stronghold had been killed in the fighting, and the leader himself had died on the spear points of Kied's own squad.

This slave must have been inside the stronghold, one of the few survivors of that battle. And he had seen Kied, had watched him giving orders to the men and women of his contingent. Kied's face had become the face of the enemy, and now fate had conspired to put the two men together in the same prison at the same time.

Kied understood there was no way to avoid this fight. He couldn't intimidate them, or talk them down. He represented the Imperial Legion to these men, a force of law that had put most of them in here. Kied would have to fight for his life—there was no other way out.

"Yes," he said. "I was at Orm'tai. I killed your friends and fellow rebels, and tonight I'm going to kill you."

He saw the effect his words had on the blonde slave. The man lost any semblance of thought as blind rage twisted his features. He screamed and charged at Kied, the man to which he was chained hurrying to keep up. The other slaves all surged forward, but were more hesitant to engage the man who had been a soldier and now seemed so confident.

But Kied's words had been calculated, and the slave's anger made him reckless. Kied easily avoided the clumsy swing of the pickaxe and then drove his foot into the side of the man's knee, a horrid snapping sound filling the tunnel. The slave's unfortunate cell-mate tried to take Kied by surprise with his own weapon, but Kied stepped inside the swing and drove the iron spike in his hand into the man's neck.

The second slave fell back, dropping his pick as he grabbed at the spike while choking on his own blood. The sight of the blood in the flickering light of the torches had the wrong effect. Instead of intimidating the other slaves, it drove them into a frenzy, and they charged at Kied in a screaming mass.

Only the cramped confines of the tunnel and the fact that the slaves got in each other's way kept them from killing Kied on the spot. The few with picks were unable to swing them without hitting their own comrades, while Kied could attack in any direction without worrying about who he struck.

Despite the momentary advantage, however, the numbers prevailed. Kied was dragged down to the floor as the slaves rained blows upon his body and head. He continued to strike out, injuring at least a couple of slaves before his arms were pinned to the ground. The blonde slave, moaning in pain, dragged himself onto Kied and wrapped his hands around Kied's neck.

Kied knew he was going to die. There was no way to break the slave's grip on his throat. With his air cut off, he began to see dark spots and felt his consciousness starting to slip away. He knew he would not wake up.

And then the pressure on his throat was suddenly released as the blonde slave was lifted up and tossed to one side, his face transforming from an expression of hatred to one of surprise. Rotos stood over Kied and the pile of slaves, and he grabbed two men by their hair and slammed their heads together with great force. A sickening crunch and spurting blood announced their demise.

Within seconds, Rotos had hammered the remaining slaves into unconsciousness, or thrown them off Kied with obvious ease.

Kied coughed and gagged as he sat up. He looked up at Rotos, and the big man just stood there, staring down at him.

"Th-thank you," he choked out, but Rotos said nothing. He merely raised his eyes and watched the guards come running into the tunnel, their swords drawn and pointed at Kied and Rotos.

*   *   *

AMBASSADOR SEAPHON STOOD AS COMMANDER NASCHECT ENTERED the tent.

"Welcome, commander," he said, smiling at her. He stepped around the small table he used as a workspace and held out his hand to her.

"Hello, Ambassador," she replied as she shook his hand. "It's a pleasure to meet you."

"Please, call me Zartay, at least when we're meeting privately. Since we're going to be working closely together over the next few months, I see no reason to stand on formality when we're not in front of the others."

She returned his smile, though it did not reach her eyes. She was being cautious, an approach Zartay could appreciate.

"Laita," she said.

"Please, make yourself comfortable, or as comfortable as one can in these surroundings," he joked as he waved her toward one of the camp chairs. "I imagine you've had a long, difficult journey. Can I get you something to drink?"

"I'm fine, thank you."

He watched as she adjusted her sword and took a seat. He sat across from her and folded his arms on the table, covering the map that spread across its surface. Zartay hadn't been sure what to expect with the new commander, and he saw it was going to take some time to get her measure.

Acting-Commander Adai had come running to Zartay yesterday afternoon to inform him about the circumstances of Laita's arrival. Chalaj had been livid, and it had taken some time for him to calm down enough to give a full account of his first meeting with the woman who was now in charge of the Second Contingent.

Zartay was concerned Laita might become a problem, and he had no desire to deal with another difficult commander right now. He hoped he could use his considerable diplomatic skills to get her onto his side. The question was, how pliable might she be?

"You are no doubt eager to get the full briefing on our mission."

Laita nodded again. "I am," she said.

"Very well. As you no doubt discovered yesterday when you arrived, the lieutenants under your command are not aware of the details of our mission. Their detachments have been tasked with establishing the base camp and preparing for mobilization, but that's about it. Even acting-Commander Adai wasn't privy to the goal of our operations here."

"I admit I was somewhat surprised he had not been given a more extensive briefing," Laita replied.

Zartay wasn't about to tell her that Chalaj had begged, cajoled, and pleaded for more information. The ambassador had kept the acting commander in the dark, however. Knowledge was power, and Zartay preferred to keep as much of that power in his own hands as possible.

"Our mission is highly delicate, and the details must remain confidential for as long as possible. Those are my orders, and now you are bound to them as well. The lieutenants are to know only what they need to know to manage their detachments."

Laita nodded a third time. She obviously understood the chain of command and the need for compartmentalizing information. She took a quick look around the tent, noting the privacy screen that separated the tent into two rooms.

"Is this a secure place to talk?" she asked. "I see that soldiers are posted outside in a wide perimeter around this tent."

Zartay smiled again. "It is. While I do have two aides who work with me, they are both out on errands that will keep them away for the next hour or more. The soldiers are outside of earshot, and will prevent anyone from approaching while we are meeting."

"I see," Laita said in a low voice, apparently beginning to understand the situation.

"Yes, this mission has the attention of the Emperor himself. The … unfortunate situation with your predecessor caused some consternation back in Ythis. Needless to say, there must be no other difficulties with this mission, or we are all going to be facing some drastic consequences."

A strange expression crossed Laita's face as Zartay mentioned the previous commander, but it was gone quickly, and he couldn't read what she might have been thinking. He made a mental note to look into any possible connection there. Any leverage was useful.

"Our objective is to occupy the handful of villages in nearby valleys and control the populace. All outlying farms and homesteads are to be taken into custody and all citizens moved into the villages for the duration of the mission. We are to lock down this region and prevent any unauthorized person from being able to move about until the mission is over."

"For what purpose," she asked.

"There is a special team coming in—they should arrive in the next few days. They have a confidential mission to perform, and I'm not permitted to give you any further details on what they will be doing. Suffice to say that their mission is the true goal of this entire operation, and we are here to make sure no one sees or interferes with what they are doing."

Laita frowned as she considered her orders.

"That's it? Just occupation and control?"

This was the delicate part. Zartay didn't want to lie to her directly—it would make things more difficult between them later. But he wouldn't make the same mistake again by revealing the secondary phase of the operation too soon. He had misjudged the previous commander, and would have to be more careful this time.

"Right now, that is the extent of this operation. However, as I said before, this entire mission has the attention of the Emperor himself. Depending on the success of the special team and what they accomplish, I would expect our orders to change and encompass new objectives."

Laita considered that for a moment. Zartay could see there was some confusion there, as if something didn't sit right with her. He had a notion of what that might be, and hoped it wouldn't cause more problems.

"Okay," she said finally. "Let's go over the details."

For the next hour, Zartay and Laita examined the maps and discussed specifics of the mission. She had a quick mind and her questions were always relevant and direct, identifying potential issues and suggesting solutions that Zartay might have missed. When she eventually left, he found himself impressed with her, wondering about the potential there after this operation was over.

Moments after she had departed, the curtain dividing the tent was pushed aside and the priest stepped out.

"I don't like her," Brother Hissiath said with a snarl.

Zartay turned to him, taking in his hunched shoulders, gnarled fingers, and stray wisps of gray hair floating about his head. The man's hooked nose, sunken cheeks, and general posture made him look like something ancient that had crawled out of a crypt and wanted to feast on the flesh of the dead.

Zartay swallowed his impulse to point out that the priest didn't like anyone. Instead, he spoke in a calm, soothing voice.

"She's competent, and seems willing to follow orders without asking too many questions," he replied.

"She'll be just like the last one," the priest argued.

"Perhaps. But we don't get to pick and choose the commander we want, and we cannot remove another one so quickly after the first. It drew too much attention. We need things to proceed smoothly, at least until the gate is located."

Brother Hissiath looked at Zartay, and the ambassador avoided the priest's eyes. The man's madness was too close to the surface, and though Zartay knew it was impossible, he had the secret worry that it was contagious somehow through the other man's gaze.

"She won't go through with it," the priest said.

"We don't know that. It'll take some time before we reach that phase of the operation. By then, I'll have taken her measure and can make other arrangements if it seems she won't accept her new orders."

He stood and crossed to a small cabinet and removed a flask of dark liquid. Taking a sip of the pungent spirits, he closed his eyes and enjoyed the taste. If he kept to no more than one taste each day, he would have enough to last him most of the way though the campaign.

Finally, after rolling it around on his tongue and savoring the flavor, he swallowed the liquor and sighed quietly.

"I will take care of Commander Naschect," he said to the priest. "You prepare yourself for what must be done when we find that cave. The Emperor awaits his prize."

Chapter Six

THE SIX LIEUTENANTS FILED INTO THE COMMAND TENT and stood at attention, waiting for Laita to acknowledge them. She kept her eyes on the report in front of her, deliberately ignoring them for the moment. She wanted to make sure she had memorized the most important details so that she could answer questions quickly and decisively.

There was a slight rustle as a couple of her subordinates shifted their feet, obviously wondering why she had not yet asked them to sit. She had heard that the acting commander she had relieved, Chalaj Adai, had treated them as equals. That was a mistake she intended to rectify.

Laita raised her eyes from the report and focused on the six men and women arrayed in front of her.

"Is something wrong?" she asked in a mild voice. No one answered, and she thought a few of them straightened their shoulders as they realized she was not impressed with their lack of discipline.

"Does anyone here feel they're out of practice in basic soldiering?"

Again, no one spoke up. Laita placed the report on her table and rose to her feet. She was a tall woman, and her height had been an advantage in the legions. She was able to meet the eyes—or even to look down upon—the lieutenants under her direct command. It helped to reinforce the dominant position she held, and allowed her to keep the full force of her personality restrained, saving it for those occasions where she really needed to unleash it.

"I understand the situation has been difficult here. Your previous commander made a grave error in judgement, and the command structure has been chaotic until my arrival. But that's over now. I require you to show the discipline that got you into the rank you now hold. The sergeants under your command, and the legionnaires under *their* command, also require it of you."

She stepped around her table and stood directly in front of the six men and women standing at attention in front of her. One by one, she looked them each in the eyes.

"Let me make it clear to each and every one of you. When I say I understand, that means I understand why this force may not have been managed effectively *in the past*. My understanding of the situation means I will excuse behaviors that occurred before I assumed command. But that's where it ends. From this moment on, that door is shut. You are lieutenants in the Imperial Legions, and you will fulfill the duties and responsibilities of that rank or you will be removed."

Laita paused and waited for her words to sink in.

"Take your seats," she said, and the lieutenants moved quickly to the large table and arranged themselves around it. Laita watched them for any signs of dissatisfaction, any expression of anger or annoyance. But they all kept themselves under control as they sat down.

The tent flap was pulled back and Namal entered. He snapped a sharp salute to Laita, and she waved him over. As she met his eyes, she raised one eyebrow, and he gave a small shake of his head. He hadn't yet found anything that couldn't be reported in front of the others.

"Lieutenants," she said, still standing in front of her own table and forcing them to turn to face her. "This is Sergeant Namal of my command squad. He came with me from the Dragon regiment in the Tenth, along with a few others. Namal speaks with my voice. Any orders he gives you will be treated as if they came from me."

That caused a few glances among the lieutenants. While it wasn't unheard of, it was uncommon that a sergeant was given such respect. Still, Laita was their commander, and they were expected to obey her orders.

"Namal, what is the situation?"

"At your orders, Saeda and I conducted a review of the camp, the perimeter, the supply depot, the general deployment, and conducted spot checks of various squads under each of the detachments."

"And what did you find?" Laita asked.

"Overall, the camp is fairly organized. There are some trouble areas—rivalries between squads in certain detachments that have escalated into a couple of fistfights, a minor racket being conducted by soldiers in the supply depot—but general discipline is still decent. However, the situation has begun to slide downhill, and it's only going to accelerate if it's not stopped immediately."

Laita nodded. "Thank you, Namal. You never know what you're going to step into when you take command of a new Contingent, but considering everything that's happened, the situation is better than it might be."

She turned to the lieutenants.

"The first order of business is to get the detachments back up to readiness. I've reviewed our orders with Ambassador Seaphon, and we must be ready to pack up and move out within three days. That means you have to put the fear of the Abyss into your sergeants and get the squads back under control."

She turned to Lieutenant Friarti.

"As you've no doubt heard by now, I ordered five lashes for two of your soldiers yesterday. Their patrol of the camp perimeter was sloppy and useless. If I was a hostile, I could have easily killed them both and entered the camp undetected. I expect that word has already spread throughout the camp that I'm a tyrant and a bitch. Personally, I couldn't care less if it puts some fear into the soldiers. I want the patrols to be alert and cautious at all times."

The lieutenant nodded at her, his eyes wide.

"Under my command, shit also rolls uphill. If things don't improve immediately, their sergeant will be the next one getting the lash. And if there's still a problem after that, guess who gets punished next?"

Lieutenant Friarti opened his mouth, and then closed it again.

"Yes, lieutenant. Is there something you want to say?"

She could see the struggle on the man's face, his caution warring with his desire to convince her to change her mind.

"Spit it out, lieutenant. I'm not going to punish you for making a suggestion."

"Commander," he said finally. "With all due respect, I'm … concerned … that punishing the sergeant in such a manner would undermine his authority over the soldiers under his command. It may have the opposite effect than you'd like."

"You're right, it might. And if that was the case, I believe I'd have to remove the sergeant from his position and replace him with someone who could get the job done. Then I wouldn't have to concern myself with punishing him, would I? Assuming the Second Contingent isn't so rotten that it's already a lost cause, I don't think I'd have to do such a thing more than once. Would I?"

"No, commander," the lieutenant answered.

"Excellent. I'm glad to see our soldiers learn from the mistakes of others. Now it's your job to make sure the sergeants understand that I'm not making an empty threat."

She didn't ask him if he was clear on her meaning. Laita knew the man understood.

"Commander," said Lieutenant Uissa. "We will have the Contingent ready to move out on time. But what *are* our orders?"

Laita finally moved to stand at the head of the large table. She looked at each of the lieutenants in turn, making sure she had their full attention.

"Our mission is delicate. We are about to take action against citizens of the Empire who have done nothing other than to be in the wrong place at the wrong time. Our job is to collect those people, every last one of them, in a small handful of central locations and keep them there."

"For what purpose?" Lieutenant Uissa asked.

"To keep them out of the way of the real mission, the details of which are on a need to know basis. But that other mission doesn't really concern us. We have one objective—to ensure that not a single living soul within these two valleys and surrounding mountain chain is free to wander that area. Some of the people we will collect will be unhappy with the situation. Some of them may resist us. And that's where the orders need to be clear and direct, and understood by every one of our soldiers in this Contingent. Because if we don't have total control over our own legionnaires, the smallest resistance could be a spark that ignites a slaughter."

*   *   *

KIED RAISED HIS HEAD AS THE DOOR TO THE CELL OPENED. THE flare of torchlight hurt his eyes and he squinted at the guards filling the narrow hallway beyond. Kied's cellmate was sound asleep, his deep snores vibrating against the stone walls of the cell.

"Get up!" shouted the guard in front, and lightly kicked the bottom of Rotos' foot to wake him up. The giant's snoring stopped immediately, and he opened his eyes. Kied pulled himself to his feet and faced the guards.

"Are we going back to work?" Rotos asked in a low voice. After the fight with the other men, the guards had surrounded Kied and Rotos and ordered them to surrender at sword point. The guards had then escorted the two men back to their cell, where they had stayed locked up for at least a day, perhaps more.

"You're going to see the commander," the guard answered. Rotos raised himself to his feet and Kied gave him a questioning look, but the big man ignored him. He hadn't said a word to Kied since they had returned to the cell.

There were at least a dozen guards in the hallway, Kied noticed as he stepped through the door. Many of them had their weapons drawn, as if they expected the prisoners to resist. But Rotos simply allowed himself to be led toward the stairs, and Kied followed his lead.

As they were climbing the stairs, Kied realized it was late afternoon—the sun would still be up. He remembered the guard's words about missing the sunlight after he had been here a while, and had to admit the man had been right. Kied had not seen sunlight for thirty-six days now, and he couldn't wait to get outside.

But as he approached the doorway, he was forced to squeeze his eyes shut against the brilliant glare. The torches held by the guards could not compare to that fiery orb in the sky, and the light reflected off the dry, dusty ground, making it too painful to see. Kied stumbled out into the daylight, unable to open his eyes against the glare.

Still, he turned his face to the sky and tried to drink in the light, even if he could not see it. He assumed the guards were leading him and Rotos to the main building, and knew the light would fade soon enough. He wanted to experience as much of it as he could.

A minute or so later, the light dimmed as they stepped into the building. He opened his eyes to see a short hallway that led into a large room ahead. He and Rotos were escorted into that room, and Kied looked around the hall.

He knew the outer walls of the building were made of stone, but was surprised to find the interior was of the same material. Thinking about it, Kied realized from the layout that this had once been a small fortress, probably on the border of the Empire. It must have been repurposed as a prison once Imperial control had expanded well beyond this region. This meant the interior walls were thick and limited the amount of space within the building. Kied estimated this hall took up the bulk of the ground floor.

A series of tables lined one wall of the room, and a half-dozen scribes managed piles of ledgers and scrolls in racks that protruded from the adjoining wall—they obviously managed logistics for the prison. A raised platform near the middle of the long wall, opposite the entrance, held a single large desk made of dark wood. Other, smaller desks were scattered across the other half of the room, though these were mostly empty.

A door along the back wall opened, and a man wearing a military uniform stepped through. He was older, perhaps in his mid-fifties, with close-cropped greying hair and a rough, unfriendly face. The man's uniform was dusty and too tight for his pudgy frame. He stepped up onto the raised platform and sat behind the desk.

The lead guard who had escorted Kied and Rotos from their cells stepped forward.

"Commander, these are the prisoners you requested."

The commander raised his eyes from the papers on his desk and looked at Kied. There was contempt in that gaze, a total disdain for the prisoners in his care. Kied could tell this man would show no mercy.

The man turned to Rotos and paused. His expression changed slightly, but Kied couldn't read him well enough yet to understand what he was thinking.

"I'm not used to seeing you in here, Rotos," the commander said in a deep, gravelly voice. "You're not usually a troublemaker."

There was a slight accusatory tone in the man's words, as if he thought they had some kind of agreement that Rotos would behave himself. The giant looked at the commander and said nothing.

From the comments the guards had made in the early days of Kied's imprisonment, he had gotten the impression that Rotos sometimes killed the prisoner to whom he was chained. He guessed the commander didn't see that as "trouble."

"Between the two of you, you killed three prisoners yesterday and injured three more. The ones who can still talk tell me this one—" and he nodded his head at Kied, "—picked a fight and then killed a man. When the others defended themselves, you waded in."

"That's not what happened, sir," Kied said. The commander looked Kied in the eyes and his mouth twisted.

"I didn't ask you a gods' damned thing," he snarled at Kied. One of the guards stepped forward and rammed a fist into Kied's stomach, doubling him over. He slowly straightened, gasping for breath. The commander turned back to Rotos.

"I've overlooked the accidents that sometimes happen to the prisoners who get chained to you," he continued. "What happens inside your locked cell, well, as long it doesn't cause me any hardship, I don't give a shit."

He looked down at his desk and heaved a sigh.

"But this ... I can't ignore this."

Kied was surprised at the man's words. It was almost as if the commander was apologizing to Rotos for what he was about to do, trying to explain himself before he pronounced judgement.

He's afraid, Kied realized. *He's worried about what will happen if he doesn't punish Rotos, but he also terrified of what damage the gi-*

ant will do if he decides to resist.

"You're my best worker, Rotos. So I'm going to reduce your punishment, because I want you back down in the pit as quickly as possible. I'm not showing you mercy here, understand. I'm just considering the production of this mine."

Kied almost smiled at that. The commander's words weren't for Rotos this time, but for the guards under his command. He didn't want to appear weak. But Kied thought it might be too late for that. It was obvious the commander was terrified of Rotos.

The man took a deep breath, and then spoke all at once.

"Ten lashes of the whip for you, Rotos. Twenty-five for this one," he said, indicating Kied again.

"Do we not get to speak our piece?" Kied asked. The commander ignored him, and the guard kicked him behind the knees to knock him to the floor, and then savagely cuffed him on the side of the head. Kied's ears rang from the force of the blow.

Kied watched the commander as the man waited for Rotos' reaction to the punishment. The big man considered, and then nodded once to the commander. The look of relief on the commander's face would have been funny if Kied had not just been sentenced to a whipping.

The guards roughly hauled Kied back to his feet, and then escorted the two men back out of the hall.

Chapter Seven

TIATH RODE THROUGH THE CAMP, HIS SQUAD FOLLOWING him in single file, and watched the soldiers around him. He recognized the flurry of activity—a rush to get the camp back in shape after letting too many duties slide, and a preparation for deployment. He wondered if this was Zartay's doing, or the direction of the new commander.

Tiath turned his horse away from the hill on which the command tent was situated, and aimed instead for the ambassador's tent, recognizable by Zartay's banner fluttering from a pole at the apex of the tent's roof. A pair of soldiers stepped forward to block his way as he neared the tent, and Tiath wordlessly handed them his identification papers.

They had obviously been briefed on his imminent arrival, as the soldiers immediately snapped salutes and then offered to take the team's horses while the squad met with the ambassador. One of the soldiers whistled to a companion standing at attention at the tent's entrance and made a quick gesture. The other soldier stepped inside to no doubt announce their arrival to Zartay.

Tiath gathered his squad, and the four of them entered the tent. Zartay was just coming around his desk and he stepped up and grasped Tiath's hand in greeting.

"Welcome, gentlemen … and lady," he said, smiling. "How was your journey?"

Tiath glanced around the tent, taking in the furnishings, the papers scattered across Zartay's desk, and the curtains around his sleeping area. This was not a secure place to discuss their mission.

"It was reasonable, Ambassador. We had hoped to make better time, but some delays are inevitable."

Zartay moved to greet the others, but Tiath interrupted him.

"I see the Contingent is active. Has the new commander arrived?"

Zartay faltered, but recovered quickly.

"Yes, I met with her yesterday morning. She seems quite organized."

Tiath glanced over at the curtains.

"I take it that's her listening to us behind the curtain?" he asked. Tiath watched Zartay's eyes as he said it, looking for the instant of surprise and guilt to cross the man's face before he was able to hide it. Zartay didn't react, however. No doubt his diplomatic training coming to the fore.

"You can rest assured," he said smoothly, "there is no one in here but us."

But Tiath knew he was lying—his own skill and experience trumping the ambassador's. The success of this mission depended on its secrecy, and he would not allow anyone to compromise that. He glanced back at his squad, and Azam and Deylista strode toward the curtains while drawing their swords.

"No, wait!" Zartay said, a note of panic in his voice. But at that moment, the curtain was swept aside and the person on the other side stepped out.

Shit, thought Tiath. *That's not what we need right now.*

Azam and Deylista stopped as the priest stepped into view, an angry expression on his face.

"Enough games," the priest snarled. "We don't have time for this nonsense."

Tiath's soldiers sheathed their weapons and stepped back. Zartay looked quickly from the priest to Tiath, realizing he had made a mistake.

"Brother Hissiath is here as an advisor," he explained to Tiath. "But his presence is to be kept strictly confidential. Only I and my personal guard are aware he is here."

Tiath looked Zartay in the eye.

"I don't like surprises, Ambassador. You lied to me when I asked if there was anyone else here. If you want this mission to be successful, you're going to have to tell me everything. We don't have the luxury of keeping secrets, because you don't know if something you omit will turn out to be vital to my operation. Am I clear?"

Zartay kept his face calm but Tiath could sense his emotions surging below the surface. This man was used to others doing his bidding, and technically Tiath was just a lieutenant in the Imperial Legions. But he was also far more than that, and Zartay knew it. If anyone here was expendable, it was the ambassador.

"Very well," Zartay replied eventually. "My apologies. It was an oversight, nothing more. I will fully disclose everything else to you from now on."

Tiath nodded at him.

"Good. Now I believe you have a package for me."

Zartay motioned for Tiath and his squad to take a seat around the table set to one side. He unlocked a large trunk and remove a black leather bag and carried it over to the table.

"Everything you need is in here."

Tiath undid the drawstring and pulled open the bag. He dumped the contents out onto the table and began to sort through it. A sheaf of parchment maps were handed to Pasill, what appeared to be an ancient book bound in leather was given to Deylista, and Tiath grabbed the scroll case that he knew would contain the specifics on his orders.

"What can you tell me about this gate?" he asked Zartay.

"Everything is in the package," the ambassador replied.

"I know, but I want to hear, in your own words, everything *you* know about it."

Zartay frowned at him, but the priest interrupted smoothly.

"You've no doubt heard of the Abyss," the priest said. Tiath nodded. "Most people don't really know what the Abyss truly is, other than where demons come from. The truth is, our world floats in an endless, dark emptiness. It is a void that we believe is alive in some manner. But it stretches out in all directions for eternity."

The priest licked his lips and watched Tiath's face for any sign that his words were making Tiath uncomfortable. If he was expecting a reaction, he was going to be disappointed. There was little that could undermine Tiath's view of the world and his place in it.

"Below us," the priest continued, grinning madly, "in the deepest pits of the Abyss at the very darkest bottom, are the spawning grounds of demons and other abominations."

"Wait a minute," Azam interrupted. "If it goes on forever, then how can it have a bottom?"

The priest's face twisted in anger at the interruption, but then he considered Azam's question and a subtle smirk came upon his face. He blinked rapidly before answering.

"The Abyss is not like our world, soldier. It operates outside of time and space as we know it. The Abyss is both unending, and has a bottom, simultaneously."

Azam frowned, but nodded and motioned for the priest to continue.

"Above us, across unfathomable distances, are the birthplaces of the gods. They dwelt there before the gates opened and brought them to our world. Iathephos, the god of Ythis, in fact, sprawls across the threshold of the gate that connects our two worlds, holding it open with his body. If he were to permit passage, one could step through the gate and visit his world."

The priest smiled, and it was a terrible thing to behold, full of madness and fanaticism.

"One would not survive such an experience, of course. We can only imagine the changes that would be wrought on a human mind and body were it to experience the alien landscape that is the original home of Iathephos."

"This is all very interesting," Tiath responded. "But are you saying that this gate for which we are searching will lead us to the birthplace of the gods?"

The priest turned serious once more.

"Of course not! That would be blasphemy. But there are other worlds out there, floating in the Abyss. Worlds perhaps not so different from ours. The Emperor is interested in one such world, and we believe this gate connects it with our own."

Tiath considered that. If the Emperor himself wanted to reach this other world, Tiath could only imagine the power that might be available there. His job was to find the gate and secure it. But you never knew what opportunities might come your way if you were ready to grab them.

*   *   *

KIED RAN HIS HAND OVER HIS SCALP, FEELING THE STUBBLE RASP against his rough palm. Sweat ran down his face, and he was thankful for the small mercy of rank that allowed him to carry his helmet rather than wear it. The dry, dusty grounds of the Imperial barracks baked in the hot sun.

Stepping into the shade of a narrow alley between two barracks buildings allowed him to get out of the direct sunlight. He leaned against the rough, wooden wall and breathed a sigh of relief. It wasn't significantly cooler in the shade, but at least the sunlight wasn't cooking him alive.

A figure stepped into sight at the other end of the alley and Kied grinned. Laita hadn't been sure she could find time to get away today, and Kied was overjoyed she had managed to come. She strode toward him and he watched the way she moved—strong, confident, and direct. It made his blood heat up even more than the burning sun overhead.

Laita's own head sported the same stubble as Kied's—the result of an infestation of lice in the barracks the army was trying to eradicate—but he didn't care. The intelligence in her eyes, the sharp wit, and the crooked smile melted his heart. Laita might not have been the most beautiful woman Kied had ever seen, but she didn't need to be. Kied loved her for who she was.

It had taken him some time to admit that to himself. But only a few days ago he had finally acknowledged that he had fallen for Laita, hard. He was pretty sure she felt the same way.

He tossed his helmet into the dust at his feet and stepped toward her, but she put one hand on his chest and shoved him back against the wall of the building. Pressing her body against his, she kissed him hard and he responded with an urgency that always came at her

55

touch. He gasped for breath as she pulled back.

"Let's go," he said, trying to push away from the wall and lead her to the unused building at the end of the row where they had gone so many times before. But she shoved him back again and put her mouth to his ear.

"No—right here, now," she whispered, and the breath on his ear sent a shiver down his spine. He hesitated only a moment—they could be flogged if caught by their superiors—but he was past the point of rational thought. She yanked his tunic up and slipped her hand into the short trousers underneath, taking him in her fist and squeezing. Kied's legs nearly buckled.

He spun her around and put her back to the wall, yanking down her own trousers. She released the clasp on her belt, and Kied slid one hand up under her tunic to cup her breast as he entered her. Laita let out a low moan and wrapped one leg around him.

Kied pulled his head back and looked her in the eyes, and she gave him that crooked grin again before kissing him passionately, her tongue sliding into his mouth. She was in complete control, and Kied knew he wouldn't be able to hold back today. He was ready to burst *now*, and they had just started.

He lost all sense of time as they ground against each other in the alley, his hands traveling over her body. It might have been hours, or minutes, or only a few seconds. She used her raised leg to control the pace, slowing down when he felt he couldn't take any more, and speeding up as soon as he managed to get a breath.

"Slow … slow down," he gasped at her, feeling the hard nub of her nipple under his thumb. "I can't … I'm going to …."

She thrust her hips back at him, once, twice, and he lost what little self-control he had. Trying to stifle his moans, he finished inside her, stars swimming in his vision.

It took him a couple of minutes to calm down enough to get his breath back. Finally they separated and she straightened her clothing and re-clasped her belt around her waist. Kied leaned back against the wall, feebly pulling his trousers back up.

"That … that was risky," he said to her. She smiled back at him.

"I didn't feel like waiting."

Then she stepped forward and kissed him again, slowly and tenderly this time. When she pulled back, her face was serious.

"I wanted our … our last one … to be memorable."

Kied blinked at her stupidly.

"Last one? What are you talking about?"

"I just found out. One of us is shipping out shortly on a special mission. There's also that position in the Tenth, Dragon Regiment."

"What special mission?" asked Kied. Laita shook her head.

"I don't know anything else. I have a friend in the command squad here. He just said that there's some special mission, and they want a good, experienced commander."

She hesitated, and he could see in her eyes that there was more.

"What?" he asked.

"We're both up for the command. We've done a good job here training the new officers, and it's time for them to move us out to another posting. One of us is getting the mission; the other is probably going to the Tenth."

Kied considered this.

"What if … what if I don't want to leave you?"

She frowned at him and opened her mouth to say something, but closed it again. Just as he was about to say more, she spoke over him.

"I don't know what you're saying, Kied."

"Maybe I don't either," he admitted. "No, that's not right. I *do* know. I … I love you. I can't just walk away from this. You are the most incredible woman I've ever known, and …."

He trailed off as she shook her head.

"You're not thinking straight," she told him. "It's been nice … no, it's been great with you. But we both knew this wasn't going to be a long-term thing. Our time at the barracks was limited, just another step in our careers. It was just a matter of time before we went our separate ways."

"Yeah, that's what I thought at first. But I have to be honest with you, Laita. I don't want us to go our separate ways."

He saw her press her lips together in a thin line.

"I know you think I'm just delirious from the sex," he said. "And that's what it was at first. But maybe you've noticed that we find ways to get together, risk breaking curfew, just to spend time with each other? We've been doing it more and more often. I—I find myself wanting to see you every day. I—"

"Stop," she said, something in her eyes telling Kied he had said too much, too soon. "I like you … quite a bit. Probably more than is healthy, to be honest. But I'm not going to let that end my career, and you can't either."

"Laita—"

"No. You've had your say, now let me have mine. If things were different, if we weren't who we are, then this would probably work. But I'm a soldier, a commander. I'm responsible for a whole Contingent, twelve hundred legionnaires who look to me to make the right decisions, to see every situation from every angle and understand the best course of action for all those under my command. And you're the same."

She closed her eyes and took a deep breath.

"You can't turn down an assignment, Kied. Not without resigning. And then what? If you did that, then you wouldn't be the man I think you are. And I'd have no interest in the man who would quit like that just for a bit of romance."

Kied wanted to argue, to protest, but he knew it would do no good.

"And you're forgetting one thing," she continued. "We're *both* up for that special mission. You may not want to leave me, but it may not even be offered to you. And if I get the posting, I will not hesitate to walk out of here and not look back."

Laita picked up Kied's helmet from the ground and handed it to him. He looked her in the eyes, and he could see the struggle there. She didn't *want* to do this, but she saw the alternatives and refused to accept them. And Laita was a soldier.

"This is the last time we will see each other like this," she said to him. "Our … whatever we had … is over. I hope you get a good posting."

She turned and walked back down the alley. When she stepped out of the shadows and the sunlight hit her, Kied found himself swallowing around a lump in his throat. He turned in the opposite direction and nearly staggered out into the sunlight. The heat hit him like a blast from behind, burning his back.

He tried to take another step, but agony shot through his back and he fell to his knees. The skin of his back was on fire, as if the sun was burning through his tunic and cooking him alive.

Kied toppled forward, and as his face hit the ground …

… his eyes snapped open and he twitched violently, sending fresh spasms of pain lancing through his body. He cried out in pain and fear, and then realized where he was.

Kied lay still on the floor of his cell, trying not to breathe too deeply. He saw Laita's face in his mind's eye—he hadn't dreamed about her, about that day, in months. He felt fresh tears drip off his nose to land in the dust beneath him.

He was unable to move without sending waves of pain across his back and he felt he had done enough screaming yesterday. After being dragged from the courtroom, both men had been chained to posts in the yard before one of the guards gave them their punishment.

Rotos, of course, had not cried out in pain. He merely stood there, his huge arms wrapped around the wooden post, and waited while the guard laid the lash across his back ten times. Kied had not lasted nearly so long. By the fourth stroke, he was grunting. By the seventh he began to cry out. And by the eleventh he had begun to scream.

Kied looked at the shadow of his cellmate, the big man lying on his side facing away from Kied and snoring deeply. He still didn't understand why Rotos had let the guard whip him. But he understood now that while the giant might help him survive, Rotos would never help him escape.

Kied lay in the dark, thinking about Laita and letting the tears run down his face.

Chapter Eight

LAITA SAT COMFORTABLY IN THE SADDLE, WATCHING HER soldiers march down toward the village at the base of the hill. Outriders already surrounded the settlement and were herding the farmers back toward the small cluster of buildings that sat on either side of the wide stream that ran through the valley. She could see by the way the villagers moved that they were terrified by the arrival of her forces.

But they would soon learn that they had little to fear. This was a temporary occupation, and her soldiers would do little except prevent anyone from traveling outside of their village for a few weeks. The farmers would be concerned about not being permitted to return to their fields until the operation was over, of course. But the lieutenants would ensure that everyone was informed about the rules, and the penalties they would face if the people broke them.

This scene was being replayed in the other neighboring valleys as the other five detachments of Laita's command took control of the villages and assorted smaller settlements within the restricted area. The cloudless sky was a bowl of blue above her, and she found herself enjoying the warm day, as her detailed plans were executed with precision by the legionnaires under her. So far, there had been no serious issues.

Laita didn't expect any trouble, though she had still prepared for it; her command squad had explicit orders on how to deal with any issues that may arise during the occupation. She would spend a day or two at each village before moving along to the next, to ensure her commands were being followed properly.

Sergeant Ellend sat beside her, watching the marching soldiers carefully. She was a good soldier, strong and built like a boulder. Ellend constantly strove to emulate Namal, trying to learn everything she could from Laita's most trusted adjunct. Laita felt Ellend would make an excellent adjunct herself one day, though most likely with another commander.

Namal himself was off with one of the other detachments, as were Saeda and Bor, acting as Laita's eyes and ears in the other valleys. She didn't trust the lieutenants in charge of the detachments—at least one and possibly more of them reported everything she said back to Ambassador Seaphon. This was not unusual. Politics played a large part in the Imperial Legions, and the success of a mission was often unduly influenced by political realities.

Laita was not a master of politics, but she understood the game and knew where her strengths and weaknesses lay. It was how she would succeed where Kied had failed.

She frowned as Kied drifted into her thoughts again. He had seemed so strong when she first met him, with a confidence and intelligence that would see him rise through the Legions' ranks. It was why she had fallen … no, best not to go down that path. She had shed her tears at the time, and she wouldn't do so again.

Kied had such promise, but then he had shown such weakness at the end. Maybe it had been there all along. His suggestion of giving up his commission to be with her—was that a sign that he would eventually find himself overwhelmed and unable to give difficult orders when needed?

All commanders eventually faced that dilemma at some point in their careers. Sometimes it was necessary to give orders you disagreed with, because those orders themselves were necessary. You had to find the strength inside yourself to reconcile your personal beliefs with your professional responsibilities. You succeeded and continued your career, or you failed and left the Legions, one way or another.

Kied was lucky he was still alive. He could have been executed ….

The thought sent a pang of despair through Laita's chest as she realized he might already be dead. The prison-mines weren't exactly conducive to a long life. Kied would spend the rest of his days there, and would eventually die a broken and empty man. Laita would never see him again, a thought she had not previously acknowledged. There had always been a glimmer in the back of her mind that maybe, one day ….

What was wrong with her today? Why was she thinking about Kied when she should be focused on the mission at hand?

"Commander, look," said Sergeant Ellend beside her, and Laita raised her head to look in the direction the other woman pointed.

In the field on the near side of the village, a farmer was arguing with one of the soldiers. The man obviously wanted to return his ox to the pen before heading into the village, but the soldier was ordering him to leave the beast and go immediately. As Laita watched, the soldier drew a weapon.

Laita swore and kicked her horse into a gallop, Sergeant Ellend following immediately behind. As she got closer, she saw that at least the soldier had pulled out his truncheon rather than a sword, but the farmer was pulling on the rope around the ox's neck, trying to turn him back toward the fenced-in pen.

The soldier urged his horse forward and moved around in front of the farmer. The other man raised his fist and punched the soldier in the leg, unable to reach any higher. Laita was close enough to see the expression on the soldier's face. Though the farmer was no threat to him, the soldier became angry and brought his truncheon down on the top of the farmer's head. The farmer staggered back, and the soldier leaned out of his saddle to strike the man a second time.

The farmer's body went limp, and he fell backward into the dirt.

The soldier looked up and saw Laita riding hard toward him, and his angry look was replaced by one of fear. Laita pulled up hard a few paces from the soldier and had to fight the urge to draw her sword.

"What in the Abyss do you think you're doing?" she demanded.

The soldier looked down at the farmer, lying unmoving in the dirt. The man's skull was obviously broken.

"H-he tried to … attack …."

Laita heard more horses and turned to see Lieutenant Friarti and one of his sergeants riding over to them. Laita forced herself to calm down. She knew something like this was inevitable. With twelve hundred soldiers engaging in an occupation, there were bound to be mistakes. But she remembered specifically telling Lieutenant Friarti to get some discipline back into his detachment. She remembered telling him what the consequences would be if he didn't.

"Commander," he said breathlessly as he rode up. He was trying and failing to hide his own fear at her presence. "I will take care of this. You don't need to—"

"Sergeant," she said directly to the other man, cutting off the lieutenant. "Is this soldier part of your squad?"

The sergeant nodded and said "Yes, ma'am."

"He is relieved of duty. He is to be docked one month pay, which will be given to the family of this farmer. He will also receive twenty lashes for killing an unarmed citizen of the Empire."

"Commander," Lieutenant Friarti said again.

"Come with me," she told the lieutenant, turned her horse away, and began to walk it back toward her vantage point on the hill. The lieutenant urged his own horse up beside hers.

"I believe," she said to him, "that I already told you I wouldn't put up with this in my contingent."

"Commander, it was simple mistake—"

"No, lieutenant. Hitting the man *once* would have been a mistake. Bashing his head in is a different situation altogether."

"Commander, if you keep ordering men to get the lash every time they—"

"There are other punishments I could order, lieutenant. Would you prefer that I revisit the list?"

"N-no, commander."

"I expect discipline, lieutenant. We are not pacifying a new territory, or punishing a rebellious province, or fighting off invaders. We are occupying a region filled with loyal citizens of the Empire. We are restricting movement, nothing more."

The lieutenant nodded, his eyes on the ground.

"This is the last warning you get, lieutenant. Next time, the lashes go to the sergeant, and the soldier gets even worse punishment."

"Commander—" he began, but she cut him off.

"And I find myself a new lieutenant," she finished. Lieutenant Friarti's mouth snapped shut.

"Dismissed," she told him. The man turned his horse and galloped back down the hill toward his own command squad. Laita looked down at the village, the soldiers having moved in among the buildings. They were ordering the villagers to gather in the central square, where they would be told about their restricted rights for the next few weeks.

Laita had a feeling things were going to get worse here before they got better.

*   *   *

KIED AWOKE AS THE CELL DOOR WAS PULLED OPEN. HE RAISED HIS head and looked up as Rotos entered the cell and sat down on the floor. Kied's back still ached, but he was healing and was now able to move without screaming.

Nine days had passed, and Kied knew they would soon put him back to work in the mine. Rotos had spent only two days recovering before he had been sent back down. The guards unchained the two men from each other at the beginning of each shift, and then reattached them when Rotos returned to the cell.

Rotos sat unmoving as the guard slipped the bolt through the hole and locked it into place. He said nothing when the guard left, and Kied sat quietly. The big man had said little since their meeting with the commander who ran this prison, and Kied didn't expect him to start now.

But Rotos took a breath and then turned to Kied.

"They're returning you to work tomorrow," he said in his low grumble. "I overheard one of the guards saying they might separate us, attach us to other prisoners since you won't be able to keep up with me anymore."

Kied felt a surge of panic. Rotos' help was the only reason Kied was still alive.

"I ... we don't really have much choice, do we?" he said in response. Rotos said nothing—just stared at him from under his mass of hair.

"You saved my life," Kied said to the giant. "You were punished because you stopped them from killing me. I haven't thanked you, but I wasn't sure you'd ...."

He drifted off, unsettled by the big man's unwavering gaze.

"You could have let me die. Why did you step in? Believe me, I'm grateful that you did. But you knew you'd be punished for it."

Kied waited in silence for Rotos to respond, but it appeared his cellmate didn't intend to answer. Kied shift uncomfortably and as he did so, the giant cleared his throat and spoke.

"I don't know," he said. Kied stopped, waiting for more, for anything. Rotos heaved a sigh and continued.

"I've been in here ... a long time. I don't know how many men have been chained to me—I lost count many years ago. They were all thieves, cutthroats, murderers, and worse. Some died in the mines, and some ... some I killed with my own hands. Every one of them deserved what they got."

Kied was afraid to say anything, worried that if he interrupted the other man, he would close up again. Rotos was a mystery, and Kied was desperate to find out anything that might help him understand the man better. The giant had become Kied's ally, and Kied hoped that was just the first step on the road to becoming the big man's friend.

"You're not like those other men," Rotos explained. "You obviously don't belong here. And there's something about you ... you stayed awake when Yarrian came here. You resisted ...."

He trailed off, but took another breath and continued.

"It's time you told me who you are, why you were sent here."

Kied hesitated. He wasn't sure if Rotos would understand the circumstances, the decisions that had brought him to this point. But he realized he had nothing left to lose. If the other man decided that Kied deserved what he had gotten, it wouldn't make much difference at this point.

Especially if the guards were going to separate the two men.

"I'm from the Twelfth Legion, Chimera Regiment. I was the commander of the Second Contingent. We were given a special mission inside the borders of the Empire, and I … it was a great opportunity for me to lead the force."

Kied turned sideways to the wall and leaned against it. He still wasn't able to put any pressure on his back.

"My orders were pretty simple. All we were supposed to do was occupy the region and keep the civilians living in the area penned up in the villages for a few weeks, and then withdraw."

"Why?" Rotos growled.

"A team of specialists was looking for something, and there were to be no witnesses, no civilians blundering through the area and causing problems. Only, once the 2nd had established a base camp just outside the valley, the ambassador revealed the rest of my orders."

Kied swallowed. He could feel Rotos tensing up, as if he was anticipating something.

"After the specialists had located their objective, I was to order the 2nd to kill every single man, woman, and child in that region. No survivors, no witnesses. We were under orders to wipe the area clean without exception.

"But these were citizens of the Empire we're talking about. These aren't enemies, they're not combatants. They're farmers and simple villagers living in the heart of the Empire. It was … it was insane. My command squad agreed with me."

Kied looked at Rotos and saw the big man hadn't moved a muscle. He was completely focused on Kied's tale.

"Or, rather, all but one of my command squad agreed with me. We talked about our options, what we were willing to do to stop this madness. We all agreed that we wouldn't go through with it. We were soldiers, legionnaires. There's supposed to be some honor in that."

"You were betrayed," Rotos said.

"Yeah, we thought we were being careful, but it only takes one spy to change everything. And we found out that, while we thought we were doing the right thing, those under us had a different outlook.

"The spy went to the ambassador, and the ambassador found a sergeant in each detachment who was willing to turn on us to further his or her own career. Our own people took us into custody and brought us to the ambassador for charges of treason."

Rotos sat silent for a moment, considering, and spoke in a low voice.

"If that's true, you should already be dead."

"I would be, except for my family name. My father … my father is a Magistrate. The ambassador wasn't going to simply have me executed without the proper protocols being followed. One doesn't just kill the son of a Magistrate, regardless of the charge.

"My father oversaw my trial himself. He decided that my execution wasn't necessary—maybe a tiny bit of sentimentality there, as I'm the last surviving son, the youngest of three. So he took *mercy* on me and sent me here."

Rotos drew in a breath and let it out slowly.

"And the rest of your command squad?"

Kied tried to keep his voice steady as he answered Rotos.

"Their fathers," he said, "weren't Imperial Magistrates."

Rotos considered Kied's story for a moment, as Kied tried to calm himself. A pressure had built up in his chest, and he felt as if he was about to burst from the inside out. Time hadn't made his tale any easier to tell—his people had looked up to him for direction, and he had led them to their deaths.

Utterly pointless deaths, as the mission was moving ahead, regardless of what he had tried to do to stop it.

"What were the specialists searching for?" Rotos asked after a moment.

"I don't know. The ambassador let slip once something about a cave. But that's it."

Rotos leaned forward, and Kied could feel the heat of the man's gaze on his face.

"*Where?*" he asked. Kied almost felt the walls of the cell rumble from the power in the man's voice.

"North," he answered. "In Aerinu Province. There is a series of valleys in the Mindistasda Mountains, and ...."

Kied trailed off as Rotos stood up.

"What's the matter?" Kied asked. "Do you know something about—?"

"I hope your back has healed enough to travel," Rotos said, cutting him off. "We're leaving this prison. *Tonight.*"

Chapter Nine

Z ARTAY GRUMBLED TO HIMSELF AS HE SORTED THROUGH his chest, searching for one of his warmer robes. A chill wind had risen over the last couple of nights, bringing with it an unpleasant scent and a reminder of the winter just past. The ambassador didn't like the cold. He was a creature of warmer climes. The sudden drop in temperature after the last few days of unseasonal warmth was a shock to his body.

He glanced around at his tent, everything out of place. The move to the outskirts of the village—he hadn't bothered to learn its name yet—had been a disruption in his orderly routine. Zartay liked disruptions about as much as he liked the cold.

Finally finding his warmer robe, he stepped behind the curtain that divided his sleeping area from the main part of the tent. As he did so, he heard one of his sentries enter and call for him.

"By the Abyss," he snarled as he pulled the heavy robe over his head. "What is it now?"

"Ambassador, the team has returned to camp and have come to see you."

The sentry didn't need to specify to whom he was referring. Zartay swallowed his annoyance and straightened his robes before stepping back out into the main part of the tent.

"Send them in," he growled at the soldier, who saluted smartly and retreated back outside. A few seconds later, Tiath and his squad entered the tent.

The specialist looked around the tent at the mess, and then his eyes went to the curtain that divided the space. Zartay ground his teeth.

"He's not here," he snapped. "You'll just have to settle for me this time."

Tiath looked at Zartay and the ambassador was sure the man was suppressing a grin. Zartay forced himself to take a breath. He needed a drink, but didn't feel like offering one to the rest of them.

"And where would he be on this fine morning, ambassador? I thought his presence here was a secret."

"It is," Zartay answered. "But he's gone into the village to move among the people. He has his own ways to avoid the notice of the soldiers."

Zartay suppressed a shudder. He didn't like to think about the things the priest could do.

"Well?" he snapped. "I believe you're here to report, so let's get on with it."

Tiath's face went blank as he looked at Zartay. In an instant, the other man transformed from an amused associate to a stone-faced killer. Zartay's blood ran cold as that gaze moved over him. He realized how easy it would be for Tiath to murder him if he offended the other man.

Perhaps it would be a good idea to swallow his annoyance and make nice with his deadly visitor. He waved his hand in a placating gesture as he strode over to the chest that held his liquor.

"You've no doubt had a hard ride. Let me pour you a drink."

Zartay pulled a few glasses from the chest and selected a middling brandy—not the cheap stuff, but nothing too good. He didn't want to waste his best alcohol on an untrained tongue. Filling the first two glasses, he turned to bring them to Tiath and his people, but stopped.

Tiath had come up to within a couple of paces behind Zartay while his back was turned. That dead look was still on his face.

"Look, I … forgive my rudeness. Moving the camp has been a serious disruption and I've let it get the better of me. Here," he said offering a glass to Tiath.

The other man stared Zartay in the eyes, and then he smiled. It was as if he had pulled off a mask to reveal a completely different face underneath. He took the glass and motioned for the others to come forward to receive a drink as well.

Zartay tried to hide his fear, but he was sure they could hear his heart pounding in his chest. He had been sure Tiath was going to kill him, just for that one instant when he turned around. He was going to have to be more careful. Between this man and the priest, this assignment was turning out to be far more dangerous than Zartay had initially thought.

"We found the stone," Tiath said after he had taken a sip of the brandy. Zartay raised his eyebrows.

"So quickly?"

"It wasn't very hard to find," the other man answered. "It's out in the open and you can see it for some distance. If you know what you're looking for, it stands out rather well."

The other members of Tiath's team spread out around the tent, making themselves comfortable.

"And the inscription?" Zartay asked.

"It's mostly faded. It took some effort, but Deylista is thorough."

Tiath glanced over at the woman seated on the floor against Zartay's larger clothing chest. She raised her glass in salute to Tiath and downed her brandy in one gulp. Zartay had to fight the urge to protest her behavior.

"We think the lost crypt is at the western end of this valley, in the pass that connects this one to the next valley over. It'll take us some time to find it, but we've recovered some clues and indications of what to look for."

"Excellent," Zartay said, nodding. He turned to his desk and searched through his papers until he found what he needed. "You'll need to carry this with you when you go back out."

Tiath took the paper and looked at it. It was an order to any soldier to render all aid to Tiath and his team should they need it. It was signed by both Zartay and the new commander. Both their seals were affixed at the bottom.

"Why do I need this?"

"It's just in case you run into any patrols."

"There shouldn't be any patrols where we're going. And besides, we're not really here."

Zartay gave the other man a tight-lipped grin.

"No, but if you're spotted by a patrol between here and the pass, they'll probably try to arrest you. This will get you out of any difficulties so you can continue on your way."

Tiath glanced around at his three companions before turning back to Zartay.

"I don't need this." He stepped forward and tossed it back on Zartay's desk.

"But what if you—"

"You need to understand a few things," Tiath interrupted, and all trace of humor was gone again from his face. "First, I don't care who you are and what connections you have. When it comes to this mission, you're the expendable one. I suggest you keep that in mind going forward."

Zartay opened his mouth, but Tiath wasn't done.

"Second, we're not going to be seen by the patrols unless we *want* them to see us. We bypassed the sentries to get into the camp, and we'll bypass them on the way out, with no one the wiser. Only you and the men directly outside your tent are aware we even set foot in the camp this morning."

Now Tiath grinned, though there was no humor in it.

"And third, if by some miracle a patrol manages to get close to us, we're not going to need that piece of paper. Dead men can't read."

Zartay snapped his mouth shut. Taking a deep breath, he said, "You can't just go around killing legionnaires."

"I've been given explicit orders to keep this mission secret. No witnesses, other than a select few who have been individually named. That means anyone who becomes aware of me or my team, or who interferes in any way or sees anything they shouldn't, will die. If not immediately, then at the end of the mission when it's time to tie up loose ends."

"Loose ends?" Zartay asked.

Tiath drank down the rest of his brandy and gently placed the glass on Zartay's worktable. As one, his three team members rose to their feet and set down their glasses.

"Don't get too attached to the men guarding your tent," Tiath said as his companions moved towards the entrance. "They'll need to be dealt with, afterwards."

After the four of them left Zartay's tent, he tried to pour himself another brandy, but his hands were shaking too much.

He couldn't help but wonder if he, himself, could also be termed a *loose end*.

*   *   *

ROTOS TURNED TO KIED, HIS FACE SERIOUS.

"Ready?" he growled in a low voice. Kied nodded once and flexed his shoulders. His back was still tight and sore, but he had discovered he had a full range of movement. As long as no one hit him in the back, he'd be okay.

It was almost time for the guards to come take the prisoners back down into the mine. Kied had been sure it would be a mistake trying to escape when they'd start off surrounded by soldiers. Rotos, however, told him that they'd need the confusion of all the other prisoners out in the hallways.

"Besides," he had said. "Getting through this door will alert every guard in this place anyway. Better that they have lots of other targets to focus on."

Kied was nervous in a way he had never been before going into battle. But he wasn't the same man who had once fought for the Imperial Legion. He was weaker, for one thing. And he had only one ally, a man he still knew so little about.

Could they really do this? Or would they both die tonight, their attempt to regain their freedom a futile gesture? It wasn't too late to back out.

Except, Kied knew Rotos wouldn't stand for that. The giant wouldn't explain why he had taken such interest in whatever was going on in that valley, the valley for which Kied had lost everything. But a change had come over the big man. He was focused in a way Kied hadn't seen in him before.

Rotos said they were getting out, and Kied wanted desperately to believe the other man was right. He knew it wouldn't be easy, but he had nothing left to lose. If he stayed in the prison, he would die. With Rotos at his side, he had a chance, though slim, of surviving his escape.

Kied could hear the cell doors being opened and the clank of chains as pairs of men were led out into the main hallway. And then the lock of their cell rattled, and a guard pushed open their door.

Kied made to move forward, and the guard held up a hand.

"Hold on," he said. "We're switching you up tonight. Face the wall."

Kied looked at Rotos, but the big man said nothing and turned to face the back wall of the cell.

They're going to unchain us, he thought. This would give the two men an unexpected edge in their escape.

As Kied turned to face the wall, he noticed a second guard step into the doorway of the cell. Once they acted, that guard would most likely try to slam the cell door shut again. If neither Kied nor Rotos was fast enough, their escape would be over before it had begun.

The guard with the key knelt at Kied's feet and began to unlock his manacle. He tried not to tense up and alert the guard that he was about to do something dangerous, but it was a struggle. Finally, he felt the weight of the manacle about his ankle fall away.

"Okay," the guard said, starting to straighten up. But Rotos spun around and his huge fist smashed into the side of the guard's head.

Kied was already moving, diving forward toward the guard in the doorway of their cell. He saw the man's eyes widen as Kied charged him. Kied hammered his fist into the man's face as he plowed into the guard, driving him backward. He could feel Rotos' presence directly behind him.

There were perhaps a half-dozen guards arrayed in the tunnels near the stairway. Only three were close enough to interfere in the escape. Rotos shoved past Kied and barreled into two of them, knocking them off their feet. Kied slammed into the third and the man fell back against a stone pillar, the back of his helmet ringing against the rough surface.

"Let's go!" yelled Rotos, looking back at the prisoners lining the walls. There was an instant of silence as everyone absorbed what had just happened, and then in a rush they suddenly leaped into action. The remaining guards went down under fists and feet, while pairs of still-chained prisoners charged into the stairwell and surged up into the courtyard above.

Rotos grabbed Kied by the arm and hauled him up the stairs as a horn sounded from above. They emerged from the doorway to see about twenty prisoners spreading out in all directions, some heading for the main gates, a few heading for other buildings, and the rest making for the walls. Guards inside the compound were drawing swords and gathering together to cover each other, while those on the walls grabbed their crossbows and took aim at the fleeing prisoners.

"This way," Rotos barked as he turned and ran toward a narrow alley between two buildings, his fist clutching the end of the chain that was still attached to the manacle around his ankle. Kied followed on his heels, looking around frantically for any signs of pursuit.

To one side, a group of four guards spotted the two men and charged toward them, angling to cut them off before they could reach the cover of the alley. Kied saw a prisoner to his right suddenly drop as a crossbow bolt punched into his chest. The man to which he was chained tripped and sprawled in the dirt, unable to free himself from the dead weight now preventing his escape.

Rotos continued to run toward the alley, and Kied realized they wouldn't reach it before the guards intercepted them. But the giant didn't slow, and the guards raised their sword points as the big man came near.

With a swipe of his huge hand, Rotos slapped away the point of one sword and crashed into the guards. Kied dove at the one guard who managed to avoid the tangle of limbs and blades. The man had dodged Rotos' charge, but couldn't recover fast enough to avoid Kied. He slammed into the guard, grabbing his wrist and twisting as they fell to the ground.

Kied managed to land with most of his weight on the guard's

arm, and he heard bone snap as they hit the ground. The guard screamed but the sword fell from his grip. Kied snatched it up and rolled away to regain his feet, the motion sending a sheet of pain though his back as it took his weight. As he rose, he expected a crossbow bolt to hit him between the shoulder blades, but there was nothing he could do about that right now.

The guard tried to sit upright, but Kied drove the point of the sword into the man's neck, shoving him back to the ground. To his right, Rotos surged upward, flinging the limp bodies of two guards backward. But the man still lying on his back at the giant's feet raised his sword and thrust upward.

Kied saw it happening and knew he was too late to stop the deadly thrust. He dove forward, but the point of the guard's sword entered Rotos' belly and slid up into his heart. The guard yanked his blade out just as Kied drove his own sword into the guard's chest.

Rotos threw back his head and bellowed in pain and rage, a huge sound that nearly shook the walls and ground around them. He staggered forward into the alley and Kied followed just as a crossbow bolt embedded itself into the wall of the building right beside his head.

"Rotos!" Kied shouted, but the giant continued to move forward despite his fatal wound. Kied had seen berserker warriors before, men who took terrible wounds and fought on for minutes after they should have collapsed. But their injuries inevitably caught up with them.

Rotos was a walking dead man, and there was no way he would ever see another dawn.

The giant emerged from the alley into the open space between the building and the outer palisade. Kied could see guards running along the wooden walkway mounted to the inside of the wall. In seconds, they'd be facing a half-dozen crossbows with no way out.

But Rotos picked up speed as he made for the wooden palisade. Kied ran beside him, glancing back to see a trail of blood darkening the ground behind the man. He couldn't believe Rotos was still on his feet, but he probably only had seconds of life left in him.

The guards on the wall closed in on either side as Rotos leaped over the pit and crashed into the palisade with a thundering blow. The wall shook and the supports holding up the walkway cracked under the assault. With a yell, the guards tumbled down off the broken ledge and fell into the pit at the base of the wall.

Kied leaped as far across the pit as he could. As he scrambled up the other side to the wall, he saw that Rotos had cracked two of the thick timbers. The big man reared back and hammered his fist against the wood a second time, and then a third. With a sharp report, the timbers shattered and fell outward, leaving a hole in the wall wide enough for the two men to pass through.

Even better, the fallen timbers made a bridge over the outer pit. Kied reached out to Rotos, who staggered as he stepped aside for Kied.

"Go," the big man growled. "I'm right behind you."

Kied knew he was lying. Rotos wouldn't follow—he was weakening rapidly from blood loss and internal damage.

"Rotos …," Kied said.

But the giant just grabbed Kied by the arm and shoved him up and out onto the timbers. Kied was surprised at the strength still in the man's grip. He was even more surprised when Rotos stepped up onto the wooden bridge and followed.

Kied was just about to step off the other side of the bridge when he heard galloping horses.

"Down!" Rotos growled and dropped off the timbers to crouch on the sloping sides of the pit. Kied knelt beside him as three riders came around the side of the wall and approached the hole. Rotos' head dropped down to his chest, and Kied knew he was finished.

What was he going to do? He was safe for only a minute or two in the darkness. But he couldn't sneak past the riders—they would spot him and ride him down. And if he stayed here, he would be spotted as soon as dawn started to creep over the horizon.

The guards on horseback were so close to him. If only there were some way ….

Kied fell back as Rotos suddenly surged into motion, rising up out of the pit to grab a guard and yank him off his horse. A second guard's sword flashed in the dim moonlight, but Rotos used the first guard's body to block the attack, and then heaved the body up to knock the second guard off his horse.

The third guard gave a yell and galloped off as Kied climbed out of the pit. Rotos, amazingly, pulled himself up onto one of the horses. Kied climbed up onto the saddle of the second horse.

"You lead," Rotos gasped. "Head northwest. There are ... gullies ...."

Kied couldn't believe the other man was still alive. He had seen the sword enter the man's body. He thought it had been a fatal wound, and most men would have died within seconds. But Rotos had managed to not only hold on, but to shatter the wooden palisade with his bare hands, and then still take down two more mounted guards.

Kied urged his horse into a gallop and glanced back to see the second horse following. Rotos leaned forward over the saddle, his arms draped on either side of the horse's neck.

Though the sword blade had obviously missed Rotos' heart, there was little chance he would recover. When the big man inevitably lost consciousness, Kied knew he would fall from the galloping horse. What then? Rotos had given his life to get Kied out of the prison.

It would be up to Kied to make sure the man's sacrifice was not in vain.

Chapter Ten

KIED WALKED HIS HORSE THROUGH THE MAZE OF GULLIES that crisscrossed the land in this region. Most were deep enough that he could not be seen from above, and he hoped he could get far enough to lose any pursuit, at least until nightfall.

Dawn had broken a few hours ago, and now Kied searched for a good shaded spot where he could rest the horses and avoid the late morning heat. He glanced back and saw that Rotos' body still lay across the other horse's back. He didn't know how long the other man had managed to live during their flight through the dark night.

But it was obvious Rotos was now dead.

He knew he should have pushed Rotos' body off the other horse—the extra weight was unnecessary and eliminated the benefit of having a second horse he could use to escape. But something inside him wouldn't let him just leave the other man's body. He didn't know why, but he felt Rotos deserved a proper goodbye, even if he couldn't give him a proper burial or cremation.

Up ahead, Kied spotted a place where some dead and broken trees on the ground above had fallen across the top of the gulley, making a deep spot of shade. It wasn't perfect, but it was as good as he was likely to find anytime soon. Reining up, he slid off the horse and led the beast into the shade.

Kied turned to the second horse and led the beast up beside the first. He placed his hand on Rotos' arm in a silent thank you to the man who had given his life to get Kied out of the prison.

Kied nearly screamed as the big man let out a low moan and

twitched his arm.

He's still alive!

Kied pulled the long hair away from the man's face and saw Rotos' eyelids flutter. The giant wasn't conscious, and he was barely breathing, but he had somehow managed to hold onto life for the entire night.

Though he was surprised by Rotos' survival so far, he had to consider that the sword wound wouldn't ultimately kill the other man. Kied decided to make the man comfortable. He pulled Rotos out of the saddle, trying to support the big man's weight as he slid off the horse. Kied only succeeded in keeping Rotos' head from hitting the ground as the giant's body nearly crushed him as it fell from the horse.

Rotos let out another low moan as he hit the ground.

Kied had to use all his strength to pull Rotos into the shade. He laid the big man out on the side of the gulley's slope, and then sat beside him. The front of Rotos' body was covered with dried blood, and Kied could see the tear in his tunic where the sword had entered his belly.

Kied lifted the man's tunic and looked at the wound. It continued to seep a pink, watery liquid, but Kied didn't know what that meant. It certainly looked like a mortal wound—the sword blade had likely sliced up Rotos' insides, possibly cutting into one of his lungs.

The weapon had obviously not pierced the giant's heart—as Kied had initially feared—or Rotos would be long dead. He didn't think it was possible to recover from what had happened, but the great strength of this man had kept him alive this long.

Might he survive such a grievous wound?

And so Kied was still faced with the decision he had not allowed himself to face last night. If Rotos died during the day, then Kied would make his peace with the man and leave him here when night fell. As much as he hated to abandon the man's body unburied or unburned, he couldn't afford the time to do either.

But what if Rotos was still alive when it was time for Kied to move on? He couldn't just leave the man to be found by wild animals? Even if Rotos never regained consciousness, it was a terrible way to die.

Kied knew it was futile to debate with himself about the rational course of action. Leaving Rotos wasn't an option until the man either woke up or passed away. He had taken the wound while helping Kied escape. Kied owed it to Rotos to stay by his side.

So Kied sat beside the giant and thought about other pressing problems. First, he'd have to find water. He needed it, and the horses needed it. It was one of the first things he'd have to do once the sun set. He would also need food, though that could wait a bit longer.

The hours passed slowly as the sun crawled across the sky. Kied dozed fitfully, always starting awake at any unfamiliar noise, grabbing for the sword that he kept at his side. He continued to check on Rotos, but there was no change in the man's condition. It was as if the man refused to let go of life, no matter how tenuously he clung to it.

Finally, after the sun had long passed over the edge of the gulley and lay touching the horizon, Kied pulled himself to his feet. He looked down at Rotos lying in the shadows. The man was still breathing.

"So now what do I do with you?" he muttered.

Rotos' eyelids fluttered, and then the man opened his eyes and focused on Kied.

"You're still here," he whispered.

Kied nearly dropped his sword. Rotos was awake.

"Rotos," he said in a low voice. "You've been … injured. It … it's bad."

"I know," the other man whispered back. "I'll … be okay. I just need a bit more time."

A bit more time? That was something they didn't have.

"It's been an entire day," Kied told him. "We're not safe here. They must be hunting us, and we can't wait here until you're okay."

Rotos frowned up at him.

"I know that," he growled. His voice was still weak, but there was a hint of his power when he spoke. "I'm not dying, but I can't just shrug off a wound like this."

Kied hesitated.

"I'm sorry, Rotos. It's just that it looks like you took a mortal wound."

"No," the giant said. "The sword won't kill me. I'll be weak for a while, but my strength will come back. I'm already healing. I'll need your help to get back into the saddle, but I will be much stronger by morning."

Kied sat back, stunned. He knew there was something special … powerful … about Rotos. No normal man could have survived the wound Rotos had taken last night. It wasn't something from which one could just heal. This was … sorcery? Something else?

"Who are you," he asked the other man in a low voice.

Rotos said nothing for long minutes. He just stared up at the tree trunks over his head. Kied could hear him taking stronger and deeper breaths the longer he lay here. It was as if his wound was nothing more than a beating.

"I'm not ready to tell you that yet," Rotos replied. "I don't intend to tell you at all, but I have a feeling you'll end up finding out the truth before this is over."

Kied didn't know what to say. Rotos *was* going to survive, and Kied wasn't sure what this meant for his own future. Suddenly, Kied had a purpose again beyond just his own survival.

Rotos raised his head and looked Kied in the eye.

"We'll wait here a bit longer, and then you'll help me back up onto the horse. We need to find water and some food. We've got a long journey ahead of us."

*   *   *

KIED USED THE BRANCH TO BRUSH THE SAND, OBSCURING THEIR trail.

"That's not going to work," Rotos rumbled.

Kied stopped and turned to the big man. Rotos sat on his horse, barely upright, barely holding on. His strength was returning, but it would be a while yet before he could easily sit a horse.

"It's better than nothing," Kied replied.

"It's a waste of time and energy," Rotos retorted. "Their trackers won't be fooled by that. If we want them to lose our trail, we have to do something more drastic."

The two men had found a small pond an hour earlier, and had watered the horses and themselves. Now, they tried to put as much distance between them and any pursuers as possible.

"What do you have in mind?" Kied asked him.

"We leave the gullies for a bit. Go up top where it's all rock. It'll be nearly impossible for them to figure out which direction we went. We'll travel for an hour or two across the rock, and then drop back down into the gullies before the sky begins to lighten."

Kied considered the plan.

"We could be spotted while we're up there."

"We could," Rotos agreed. "Though it's a dark night, and I think we've put some distance between us and them. Still, if they're close, they'll probably see us."

"You're in no condition to fight, not yet at least. If we're spotted, it's all over."

Rotos nodded but said nothing. Kied worried about how close their pursuers might be. He had no way of knowing their location, but little choice. By dawn, they would reach the edge of this region, and the gullies would give way to grassland that stretched to the mountains.

Kied knew they would need to spend tomorrow night crossing as much of the grassland as they could. There were very few trees, and no place to hide. Anyone following them would easily spot them once the sun came up.

"Okay, we do it," he decided. "There's a path just back there that leads up to the surface."

He led his horse back to the rocks that formed a natural ramp up out of the gully, Rotos riding slowly behind him.

"My horse isn't going to make it up with me on it," he said in a low voice. Rotos slowly slid off his horse and stood unsteadily, leaning heavily against the beast. Kied stepped over to him and Rotos put his arm over Kied's shoulders.

"You sure you can do this?" Rotos asked.

"No, but what choice do we have?"

Rotos snorted and let go of the horse. He tried to keep most of his weight off Kied—both men knew Kied would never be able to fully support the big man—and he staggered slightly as he stepped up onto the ramp.

More than once, Kied was sure they were going to topple back down into the gully. But slowly, and with great care, they managed to ascend to the surface. Rotos sank onto the hard rock and took a deep breath. Kied looked around but could see nothing in the darkness.

He returned to the gully and began to lead his horse up to the surface. The animal balked at first, not wanting to step up onto the stone ramp. Kied swore under his breath and then forced himself to remain—and sound—calm. He spoke gently to the horse, urging it forward.

The animal's hooves slid on the sandy surface of the ramp, and its eyes rolled in their sockets. Kied gripped the reins with all his strength and continued to speak soothingly to the animal. Finally, the horse stepped up onto the rocky ground above and Kied handed the reins to Rotos.

The second animal was less trouble—Kied figured it was exhausted from carrying Rotos, or perhaps it merely wanted to join its partner on the surface above. Regardless, the animal came up with a minimum of fuss, and soon they were ready to depart again.

Kied had just mounted his horse when Rotos hissed at him. He stopped and listened, glancing at the other man. Rotos was staring off into the distance to their right. Kied held his own breath, though his horse's breathing would cover any light noise from anyone out in the darkness.

He gripped the hilt of his sword and stared out into the darkness, willing his eyes to pierce the veil that hid their pursuers. But he could see nothing. Perhaps whoever was out there was equally blinded by the near impenetrable darkness.

And then, so slowly that at first he thought it was his imagination, or that his eyes were playing tricks on him, he saw a glow begin to appear from within the same gully from which they had just climbed. It was farther down the path, but the source of the light was moving slowly closer.

Faintly, on the very edge of his hearing, Kied could make out a slithering noise, as of silk garments being rubbed together. Rotos was rooted to the spot, staring at the same pale glow.

"That's not torchlight," Kied whispered. Rotos didn't respond.

The slithering noise took on a strange quality, and Kied focused on it. There was a pattern buried in the noise, gaps and changes in pitch that resembled ….

With a start Kied realized he could hear words, unintelligible yet, but speech, nonetheless. He realized at the same moment that the glow was not caused by a lantern either. This light was white, and had a strange, surreal quality about it.

Off in the distance, from another direction, Kied heard a cry. It sounded like an infant.

What would a baby be doing out here in this land? Kied thought to himself. A second voice joined it from another direction, and then a third. The children screamed as if they were in great pain, their howls arising from out of the darkness in a great semi-circle around the two men.

Rotos turned to Kied, his eyes wide and his mouth open. The look of horror on the giant's face turned Kied's blood to ice.

"Ride!" he said out loud, his lips barely moving. "Ride and don't look back."

Rotos spun his horse around and kicked it into a gallop. From the edge of the gully, Kied saw pale white arms rise up and slowly reach for the rock surface. Some small part of his mind noted the arms had too many joints in them, and there were too many fingers on the delicate hands that grasped the edge of the rock.

He wheeled his horse and galloped off after Rotos, not knowing what was behind them and not wanting to find out. He understood that this reckless ride across the rocky surface was possibly just as dangerous as whatever was back in the gully. It was too dark to see where they were going, and this region was riddled with gullies like the one from which they fled.

It was quite possible they would come to a gap before they could see what was ahead of them. If they toppled into a gully with their horses, they might not survive the fall.

But luck was with them as they spotted a gaping pit to one side in time to avoid it, and angled their path to gallop alongside the edge. The cries of the infants behind them faded, but Kied didn't look back to check if the glow was still following them. Rotos obviously knew more about whatever was behind them than he did.

Minute after minute passed, and eventually Rotos drew rein and slowed his horse to a walk. The beast's ribs heaved as the exhausted creature tried to catch its breath. Kied moved up beside the other man.

"What was that thing?" he asked. Rotos rode on in silence for a minute, and then brought his horse to a stop.

"This land wasn't always like this," he said. "This all used to be grassland, a very long time ago. People lived here. Whole villages of mud and stick huts."

Rotos turned and looked back into the darkness in the direction from which they had come. Kied followed his gaze, but the glow was gone and a wall of darkness faced him.

"They had certain beliefs, certain rituals. Their shamans led the villages in worship, and the people joined in willingly."

Kied turned to look at Rotos. The fear was gone, but he spoke as if he was watching something far away.

"Their rites were foul, awful affairs. They brought this on themselves. They brought that," he said, gesturing into the darkness, "on themselves. The people are long dead, but the world still recoils from the things they brought forth in their ignorance and arrogance. All they can do is cry warnings into the night."

"Wait," said Kied. "You mean those infants were …? But you said they're all dead …."

Rotos turned and looked at Kied, and then gently shook his head.

"They are not worth discussing. Their lessons haven't been learned, and the same mistakes keep being made."

Rotos slid off his horse and began to walk, slowly but without needing any assistance. Kied could do nothing but follow.

Chapter Eleven

TIATH BLINKED AWAY TEARS AS HE LOOKED AT THE entrance to the pass between the valleys. The chill wind cut across the valley mouth, making his eyes water and his skin tighten. It might be springtime further down the slopes, but up here it still felt like the remnants of winter had its claws dug into the peaks and refused to be swept away.

He reined in his horse and looked back at his companions, riding single file up the trail behind him. Azam drew up as he neared, the others following suit.

"We'll camp over there, in the lee of those rocks," said Tiath. The others simply nodded, and he turned his horse and led the way.

As soon as they reached the spot where they would build their campsite, all four quickly got to work. Pasill began to build the fire, while Deylista and Azam took care of the horses. Tiath climbed up on the rocks and looked around, carefully scanning for any signs of life.

By now, no one should be freely wandering in the valley or anywhere near the pass. But Tiath took his own precautions—he had long ago learned to rely only on a select few he had hand-picked and trained himself. His three companions were the best of the best, true professionals who were utterly reliable.

By the time the fire was roaring and the horses were settled, Tiath was satisfied that no one was near. The sun had moved well beyond the edge of the peaks by this point, and shadows were thickening the air around them. He climbed back down the rocks and rejoined the others. Pasill and Deylista pulled the rations out of the packs and handed them out to Azam and Tiath. They seated themselves around the fire and began to eat in silence.

Finally, when they had finished, Azam left the fire and climbed up onto the rocks to settle in for his watch. He was far enough away from the fire that it wouldn't ruin his night vision, but close enough that he could quickly return to the camp and wake the others if anyone—or anything—approached.

Tiath watched Pasill as Azam left the circle of firelight. He didn't know precisely when the two men had become involved, and that worried him. He was usually more aware of the lives of his people, and wondered what else he might have missed.

Tiath briefly considered talking to the two men about their situation, but decided to hold off. He trusted both of them to remain professional and to do their jobs to the best of their ability. Though, he had to admit to himself that he wasn't entirely happy about it. This team regularly put itself into dangerous situations, and none of them could afford misjudgments based on emotional attachments to the other members of the team.

Still, both men had proven themselves time and again, and Tiath trusted them to react properly when they inevitably faced the next threat to their lives.

His gaze shifted to Deylista, sitting just back far enough from the fire that her face was in shadows. She had always preferred the darkness, the secret ways, the blade from out of nowhere. But he could also tell she was troubled by something. He stood and stretched.

"Deylista," he said. "Walk with me."

She rose to her feet like a spring uncoiling, a smooth economy of movement marking a deadly grace. She was the one member of the squad Tiath believed could best him in a fight. He hoped he'd never find out.

The two walked into the darkness some distance from the fire. The night was a wall of black in front of him as he waited for his eyes to adjust after the brightness of the flames.

"What's bothering you?" he asked her bluntly. She preferred the direct approach.

She stood silently beside him for a moment, contemplating.

When she answered, her voice was tight, her words clipped. Tiath could feel her body practically humming beside him, like a rope that was stretched too tight.

"I don't trust them," she said finally.

"Who?"

"The ambassador … and the priest. They are keeping back something important."

Tiath nodded. "No doubt. We would be fools to trust them. But we've been in this kind of situation before. We can never fully trust those who give us orders."

"This is different," Deylista said, her voice harsh. "I …."

Tiath waited for her to finish her thought, but she remained silent.

"Do you remember when we met?" he asked. She turned fully to him, staring into his face.

"I would never forget," she said. "You saved my life. You gave me purpose."

"I gave you a chance. But do you know why I picked you over anyone else?"

"Because I am a killer."

Tiath frowned at her. "After everything we've been through so far, is that what you really think?"

"No, I … I'm sorry, sir. I know you saw … something in me. I've tried not to let you down."

"You haven't yet, Deylista. And I honestly don't believe you will. I chose you to join my squad back then not because you were a killer. Anyone can kill. I chose you because you're smart, and you're brave."

He could see the confusion on her face.

"What you did took guts, it took planning, it took attention to detail. You conceived of a mission, you put it together, and you executed it without any backup, with no resources, and with everyone against you."

"I was caught," she said simply.

"No, you were betrayed," he corrected. "Otherwise, they would never have caught you."

"Do … do you ever think about what I did? That I murdered my commanding officer and some of my fellow soldiers?"

Tiath couldn't help but smile.

"Oh, I considered that quite thoroughly before I requested your pardon. But when you're guarding my back, I feel safe, not threatened."

He could feel her relaxing as he spoke. It was time to get to the truth.

"What's really bothering you?" he asked. She froze, but then seemed to deflate.

"Sir, we're not priests … or sorcerers. We don't know what kind of guardians we'll face, or—"

"We've faced our share of eldritch threats before," he said interrupting her.

"This is a gateway to another world," she hissed. "Like where the gods come from. We can't imagine what might be waiting for us. We can't prepare the way we should."

"We're going in blind," Tiath finished.

Deylista nodded at him.

"Listen, I don't disagree with you. This is pretty far from ideal. But you trust me, right?"

"Of course, sir."

"No, not as your commanding officer. As me, as Tiath. Do you trust me?"

"Sir, I trust you with my life, and with my soul."

"Then trust me when I tell you this mission is an opportunity. I'm not going to say anything more than that right now. But if you trust me like you say you do, then understand I have no intention of getting us all killed, or worse. I don't leave anything up to chance."

Deylista looked into his eyes. And then she lowered her head and stared at the ground.

"Sir, please accept my apologies—"

"No," he said. "There's nothing to apologize for. We've never done a mission quite like this before, and we're all a bit on edge. I'm responsible for you, but I also rely on you. I need to know when something troubles you, because you have great instincts. Never apologize for bringing your troubles to me. Your opinion informs my choices."

He could see Deylista relax. She nodded at him, but didn't smile. He had never seen her smile in the entire time he had known her.

"All right," he said. "It's time to get some rest. We've still got a lot of work ahead of us."

*   *   *

THE MOUNTAINS ROSE UP BEFORE THEM LIKE THE RAMPARTS OF some colossal fortress, the abode of giants reaching into the sky. A swiftly flowing river emerged from a narrow valley ahead of them, twisting and turning among the foothills clustered at the base of those impossible peaks. The pass they sought was not yet visible from their vantage point, and it seemed as if the wall of stone above them was unbroken.

"You sure you know where you're going?" Kied asked his companion who stood at his side. The horses rested at the base of the hill, drinking from the edge of the river that twisted away to their left.

Rotos grunted and waved a hand at the river. Kied was left to assume the river indicated something about their path, as Rotos was obviously not inclined to elaborate. He had withdrawn into himself since they had ridden out of the broken lands four days ago, and Kied was now unable to get more than a dozen words out of him each day, and never so many all at once.

A cool breeze wafted among the foothills and Kied shivered. Winter was barely over up there among the heights, and neither man was dressed for traveling in such a climate. He returned to the horses and picked up one of the saddles. It was time to get moving again.

"Leave them," Rotos growled from behind him.

"What? Why?"

"Can't climb," the big man grunted and looked back up the slopes to the peaks above.

"I thought you said there was a pass." Rotos ignored his question and continued to stare upward.

Kied wanted to swear at his companion, tell the man exactly how much he appreciated being kept in the dark. But he knew it would do no good. Rotos would talk to him when he decided it was time and not before.

He wasn't sure exactly where they were, nor in what direction their destination lay. Regardless, some hard travel faced the two men, and it would only get more difficult as they ascended the slopes of the mountain range.

Kied removed the bridles from the horses while Rotos continued to scan the heights. The animals grazed on the grass at the edge of the river even after they were free. He expected they would stay here for the rest of today and perhaps during the night, before wandering off when the sun rose.

Neither man was worried about pursuit at this point. When they had crossed from the scrubland into the waving fields of long grass, they were completely in the open. If pursuers had been following, that was the point at which the fugitives would have been spotted. But there had been no sign of anyone on their trail for days now.

Their escape from the prison seemed to have been successful.

But instead of hiding out in some town on the other end of the Empire, like any normal man might do in these circumstances, Kied and Rotos were heading right for a contingent of the Imperial Legion. A contingent that Kied had once led, the leaders of which had betrayed him and sent him to be court-martialed and tried for treason.

He shook his head at his own stupidity. He had freely taken an oath to the spirits of his comrades who had followed and supported him. Their deaths weighed heavily on his mind and his heart, and he knew he couldn't stop until he had done something to lay them to proper rest.

And there was only one way he could do that.

Rotos was already walking up the final hill toward the slopes of the mountain, and Kied slung the saddle bags over his shoulder and hurried to catch up with the man. They traveled in silence for some time as they climbed, the sun and the physical exertion warming them up until both men were sweating.

Kied's blood pounded in his ears, and he stopped and shook his head, trying to get rid of the rushing sound that he realized had been sounding in his head for some time now.

"I need to rest," he told the giant. Rotos stopped and looked back at Kied, his eyebrows raised.

"My ears are … I hear—"

"Water," Rotos interrupted. Kied looked at him dumbly.

"You hear water," Rotos repeated. "We're not far, now."

"Far from what?"

Rotos turned and looked at the slope, both above and behind.

"The waterfall. That's what you hear. Near its head is a passage that cuts through the rock and will take us right through the side of the mountain into one of the valleys."

It was the most Rotos had said to Kied all at once for two days. Kied looked around, as if he might spot the waterfall himself.

"The waterfall is the source of the river where we watered the horses?"

Rotos nodded. Kied felt a new energy in his limbs.

"Let's go," he said.

Rotos held up a hand.

"We need to catch some food before we go in. There isn't anything to eat in that passage, and we'll be underground for at least a day."

The hunt took the rest of the afternoon, as neither man was particular skilled at catching animals. But they were still below the tree line and there was an abundance of small game in among the needle-covered boughs. Eventually, they captured and killed enough food for a couple of days.

Rotos quickly set a fire, screened by a copse of trees on the downward slope so that no one below them would be able to spot their camp in the rapidly growing darkness.

As they cooked the meat, Kied watched Rotos over the flames. The big man was lost in his own thoughts and said little.

"What are they looking for?" Kied asked him.

Rotos raised his eyes and blinked.

"What?"

"I asked you what they're looking for. You obviously know the prize they seek. What's hidden in those valleys? What's worth killing all those innocent people for?"

Rotos lowered his eyes to the sizzling meat once more.

"Something dangerous."

"I figured that much myself. What's in this cave they want to find so much?"

Rotos sat in silence, saying nothing. Kied had learned that if he also stayed silent, the other man might eventually answer his questions. But tonight, Kied was in for disappointment.

"It's better you don't know," Rotos said in a low voice.

Kied sat up and glared at his companion.

"Don't even try that shit with me. You wouldn't even know the contingent was up there if I hadn't told you. We're in this together. You owe me an answer."

The firelight reflected in Rotos' eyes and he raised his gaze and focused on Kied. When he spoke, there was a tone in his voice that said Kied had just done something stupid.

"Owe you?" Rotos growled at him. "You've obviously lost your wits. Not only have I saved your worthless hide over and over again, I got you out of that prison in one piece. If not for me, you'd still be in that cell, or dead at the hands of your admirers."

Kied raised his hands in surrender, hoping Rotos would calm down. But the big man was just getting started.

"I stopped them from killing you, took lashes from the guards, took a sword wound that would have killed any other man. Crossing paths with you is the worst thing that could have happened to me. It wasn't time for me to leave that prison yet. But here I am, breaking an oath that—"

Rotos suddenly choked off his words, his eyes bulging. Kied realized the other man had been about to say something about why he had been in prison, why he had stayed there when he could have escaped any time he wanted to do so. He needn't even have fought his way out—his brother Yarrian could have spirited him away with the guards never realizing until it was too late to do anything about it.

"I'm sorry—" Kied began, but Rotos thrust himself to his feet.

Kied flinched back, sure that the big man was going to lash out at him. But Rotos just stood there, glaring down at Kied, the light from the fire dancing over his face. In that moment Rotos was more than a man—he was a malevolent god looking down on a mortal servant in judgement.

Kied felt an overwhelming urge to abase himself at the feet of his companion.

Rotos spun on his heel and stalked away into the darkness, and the feeling drained away. Kied gasped as if someone had thrown a bucket of ice-cold water over his head. The stars spun in the sky far above.

Kied toppled backward, staring up at the glittering blanket above him. The patterns of the stars twisted and writhed, and Kied was sure he could glimpse terrible truths and horrid meaning in the shifting pinpricks of light.

He closed his eyes and jammed his fists over them to keep the ideas away, and he fought to hold onto consciousness as it tried to slip away from him.

He didn't know how long he lay there like that, trying to concentrate on anything other than those fleeting glimpses that had tried to burn themselves into his brain. But eventually he felt reality slip back into place around him. He slowly lowered his hands and fearfully opened his eyes.

The night sky was full of stars, but they were no longer moving. It was the same sky he had seen his whole life, familiar and comforting.

Kied pulled himself back into a sitting position and looked around. He couldn't see where Rotos had gone, and worried that the man had abandoned Kied there on the side of the mountain. But if so, there was nothing he would be able to do about it until morning.

Eventually, his exhaustion caught up with him, and he felt himself nodding off in front of the fire. Kied stretched out and tried to make himself as comfortable as possible on the hard ground. Moments later, he was fast asleep.

Chapter Twelve

THE GLASS WAS EMPTY AGAIN. ZARTAY LOOKED AT IT, HIS eyes narrowed. He wanted to pick it up and throw it, to hear the satisfying smashing sound as the glass shattered against a hard surface. But the canvas walls of his pavilion stymied him.

Besides, he would then have to wait for someone to find a new glass before he could drink again.

Zartay was in a foul mood, and needed someone to take it out on. As a diplomat, he rarely allowed himself to let his emotions go. But tonight he wanted to be cruel to someone. As his eyes focused on the soldier, he considering making this man the target of his ire.

No, that will just come back to bite me, he thought to himself.

Zartay had been drinking, but wasn't drunk. His patience had run out, however. He didn't want to be here, in this godsforsaken village sitting in this pathetic valley high up in the barren mountains. Zartay belonged in Ythis, or at least Caladur or Svislen or some other large city where he could get decent liquor, attractive company, and all the other comforts of home.

He realized the soldier was waiting to be acknowledged. No doubt there was some message from Commander Naschect, or a question perhaps about Tiath's specialist team out there somewhere searching for the tomb.

"What is it?" he snapped. The guard didn't flinch or otherwise give any indication he was aware of Zartay's tone.

"Sir, Commander Naschect is here to speak with you."

Zartay closed his eyes and forced himself to take a deep breath.

The bloody woman was here, bothering him in person. But he couldn't very well ignore her, and she knew it. Right now, the ambassador really had nothing to do. Boredom was one of the reasons he was so irritable.

It occurred to him that the priest had not been seen in three days. No doubt he was out in the village—perhaps this one, perhaps one in another valley—wreaking havoc with some poor family. Zartay suppressed a shudder. He didn't want to think about what the insane priest was up to.

He supposed he should have kept a firmer grip on Brother Hissiath, but he wasn't about to deny the man permission to leave the tent the whole time he was here. Zartay didn't want to be around the priest any more than the villagers would. Better that he work out his psychosis on other people than stay cooped up here with Zartay.

It was probably better that Zartay was still mostly sober. If the commander was here, it was because there was a problem somewhere. He heaved a sigh and looked at the soldier.

"Send her in," he said, modifying his tone somewhat.

The soldier saluted and stepped back outside. A few seconds later, Commander Laita Naschect stepped into his tent. Despite the late hour, the woman looked as if she had just finished preparing herself for the day. She was certainly disciplined, he'd give her that. But, like all officers in the Legions, she was an annoyance, though a necessary one.

"To what do I owe the pleasure," he said, though he put no welcome in it. She looked him over before answering, but kept her expression neutral. He knew she was judging him, could tell he'd been drinking though he slurred none of his words.

"Ambassador, we need to talk," she said.

"Is there a problem?"

She considered that a moment before answering, "You tell me."

Zartay waved her over to a chair and grabbed a second glass. When he went to hand it to her, she gave a small shake of her head.

"No, thank you."

"I've been waiting for this talk," he replied to her. "It was going to come sooner or later, and we might be here a while. Have a drink and relax, and I'll try to answer as many of your questions as I can."

She took the glass from his hand and he poured a generous helping of fine Girian brandy into it. He sat in another chair facing her and raised his glass in toast. She nodded at him, raised her own glass, and then brought it to her lips. But he could tell that was as far as the liquor went, though she pretended to take a sip.

Stupid bitch, he thought to himself. That brandy is worth more than your life, and you think you can fool me.

"I'd like the truth," she said to him, her voice even.

"Everything I've told you about our mission is true, commander. Though there are elements of which I cannot speak, I haven't lied to you about anything."

"You said this was merely an occupation of the region. We are to hold the people in their villages until the classified part of our mission is complete."

"That's correct," Zartay replied.

"And how much resistance were we expecting, Ambassador? By all accounts this is a peaceful region, sparsely settled. Is there something about the people here, some special abilities or combat experience that I should know about?"

Zartay frowned at her, trying to figure out where she was going with this. He had expected her to ask him about the mission, the timing, and the withdrawal plans. She was smart enough to have figured out that whatever it was they were looking for might not be portable. And if that was the case, the occupation wouldn't just suddenly end as soon as the prize was located.

But she was coming at him from an unexpected angle, and that worried him. He preferred her to remain predictable.

"There is nothing I'm aware of that the people here possess," he answered slowly. "But you are surely concerned about something specific. It would help if you explained the cause of your worry."

"Okay, then," she said, taking a deep breath. "Do you know why we have enough arrows and crossbow bolts with us to fill every living thing in these valleys with feathered shafts? We have munitions enough to flatten every building in every village, enough oil to burn every field. This Contingent is outfitted to conduct a whole lot more than just an occupation and withdrawal, Ambassador."

"Perhaps there is a mistake," suggested Zartay, trying to think fast. The bloody Quartermaster was under orders to keep quiet about the full extent of their supplies until it was needed.

"That's what I thought," she continued. "When I asked my Quartermaster to give me the full accounting of our supplies, he kept only providing counts of the food stores, medical supplies, and the like. He became quite nervous when I demanded to see the full accounting of everything in the supply wagons. He nearly cried when I confiscated his ledgers to review them myself."

Zartay considered his options. Commanders didn't usually delve this deeply into the Quartermaster's business—most couldn't read the ledgers well enough to figure out the exact state of affairs at any given time. He wanted to curse out loud, but held his tongue.

"Have you considered the possibility the Quartermaster is mistaken? Incompetence is not unknown—"

"That was my thought until I had my squad search his tent. The Quartermaster had orders, written orders, about the military supplies he was to bring on this mission. He had hidden them well, but my people are thorough. The orders prove he was doing his job correctly. And they were signed by you."

She leaned forward, put the glass on a small table to one side, and stared Zartay in the eyes.

"Now I have to ask you, are you sure you're telling me the truth?"

The look in her eyes would have pinned Zartay to his chair if he had been anyone else. But, though he had been taken by surprise by her words tonight, he wasn't afraid of her. Zartay had been in the same room as the Undying Emperor himself—a mere commander in the Legions was nothing compared to the overwhelming presence of that being.

He smiled at her, a friendly smile that looked almost, but not quite, sincere.

"Commander, I've made it clear to you that there are some elements of this mission to which you are not privy. At some point in the future, new orders will be handed to you, and you will execute them to the best of your ability."

He leaned forward to match her posture, still smiling, though he let steel show in his eyes.

"Making attempts to learn of classified orders before you are authorized to see them is a gross violation of the law. You have a promising career ahead of you. And you will be, at times, required to execute orders which you might find surprising … or distasteful. But your personal feelings are not relevant."

He sat back in his chair and took another sip of his brandy.

"I'm sure you are busy," he said to her. "Don't let me take up any more of your time."

It wasn't the politest of dismissals, but it got the point across. He was in charge here, not the commander.

Laita stood up and looked down at him. She was obviously unsatisfied by his answers and wanted to demand more, but she knew she had no authority to do so. Still, there were no regulations against asking.

"What are we going to do to these people when the mission is over?" she said in a low voice.

Zartay sat there, staring at her, making her wait for his answer. Just when she was about to say something else, he spoke over her.

"You will do what is necessary. I have no doubt you already know about your predecessor. He made the wrong decision, and paid the consequences for it. I believe you're smarter than he was. I would hate for you to prove me wrong."

Laita's eyes widened slightly at Zartay's words, and he relished the feeling of power he had over her. Turning on her heel, she marched out of his tent.

This time, his smile was real.

*   *   *

THE ENTRANCE TO THE CAVE WAS SURROUNDED BY THE exposed roots of a large tree clinging to the slope above. Kied could see it was pitch dark inside. Off to one side, the waterfall roared out of a crack in the rock, water spilling down into a deep crevasse that eventually cut through the hills far below.

Kied glanced over at Rotos, who was looking around, scanning the area for any sign of other people, either pursuers or witnesses.

The big man had been seated near the fire when Kied awoke this morning. Beside him was a pile of thick branches, and he had already prepared a dozen torches and was working on another. He hadn't acknowledged Kied except to grunt at him when it was time to leave. The men had walked in silence until they reached the entrance to the cave.

Rotos turned and stepped up to the dark entrance and peered inside. Kied could see him sniffing the air and examining the thick, twisted roots around the sides of the opening. Finally, he stepped into the cave mouth and took out one of the torches.

Kied waited until Rotos had the torch fully lit. Then the big man moved farther into the cave and Kied followed him. As he entered, Kied noticed how large the passage was—Rotos was able to walk upright, and the big man's shoulders didn't brush the walls on either side.

The walls and roof were packed dirt, with exposed rock at their feet. The sound of the waterfall became muted as soon as they stepped into the cave. The smell of wet earth filled Kied's nose, mixed with the scent of burning oil from the torch in Rotos' hand.

The big man turned slightly and spoke to Kied over his shoulder. "Stay close to me. Don't wander down any side passages. If you see anything wrong, tell me right away."

"What might I see?" he asked the giant.

"Anything you think shouldn't be in a tunnel that cuts through the ground. Some of the passages might be inhabited. You don't want to meet whatever is living in there. If you see any sign of another ... of anything that doesn't feel right, tell me. I'm safe, but you're not."

Kied wanted to ask why Rotos was safe—he knew it had nothing to do with the man's size or strength—but knew it would be futile. When Rotos had walked away last night, Kied had been pretty sure the other man wouldn't just abandon him, but he was still relieved to find Rotos at the fire this morning. He wasn't going to push his companion today.

Let him have his secrets.

The light of the torch was mostly blocked by Rotos' body, but it was still bright enough that Kied could walk easily and not worry about tripping or falling behind. They walked for nearly an hour, and then Rotos called a halt and lit a new torch, as the first one was beginning to gutter.

"How long will it take for us to get through here?" he asked. Rotos considered the question before answering.

"It shouldn't be more than about ten hours, plus resting time. I would say about twelve or thirteen total. We'll need to stop to eat and rest—some of the going is hard and will tire you out."

"Do we have enough torches?"

Rotos nodded. "We've got enough, plus spares. I made sure of that. If we run out of light, there's no way we'll make it out the other side."

Kied didn't like the sound of that, but there was nothing he could do about it. Rotos dropped the spent torch and continued on. Kied made sure to stay within reach of his companion.

By the end of the second hour, the dirt walls and floor had given way to bare rock. It still seemed like a natural passage, rather than carved. Kied wondered how deep below the surface they were traveling, but he had no way to know and he wasn't going to bother Rotos about it.

As the big man lit the next torch, he looked at Kied.

"The passage is going to change soon. This next section was carved out of the rock. There are symbols and images carved into the walls and ceiling—don't stare at them for too long."

"Why, what will happen?" Kied asked.

"You'll call attention to yourself. We don't want that. Just watch my back and stay close to me. We'll also start to pass side tunnels. Once we do that, things get more dangerous. Our light could attract others. Let's hope they're all sleeping."

"What lives down here?"

Rotos looked down the tunnel in the direction they were about to go, and then back at Kied.

"Some things that are very old, and probably very hungry. They don't belong to this world. Ask me again when we come out the other side. For now, avoid talking unless you must."

Kied nodded and they proceeded on.

The transition from natural cavern to carved passage was abrupt. They reached an opening and stepped down onto a floor of carved obsidian blocks. The walls and ceiling were made up of fitted gray stones with barely a visible seam between them. The air was dry and dusty, and Kied was forced to stifle a sneeze.

His eyes caught a carved symbol in one of the stones, and he focused on it before yanking his eyes away. He had no desire to meet any of the denizens of this place. His nerves were tingling, and he realized he could almost hear a low hum, little more than a deep vibration in his bones. Kied wondered if he had caused that by looking at the symbol on the stone.

Rotos turned to Kied and said in a low voice, "You may feel a deep rumble, though it's probably too low for you to notice. You can ignore it."

"I feel it," he whispered back to Rotos, who raised his eyebrows slightly. Then the big man turned back and continued along the passage.

Minutes later, they passed the first side tunnel. The stones around the tunnel entrance were different, framing the door in a narrow set of greenish bricks with golden symbols carved into them. Rotos held up the torch and peered down the passage, but it led straight on into darkness. He continued along the main tunnel, Kied at his back.

More and more side tunnels appeared, at irregular intervals. Rotos took a quick look down each one as they passed, but kept up his steady pace. Kied was getting tired—they had been walking steadily for over three hours without even a short rest. Still, he had no desire to stop anywhere along this part of their journey, and so continued to follow his companion.

Moments later, he stopped suddenly when he heard a woman's voice call his name. The sound echoed off the stone walls, but Kied knew that voice.

It was Laita.

Rotos continued to walk on as if he hadn't heard anything. Kied opened his mouth to call out to the other man, but Laita's voice came out of the darkness again, calling his name a second time. She sounded as if she was in some pain. He turned and looked back into the darkness, but could see nothing.

To his left sat the entrance to one of the side passages. He stepped up to it, trying to peer into the shadows.

"Laita?" he whispered. What could she possibly be doing down here? Had soldiers from the Contingent found the entrance to this tunnel and were exploring it even now?

Kied shook his head. Something was wrong, but he couldn't quite grasp the idea that seemed to float just out of reach. Laita was somewhere down there. Maybe she was lost without a light. He couldn't just leave her ….

A large hand grabbed his arm just as he was about to step through the entrance into the other tunnel. Kied was spun around to find Rotos standing there. The light of the torch flared in Kied's eyes and he squinted in the sudden light.

"What are you doing?" the man growled at Kied.

"Laita … she …."

"Laita is someone you know?" Rotos asked.

"Yes, I heard her voice," Kied said.

"I told you to tell me if you saw or heard anything strange."

"I tried …," Kied attempted to explain, but his thoughts were muddled.

"We have to leave this place. Now," Rotos said and hauled Kied away from the mouth of the side passage.

It was some minutes before Kied's senses returned to him. Rotos was marching forward, no longer slowing to look into each side passage as he moved. Kied was nearly running to keep up with the large man's long strides.

"I … I …."

"Quiet," Rotos ordered, and Kied stopped trying to explain that he was better now.

Without warning, the tunnel suddenly opened up into a vast cavern, the walls curving away into darkness beyond the light of their torch. A bridge extended out over a drop that seemed bottomless from their vantage. A short way out from the edge, the bridge turned into a staircase that led upward into darkness.

"I'm tired," Kied said, eyeing the staircase. "Can we rest a few minutes before we tackle that?"

Rotos looked back into the tunnel behind them. Kied followed his gaze and for an instant he was sure he could see something moving in the shadows. He got the sense of many eyes and long, segmented legs.

"Never mind," he said as Rotos hauled him up onto the bridge and towards the staircase. Whatever had been behind them didn't follow them out into the cavern, and they began to climb. The steps had no railing, only a sudden drop off into endless darkness. Kied, already tired, went slowly so that he didn't make a misstep and tumble off the stairs.

Eventually, they reached the top of the staircase, which led to the other half of the bridge taking them back into a hole in the cavern wall. They stepped through the doorway into a round room about thirty paces in diameter. Rotos stepped to one side and let go of Kied's arm.

"We'll rest here a bit before going on. We're not far from where the tunnels turn back into natural passages. The going there is tough—we'll have to do some climbing over rocks and some crawling—but the danger is past."

Kied sank to the floor and nodded wearily. He couldn't wait to get out under the sky once more.

Chapter Thirteen

THREE SOLDIERS STANDING NEAR THE LOW STONE WALL eyed Laita sullenly as she rode up the track toward the village. The salute they gave her was barely acceptable, but she let it pass. There were bigger problems to deal with right now.

The soldiers knew what was about to happen, and they had little choice but to accept it, though they would do so grudgingly. Laita didn't care what they thought of her as long as they followed orders. And the truth was, career soldiers always willingly followed strong leaders, even when they hated the people giving commands.

Respect and love were unrelated when it came to the Imperial Legions.

Namal waited at the edge of the village for her. He turned his horse as Laita passed and fell into step beside her.

"Anyone else?" she asked curtly. Namal shook his head.

"No one else is stupid enough to escalate anything right now. They know you're coming to deal with it personally."

They reached the small tent that served as a makeshift command headquarters when Laita was in this area. Dismounting, she led Namal into the tent. He had temporarily taken it as his own quarters, but she found it neat and tidy and ready for her use.

"Where are the two men?" she asked, grabbing a camp chair and sitting near the small iron stove that gave off waves of heat. Namal sat across from her and leaned forward.

"I've got them under house arrest in one of the outbuildings. Four soldiers are guarding them, with orders to send a runner for me if the villagers get themselves worked up again."

"Is there any doubt about what happened?"

Namal heaved a sigh before answering. "None. One of them admitted it to me directly once I got the villagers to stand down. Trial's a formality at this point."

Laita cursed under her breath.

"I'm going to have to execute both of them."

Namal raised his eyebrows but said nothing.

"Don't give me that look," Laita told him. "You know it as well as I do. They murdered that family. They are directly responsible for the riot, which resulted in the deaths of three more citizens of the Empire, and one seriously—possibly fatally—injured soldier."

Namal grimaced. "It's not quite as simple as that. They are claiming self-defense for the killings."

Laita realized she had clenched her fists and forced herself to relax.

"It's not self-defense when you're raping a woman and her husband tries to stop you."

"It's not me you have to convince," Namal replied.

"I don't have to convince anyone," she told him. "I have the authority to deal with the soldiers under my command, to sentence them to whatever punishment I deem appropriate to the crime. Those two men raped a woman, and then killed her husband and her son when they walked in and found them. I don't care that the two villagers attacked those soldiers. As far as I am concerned, it's rape and murder."

Namal pondered that for a moment before speaking.

"What about the other dead villagers? They did attack us first, trying to get to the accused."

"I don't intend to lay any other charges," she replied. "I'm laying this entire situation at the feet of those two men. We're here to keep these people from going where we don't want them to go. But we're also here to protect them. They're all citizens of the Empire, and the Legion failed them. We can't just murder our own people. We have a responsibility."

Namal was looking at her wide-eyed, and she realized she was shouting. Her fists were clenched again, and her blood nearly boiled with rage.

"What aren't you telling me?" he asked her. The question took her off guard and she stammered.

"I … I … what do you mean?"

Namal reached out and took her hands in his. Though she was his commanding officer, he had been a soldier far longer and was almost a father figure to her. There was a certain familiarity she allowed him, and he never abused it. But he knew how to help her regain her focus, and there was little she could keep from him.

Laita valued his advice and his skills more than any other. With Namal at her back, she felt she could face any difficulty and come out on top.

She took a deep breath and let herself regain her calm under the warmth of his rough hands on hers.

"You've never been moody in all the time I've served with you. You don't get angry, you get serious. I'm the sergeant—it's my job to yell, not yours. So something else is wrong if you're losing control like this."

She nodded wearily.

"Yes, well I do think something is very, very wrong here. I had Saeda conduct her own inventory of the supplies. She found some discrepancies, and I went to see the Quartermaster directly to talk about them. He tried to put me off, but I forced the issue until he caved in and showed me his orders … special orders directly from Ambassador Seaphon."

"What was he doing?" Namal asked.

"We've got enough weaponry and munitions to conduct a major operation here. I'm not talking about padding out his supplies and selling them to the soldiers for some extra cash. He's got a supply dump that could support us through the beginning of a pacification campaign."

Namal let go of Laita's hands and sat back, whistling a low note that trailed off as she stood up from her chair and began to pace.

"I went to see the Ambassador the night before last to confront him about it. He refused to answer my questions."

"Not much you can do about that," Namal muttered.

"No, but he had enough to drink that his defenses slipped just a little. I got the impression that when this phase of our operation is over, and we get the rest of our orders, it's going to be bad."

"We've had tough orders before," said Namal.

"Not tough, Namal," she replied. "I think … I have the feeling—and this is just my gut saying this, so take that for what it's worth—that we're going to attack the villages."

Namal considered her words.

"Why?" he asked. "What benefit would it be to the Empire to wipe all these people out?"

"I don't know. And the Ambassador didn't confirm my suspicions. But he did threaten me, and reminded me about Kied."

"What did he say?"

Laita thought about it. "He reminded me that my 'predecessor made the wrong decision' and paid the consequences for it. Seaphon seems to think that's going to put me in my place. But, instead, it got me thinking about Kied."

She saw Namal's frown and waved him off.

"I know, but I've been fine—I haven't really been thinking about him much, if at all. I've been too busy most of the time. But I realize now what Ambassador Seaphon unintentionally told me. Kied was charged with treason, court-martialed, and sent to prison. He was only saved from death by his father."

"Didn't help those who followed him, did it?" Namal growled. Laita knew he blamed the deaths of the command squad on whatever it was Kied had done. As a veteran sergeant, Namal was acutely conscious of the collateral damage that could be inflicted when a commander made a bad decision.

"That's not the point right now, Namal," she said. "What if Kied found out what the next phase of our orders were and refused to go along with them? He wouldn't have agreed to wipe out the people in these valleys. What if he sacrificed himself for—?"

"For nothing," Namal said, interrupting her. "Even if you're right, his little rebellion did absolutely nothing but get his people killed and himself tossed in a prison where he'll probably die sooner rather than later."

Laita knew Namal was correct. She was mostly guessing at this point, and that's what frustrated her the most.

But what scared her was the thought that if she was right, if her orders did include slaughtering the people of this region, she didn't think she'd be able to follow them. And that led down a path she had never contemplated before.

"If I'm right," she said aloud to Namal, "then you are willing to execute the orders no matter what they are?"

Namal didn't answer, but looked at her with sad eyes, eyes that had seen so much in his career as a soldier in the Legion.

"Can I do it?" she asked him. "Can you do it? When I come to you and give you those orders, what will you do?"

"I don't know," he said finally. There was something in his tone and in his gaze that said this talk had disturbed him greatly. His fingers twitched with nervous energy, something she had never seen in him before today. He stood and went to the door, peering out at the cloudy sky.

"Namal," she said to him, "I could be wrong. I don't know enough to make any decisions at this point. Right now, we need to fix the situation here, in this village."

Namal turned to her, and his expression had become stone. She couldn't read anything in his face as he looked at her.

"You're right, commander. Let me know when you're ready, and I'll have the accused brought before you for the trial. We need to deal with this first."

Laita nodded at Namal and he left the tent. It was her responsibility to administer justice, to order the execution of two Legionnaires who had committed heinous crimes against citizens of the Empire. And then she'd need to meet with the villagers and calm their worries and give them a chance to vent their own anger and sadness at what had happened here.

Her own anger and fear would just have to wait.

*　　　　*　　　　*

THE HEAVY, LOW CLOUDS RESEMBLED THE ROUGH, DARK ROCK that had pressed down over their heads as they made their way through the tunnel under the mountain. Still, Kied was grateful to have actual sky above him once more, regardless of how it appeared. Any weather was better than what he had just experienced deep below ground.

The two men had encountered no other creatures, and for that Kied was grateful. But the rest of the trip had been exhausting. They had been forced to climb steep rock slopes, crawl through low tunnels, and balance precariously on narrow ledges over endlessly deep gorges as they made their way toward the exit.

Now Kied nearly staggered as they crested a slope and started down the other side. He needed rest, though he knew none was coming anytime soon. They had reached one of the occupied valleys and must avoid the mounted patrols that surely swept through this area on a regular basis.

Kied was relying on Rotos to alert him to any movement in the valley—his own vision was blurry and unfocused. Never mind the cold, or the hard ground. When they camped for the night, Kied was sure to fall into unconsciousness and sleep like the dead.

He heard Rotos' voice rumble something and had to force himself to focus on the other man's words.

"Down!" Rotos barked at him, and Kied dropped to the ground without another thought. The grass was long and waved in the wind, allowing them to hide easily from distant observers. Rotos crouched beside Kied and peered over the top of the shifting stalks.

"What is it?" Kied whispered. Rotos didn't pull his eyes away from whatever it was he was watching.

"Mounted patrol," he replied. "Four soldiers. They're angling away from us."

So the patrol hadn't spotted Kied and Rotos yet. It was a small bit of luck that they sorely needed.

"We wait here until they're gone, and then find a place to rest until dark. From now on, we travel only at night."

Kied groaned inwardly. He had been desperately looking forward to getting some real sleep.

"Wait," Rotos said and Kied could almost feel the other man tense. "They're changing direction."

Kied wanted to rise up and take his own look, but he knew his movement might be spotted by the soldiers. Rotos stayed as still as a stone as he watched the patrol ride closer.

"We're going to have to move," he said quietly. "They're not coming straight for us, but they'll be close enough to see us hiding here. There's a small copse of trees about two to three hundred strides down this slope. We'll make our way toward that."

Rotos slowly lowered himself down and then began to crawl forward at an angle away from the riders. Kied followed closely behind.

They traveled erratically, constantly starting and stopping, changing directions often. The wind blowing the grass around was their ally, making it harder for observers to spot movement among the stalks. But they were still creating a trail of trampled grass, and even from a distance it might be visible as they pushed through the green waves.

After some minutes, Kied heard the sound of horses coming nearer, off to his left. Rotos stopped and remained still and Kied follow suit. He could hear the soldiers' voices, but was still too far away to make out their words.

The two men remained hidden as the patrol passed by. Rotos held still as a minute passed, and then another. Finally, he started crawling once more. They continued to move forward for some time as the sound of the horses receded into the distance, fading into the constant rush of the wind.

Kied raised his head and saw the trees not far off, the blue-green needles rustling in the chill gusts. A few minutes later, they crawled into the deep shadows that clustered among the trunks. Once they were safely hidden, both men turned and peered out at the mounted soldiers.

The patrol had ridden up the slope and then stopped. They were talking with one another.

"They've found our tracks," Rotos growled in a low voice. As he spoke, one of the soldiers dismounted and knelt down in the long grass.

"If any of them are trackers, we'll have a fight on our hands," he said.

Kied considered the possibility.

"The Contingent has some skilled trackers, but not nearly enough to have one with every patrol."

Rotos remained silent, watching.

The soldier who had dismounted stood back up and spoke with the others. Kied's muscles tensed as one of the soldiers on the horse raised an arm and pointed at the copse where the two men were hiding.

"If they come over here, we're in trouble," he said to Rotos. "Standard procedure is for one of them to remain mounted and outside of any threat range. If the others are attacked, the mounted soldier will ride away and bring back reinforcements."

The one who had dismounted now climbed back up into the saddle.

Rotos sat down and closed his eyes.

"What are you doing?" Kied asked him.

"Keep silent, and don't move," the big man said.

Kied looked back out at the soldiers, who were walking their horses toward the trees. They were following the trail, and it would take them only a couple of minutes to arrive. He looked back down at Rotos, whose face had twisted into a grimace. He was concentrating hard on something, though Kied didn't know what.

And then a great weight seemed to settle down across Kied's shoulders, and he lowered himself to his knees and fought to keep his head up and his eyes open. This was similar to what he had experienced before when Rotos was angry, though this time it was not directed at him.

A thick, pungent odor filled his nostrils, and Kied nearly gagged. It was an animal smell, though stronger than anything he had encountered before.

And then, from the shadows behind Kied, something big and dark burst forth and rushed past him, nearly knocking him over as it passed. The creature barreled out from under the trees into the grass, and Kied caught a glimpse of something resembling a small bear with dark, oily fur.

The soldiers saw the beast charge out into the grass, and they kicked their horses forward, only to recoil as they caught a whiff of the animal's scent.

"Wolverine!" cried one of the soldiers and yanked on the reins to stop his horse from getting any nearer. The other soldiers pulled back as well as the animal ran through the grass, carving a trail away from the trees and up the slope to the rocky ground above.

Kied and the soldiers watched the beast retreat from the area, and one of the mounted men laughed nervously, the sound carried on the wind. The others looked around, and one pulled out a bow and grabbed an arrow.

The feeling of being pushed down under a heavy weight had disappeared, though now Rotos sagged sideways. Kied grabbed him and held him still as the soldiers discussed their next move. He heaved a sigh of relief as the patrol turned and started riding away in the direction they had been traveling when Rotos first spotted them.

Rotos opened his eyes and seemed to gather his strength back.

"Was ... was that animal in here with us the whole time?" Kied asked, thinking about what would have happened if the wolverine had decided to attack instead of run.

"No," Rotos said, and his voice was thick and slow. "I brought it here."

"What do you mean—" Kied started, but Rotos held up his hand.

"We're safe for now. Get some rest. We move out once it's dark."

Dropping his hand, Rotos closed his eyes and almost immediately began to snore. Kied sat in the gloom under the trees for some time before sleep finally found him.

Chapter Fourteen

THE ROCK WALLS OF THE PASS STRETCHED UP ON EITHER side of the group, sheer slopes that swept up towards the peaks far above. The highest slopes were hidden by the clouds, and it looked as though the mountains faded into nothingness as they rose above the valleys.

Tiath glanced up once or twice, but mostly focused his attention on what immediately surrounded him and his people. Somewhere near here was the doorway he sought, a hidden entrance to a crypt that held the next piece of the puzzle.

There was only another hour of sunlight left before the orb would creep behind the mountain ranges and darkness would swiftly fall. Tiath silently cursed the clouds and the short days—he needed light to find his prize, and daylight hours passed too quickly.

Still, his day was not over yet, and his team was spread across the width of the pass, carefully examining the walls on either side for any sign of the hidden entrance. They rode on in silence, only the sound of the horses' hooves and the creaking of their saddles echoing off the blank stone.

At least we're out of that cursed wind, he thought to himself.

"Hold up," Pasill called from the far side.

They all reined in and waited as he explored an irregularity in the rock that had caught his attention. Some of the cuts and ridges could look almost man-made at times, and they had to carefully check each one for any indication it might be their doorway.

Finally, after some minutes, he waved them off.

"It's clear," he called over and moved on.

Minute after minute passed, and Tiath had to force himself to remain focused. After a few hours of searching, all the rock began to look the same. The last thing he wanted was to miss the door and have to explore the entire pass a second time. He checked on the others, but they all seemed alert.

Once more Tiath thought of the gateway that was their ultimate goal. He knew they were walking toward danger, but real opportunities never lay along the safe path. What kind of power sat on the other side of that gate? And could he take some of it for himself before the Emperor claimed the rest?

Tiath shook his head and brought his thoughts back to the task at hand. He didn't want to be the one to miss the sign that showed the location of the doorway. And it could be anything. The sparse information he had indicated there was some marking—some sigil or carving—that would signal the entrance to the crypt. But he didn't know what that mark might be.

He felt a shiver run up his spine as he passed a spot where a slight indent in the rock cast a shadow down the face of the wall. Nothing else about the spot was unusual, and he rode on another few paces before reining in.

"Hold up," he called out and the others came to a stop.

Turning his horse, Tiath rode back to that spot and faced the shadowed alcove. A feeling of dread washed over him as he looked at it, and then faded away. He dismounted and stepped up to the indent. Looking up, he gasped involuntarily and took a step back.

Carved into the slight overhang, a stone eye looked down at him. There was something wrong, something unnatural about that eye, though it appeared ordinary enough.

"This is it," he whispered. He cleared his throat and then spoke louder. "I think I've found it!"

The others hurried over and clustered around the spot.

"Shit," Azam muttered as he neared the alcove. "That doesn't feel right."

"I feel it, too," replied Deylista in a solemn voice.

"We all feel it," Tiath told them. "There's an eye carved under the overhang, and it gives me the creeps something fierce. This has to be it."

Tiath glanced around and realized all the shadows were lengthening and the pass was filling with gloom.

"It'll be dark shortly," Azam said aloud. "Do we camp here overnight, or try to open it before it gets too dark to see?"

Neither of the options appealed to Tiath, and he was sure the others felt the same. They'd sleep poorly near the crypt—he was sure of it. And yet, he was uncertain about opening it right before darkness fell fully in the pass. What kind of guardians might be waiting on the other side of the door?

"We camp," he said finally. "This thing isn't going to open with a good shove. We'll need light to figure out how to unlock it and reach the crypt."

They all stood there, staring at the dark alcove. None of them relished the thought of sleeping near that shadowed doorway.

"We'll camp over there," said Tiath, pointing to the other side of the pass. "Double watches. No one goes anywhere alone tonight."

As the team led their horses away from the doorway and began to make a simple camp, Tiath opened one of the two small wooden cages on the packhorse and drew forth a small, grey bird. He stepped away from the horses and flung the bird up into the air. Wings fluttering, the bird circled once and then flew off back down the pass toward the valley they had just left.

By morning, Zartay would know they had found the crypt. The other bird would be released when they found the cave that housed the gate itself. And then ….

Tiath looked over at the alcove and suppressed a shudder. He had a feeling entering the crypt was going to be unpleasant at best. He could only imagine what might wait for them in there, protecting the remains of whoever had been interred.

He wished, not for the first time, that he had more information. But he was dealing with ancient history here. Scant writings were all he had as resources. Ultimately, it didn't matter. He would prepare himself and his team, and they would go into the crypt and extract what they needed.

It was what they did, regardless of the difficulty of the task. One way or another, Tiath was going to find that gateway.

Azam and Deylista were on the first watch, and Tiath wrapped himself in the thick blanket and jammed his body into the corner where the stone wall met the floor of the pass. He couldn't fall asleep for some time, but he kept his eyes closed and rested as best as he was able.

Eventually sleep took him, and his mind was filled with dark thoughts of twisting passages and cold hands reaching out of the shadows to claw at his skin, leaving burning scratches on his arms and chest that would not stop bleeding. Above him, the eye was always present, watching him with a cold, alien gaze.

When Azam woke him for his own watch, he couldn't shake the feelings of despair and loneliness that had filled his dreams. Azam bedded down and seemed to find sleep much faster than Tiath had managed. Deylista sat near the small fire, glancing over at the doorway every few seconds.

"Did you sleep?" she whispered to him. He nodded.

"Don't expect happy dreams," he told her.

By the time it was Deylista's turn to sleep, Pasill was moaning in a low voice. Tiath woke him, and Pasill bolted upright breathing heavily.

"It's okay," Tiath told him. "Our dreams are bad here."

It took a couple of minutes for Pasill to fully calm down. When he joined Tiath at the fire, he seemed embarrassed.

"Don't worry about it," Tiath told him. "This is one of the stronger ones I've encountered, and you were asleep the longest so far. If we can get that door open early, we can be well away from here before we have to make camp again."

Pasill nodded wordlessly. Just like Deylista, he kept glancing at the hidden doorway every so often.

Tiath sighed. He couldn't wait for dawn to arrive.

*   *   *

SMALL PLUMES OF SMOKE WAFTED UP FROM THE CHIMNEYS BEFORE shredding apart in the brisk wind. The low clouds seemed to press down on the dark wooden walls and thatched roofs. A cluster of tents squatted on the field directly south of the village, the canvas snapping and rippling under the caress of the chill breeze.

Kied could see four soldiers walking a slow patrol down the single road that passed through the town. It was little more than a pair of wheel ruts surrounded by flattened grass and churned-up mud. No villagers were visible from Kied's vantage point just behind the top of a hill a few hundred strides away.

He knelt down and told Rotos what he saw.

"We need to find the main camp," the other man rumbled. "I need to see the maps, see if the cave has been located."

"I thought you knew where we were going."

Rotos hesitated before answering.

"I don't … I can't remember where the cave is located, precisely."

"What?" Kied nearly shouted, and then immediately lowered his voice again. "If this cave is so important, how could you forget something like that?"

"It is important," Rotos replied. "But that cave has been hidden for … for a very long time. I've spent cent … many, many years trying to forget where it is. The location is not supposed to be known. That's why your Legion is here, and why that special team of yours is searching these valleys. They don't know its exact location. And I no longer remember."

"If it's so well hidden, how likely are they to find it?" Kied asked.

"If your Emperor has sent this force here, then he's found something that gives him a clue, a point in the right direction. Given enough time, they'll find it. We have to reach it first."

"That'll be dangerous," Kied replied. "The main camp will have more soldiers, and more people who might recognize me."

"Then we'll just have to be careful."

Kied nodded and returned to his position at the top of the hill. The patrol had reached the end of the road and was now returning to one of the tents. Kied scanned the camp and counted the tents he could see. If his calculations were correct, there was a half-detachment quartered here.

Most likely part of this group were tasked with controlling the village, and others would be out on patrol, returning here every couple of days to report in. He figured about one hundred soldiers were stationed here, with perhaps half out on patrol at any given time.

"There could be close to fifty soldiers in that camp," he whispered down to Rotos. The big man shrugged.

"We need food and weapons. Horses, too, if we can manage it. How long do you think a couple of horses can go missing before anyone notices?"

Kied thought about it.

"If the camp quartermaster is halfway decent, no more than a day."

Rotos considered the problem.

"I prefer to not let on that they've been robbed," he said finally. "The longer they go without realizing we're here, the better for us. We'll stick to food and weapons and do without the horses for now."

Kied and Rotos returned to the line of trees that ended less than a hundred paces from where they had spied on the town. It was only mid-morning, and they would have to make their move once it was dark. They settled down among the tree roots, Kied offering to take the first watch, and Rotos was quickly asleep.

Kied rubbed his hands together in a futile attempt to warm them up. The trees provided some shelter from the wind, but the ground was cold and uncomfortable. He pushed needle-covered branches apart and leaned back against the trunk of the tree.

To his left, a twig snapped.

He leaned forward and peered around the branches. No person or animal was visible. Kied pushed himself to his feet slowly and quietly and took a careful step away from his tree, the sword hilt gripped in his right hand. The wind was loud in his ears, masking the sound of anyone—or anything—breathing just out of sight.

Kied took a wide step to his right, giving a better view around the next tree. As he did so, he spotted a figure waiting just around the far edge of the tree. Kied could see the brown leather cloak and the armor of an Imperial soldier.

He sensed movement behind him and spun just in time for the

pommel of a sword to strike him in the face. A searing pain flared in his cheek as he was knocked backward, losing his balance and sprawling on his back in the mud. A second soldier had snuck up behind him, and now the first came out from behind the tree. In seconds, they were joined by two more.

Rotos continued to snore softly among the roots of another tree. The soldier who had struck Kied in the face placed the tip of his sword against Kied's neck and made a gesture to keep silent while his companion pulled a length of twine from a pouch. They quietly and methodically tied Kied's hands behind his back and sat him up on his knees.

One soldier stood behind Kied while the other three approached the sleeping giant. One of the soldiers had a spear, and he stepped forward and poked the tip into the big man's leg.

"Wake up!" ordered the soldier, and Rotos' sleep ended with a snort. He opened one eye to see a spear tip inches from his neck.

"Guh," he said, and Kied could see fear in the man's eyes. A thin trickle of drool oozed out of his open mouth and reached toward the ground.

"Put your hands behind your back!" the soldier ordered, and Rotos' eyes rolled wildly. His hands shook as he slowly moved his arms backward.

One of the other soldiers tied the giant's wrists together behind his back. Kied noticed he used a fair bit of twine to make sure the big man couldn't just snap his bonds apart.

"What's his problem?" a soldier asked Kied. Rotos was moaning softly, and he looked as if he was about to cry.

"Guh," Rotos repeated and looked fearfully up at the soldiers.

"He … he's simple," Kied told them, trying to sound as if he was an uneducated drifter. "He don't speak."

The soldier with the spear kept it aimed at Rotos' throat while one of the other men, a sergeant by the patch on his uniform, turned to Kied.

"Then you'll have to answer all our questions," he said. "Who are you?"

Kied thought furiously.

"G-Gunt," he replied. "That's Danz. We live … farther up the mountain."

"Where, exactly?" the sergeant asked him. Kied jerked his head toward the slopes in the distance.

"Up there. We got us a cave."

The soldiers looked at each other, and Kied was sure they saw right through his lies.

"What are you doing down here?" demanded the sergeant.

"We wanted to trade work for food," Kied answered. "Game's been scarce lately and it was a long winter. We run out of food."

"So you've been here before?"

The question was asked almost as an afterthought, but Kied realized what it meant. If he was telling the truth, someone in the village should know him and his companion. But if no one recognized them ….

"Uh, yeah."

The sergeant turned to Rotos but still addressed Kied.

"Is he violent?" the man asked. Kied shook his head.

"No, he never hurt no one. Don't think he knows how to fight."

"Does he understand when you talk to him?"

"Sure," Kied answered. "He don't speak, but he knows what you're saying."

The sergeant stepped over to Rotos and looked down at the big man.

"Both of you are trespassing in restricted territory. You are under arrest until I can check out your story. If you're telling the truth, you'll stay in the village. If not …."

The sergeant let the threat hang in the air.

"Now stand up."

Kied rose to his feet and Rotos struggled to right himself. None of the soldiers gave him a hand, and Kied marveled at his ability to assume the guise of a clumsy simpleton. The look in the big man's eyes was dull and fearful and his mouth hung open while drool collected in the corners.

The soldier behind Kied shoved him forward and he marched out of the trees toward the village. Rotos followed, stumbling every so often and occasionally moaning in a low voice. It was obvious his companion was letting Kied take the lead. But they were marching toward even more trouble.

None of the villagers could possibly vouch for them. They'd be identified as strangers, and then the soldiers would start to question them with more vigor.

Kied felt well and truly trapped.

Chapter Fifteen

Z ARTAY COVERED HIS EYES AND MOANED AS THE TENT FLAP was pulled aside by one of his soldiers. Even with the heavy cloud cover, it was too bright outside for Zartay's sensitive eyes. His head pounded and his tongue felt like one of the thick rugs that covered the floor of his pavilion.

He knew he shouldn't have had so much to drink last night, but it was the only way he could deal with the tedium of this horrid posting. He cursed under his breath as the soldier stood at attention just inside the entryway.

"What is it?" he asked in a low voice. The soldier stared straight ahead and kept his face emotionless as he answered.

"A message just arrived for you, Ambassador."

That caught Zartay's attention. Finally, something good might be happening.

"Bird?" he asked, almost forgetting about his splitting headache.

"Yes, Ambassador."

Zartay dragged himself to his feet and lurched over to the soldier. "Where is it?"

The soldier handed him a small rolled piece of parchment and withdrew. Zartay unrolled it and forced his bleary eyes to focus on the small handwriting.

Have located first target.

A thrill ran down Zartay's spine. As much as Tiath's squad was legendary among those who worked in the shadows, the ambassador had still harbored his doubts about the success of this mission. He knew the odds of finding their prize was small, no matter what the priest believed.

Zartay turned and tossed the parchment into a brazier, watching to make sure the paper was consumed by the flames before he turned away.

The tent flap was pulled back once again and dreary daylight speared into Zartay's eyes. He squinted and made out a figure stepping into the tent and yanking the flap back into place. Zartay wiped his eyes and focused on a dirty figure dressed in simple farmer rags. But this was no ordinary farmer.

Brother Hissiath's eyes almost glowed with malicious pleasure as he regarded Zartay. The ambassador didn't want to imagine what the priest had been up to these past nights. No doubt some family in the village had become his victims, and it was obvious the mad zealot had indulged his vilest inclinations until he was fully sated.

The priest stepped forward and smiled, a ghastly grin that sent shivers down Zartay's spine.

"Well?" the priest said. "Any news?"

Zartay blinked at him, not sure how to respond. The man had left the tent some nights ago, ordering Zartay to let him be and wait for him to return. It felt as if so much had happened since then. Laita Naschect had questioned him about her orders. She had executed two of her own soldiers for murdering "innocent" citizens of the Empire. And now Tiath had found the tomb.

The priest walked past Zartay and stepped behind the curtain that separated the sleeping area from the rest of the tent. He stripped off his clothes and grabbed a rag from the bucket of water that served as a washbasin. Zartay saw dried blood covering the other man's arms and legs and turned away.

He sat in a chair and looked over at the chest that carried the remains of his stock of liquor. There wasn't much left, but he craved a drink right now more than anything. He forced himself to ignore the demands of his body. It was time to assume his role as master of this operation once more.

Zartay took a deep breath and began to explain everything to Brother Hissiath. It took some time to fully update the other man. By the time he was finished, the priest was dressing himself once more in his robes, the water in the washbasin a rusty brown.

"I have news for you as well," the priest said as he sat himself at the small table and grabbed some cheese and bread from the platter that rested there. He stuffed his mouth and chewed noisily. Finally, he swallowed and then continued talking.

"The commander has been busier than you think," he said. Zartay waited for him to continue, but Brother Hissiath turned and regarded the ambassador with a strange look in his eye. Finally, just as Zartay was about to urge the priest to continue, the man began speaking again.

"She's been talking to her soldiers."

"That's not unusual," Zartay replied. "She's their commander."

"She's been asking questions about matters that don't concern her."

Ice began to fill Zartay's bowels.

"What kind of questions?" he asked in a low voice.

The priest smiled again, and it was no less ghastly the second time around.

"She's been asking about her predecessor—about what really happened."

Zartay cursed loudly. Why did the damned woman have to go causing trouble right now? What was it about the current crop of leaders in the Imperial Legions? Were they all too squeamish to do the job that needed to be done? Maybe there hadn't been a culling of their numbers for so long they were breeding a whole generation of caregivers instead of soldiers.

"Who has she spoken to?" Zartay asked.

"As far as I can tell, she's been avoiding her own lieutenants. She's going straight to the Legionnaires—asking them directly what they saw, what they were told."

Brother Hissiath's smile disappeared and his eyes went cold.

"I thought that business was behind us," he snarled. "Now they're all talking about it again. The man they were only too happy to betray is gaining some sympathy now that he's no longer around. And that woman is now questioning you about her orders."

Zartay saw where this was going and knew he needed to do something to head it off.

"She's not like her predecessor. Kied Leele thought he was the perfect soldier, the perfect leader. He refused to get his hands dirty because he thought he was above the politics of a career soldier. Commander Naschect is different. She's a realist."

The priest raised an eyebrow.

"Oh, really?" he asked sarcastically.

"She executed a couple of her own soldiers yesterday. Pronounced sentence and watched it being carried out. She's a pain in my ass, but she's not going to be any real trouble. She understands the reality of her position. And she has Commander Leele as an example if she starts to really question her options."

Brother Hissiath squinted slightly at Zartay, a thoughtful look on his face.

"You're not getting attached to the commander, are you, Ambassador?"

Zartay would have laughed out loud if it had been anyone but this mad priest asking the question.

"I can assure, you Brother Hissiath, there is no concern there. I will order her death tonight if it furthers our mission. But I know that at this juncture it would do the opposite. We need a commander who can hold this Contingent together. There's been too much trouble here already. We must play this out with the pieces we have. To do otherwise is to risk it all."

The priest watched him for a moment longer and then his expression changed, as if he had made a decision and it had now disappeared from his mind.

"Very well," he said. "For now we do nothing. But if she stirs up her soldiers with talk of Kied Leele, it could well come back to bite us. That is also a risk, and one you cannot ignore."

"I'm not going to ignore it," Zartay replied. "My job is to manage the Legion as well as our team of specialists. I understand Commander Naschect, and I know how to direct her to do what we want."

"You're saying there's no risk?" Brother Hissiath asked.

"Of course there's a risk," Zartay snapped. "There are risks with everything we do here. But I prefer a calculated risk over throwing the entire situation into chaos and hoping for the best."

The priest sat there considering Zartay's words for a moment and then turned back to the table and began stuffing his mouth with food once more. Zartay might have won some respite for now, but he knew that chaos was what the priest truly sought, regardless of the desires of the Emperor.

The ambassador understood he would have to play each side even more carefully from now on, or the whole game might well be lost.

* * *

THE SERGEANT STOOD TALKING TO THE VILLAGE HEADWOMAN JUST far enough away that Kied couldn't hear what they were saying. He stood to one side of the main track, near the cluster of soldiers' tents, waiting for his ruse to fall apart. Rotos stood beside him, his eyes vacant and a string of spittle hanging from his lower lip.

The headwoman was skeletal, her skin hanging loose over a thin frame as if she was wearing an outfit too large for her. Her eyes, though, were piercing and attentive. Kied could see any attempt to bluff her would be futile.

As he watched, she pushed her way past the sergeant and strode over to where Kied and Rotos waited, surrounded by the other soldiers. She stopped a dozen paces away and looked Kied in the eyes. He returned her gaze, unflinching.

When she turned her attention to Rotos, Kied saw her give a tiny start, little more than a momentary tightening of her neck muscles. She recovered almost instantly, and it appeared none of the soldiers noticed. Kied couldn't be sure, but it was almost as if she recognized the big man.

She returned her gaze to Kied and took a deep breath.

"I always said you were a fool," she said to him, resignation in her voice. "I'm getting tired of pulling you out of trouble."

The sergeant stepped up and looked from the headwoman to Kied and back.

"So you know these two?"

"To my misfortune, yes. Useless vagabonds, the both of them. Although the big one at least has an excuse."

She turned her eyes back to Rotos and stared at him. Kied wanted to turn and look at his companion's face, to see if there was any recognition there of the headwoman, but he kept his eyes forward. He didn't want to call the soldiers' attention to whatever was going on between Rotos and the headwoman.

"So they're criminals?" asked the sergeant, and Kied could hear the tone in his voice that meant there would be no mercy for them if the headwoman gave them up. Kied almost held his breath—he didn't know why she had claimed to know the two men, and he feared she would change her story.

"No, not criminals."

She turned back to Kied and said, "I see you're at least taking care of him—he seems to be well fed."

Kied nodded.

"We got good at catching animals up there. And our cave is warm. But we just ran out of our winter stores and we want to trade work for some food for a bit."

He could see understanding dawn in her gaze as she realized the story he had woven for the soldiers.

"You picked a damned poor time to come down here," she said sharply. "You should have stayed up in your cave. There's no work to be done while these men occupy our town."

Kied saw the sergeant frown.

"But you're here, so you're my responsibility now. And you couldn't leave even if you wanted to. There'll be a rush to till and sow once the soldiers leave so we don't starve next winter. Extra hands will be useful."

She turned to the sergeant.

"I'll take these men and get them settled somewhere in the village."

It wasn't phrased as a request, and the sergeant hesitated, not wanting to appear as if he was taking orders from the headwoman. But he had no good reason to argue the point.

"I'm releasing them into your custody," he said gruffly. "You're responsible for them now, so make sure they don't cause any more trouble, or you'll also face the consequences."

The headwoman nodded to the sergeant but didn't even glance at him. The sergeant motioned and the soldiers cut the twine from around Kied's and Rotos' wrists. The headwoman turned and marched back into the village, and Kied hurried after her, Rotos at his heels.

They followed the woman down the main track until they came to what he saw was a general merchant, easily the largest building in the village though it was still only a single story high with the same thatched roof as all the other structures clustered along the track. She entered without looking back, and Kied followed her through the door. Rotos had to duck his head as he passed through the entryway.

They stood in a large room, shelves lining the walls, and barrels and crates stacked in rows forming aisles down the center. A counter stood out from the wall on one side and a heavyset man with a few wisps of gray hair stood behind, staring at Kied and Rotos as they entered.

The headwoman turned to the man and asked, "Anyone here?" He gave her a shake of his head. She turned back to look at Rotos.

"It's really you, isn't it?" she asked him in barely a whisper. Kied turned to see the vacant look vanish from his eyes. He was suddenly Rotos again, and he wiped the drool from his mouth with the back of his hand.

"You still remember?" he asked her, disbelief in his voice.

"Of course I remember," she replied. "Even a child doesn't forget something like that. It's mad, but I always felt I would see you again some day. Even though I knew you had probably died of old age long before now, that feeling never left me."

A tear ran down her cheek.

"And here you are."

"We need your help," Kied said to her.

"That's obvious," she said to him in that same sharp voice she had used with the sergeant outside. "I'll do whatever I can, but this is a terrible time to come back here. The Legion has rounded up everyone who lives in the valley and confined us to the villages. No one is permitted to travel, and they won't say how long this will last. We can't even work in the fields."

"We know," Rotos told her, his voice gentle. "That's why we're here. I'm going to the main camp to see the commander of these forces. I'll do something about this."

Kied looked at Rotos in surprise. That had certainly not been their intention this morning.

"We're leaving as soon as it's dark," the giant told her.

"What can I do to help?"

"Nothing," he said, and there was no room for argument in his tone. "We can take care of ourselves, and there's no reason for you to endanger yourself for us. Wait a day or two, and then report to the soldiers that we have disappeared. The sergeant will be angry with you, but I don't believe he'll punish you."

"Won't they come looking for you?"

Rotos shrugged.

"They'll send out patrols to find us, but there's no reason for them to think we're heading deeper into the valley. Tell them Gunt …," he gestured at Kied, "… was talking about wanting to go back up to our cave. They'll end up searching in the wrong direction."

The headwoman nodded but continued to stare at Rotos' face.

"You haven't changed at all," she murmured at him. "You look exactly how I remember you. It's been—"

"A long time," Rotos said, interrupting her and glancing at Kied. "I hope you've had a good life."

She glanced at the man behind the counter and gave him a small smile.

"It's been good enough," she said. "Hard at times, easier at others. But it was a life you gave me. There were times, over the years, when I wondered if I imagined you. If the tragedy had wiped away my real memories and I dreamed you up as my protector. If not for you …."

She trailed off and Kied could see her eyes were wet once more. Rotos stepped forward and wrapped his big arms around her. She pressed her face into his chest and muffled sobs came from her thin frame.

After a couple of minutes, she pulled away from Rotos and wiped her eyes with the sleeve of her dress.

"You'll need supplies for your journey: food, warm clothing, and other essentials. I can supply all that."

"We had a sword," Kied said to her. "The soldiers confiscated it. Do you have any weapons?"

The woman frowned and glanced at the door.

"They confiscated all our weapons when they occupied the village. Did a search of every building and took anything we could use against them."

Kied wasn't surprised—it was standard procedure during an occupation. They would just have to make do without a sword and hope they didn't have to fight. If they reached the main camp without being caught, he was sure they would have an opportunity to rearm themselves.

"You look exhausted," the headwoman said to Kied. "We have a couple of real beds in the back. Get some rest, and we'll wake you just before dusk and get you outfitted for your journey."

Kied shivered at the thought of sleeping in a real bed. He needed some good sleep or he was going to be unable to keep up with Rotos.

The big man nodded at the headwoman and they followed her into a narrow hallway at the back of the main room. She led them to a bedroom with a pair of beds with solid, wooden frames. Kied stretched out on one of the beds and gave a huge yawn. It felt like the most comfortable thing he had experienced in his entire life.

Rotos took one look at the small bed and shook his head.

"I've been sleeping on a hard surface for too long to appreciate the bed. Besides, I'm too tall for it."

He lay on the floor and gave a small smile to the headwoman.

"Thank you," he said to her.

"No," she said in a voice that wavered with emotion. "Thank you for coming back to me. I'll see you at dusk."

She closed the door and moments later, Kied was unconscious.

Chapter Sixteen

THE TWO SOLDIERS GLANCED AT ONE ANOTHER AND THEN back to Laita. It was an unusual request, and they weren't sure if they were in trouble or not. And many of the legionnaires under her command were resentful of her actions yesterday.

She had ordered the execution of two of their own.

The trial was short and simple. There was no question of innocence, or mitigating circumstances. Laita listened to their short statements—more pleas of mercy than anything else—and then, witnessed by the village headman and a few others who were related to the dead villagers, she pronounced sentence on them.

Both men were escorted out of the command tent and marched out to an open field. They were forced to kneel over a block of wood, and Namal took their heads off with an axe, one by one.

Laita had wished she could do it herself. Despite the fact that she had given the order, Namal would be seen by the other soldiers as a betrayer. No one would be foolish enough to attempt to harm him, but they could make his life difficult in so many subtle ways.

She would have gladly taken it on herself, but commanders were not permitted to perform executions unless in extreme situations. Her rank put her above such tasks during normal operations. And so she had watched while the two men were beheaded on her order.

The two soldiers standing in front of her now were obviously nervous. They had not likely ever spoken directly to a commander before.

Laita almost explained that they weren't in any kind of trouble, but someone in her position was not required—nor encouraged—to explain themselves to those of lower rank.

"Follow me," she said, and turned on her heel and marched toward her command tent. She heard the two men fall into step behind her.

As she approached the tent, she saw Namal off in the distance talking to one of the patrols. He noticed her companions and gave her a questioning glance, but she waved him off with a curt gesture.

The two soldiers followed her into the tent and stood at attention as she ordered the attendant who was setting out food to give her some privacy. The man saluted and withdrew.

"At ease," she said to them as she sat in a chair. "You're in no trouble. But you are in a position to provide some information to me. Before we begin, however, you are both to understand that this discussion does not, under any circumstances, leave this tent. Am I clear?"

"Commander, yes ma'am," both men said in unison.

"Good. Legionnaire Heudai, you've been in the 2nd for some years now, correct?"

"Yes, ma'am."

"So you were here when my predecessor, Commander Kied Leele, was given his commission."

Heudai's eyes went wide. The subject of Kied was off limits to the soldiers—though Laita knew rumors had spread like wildfire when their superiors weren't in earshot—but this soldier was being asked a direct question by his commander.

He swallowed before answering.

"Yes, ma'am."

"And you were here when the entire command squad of the 2nd was placed under arrest, were you not?"

The other soldier, Miaseyk, stared at Laita, his eyes bulging. Heudai sputtered before getting himself under control. Laita could see perspiration run down his brow despite the chill air and he wiped it away quickly with the back of his hand.

"Well?" she said, waiting for his answer.

"Uh, well, yes ma'am. I don't think—"

"You're not here to think, soldier," she said sharply, interrupting him. "You're here to answer my questions. Nothing you say here will leave this tent. But I want you to tell me everything you know, and everything you heard when it happened. Rumors that went through the camp are fine, but I don't want you making anything up right now just to satisfy me. Understand?"

He nodded and gulped a breath.

"Ma'am, I was given orders—"

"To the Abyss with your previous orders, soldier! I'm giving you an order right now."

The man looked at her helplessly then glanced sideways at his companion. Finally, his shoulders slumped, and he looked down at the ground.

"Ma'am, I don't really know anything for sure. Just stuff I heard. But it was all rumors and such. You know how it is in the Legions ...."

"Yes, I do," Laita replied not unkindly. "But there's often a grain of truth in rumors. Sometimes they're just wild stories, sure. But often someone takes a tiny piece of real information and uses it as the basis for their own speculation. I want to hear the rumors."

Heudai nodded again.

"Ma'am, I heard Commander Leele was planning to take the 2nd and start a rebellion against the Emperor himself. He intended to march on Ythis. By the time anyone knew what he was planning we'd be at the palace gates."

Laita tried not to laugh out loud.

"Okay, what else?"

"Well, I also heard he was planning to desert the Legion. He was going to take his whole command squad and become mercenaries in the south. I heard he had a whole plan to rearrange the men so that he'd have at least a couple of the detachments go with him."

"And?"

"Someone said he was an imposter. The real Commander Leele had been murdered and this guy took his place. But one of the soldiers had met the real man, and knew this guy wasn't him."

"Imaginative," Laita replied. "Anything else?"

Heudai thought hard, his face in a frown. Suddenly, Miaseyk

spoke up.

"I've got one," he said in a quiet voice. Laita nodded at him to continue. Heudai stepped back with obvious relief.

"Commander Leele didn't get on with that ambassador, the one who's been in the main camp all this time. Some say the ambassador was giving orders to the commander instead of them coming down from Chimera Regiment."

Laita sat forward in her chair.

"What kind of orders?"

"Don't know," he answered. "But a' couple guys heard the commander and the ambassador yellin' at each other a few times. No one could make out what they was fighting about, but over a few days they had a bunch of arguments. And then the day after the last fight, the command squad was arrested by the lieutenants on charges of treason."

"What did the sergeants tell you about what had happened?"

Miaseyk frowned, trying to remember the incident many weeks back.

"They didn't tell us much. Just that some sergeants had relieved the command squad of their duties and arrested them. And that the Regimental Command was aware of it and had given the orders … through the ambassador."

Laita leaned back in her chair and considered the man's story.

"We were never told what the commander done. They just said it was treason and a new commander was going to be sent to take over. In the meantime, those sergeants were given field promotion to lieutenant and they all spent most of their time with the ambassador."

"Tell me, Miaseyk, did the sergeants meet with the ambassador much before Commander Leele was arrested?"

Miaseyk glanced over at Heudai as all color drained out of his face. Then he planted his eyes on the floor of the tent.

"I don't know …." he muttered in a low voice.

Laita felt a chill rush though her body.

"Soldier, look at me when you answer my questions."

Miaseyk raised his eyes from the floor. Fear danced in his gaze—

he was terrified of answering her questions any further. She turned her attention to the other man.

"Heudai? What about you? Did the sergeants spend time with the ambassador before the commander was arrested?"

Heudai's mouth opened and closed. He swallowed nervously before answering.

"Uh, no ma'am," he said.

They're lying, Laita realized. They don't trust their new lieutenants, and they don't want to get caught between them and me.

Laita knew she had pushed this far enough. She had gotten what she expected out of these men, and it was time to let them go back to their duties.

"Okay," she said. "You've been a help, both of you. You're dismissed."

The men straightened up and saluted before beating a hasty retreat. Tomorrow morning, Laita would return to the main camp where Ambassador Seaphon was waiting. She knew the man was watching her closely. She would have to tread carefully around him until she could figure out a plan of action.

Laita stepped over to the platter of food that had been left for her. She stared at it, her appetite gone and her thoughts swirling around the fate of Commander Kied Leele.

*   *   *

KIED KNELT DOWN AND STARTED UNDRESSING THE SOLDIER AT his feet. He was careful to avoid letting the blood leaking out of the dead man's skull touch the uniform. Telltale bloodstains could make the difference between success and failure.

Rotos finished examining the other three bodies. Kied didn't have to ask to know that none of them were nearly big enough to have a uniform to fit his companion. The odds of them encountering someone the same size as Rotos were slim at best. No, they would have to find another way to get the big man into the main camp when they reached it in a couple of hours.

He carefully stripped the leather armor off the soldier and then began to remove the man's tunic.

Rotos grabbed a short sword in its scabbard and hooked it on his belt. The sword looked more like a large dagger in the man's hand.

Attacking a patrol had been a huge gamble. If even one of the soldiers had managed to get away on his or her horse, this area would be crawling with legionnaires by morning. But luck had been on their side.

The patrol had been looking for a place to stop and rest, and a nearby copse of trees had looked inviting. By chance, Rotos and Kied were hiding among those trees. With this patrol, complacency had begun to set in—the occupation seemed to be going well, with few incidents. Perhaps they hadn't encountered any trouble for days.

Regardless, the soldiers had been lax about their own safety. They moved into the trees and began to prepare a meal, not bothering to set one of their number as a sentry. When Rotos and Kied launched their attack, none of the soldiers were prepared to defend themselves.

Rotos had stepped out from behind a couple of trees and grabbed two soldiers from behind, smashing their skulls together with enough force to shatter bone. Kied took down a third, managing to get a chokehold in place before the soldier could react to Rotos' sudden attack.

The last soldier had tried to get to his horse, but Rotos reached him before he could untie the animal's reins from the branch of the tree. The soldier tried to draw his weapon, but Rotos knocked the man down and grabbed his head, twisting it violently to one side. Kied had heard the man's neck snap.

Now, with the sun about to slip behind the mountains, the two men armed themselves and prepared to approach the main camp.

"None of these fit me," Rotos rumbled. "You'll have to escort me into the camp."

Kied considered their options. If he brought Rotos in with the big man posing as a prisoner, it would attract too much attention. Rotos' size would bring at least a few soldiers to assist Kied and then they would not have the freedom of movement they needed.

No, Rotos would have to pose as a villager who was helping the

Legion. That way, Kied could more easily bluff his way into the camp—he'd merely be escorting Rotos to see a lieutenant and wouldn't need any assistance.

Kied knew getting into the camp wouldn't be too difficult. With his experience, he could easily assume the role of a common soldier and talk his way past any sentries. The danger was that someone might recognize him. Most of the individual soldiers had no idea what he looked like, but there was always a chance he could run into a sergeant, or even worse, a lieutenant. If that happened, everything would fall apart.

No matter how good his act, Kied knew that luck would rule the night. It was something on which he hated to rely. But, in this case, they had no other choice.

Kied and Rotos mounted two of the horses and rode out of the trees, heading for the main camp. They remained silent as they rode, neither man feeling like talking. Kied was aware that he might die tonight, but the threat of death had been near constant for so long now that he was almost numb to it.

He wondered about the current commander of this contingent. He hadn't wanted to think too much about it, and he admitted to himself now that he was trying to avoid the thought that Laita might have been given the assignment. He needed to enter the commander's tent and examine the maps, see if there was any indication of where they were looking.

Kied had managed to avoid thinking of Laita, focusing on the task of escaping, surviving, and then making his way back here. But now he realized he might really see her again.

It could complicate things dramatically. Kied was prepared to kill people who had been his fellow soldiers to stop the Emperor from finding whatever was hidden in that cave. He had assumed he might need to kill the new commander, if necessary, to get the maps.

But Kied knew he could not kill Laita. More, he wouldn't let Rotos harm her, either.

He could only hope she wasn't the new commander of this contingent. If she had been sent to the Tenth, it might have been more convenient for the Legion to bring in someone else to command this mission.

Kied held onto that thought, hoping he wasn't wrong.

The sky darkened as they rode on towards the main camp. Eventually, they topped a rise and saw before them the fires of the camp spread out around one side of a village. The camp was much smaller than the base they had first established while preparing for the mission—he figured four of six detachments were stationed in strategic locations across these valleys, leaving about four hundred soldiers here.

Still more than enough to stop Rotos and Kied.

Rotos dismounted and waved for Kied to do the same. They would walk the rest of the way, keeping silent and attempting to enter the town on the opposite side from the camp. Only once they were within the perimeter of the village would they step out into the open and stride boldly into the camp itself.

The question was whether there were sentries posted all around the village, and whether the two men could sneak by the soldiers and get into the village without being seen.

Kied had considered riding right up to the camp and claiming that a horse had been lent to Rotos to bring him here from another village. But that would bring too much attention to them. At the very least, a sergeant would be summoned to talk to Kied.

He would have to walk the fine line between being both bold enough to allay suspicion and subtle enough to avoid the wrong kind of attention.

Kied and Rotos led the horses back down the opposite side of the rise and tied their reins to a small bush growing out of the rough grass.

"If something spooks them, the horses will pull this thing right out of the ground," Kied said.

"It's a risk we'll have to take. The beasts will wander back to the camp if we leave them here. Besides, if everything goes well, we can return here and recover them. They'll be handy to have if we must travel any distance though these valleys."

Kied nodded, agreeing.

The two men turned and walked back up to the top of the rise, looking over the camp once more. A small stream came down from the slopes in the distance and ran beside the town.

Kied turned to his companion.

"We'll follow the stream—the sound of it will mask any noise we might make. Follow my lead. Once we get closer, I'll be able to figure out the most likely spots where the sentries are posted."

Rotos nodded at him, and the two men started down the rise toward the village.

Chapter Seventeen

ZARTAY SAT ACROSS THE SMALL TABLE FROM COMMANDER Laita Naschect and looked her in the eyes. She returned his gaze, but her expression was guarded.

"I wish to apologize," he said to her. "My behavior a few days ago was … unacceptable. I was rude and unprofessional, and there is no excuse for that. I've found myself letting this place get the best of me, and that's not something I've allowed to happen before."

Laita gave him a small nod of acknowledgement, but said nothing.

"I'm not going to pretend that we can be friends, commander. But despite what you think at the moment, we are on the same side. I've been given orders to conduct this mission to the best of my ability, and from your record I've seen that you do everything to the best of yours."

"Thank you," she said, but Zartay could see she still didn't trust him or his motives for inviting her here tonight.

Zartay had considered his options since the return of Brother Hissiath. The priest wanted Laita removed, but that would prove disastrous for the mission. They were at a critical juncture, and Hissiath didn't understand the subtlety needed to bring them success.

Hence Zartay's invitation to Commander Naschect to join him for dinner this evening. He needed her to fall in line for a short while, to give the priest no reason to do something drastic. Brother Hissiath was an element over which Zartay had absolutely no control.

He knew honeyed words and empty platitudes were not going to be enough to get Laita to trust him. That ship had sailed. But Zartay didn't need her trust. He needed her cooperation, and he understood those were not the same thing.

What he was going to do tonight was give her the truth, or at least enough truth to support the specific lies he would also have to tell.

"I'm not used to all this," he continued, waving a hand around at the tent. "I spend most of my time in palaces, with the occasional voyage in a comfortable and safe cabin aboard a large ship. I meet with foreign rulers, or their ambassadors, and I'm never called upon to speak directly when prevarication and obfuscation will do."

He gave her a rueful smile.

"To tell the truth, I've never given much thought to the Legions. I held them in no disrespect, understand, but neither did I consider the individuals who make up the greater forces. The Legions have always seemed to me to be a vast organism directed by the will of the Emperor, not a group of people who work together to protect the Empire."

She frowned at his words, but he continued before she could say anything.

"It's unfair, of course. And I've been confronted with my own ignorance here, and I reacted poorly to it. I operated under the assumption that you were all here to serve my purpose, to take my orders, to do what I wanted. The harsh reality was difficult to accept."

She picked up her fork and took another bite of the steak. Zartay knew she hadn't eaten food this good in quite some time, if ever. Laita savored the bite, chewing slowly before swallowing it down.

"I accept and appreciate your apology," she said carefully. "You are a proud man, for good reason, and I know it's difficult sometimes to admit mistakes. So I understand what you're trying to do here."

She put down her fork and gave him an even look.

"But none of that changes the situation, Ambassador. Our mission here, how it will end, that still concerns me."

Zartay heaved a sigh and sat back in his chair.

"As it should," he answered. "It took me some time to come to grips with the entirety of this mission, myself. And I'm sure you understand that I am also under orders, and I cannot give you the complete picture until it's time. The expectation is that, as the commander of this Contingent, you will receive your orders and find the best way to execute them quickly and efficiently, because that's what you're trained to do. You're a professional soldier, a leader of the men and women who make up the Legions."

"You're asking me to blindly—"

"I'm not asking anything," he said, interrupting her but holding up his hands, palms out, to show he wasn't trying to be aggressive. "I serve two purposes here. The first is to hand out orders from the Emperor and the General based on the current situation. I had no hand in the orders you receive. I'm a messenger, nothing more."

"And the second purpose?"

"To monitor the situation and determine if the mission is under threat of failure. If that threat arises, I have some small power to take temporary control of certain elements to bring things back into alignment, but—and this is important—only long enough for me to get a message out and receive instructions back on how to proceed from those who are truly in charge."

Laita's mouth was set in a thin line, and Zartay knew he sounded as if he was weaseling out of any responsibility.

"Is that what happened with Commander Leele?"

Zartay had known this was coming.

"I'm not supposed to discuss that with you, or anyone else," he replied. "I would be defying orders to do so."

Laita opened her mouth to speak, but he cut her off.

"However, since I have some leeway to ensure the successful completion of this mission, I will step around those orders temporarily to explain a few important details to you, on the understanding that you never speak of this to anyone outside this tent. Understood?"

Laita narrowed her eyes at him. He knew what she was thinking, that she couldn't trust anything he'd tell her. But he was counting on the fact she didn't know he was aware of her questioning of the soldiers under her command.

"Do you agree?" Zartay asked her again. She nodded.

"Yes, I agree," she said in a low voice.

"Kied Leele was a good commander. He was smart, he was efficient, and he was capable. I was relieved when I met him and saw him work with his command squad. I'm not going to say I liked the man or that we were friends—that would be silly. But I thought things would go smoothly and I'd have no trouble from him."

The story Zartay had woven had to be believable. He couldn't claim that Kied was a lousy commander—Laita had known the man before he was posted here.

Always build lies on top of a foundation of truth.

"But Kied made one, very large mistake. He became romantically involved with one of the lieutenants."

Laita did a good job hiding her reaction, but Zartay was well practiced at reading people and saw it for what it was. A slight twitch, a tiny expression, and then it was gone. Zartay had to fight to keep himself from grinning. It had been a guess, a gamble. He had figured that Kied's actions indicated the man was a romantic rather than a realist.

And Zartay had guessed correctly. He wondered if anything had happened between Kied and Laita, but decided to stick with what he had planned.

"On its own, it would have been a minor problem. But the lieutenant had also been involved with another member of the command squad before Kied showed up. It did more than just cause a problem amongst those three. The rest of the command squad took sides. In a matter of two weeks, small, barely noticeable acts of insubordination started cropping up. That's how I heard about it."

Laita was listening carefully to every word Zartay said. He had hoped to undermine her determination to find out the truth about Kied Leele, but this was obviously working far better than he could ever have guessed.

"A couple of the sergeants came to me. They didn't know where else to go, and there was some belief that I was the one giving orders—you know how rumors and such work. Regardless, they told me that the lieutenants were starting to work against each other. They were deliberately sabotaging each other's efforts, and had started bringing their sergeants into this petty, ridiculous conflict."

Zartay stopped and took a deep breath. It was all just for show, and he reveled in his own performance.

"I spoke to Kied privately about it. He knew he had lost control of his Contingent, but didn't know how to resolve it. He was trying not to play favorites, trying to be fair to everyone, but of course there was no salvaging the situation by that point. I spoke to him a few times, but he told me to stay out of it. We argued, more than once, but there was nothing I could do here. I sent a message to the Major of Chimera Regiment and waited for a response."

Zartay put on a grim expression.

"Unfortunately, events happened too quickly for the Legion to resolve the situation. The lieutenant who had been involved with Kied's lover lost control of himself. During a meeting of the command squad, the lieutenant pulled a knife on Commander Leele and tried to kill him. Everyone jumped to the defense of their favored faction, and suddenly the command squad was brawling amongst itself.

"From what I could piece together afterward, Kied and the lieutenant struggled and fell over the table. The lieutenant was stabbed in the chest with his own knife, probably accidentally. Regardless, the commander of this Contingent had just killed one of his own lieutenants.

"One of the soldiers stationed outside the command tent came and told me, and I summoned the sergeants. By the time we got there, the fight was over. The lieutenants were all in shock over what had happened, what they had done. I had the sergeants arrest the entire command squad and relieved Commander Leele of his duties."

Zartay looked Laita in the eye. He could see she was barely keeping herself together. Her fists were clenched and her jaw was tight. Despite her mistrust of Zartay, she believed him.

He could not have imagined how successful this dinner would be. By the time she left this tent, he was sure she'd return to being the commander he needed here.

It was time to wrap it all up.

"I'm sure you've heard what happened next, when the Legion heard about the situation …."

*　　　　*　　　　*

KIED CROUCHED IN THE WEEDS AT THE SIDE OF THE STREAM AND scanned the darkness, searching for any telltale signs of posted sentries. He was sure at least one soldier would be posted near here. The variable was how alert the sentry might be. It was still early—the sun had just set a short time ago.

The best time to sneak into the camp would, in truth, be long into the night, a couple of hours before dawn. That was the time when sentries found it hardest to maintain vigilance, when even those who stayed up late drinking or playing cards would have found their bedrolls.

But Kied and Rotos couldn't wait that long. They had to be long gone by the time the sun broke over the mountain peaks or the chance of them being spotted would increase dramatically.

A slightly darker shadow behind one of the small homes that squatted near the stream caught Kied's eye. He watched carefully, and after a moment was sure he had spotted movement. Turning to Rotos, he leaned in and whispered in the other man's ear.

"Sentry is behind the first house on the right."

Kied knew both men wouldn't be able to sneak past the sentry without making some noise. Rotos was too large—the sentry would spot him before he could get close enough. Kied knew a few other soldiers were always stationed with shouting distance of each of the sentries, to respond to any calls for alarm. If this soldier spotted anyone approaching the village, he would call out a warning before approaching to investigate.

"Stay here and remain quiet," he whispered to Rotos. "I'll take care of this."

The big man gave Kied an appraising look and then nodded once.

Moving off down the edge of the stream, Kied tried to avoid brushing the long stalks of the weeds. He stayed crouched low, his feet on the very edge of the bank. The noise of the rushing water masked his footsteps as he approached, and he knew he could get quite close without too much difficulty.

Still, Kied moved slowly and carefully, not taking any chances.

Step-by-step, he approached the edge of the village until the weeds became sparse enough that they no longer provided enough cover to shield him from the eyes of the sentry.

He could slip into the water and make his way forward, but that would cause other problems once he was past the soldier. Fortunately, the mud on the banks of the stream was still hard, not yet fully thawed from the cold weather recently past. Kied sprawled out and began to inch his way forward.

The slope of the bank should be enough to keep him hidden from the sentry, though Kied couldn't be completely sure. He wanted to move faster, to get into the camp, but he knew this was a critical point. If the sentry spotted him and called out to the other soldiers, Kied would be caught.

He didn't know how much time passed as he shifted himself forward slightly, over and over, bit by bit. At times it seemed as if the small house wasn't getting any closer. But he made slow progress and the sentry didn't call out.

The stream cut through part of the village, a small wooden bridge spanning the water in the midst of the few structures that stood on the far side. Kied continued to crawl along until he had moved just past the edge of the small house, cutting himself off from the sentry's line of sight.

He scanned the buildings in front of him for any sign of the other soldiers, but didn't see anyone else. Rising from the mud, Kied stepped up onto the hard-packed earth that substituted for a proper road in the village. He took a deep breath and prepared himself for what he had to do next.

Staggering slightly, Kied walked back out of the village directly into the sight of the sentry. He stumbled as he moved toward the edge of the river and turned his back on the spot where he knew the sentry was keeping watch.

It all came down to this instant. Since the sentry had seen Kied come from inside the village, he probably wouldn't call out a warning to any other soldiers. The fact that Kied was wearing a soldier's uniform also played into the ruse.

But there was still a chance the soldier would play it safe and perform a proper challenge. Kied was gambling on a certain lack of discipline in the camp, a lack that no commander, no matter how strict, could ever entirely eliminate.

Kied pretended to loosen his breeches so that he could urinate in the stream. He heard the sentry mutter a low curse.

"Hey!" the soldier called out to Kied. It wasn't particularly loud, and Kied didn't know how close the other soldiers were stationed, but he had to force himself not to tense up at the sound of the sentry's voice.

Kied's head wavered on his neck as he slowly looked back over his shoulder at the soldier.

"Wha?" he slurred at the man.

The sentry stepped out of the shadows and approached Kied.

"What do you think you're doing?" the sentry demanded.

"Gotta piss," Kied replied, looking back down at his crotch.

"You're upstream, you ass," the sentry replied, obviously annoyed at having to explain this simple fact to what he thought was yet another drunken soldier. "Go piss somewhere else."

Kied looked around as if unsure of where he was.

"But I thought …," he trailed off as if too confused to understand what the sentry was saying. The soldier stepped up behind Kied, angry now.

Kied spun and drove his knuckles into the other man's throat. The sentry fell backwards, taken entirely by surprise at the unexpected attack, and unable to call out as he clutched at his throat. Kied leaped forward and drove his knee into the sentry's gut, doubling the other man over and taking away what breath he still had.

Planting his feet to steady himself, Kied brought his elbow down on the back of the soldier's neck. The sentry sprawled on the ground, barely conscious. Kied knelt down on the man's back and grabbed the sentry's knife. He thrust the blade into the soldier's neck at the base of his skull, and the sentry twitched a couple of times and lay still.

Raising himself to his feet, Kied looked around for other soldiers, but it appeared his short fight had not been seen. A huge shadow rose up out of the night and Kied flinched back, but Rotos stepped forward and looked Kied over.

"You killed him," the big man said.

Kied nodded. He didn't want to think about it. He had once been the leader of these men and women, and now he was murdering them. He believed Rotos when the giant said they were doing something important, but these were still fellow Legionnaires who were dying at his hand.

But Kied couldn't spend time thinking about this, couldn't let it stop him now. He tucked it away to resolve later as Rotos picked up the sentry and carried the body off into the shadows. Now there was a more urgent time limit to their activities here—if the body was discovered, the entire camp would go on alert.

Rotos returned and looked around at the village buildings.

"Now what?"

"Now we walk right through the village and approach the camp. You'll go a few paces ahead of me, but let me direct you. You're not my prisoner, but you are in my custody. Let me do the talking and defer to any soldiers you encounter, you know, as if you're not the deadliest man on these mountains."

Rotos snorted in what Kied took as amusement.

Kied fell into step behind the big man as they walked into the village and turned onto the main track. In the next few seconds they would be spotted by the soldiers of the Legion.

What happened next would determine the fate of their mission.

Chapter Eighteen

FLICKERING TORCHES CAUSED THE SHADOWS TO DANCE ON the walls of the pass, as if the souls of the damned were capering around them while they worked. Tiath threw down his tools and cursed.

The team had spent the whole day working on the door and they were no closer to their prize than they had been at dawn. Now they faced another night camped near this horrifying portal. Another night of twisted dreams and crawling fears.

Deylista and Pasill stopped working and leaned against the rock wall on either side of the alcove. Despite the many hours of work, the rock was barely scratched. They hadn't managed to find a seam for any door, and that eye carved into to the top of the indent watched them with a deep malevolence that made their skin crawl.

"Maybe this isn't it," Azam suggested. The thought had occurred to Tiath earlier today as the sun had passed its zenith and began its journey down toward the mountain ridges. It was possible they were wasting their time in this spot, chasing a false lead.

But if that was the case, what was this alcove? Why did they all feel the horrible presence on the other side of the rock, waiting for them?

Deylista met Tiath's look and he clenched his jaw. She had suggested performing a particular ritual to gain some insight into what was here. Tiath had turned down that idea—he wanted to avoid anything that might cause the inhabitant of this crypt to awaken enough to take an active hand against them.

When dealing with entities such as this, death was not always a final end. They had ways of coming back if one attracted their attention strongly enough. But now Tiath was running out of ideas, and he knew Deylista wanted to get this over with.

He met her gaze and gave her a nod. She pushed away from the rock wall and went back over to their makeshift camp.

"We should have done this hours ago," Tiath admitted to the others. "Deylista was right."

"We could wait until morning," Pasill suggested. He wasn't eager to enter the crypt at night.

Tiath shook his head.

"No, I don't want to be here any longer than we have to. One night was enough, and I'm no longer sure opening this thing in the dark is any worse than trying to sleep near its presence. There's danger in either option, and I'd prefer to take action than wait for … whatever might happen."

Deylista returned with a small bundle that she unwrapped, withdrawing four fat, red candles and some yellow chalk. Tiath's fingers hummed as he took the chalk from her and began to draw a circle on the rock floor of the pass. He took a deep breath and drew eight symbols around the circumference of the circle.

His stomach roiled and he tasted bile, but Tiath made sure each symbol was exact. Deylista handed two small, rolled parchments to Azam and Pasill as they took up position on either side of the circle. Tiath replaced the chalk in the bundle and placed the candles at the four compass points on the circle.

Deylista began to read from her own scroll as Tiath drew his knife. Her voice sounded wrong to his ears as she carefully pronounced the alien words drawn on the scroll. It was as if a second voice, deep and full of blood, was speaking along with her just under his hearing. But he could feel it, that second voice, and it made him want to vomit.

Tiath placed the edge of his knife over his palm and waited. When Deylista reached the correct part of the ritual, Tiath opened his flesh and dripped blood on the first candle. It burst alight as his blood hit the wick, a deep red flame that did not flicker in the wind blowing through the pass.

Now Azam joined in, reading words in counterpoint to Deylista's chanting. A wave of dizziness swept through Tiath and he waited until it passed. Then he positioned himself over the next candle and dripped his blood onto it at the right moment. A second red flame joined the first.

Pasill's voice wove into the chanting, creating yet a third thread. Stars swam in front of Tiath's eyes, but he focused and moved to the third candle. When the time was right, his blood ignited the flame.

Tiath didn't need a scroll—his part of the ritual was burned into his memory. It was only a few words, but it ended the ritual and opened his eyes to the other sight, the sight that would reveal the truth about this alcove.

He stepped into the circle and waited for the right moment. When the voices of his three companions reached a crescendo, Tiath shouted the alien phrase. He tasted his own blood as the final candle burst alight and the world around him faded to black and all went silent.

Tiath was blind for a moment and he remained still. A swirling gray fog rose up out of the darkness and surrounded him. Something vast and ancient moved in the depths of that fog and Tiath felt he stood on the edge of a precipice over some endless abyss.

And then a powerful wind rose up and blew away the fog, revealing the pass and the alcove in front of him. Dark shapes slithered over the rock around the alcove, and the eye carved into the stone moved and blinked, the flesh around it purple and red and its pupil a black so deep Tiath thought he might fall into it and drift forever.

He could see a tunnel on the other side of the stone leading deep into the mountain. Hundreds of bodies were buried there, and blackened, twisted shadows struggled and fought to break free of their corpse-prisons. At the bottom of an ancient staircase squatted a warded room holding a stone sarcophagus.

Eldritch energies pulsed from the stone and Tiath saw they flexed and bulged as the inhabitant rested uneasily in its death-sleep. Whatever being was interred in this crypt, it was slowly awakening, gaining awareness. Another year, or ten thousand years, might pass before it returned, and Tiath shuddered to think what might emerge when the wards finally failed.

But he had his confirmation—this was indeed the place they sought. And he understood now how the entrance to this crypt might be opened.

As he realized the thought, it happened—the stone pulling back and away to reveal the dark tunnel beyond.

Tiath's mind flew down over the sarcophagus, and then up and away. His vision soared above the pass and out over the valley and in an instant was at the cave. Too fast to register what he was seeing, his mind entered the cave and then he was somewhere else, buildings flashing by, a window, a ... throne?

With a flash, he was back in the pass, standing before the entrance to the tunnel. He could still see through the rock, down to where they would find the amulet.

A darkness reached up from the sarcophagus at the bottom of the crypt. A tendril of utter blackness, a tentacle of void, reached up through the stone toward Tiath. He saw it coming and fear took hold of him. He tried to utter the words to end the ritual, to return him to the world above, but terror drove the knowledge from his mind.

The void probed upwards, coming ever closer, and Tiath recoiled but could not retreat. He was rooted to the spot by the circle around him, by the ritual itself. There was no way out, and he did not want to imagine what would happen when that tentacle wrapped itself around him and drew him back down to the being waiting below.

Faintly, a voice came to him on the wind, screaming words that made no sense. The tip of the tendril touched the edge of the circle and the outline flexed, sending agony through Tiath's body. Again, he heard the voice screaming.

Deylista's voice.

The words to end the ritual.

Seizing on the knowledge of his salvation, Tiath focused and remembered. As the tendril pushed in at the circle and he felt the protection around him unraveling, Tiath shouted the words.

"Ehtjima! Falqomva! Xilschreator! Jh'bmaal!"

Darkness fell over Tiath and he felt himself falling backwards. A pulse of energy hit him and lifted him up, tossing him like a strip of cloth in a strong wind.

The stone of the pass hit him in the back and his head bounced off the hard surface. He gasped for breath and heard Azam moan painfully beside him.

Tiath opened his eyes and the cold stars above seemed to be the points of needles hung suspended over his face. He turned his head to see his team sprawled out on the ground around him.

Pasill pushed himself up into a sitting position and grabbed his head. Azam rolled over and climbed up onto his hands and knees. He vomited suddenly, his body shuddering with the force of his expulsion.

Tiath crawled over to Deylista. She lay on her back, staring up at the sky, breathing slowly.

"Deylista?"

She turned her head to him. For an instant, he could see nothing but madness in her eyes. And then she blinked and it was gone, and he wondered if he had really seen it.

"It worked," she whispered, her gaze going to the alcove. Tiath turned his head and looked for himself.

The rock wall was pierced by an irregular opening, thick with darkness.

He sat up and glanced sideways at Deylista as she pulled herself to her feet. It was still there, the madness in her eyes, hiding deep inside but not gone. Or maybe it was just his imagination.

One by one they stood and faced the open doorway. They would need to gather their wits, and then their equipment.

And then it would be time to descend to the crypt from which Tiath had so recently fled.

*   *   *

THE SOLDIER LOOKED ROTOS UP AND DOWN AND GLANCED nervously at Kied. He couldn't have been more than eighteen, probably a raw recruit on his first mission.

"He's your prisoner?"

Kied sighed, visibly annoyed.

"No," he said slowly, as if talking to a child. "He's in my custody. He's a villager, and he's got information that the lieutenant needs to hear."

The soldier turned to look at his companion. The other soldier was older, but not by much. She, however, didn't appear to be intimidated by Rotos' size.

"What's this about?" she asked.

Kied stepped forward and leaned in close.

"He spotted someone doing something they weren't supposed to be doing. Something the lieutenant would want to know about so he could take care of it quietly."

Kied knew it was better to let the soldier's imagination run wild rather than make up something specific himself. The fact that he was trying to save a lieutenant some embarrassment would plant the idea that there was some benefit in cooperating with him.

"What's your sergeant say about this?" she asked him shrewdly. He was bypassing the chain of command and they both knew it.

Kied gave her a look that said he was tired of prevaricating.

"Look, do I need to spell it out for you? My sergeant's not here, and I'm trying to quietly go see the lieutenant."

He said nothing else, hoping she wouldn't demand to know the full story. Soldiers loved gossip, and it was possible she might take this opportunity to learn something juicy.

But she was obviously far smarter than her fellow soldier. She nodded at Kied and stepped aside.

"Favors and favors," she muttered at him as he passed.

"One and back," he answered, the time-honored phrase that meant he understood she was sticking her neck out for him and he owed her something in return.

The younger soldier watched, wide-eyed, as Rotos followed Kied up the path into the officers' camp.

It was quiet here, the lieutenants still in camp either asleep or out drinking in the mess tent. Kied led the way toward where he figured the local lieutenant was camped and then ducked into a shadow between a tent and a large wagon. Rotos followed suit.

"The easy part is over," Kied whispered to him. "There are going to be a couple of guards stationed at the command tent. This isn't a war zone, so they'll be pretty lax. Still, we have to be careful."

"We need weapons and other equipment," Rotos rumbled. "You go get the maps and I'll find us what we need."

Kied didn't like the sound of that.

"How are you going to walk around in the camp without raising an alarm? You don't have a uniform."

Rotos shrugged.

"I'm not without some skill of my own. We don't both need to sneak into the command tent, and it's faster if we split up."

"You know that's not going to work," Kied argued. "If you get challenged, you can't just kill whoever stops you. The alarm will be raised so fast, we'll both be caught."

"I wasn't asking," Rotos said, and the edge in his voice gave Kied the shivers. "I'll meet you behind the command tent in ten minutes."

The big man stood up and stepped out onto the track between the tents. He looked left and right, and then strolled casually off as if he belonged in the camp.

Kied wanted to scream. Rotos would wreck everything if he was caught. He didn't understand the size of the force here in this camp.

Kied almost followed his companion in a vain attempt to stop him. But he realized as he stood up that Rotos couldn't be stopped. He would do what he wanted, and would be angry at Kied for not following his orders.

Taking a deep breath, Kied forced himself to remain calm. He had his own mission, and he needed to concentrate on that instead of worrying about the giant. He moved off toward the command tent, taking care not to be spotted by any sentries or patrolling soldiers.

The tent was situated on the top of a low rise, away from the other tents. A second large tent sat some distance away, and Kied recognized it as Ambassador Zartay Seaphon's pavilion. He felt his blood run cold—he hadn't given the Ambassador much thought since Kied had been sentenced to slave-prison by his own father.

But now he wanted nothing more than to go into that tent and choke the life out of the Ambassador with his bare hands. It had been Zartay who had planted the spy in their midst, who had convinced a handful of sergeants to betray their leaders in return for field promotions.

This man was responsible for the deaths of Kied's command squad.

Without thinking, he placed his hand on the hilt of his sword and started walking toward the Ambassador's tent. Two soldiers stood guard outside the entrance, men sworn to Zartay rather than to the Legion.

Kied could see light inside the tent. No doubt the Ambassador was relaxing with a glass of some expensive liquor, planning his next betrayal. The look on his face when he saw Kied would be priceless ….

Kied forced himself to stop. To get to Zartay, he would have to kill both guards outside—without raising an alarm, without anyone seeing the fight. And that spineless coward would no doubt start screaming when Kied came into his tent.

The risk was too great. As much as he had cursed Rotos a few minutes earlier for going off on his own mission, Kied knew he would destroy any chance of success if he went after the Ambassador. There was more at stake here than just revenge on that one man, as loathsome as he was.

He crouched down in the grass and looked around, hoping he hadn't been spotted in his moment of weakness. But the two soldiers in front of the command tent were seated at a small table, playing cards. They expected no trouble and were only there because of protocol, not necessity.

Kied snuck around to the back of the tent and crawled slowly through the grass to the edge of the canvas. He listened carefully for anyone inside, but the chill breeze was the only sound.

Using the tip of his sword, Kied carefully poked a small hole in the wall of the tent and pressed his eye to the opening. The inside was mostly dark, the glowing coals of the brazier giving off a faint, red glow. The curtains to the sleeping area were open, indicating that the current commander—again Kied hoped it wasn't Laita—was out.

Kied slowly lifted the heavy canvas, trying not to shake the tent or make any noise. He wriggled under the wall and let it back down gently. Regaining his feet, he made his way over to the commander's desk.

It was neat and tidy, everything in its place. No maps were left out on the larger table where the lieutenants gathered for instruction, and all papers were stored safely away.

Kied clenched his jaw. It wouldn't be easy to search the command tent with two soldiers right outside the entrance. Any noise would bring them in to investigate.

He moved over to a large chest and tried to open the lid. When it didn't budge, he realized the clasp was engaged. With a sinking feeling, he tried to undo the clasp, only to find it locked.

The empty keyhole mocked him. He knew the maps would be inside, but the key was likely hanging around the neck of the commander. If sound hadn't been a problem, he could probably have smashed it open. But that wasn't an option.

"Commander!"

Kied nearly jumped into the air as the soldier's voice cut through the silence. He heard the two soldiers leap to their feet, and Kied flung himself over the chest and dove behind it.

"At ease," he heard the commander say in a tired voice.

Her voice.

Kied lay still behind the chest as Laita walked into the tent.

Chapter Nineteen

THE SUNLIGHT GLARED INTO HIS EYES AS LIEUTENANT KIED Leele snapped a salute at the officer in front of him. She saluted back and then clasped his hand in a firm grip.

"It's nice to meet you, lieutenant," she said. "I'm Lieutenant Laita Naschect."

Kied nodded and returned the handshake.

"You're from the Eleventh, aren't you?" he asked her.

"I am," she replied, smiling. "Ninth Contingent. It was a great posting. I learned a great deal."

Kied turned to survey the barracks buildings spread out before them. The heat shimmered on the dusty ground. No breeze stirred the air.

"And now you get to teach a whole new wave of recruits everything you know."

"Hardly," she snorted. "We don't have them long enough for that."

Kied found himself admiring her confidence ... and her smile.

He pulled his thoughts back from the past, from that first meeting, and concentrated on now. He could hear Laita stir the coals in the brazier and then move over to a lamp. Kied was pretty sure he was hidden but worried that Laita would go around and light all the lamps before settling down to work.

He remembered how late she liked to stay up.

But one lamp seemed to be enough, and she went into the sleeping area.

By the Abyss! I need to get out of here!

But he hadn't managed to grab a map yet, and this was their only chance. If it had been anyone but Laita, Kied might have tried to eliminate the commander and take the key for the chest.

I can't do that to her. There has to be some other way.

The longer he stayed in this tent, the more likely he was to be discovered. And the truth was, he honestly didn't know what she would do if she found him here.

Her first reaction might be to run him through before she even realized it was him.

At the very least, she'd raise an alarm and bring in the guards from outside. And then it would all be over. She'd have no choice but to place him under arrest and return him to the Magistrates.

This time, his father wouldn't be able to save his life.

Kied cursed his luck, that he'd be faced with such a dilemma. He was torn between his desire to just sneak back out of the tent and try something else, and the certainty that stopping the Emperor from reaching that cave was so very necessary.

He didn't fully know why he believed Rotos, trusted that the man was telling the truth. Yes, Rotos had saved Kied's life. But there was something more than that. Kied knew he had no real reason for believing in what small amount the giant had told him.

But there was something about the man—something strange and powerful—and Kied understood that Rotos was willing to sacrifice his life, sacrifice anything, to stop the Legion from finding that cave. Despite the lack of a reason, Kied couldn't help but believe and accept everything Rotos had said about the danger of that coming to pass.

Laita came out of the sleeping area and approached the chest. Kied held his breath, hoping he was fully hidden among the bags and boxes stacked behind the chest. He heard her put the key in the lock, unlock the clasp, and then lift the lid.

If she hadn't spotted him before, he was certainly well-hidden now with the lid of the chest raised and hanging over him.

But Kied was trapped. He had missed his chance to escape while she was behind the curtains, and now she would likely work for some time at her desk before going to sleep. Not only would Kied not be able to get the maps, but neither would he be able to get himself out of the tent to meet Rotos.

The other man would … what? When Kied didn't appear, how would Rotos react? With no alarm raised throughout the camp, he would know Kied hadn't been found. Would Rotos wait patiently, or come looking for Kied? Would he leave after a short time, or try to get the maps himself?

Kied listened as Laita sorted through some papers in the chest, and then pulled out whatever she was looking for. She sat at her desk and he heard her spread the papers out.

From the short time he had spent examining the tent, he knew that when she was seated at the desk, the chest was on her right and slightly behind her. It was possible he might be able to move without her catching a glimpse of him in her peripheral vision. He knew how to move quietly—he might have a chance to reach the tent wall.

But that was where his escape would end. There was no way he'd be able to crawl out of the tent without making any noise. She was too close, and the slightest sound would alert her to his presence.

There was the other option, of course. If he managed to get behind her, he could grab her from behind and ….

But that was just as much of a problem. The fastest way to silence her was to kill her from behind. Kied had been trained well and knew how to take out an unprepared enemy quickly and quietly.

The other option was to grab her and put her into a choke hold. If he did it correctly, she'd be unconscious in seconds. He'd get what he wanted, and she would still be alive.

The risk, of course, was what she would do in those few seconds. Laita had been trained just as well as Kied. She knew the guards were close. She'd try to alert them by making some kind of noise that would bring them to investigate, like kicking over her desk.

She was also a skilled unarmed combatant. He couldn't guarantee his attack would be successful.

Wracked by indecision, Kied knew his time was almost up. Assuming he hadn't been caught, Rotos would be returning to their rendezvous point by now. Kied would have to make his choice and act or everything would be left in the hands of the other man. And

Kied was worried about what Rotos might do.

I can't kill her.

Ultimately, Kied knew this was true. No matter what was at stake, he wasn't going to murder Laita. There was no way he'd be able to bring himself to do it.

No matter the risk, he was going to have to try to subdue her. It was the only choice he had.

He slowly pushed himself up onto his hands and knees and leaned forward to peer around the edge of the chest's open lid.

Laita sat at the desk, examining the papers spread out before her. She was turned away enough that Kied was sure he could move out of his hiding spot without her noticing him—as long as he didn't make any noise.

Without warning, she spun and rose to her feet. Fortunately, she had turned away from Kied instead of toward him. She walked back into the curtained sleeping area and disappeared from his view.

This was his chance. He might only have seconds, but if he hesitated now, all would be lost. He rose to his feet and stepped around the chest, ready to bolt for the wall at the back of the tent. But he stopped when he realized Laita's desk was covered with maps of this region.

This was what he had come to retrieve.

He stepped lightly over to the desk and carefully picked up the sheets of parchment, trying not to make any noise. Laita might return at any second, and he was fully visible and too far away from the chest to regain his hiding place if he heard her returning.

Kied quickly rolled the parchments up and tucked them into his belt as he quietly picked his way over to the wall where he had entered. He knew he was probably late to meet Rotos, and he hoped the other man would wait at least a few minutes for Kied to return.

He knelt down at the foot of the wall and was reaching for the canvas when he heard Laita's voice behind him.

"Don't move," she said in an even tone. "I have a crossbow pointed at your head. Stand up and turn around slowly."

Kied froze in place. Despite his attempt to be silent, she had obviously heard him. It was over. He had failed to get the maps, and failed to escape the tent. Her soldiers would come and take him into custody. He would be executed for sure this time.

He slowly rose from the floor and raised his hands to show her he held no weapon. He wondered how she would react when she saw his face. It would be a shock, for sure.

Kied took a deep breath and turned to face Laita. She stood a half-dozen paces behind him, her crossbow held steady, the bolt aimed at his throat. Her eyes widened as she saw his face and realized who was in her tent.

She looked the same as she had the last time he had seen her, serious and professional. Seeing her now, he realized how much he had missed her. Nothing had changed for him since the day she had told him it was over.

He took this opportunity to see her one last time.

*   *   *

THE SHADOWS WERE A HEAVY WEIGHT PRESSING DOWN ON THEM as they cautiously moved forward along the tunnel. Azam was in the lead, his torch held high as he scanned the walls, floor, and ceiling for any threats. Crypts like these often held devious traps to maim or kill intruders. Tiath had no intention of losing any of his people in these deep tunnels.

Tiath moved along behind Azam, Deylista at his back and Pasill bringing up the rear. The air was still and thick with the smell of earth and mold. Patches of black fungus spread over the fitted stones of the tunnel and many of the flat stones at their feet were cracked and broken, revealing the dark, packed earth beneath.

Azam halted and held up one hand, the rest of the team freezing in place at his signal.

"There's an opening up ahead, both sides, like a cross-passage," he said.

"Everyone remain alert," Tiath told his team. "If there's a trigger along here, this is the most likely area for it."

"Why here?" Deylista asked him.

"That cross-passage acts as a distraction for anyone intruding down here. Curiosity draws a person's focus. That's when you hit them with a trap."

Azam proceeded cautiously and had taken a dozen steps when he stopped again.

"There's something here," he announced.

Tiath moved up beside him and looked where he pointed. At the top of the passage in the corner where the ceiling met the wall, a small stone protruded from the surface of the wall. It was perhaps the width of a person's finger, and barely noticeable.

But it was an irregularity, and therefore a potential threat.

Tiath carefully examined the area around that tiny stone from a distance, but could see no sign of anything that might reveal its purpose.

"There's another one," Azam reported. This time, the small protrusion was at the bottom of the other wall, exactly opposite the first.

"Hold up your lantern and stay still," Tiath ordered Azam. The man lifted the lantern and Tiath knelt down and slid forward, stopping just before he came abreast of the small stone at the bottom of the wall.

He could see nothing special about it at first, but as he inched closer, he noticed a miniscule hole in the top of the tiny stone. Tiath pulled back slightly and blew a breath at the stone. Something shimmered in front of his eyes and disappeared.

He blew again, and the shimmer appeared before vanishing once more.

Tiath carefully retreated before standing up and facing his team.

"There's a tripwire strung between those two stones. It's so fine as to be almost invisible. I could only see it when it vibrated under my breath. It stretches from the bottom left to the top right of the passage."

"How do we get past it?" Pasill asked.

"We crawl," Tiath told him.

One-by-one, the team members stretched out on the floor of the tunnel, hugging the bottom right corner of the passage. They couldn't see the tripwire, and so had to remain as low and as close to the right-hand wall as possible.

Tiath went first, inching his way forward until he was well past the small stones. Azam came next, then Deylista. Finally, when Pasill had successfully passed the trap, the team moved back into their designated positions and continued on toward the branching passages.

As they reached the first junction, Azam spotted another a short distance ahead. Tiath took the second lantern and examined the cross-passage. The walls of this tunnel were carved with strange patterns of swirls and circles. Though no particular groupings of carvings resembled anything recognizable when looked at directly, the overall effect on the edge of Tiath's vision was of thousands of eyes staring out from the walls.

Spaced at regular intervals, stone slabs were embedded in the walls.

"Stone coffins, built right into the sides of the passage," Tiath told the others.

"It's the same in the passage on the other side," Azam reported.

Tiath stepped back into the main corridor and motioned for Azam to continue onward.

At the next junction, both side passages were the same. The team continued on like this for some time, passing junction after junction.

"There must be hundreds of bodies interred down here," Deylista murmured.

"There are," Tiath answered, remembering his vision from earlier. "And they don't rest easy."

They followed the main tunnel until it opened up into a large chamber. A single pillar in the center supported the domed ceiling. The pillar was studded with stone eyes like the one they had encountered on the entrance to the crypt. Tiath could feel the power in this room, a low vibration just below the level of hearing. Looking at the pillar made his blood run cold.

From the wall opposite the tunnel through which they had entered the chamber, a wide archway led to a set of stone stairs leading down into darkness.

"That's where we need to go. It's a long walk down to the chamber we need."

"It'll feel a lot longer coming back up," Pasill noted. Tiath ignored the comment.

He was just motioning for Azam to proceed when Pasill screamed.

Tiath spun around to see Pasill standing rooted to the spot, his head thrown back and his eyes wide as he continued to shriek. A black shadow in the rough shape of a cloaked figured had oozed up out of the floor and a black, skeletal hand was wrapped around Pasill's ankle.

Deylista reacted first, flinging off her backpack as Tiath lunged toward Pasill. He caught the man around the waist and tackled him, throwing Pasill backward away from the shadow figure. The two men hit the stone floor with a bone-jarring impact.

Pasill rolled to one side and vomited, black bile spewing from his mouth as his eyes nearly burst from his skull. Wisps of smoke floated up from his boot where the shadow had grabbed him.

The figure clawed at the floor and dragged itself toward Tiath and Pasill as more of its substance emerged from the cracks between the flagstones. Tiath yelled a warning at Azam as another black shape emerged from the floor behind him.

Pasill vomited again, the dark liquid bubbling as it hit the stone floor. Tiath tried to drag him away from the approaching shadow, but couldn't move Pasill fast enough. He felt the wall at his back and realized he had reached the edge of the chamber and there was nowhere else to go.

He glanced over at Deylista to see her empty a small bag of powder into her open palm. She raised her palm up to her mouth and blew on it. The powder burst outward from her hand as if blown by a great wind and filled the room with swirling flakes.

The shadow creatures shrieked and thrashed as the powder touched them. Deylista raised her other hand and Tiath saw a red crystal clenched in her fist. He shut his eyes and raised his arm over them, knowing what was coming, as he heard her say the words to activate the ritual.

The powder ignited with a flame that filled the room. The flash would have been blinding if Tiath had not covered his eyes. He felt the heat faintly as it washed over him and then faded.

Opening his eyes and looking around, Tiath saw the shadowy figures had been blasted into ashes that scattered under a wind he couldn't feel. The explosion of flame had occurred on the other side of the veil that separated these dead creatures from the world the living inhabited. The wraiths had been incinerated while all Tiath felt was a faint warmth.

Pasill moaned and Tiath returned his attention to the wounded man. Black bile stained his chin and his eyes were full of blood. Deylista grabbed her pack and rushed to his side. They would have to work fast if they were going to save Pasill from joining the ranks of the damned.

Chapter Twenty

THE SOLDIERS SNAPPED TO ATTENTION AS LAITA STRODE UP the path to her tent. They had been relaxing and playing cards.

"Commander!" one of them said as she reached their table.

"At ease," she said, too tired to berate them for not paying attention to their duty. She knew their post was painfully boring and didn't begrudge them a small amount of distraction to keep themselves occupied.

Besides, it wasn't like the villagers were suddenly going to rise up and attack the camp. The threats against Laita took a different form.

Son of a bitch thinks he can play me like a fiddle, does he?

She had managed to remain calm during her dinner with Ambassador Seaphon, but there had been moments when it was a close thing. At first, Laita had to admit she had been taken aback by Zartay's apology. She didn't think the man had it in him.

But it was all an act, and Laita knew it. The man had no respect for her. As far as she was concerned, the feeling was mutual. They were forced by circumstance to work together and it was only a matter of time before she would find herself in total conflict with that man.

She suppressed an urge to grumble to herself as she stirred the coals in the brazier to life.

And his lies about Kied ….

Fists clenched, she stormed into the curtained sleeping area and threw her cloak to the floor beside her pallet.

As if she would ever believe Kied had thrown everything away over a woman.

A woman who wasn't me, you mean.

Laita paused and looked at herself in the small mirror nailed to one tent post. She was still attractive, if a bit severe these days with her hair pulled back and a constant scowl on her face. There was no reason to be jealous ….

By the Abyss, I'm not jealous!

But her own thoughts rang hollow. She was lying to herself, trying to convince herself that she didn't believe the Ambassador, that she didn't care what Kied had done even if the story was true.

Only, she did care. Laita didn't trust Zartay and figured it was all a story he had made up to distract her, to give her something else to think about. But she knew, deep down, she wanted it all to be a lie.

She felt ridiculous. Kied was as good as dead. As far as she knew, he might have died already through accident or malice. It didn't matter anymore if he had found someone else. She would never see him again.

Laita returned to the main section of the tent and opened the chest where she kept her papers. She wasn't ready to sleep yet—she was too wound up over her meeting with Zartay.

Returning to her desk, she spread the maps of the region out and studied them. Her troops were deployed well and there had been no further incidents after she had the two rapists executed. So far, the mission was proceeding exactly according to plan.

Yeah, the plan.

Halfway through the dinner, Laita had realized something important. Zartay Seaphon—despite his position and his power—needed her. Kied had caused a serious interruption in the overall mission. Laita was brought in to bring everything back into line, and she had done a fine job so far.

But if Zartay decided she was too much trouble and tried to replace her, it would cause even more attention to be paid to this mission by his superiors. If he kept losing commanders, it would begin to appear that the Ambassador was the problem, not the Legion. His own career, his well-being, relied on Laita's skill.

Of course, he could simply have her murdered by another soldier. Then it would be an internal Legion matter and he'd still look clean.

He could even lament her loss.

When the faint sound came from her right, Laita felt her blood turn cold. She almost spun about, but managed to remain still.

There's someone in here with me.

Maybe Zartay had invited her to dinner to do more than distract her. Maybe he had arranged for an assassin to enter her tent while she was out.

She heard the intruder take a soft breath. Whoever it was, he or she was good. The assassin was nearly silent. Only the stillness of the air in the tent had allowed Laita the chance to hear the assassin approaching.

Laita nearly leaped up and called for the soldiers outside. They'd be in here quickly enough and she could defend herself until she had reinforcements. But she hesitated.

The assassin had obviously not come in the front entrance of the tent. If Laita called out, the assassin would likely flee. Laita wanted to capture whoever it was behind her. It would be the only way to prove Ambassador Seaphon's complicity in the crime.

Without warning, she stood up and walked back toward her sleeping area, acting as if she didn't know someone else was in here. She grabbed a short sword and belted it around her waist before lifting up her sleeping pallet and pulling out a small crossbow.

This crossbow lacked a crank, but it allowed her to draw and load the weapon without making any noise.

Raising the crossbow, she stepped out to see the assassin heading for the far wall of the tent. The figure knelt down and began to lift the canvas.

"Don't move," she told the figure. "I have a crossbow pointed at your head. Stand up and turn around slowly."

The figure froze and then slowly stood up. She could tell it was a man, and he raised his hands to show he held no weapon.

A terrible feeling of foreboding dropped over her like a thick blanket as the figure turned around to face her. She stared into a face she had never expected to see again, the face of a convicted traitor, the face of the man she had—for a too-short time—loved.

He looked at her and she saw the emotion in his eyes. His face was too thin, almost gaunt. He was dressed in a soldier's uniform, but she could instantly tell it wasn't his—it didn't fit his thin body.

"What … how did you …?"

Kied stared into her eyes and took a deep breath.

"I'm sorry, Laita. I had hoped you weren't the commander here. I—"

Laita's gaze dropped to the roll of papers tucked in Kied's belt.

"You're stealing the maps," she said. Despite her shock, she realized she hadn't lowered the crossbow and as much as she felt Kied wouldn't hurt her, Laita continued to keep it aimed at him.

"I need them, Laita. There's more going on here than—"

"Halt and identify yourself." The voice that intruded came from one of the soldiers outside. Laita had a moment of panic. Who was coming to her tent this late? She hadn't decided yet what to do about Kied.

A meaty thud sounded from outside, and then another, and all was silent. Laita looked back and forth between Kied and the doorway, for the first time in her life paralyzed by indecision.

And then a huge man stepped into the tent. He had to duck to come through the entrance, and his long hair brushed the top of the tent as he straightened to his full height. The man radiated menace, and Laita instantly spun her crossbow around to aim at the man's face.

"Laita, no!" Kied yelled, and the giant stood and stared at her. She felt as if his gaze was penetrating her skin, flowing along with her blood right to her heart. Laita could hear her own heartbeat in her ears, and she felt the crossbow wavering, the point sinking down toward the floor.

She heard Kied yell something else, and then he was standing in front of her and the feeling lessened though did not disappear completely.

Laita stood and brought the crossbow up, the bolt aimed just over Kied's right shoulder at the giant facing them across the tent.

*　　　　*　　　　*

"ROTOS, STOP THIS! SHE'S NOT THE ENEMY!"

The big man focused on Kied, and he could see the anger in Rotos' eyes.

"You don't know who our enemies are," Rotos answered in his low rumble. "She's the commander of this force. She'll bring them all down on us."

"Your gods-damned right I will," Laita snarled from behind Kied. "Right after I take you down myself."

Kied spun to face her and saw her hands tight on the crossbow. He knew if she decided to release the bolt, Rotos would take it in the throat.

"Laita, please, just listen to me. We're not here to hurt you or anyone else. But we need these maps. There's more going on here than you've been told, and we need your help."

Laita's eyes never left Rotos' face as she answered Kied.

"You're a convicted traitor, Kied. Why in the Abyss should I listen to anything you tell me?"

Kied could see she was furious, at Rotos for hurting—possibly killing—her guards, and at him for showing up here and putting her in this spot. But he needed her to listen or Rotos would do something drastic.

"Laita, if what we shared in the past meant anything to you, anything, I need you to listen to me."

Kied saw it coming but couldn't decide how to react quickly enough as Laita took her hand off the trigger and hammered her fist into the side of his face. He was knocked off balance and tripped over the chair behind her desk, sprawling on his back at her feet.

"How dare you?" she growled at him.

And then a vast weight settled over him and the room darkened as Rotos exercised the force of his will. The crossbow slipped from Laita's grasp as she dropped to her knees, her head sinking down toward her chest.

Kied fought for consciousness as Laita fell to her side near him. Rotos stood over her, looking down at her face as she moaned and writhed on the floor. The giant was going to kill her, and Kied could only watch helplessly as the woman he loved would die just beyond the reach of his arms.

And then, as suddenly as it had descended, the weight dissolved into nothingness. Kied blinked and tried to sit up, but there was little strength in his limbs. Rotos reached down and picked up the crossbow, removing the bolt and setting it aside.

Laita rolled onto her side and looked up at the giant standing over her.

"Who in the Abyss are you?"

Rotos looked from Laita to Kied and back.

"I'm the man who's trying to stop you from destroying everything you have."

Laita sat up slowly and massaged her temples.

"So I take it you're not going to kill me after all," she said. "Why? What changed your mind?"

Again, Rotos' gaze settled on Kied. He understood the message in that look—the giant had seen Kied's feelings for Laita and decided to take mercy on her. But it was a tenuous thing.

"Laita, please let us explain."

Kied gingerly probed his face where she had punched him. He would have a serious bruise by tomorrow.

"Is it true, what they said about you?" she asked him. "Are you a traitor?"

Kied considered the question and then nodded at her.

"Yes, I suppose I am. I never thought I'd reach a point where I'd be asked to do something I knew I wouldn't be able to do. When I reached that point here, it turned out I wasn't alone."

"Why are you here, Kied?"

Kied looked up at Rotos. The big man reached out a hand and helped Kied to his feet. He didn't offer any assistance to Laita. Kied held out his hand, but Laita ignored it and pushed herself to her feet without any help.

"There's a special unit somewhere in these valleys. They're looking for a cave. We can't let them find whatever is hidden there. It would be bad for ... well, everyone."

"You don't know what they're looking for?" she said, disbelief in her voice.

"I do," Rotos answered. "You don't need to know."

"So you want to steal my maps to go stop this mission, and I'm just supposed to take your word that it's a bad thing if they find whatever it is they're searching for. You want me to be a traitor, too."

Kied couldn't help but grimace when she said that. As much as it was true—he had betrayed the Emperor by refusing his orders—Kied had tried to believe what he was doing was the right thing for the Empire, if not its ruler. But to everyone else, he was just a man who had turned his back on the Legion.

"Laita—"

"Are my men still alive, or did you kill them?"

"They live," Rotos answered. "They'll need medical help."

"Get out," she told them.

Rotos raised his eyebrows at her.

"Take the maps and leave. Don't tell me where you're going, and don't wait around. I'll give you a bit of time to get some distance from the camp, and then I'm going to raise the alarm. Don't expect any help if we catch you."

Kied couldn't believe she was letting them go. He wanted to touch her, to wrap his arms around her, but he could see she was still angry.

"I'm sorry—"

"Shut up, Kied. I don't want to hear your apologies. I had a career before this, before you. Now everything is a mess."

Kied didn't fully understand what she was talking about but knew better than to ask her for clarification. It was time for the two men to leave.

Laita was giving them a chance. It was more than they had when they entered the camp earlier tonight. She owed them nothing.

"You're special, too," Rotos said, staring into Laita's face. "Like him, but different. It's why he loves you and why you feel the same. Meeting both of you at this time was no accident, no coincidence."

Kied turned to face Rotos.

"What are you talking about?"

"I told you once there is more to you than I understand. She is the same. There's something greater happening here, but I can't see where it's leading."

Laita looked at Rotos, and then glanced at Kied. There was something in her eyes when she looked at him—the anger was still there, but there was something subtly different in her gaze.

"Thank you," Kied said to her. "Stay safe."

Rotos turned and ducked low as he stepped out of the tent. Laita opened her mouth to say something, and then shut it again with an audible snap. Kied looked at her, wanting to say something to make it all right between them. But he didn't have the words he needed, and time was running out.

She nodded at him, once, and he understood the message. She was doing this because—despite his inability to prove himself to her—she believed in him. Laita was telling him to go and do what needed to be done.

It was more than he could have ever hoped.

He straightened and marched out of the tent, following Rotos. The two guards were sprawled unconscious on the ground beside their small table, the cards scattered across the dirt like windblown leaves. The camp lay spread around them, a mire of unseen threats. The two men would still have to make it past the sleeping soldiers and the sentries without raising any alarms.

But Kied knew they would make it out. Laita had given them the maps, and the chance they needed to escape.

He only hoped he could live up to her faith in him.

Chapter Twenty-One

THE DARKNESS FOUGHT AGAINST THE LIGHT FROM THE lanterns, retreating reluctantly in the face of the flames. Azam stepped back from the door and looked over the portal one last time.

"It's clear," he said. Tiath detected the slightest hesitation in the man's words, but didn't voice it. They were all on edge, having found and bypassed another three deadly traps on their way down the stairs to this final chamber. Azam knew their lives rested on his ability to notice and identify the devices set up to kill any intruders into this crypt.

Tiath stepped forward and placed his hand on the door. He looked back over his shoulder at his team.

Azam rolled his shoulders, trying to loosen up and prepare for whatever might be waiting for them behind the large, stone door. He would follow right behind Tiath and cover the leader's back.

Deylista had her knives in her hands. The drawstring on her backpack hung loose in case she needed to grab any ritual components quickly. Her gaze was fixed on the portal, and Tiath knew she was ready for what lay ahead.

Pasill carried the second lantern, his face drawn and his mouth slack. Tiath knew the man was fighting to stay upright, exhausted by the energies that had surged through his body in the chamber back at the top of the stairs they had just descended. It had been a close thing, keeping him alive long enough for the ritual to purge the infection from his soul.

Tiath would have preferred Pasill to have retreated from the tomb to remain at the campsite out in the pass. But it was folly to send the man alone, and they couldn't afford to split their small team in two. Tiath only hoped they wouldn't have to retreat in a hurry—Pasill would need many rests on the way back up what had felt like endless stairs leading down to this chamber.

His people were ready. He turned back to the stone slab and pushed. A small amount of dust fell from the top of the door, but the portal didn't move. Tiath put his shoulder against the stone and planted his feet, driving forward with his legs.

Stone grated against stone as the portal budged slightly. A second heave got it moving slowly inward, the vibrations through the stone walls and floor setting everyone's teeth on edge.

A crack appeared between the door and the frame, a sliver of cold darkness that pulled at Tiath's eyes as if it was a vacuum inside the room, though a chilled breath of air blew out from the opening. There was no scent on the air—an unnatural absence—and Tiath automatically held his breath as the breeze caressed his face, seemingly searching for a way inside his body.

Azam stepped forward and raised the lantern, but the darkness beyond the door seemed to drink in the light, swallowing it down into that stygian blackness. Pasill moved up and raised the second lantern, and the combined flames pushed the darkness back a few paces.

Tiath stopped pushing once the slab was perpendicular to the wall. Though the team members could have squeezed through a narrower opening, Tiath didn't want to leave a bottleneck at their backs. His earlier vision of this chamber replayed over and over in his mind, sending a shiver up his spine.

"Don't step out of the circle of light," he told the others. "You may not be able to get back in."

Tiath moved forward, Azam and Pasill following immediately behind, and Deylista bringing up the rear. The four remained within a few paces of each other, the darkness shoving at the edges of the circle of light created by the two lanterns.

As they entered the chamber, Tiath glanced back at the walls around the doorway and quickly averted his eyes. The stone blocks were covered with bas reliefs of impossible vistas, horrific creatures, and other mind-twisting images. He realized the impenetrable darkness surrounding them blocked their sight of the outer reaches of the chamber, protecting their minds from the ghastly carvings that covered the walls.

The center of the room was dominated by a great stone sarcophagus. Strange runes covered its surface, flowing and twisting around hundreds of carven eyes that stared out in all directions from its sides and top.

"Lovely," Deylista murmured sarcastically.

"Do we open it?" Azam asked. Tiath shook his head.

"No, that's the last thing we want to do. The amulet isn't in there, anyway. Follow me."

Tiath led his people past the sarcophagus, many of the stone eyes turning to follow the team's progress through the room.

A dozen paces past the sarcophagus stood a short, stone pillar that came up to Tiath's waist. A small metal box rested in the center of its surface. The top of the box appeared to have no clasp or other locking mechanism.

"Should I …?" Azam asked, stepping forward.

"No," Tiath told him. "You cannot see what protects this box."

"Then how do we open it?" Deylista asked him.

"We don't. We take the amulet out without opening or even touching the box."

Tiath glanced back at Deylista and met her gaze, and she understood. Shrugging out of her backpack, she knelt down and searched inside for what Tiath needed. Finally, she handed him a small rolled scroll tube and a leather pouch.

Tiath opened the pouch and drew out a dusty gray stick of chalk. As the chalk was pulled from the pouch, the darkness pressed down on their small circle of light, and the flames dimmed.

"Shit!" Deylista yelled and grabbed for her pack, which was now partially in shadow. She tried to yank it into the light, but something in the darkness had taken hold of the pack and was pulling it inexorably into the blackness that surrounded them.

"Let it go!" Tiath ordered and Deylista released her grip just as whatever was in the darkness gave a final heave. The pack disappeared into the inky dark. Tiath let out a short breath. If Deylista had held on for another second, she would have been pulled off balance and might have fallen out of the tiny protective circle and been lost to them forever.

Tiath turned back to the pillar and began to draw symbols on its surface around the small metal box. As he worked, he began to notice, at the very edges of his hearing, slithering and snarling in the darkness that pressed in around them. Whatever was out there didn't like what he was doing.

He could only hope the light continued to keep them at bay.

Tiath finally completed the runes and replaced the chalk in the leather pouch. He uncapped the tube and pulled out an ancient parchment. Carefully unrolling the sheet, he licked his lips and prepared to speak the alien words written across its surface.

This was the moment of truth. Once he began the ritual, he would be unable to stop. The living darkness would fight to prevent him from completing the ritual, and it would all depend on the flames inside the two lanterns. If they weren't enough to keep the darkness back, Tiath and his people would fail and … he didn't want to think about what would happen to them here.

He wished he could have done something to shore up his defenses against the writhing blackness surrounding them, but only natural light—natural flame—would work down here.

He had to hope it was enough.

Tiath took a deep breath and began to read. The words burned on his tongue and he tasted blood and bile as he spoke them. The shadows twisted and shifted around them, pressing even closer and shrinking the circle of light around them. But as Tiath continued, the shadows seemed unable to collapse the dome of protective light that separated them from whatever moved in that ebon sea.

The runes on the surface of the pillar glowed blue and then white, and Tiath kept reading. He could feel his tongue thickening and slowing as he neared the climax of the ritual and took extra care to pronounce every syllable, to maintain the proper cadence, and to enunciate as much as he was able.

To his left, the darkness suddenly drew back, and the lantern light illuminated a wide path across the chamber to one of the walls. Pasill looked at the images across the surface of the wall and moaned, and Tiath heard Azam order the others to shut their eyes.

He continued reading while Pasill whimpered behind him and his tongue was burning and bleeding as he neared the final words of the ritual. His mouth was in agony, but he continued, shouting out the last words as the powdered runes on the pillar burned white hot and sizzled away.

Tiath felt his tongue split open and he leaned forward and vomited blood out onto his hand as the parchment crumbled away into dust. Something hard and heavy landed in his palm. He looked down to see a blood-spattered black gemstone set in an iron clasp resting in his grip.

He nudged Azam, who opened his eyes and looked down at their prize.

"Okay, everyone," Azam announced. "It's time to get out of this fucking place."

*　　　*　　　*

THE SUN'S WARMTH WAS A WELCOME CARESS AS KIED CLOSED HIS eyes and turned his face up to the cloudless sky. After the sweltering heat of the badlands where the prison squatted like some great hungry beast, Kied had thought the coolness in the mountains was refreshing. But without proper clothing, he had soon tired of the biting wind and bone-numbing chill.

As much as winter had tried to hold on in these mountains as long as possible, spring was forcing its way onto the heights, thawing the ground and swelling the streams and rivers that wound down out from among the peaks.

Kied drank in the warmth for a few moments before returning to Rotos. The giant was on his knees in the grass, the maps spread out on the ground in front of him. A few stones held the edges of the parchments down as the breeze struggled to steal away the precious maps.

Rotos grunted as Kied moved up beside him.

"Anything?" he asked the big man.

Rotos sat back on his haunches and grumbled under his breath.

"It looks familiar. That's the problem—it all looks familiar. It's not coming back to me like I thought it would."

"Take a break," Kied suggested. "You've been concentrating on it for about an hour or so. You need to think about something else. The answer may sneak up on you the next time you look at the map."

Rotos grumbled again, and Kied was sure he heard the man say, "It's been too long." Rotos looked up at him and frowned.

"Any signs of pursuit?"

Kied shook his head.

"Nothing so far. Remember, they don't know where we're heading any more than we do."

"What about their trackers?"

"There are so many tracks around the camp, it'll be a miracle if anyone manages to ferret out ours from the patrols, supply wagons, and everything else that's stamped through the area. We're safe enough for now."

He knew, though, that riders would be heading out to find the patrols who hadn't yet returned to camp. He and Rotos had a day, at most, to put some distance between themselves and the camps before everyone in the valley knew the Legion was now specifically searching for intruders.

"Is the cave hidden?" he asked. Rotos slowly rose to his feet and looked out across the valley, searching for any sign of other riders. Kied knew he was deliberately avoiding answering the question about the cave. Despite the fact he was bringing Kied along on this mission, Rotos was still unwilling to share any information unless he had no choice.

"Rotos, I asked you a question."

The giant turned back to Kied, his face impassive.

"Is the cave hidden? Could somebody just stumble upon it? Or are we going to have to do some searching for the entrance?"

Rotos drew in a deep breath through his nose and then slowly let it out.

182

"It's hidden."

"So even when we get to the actual spot, we'll have to search around?" Kied asked.

"No. The entrance will be obvious to us. Just not to anyone else."

"What, there's some kind of magic that hides it from other people?"

At the mention of magic, Kied saw Rotos grimace as if he had just tasted something unpleasant.

"Not magic?" he asked, knowing he was pushing hard but unwilling to just give up this time.

"Not what you think of when you say that word," Rotos answered. "The cave is old, ancient. It doesn't want to be found. But it can't hide itself from those who know it's there."

Kied didn't like how that sounded. Rotos turned and knelt in front of the maps again. He ran a finger along a ridge marked on the parchment and began to mutter under his breath again. The sun dimmed and a chill wind rose around them, sending a shiver down Kied's spine. He glanced up, expecting to see clouds floating across the sky.

But no clouds blocked the sunlight. Instead, the sky had turned blood red and the sun was a dark disk, almost a black hole in that crimson curtain. Kied felt his gaze lock onto that black orb, felt a pressure begin to build behind his eyes, as if it was drawing his eyes out of their sockets.

He tried to pull his gaze away from that hole, but he felt his will draining away. And then he realized the black disk wasn't a hole, but an eye. The eye looked down on Kied, and he could feel himself shrinking under that alien gaze, dissolving into dust as a thousand years passed in an instant.

Something hammered into his chest and Kied screamed as he was flung down to the ground, the breath driven from his lungs as his back hit the dirt and a great weight landed on his chest. His head bounced off the surface and his eyes snapped shut, severing the link to whatever watched him through that ebon orb.

Kied blinked his eyes open to see the blue sky above him, the sun shining down and stabbing into his eyes. The chill wind died away and he was able to feel the warmth of the sunlight on his wet cheeks. He wiped his hand on his face and pulled it back to see blood smeared across his fingertips.

Rotos climbed off his chest and looked down at him with concern on his face.

"My eyes ...," Kied said.

"It's just a bit of blood. You'll be all right."

"What ... what happened?" he asked the big man.

A guilty look crossed Rotos' face for an instant and was gone.

"You shouldn't have been able to see that," Rotos explained. "I voiced some things I should have kept silent. But you shouldn't have seen ... what you saw."

Kied pushed himself up into a sitting position.

"What did I see, Rotos? The sky was red, and the sun was a black disk that became an eye. All because you muttered something under your breath. Tell me what that was."

He heard an edge in his voice he had never used with Rotos before. Kied realized he was on the verge of panic, and anger was the only emotion he could cling to, like a broken board in a stormy sea of fear and frustration.

Rotos stood up and held out his hand to Kied. He let the giant help him to his feet, but didn't let go of the big man's hand.

"I'm not taking another step until you tell me what that was."

Rotos looked down at their clasped hands. When he spoke, his voice was full of resignation.

"I said something in a language that hasn't been used in a long time. It was a mistake. I called attention to myself, and to you. But what you saw should have been hidden from you."

"You tackled me."

Rotos nodded once.

"It was the fastest way to break the connection between you and ... it."

"Is it still watching us?" Kied asked and could hear the fear in his own voice. He realized his bladder was full, and his stomach roiled and twisted.

"No," Rotos answered. "When I stopped talking, and when you

closed your eyes, there was nothing left for it to hold onto. It's gone."

Kied didn't feel any relief at Rotos' words.

"What was it?"

As soon as he asked the question, he could see on Rotos' face that the other man wasn't going to answer him this time.

"I need to know, Rotos."

"No," Rotos said, his rough voice low and serious. "You think you want to know, but it's far better for you that you don't. Some questions are better left unanswered."

"Better for me? Or better for you?" Kied tried to hold onto his anger to help stem the tide of fear that threatened to overwhelm him.

"It's time we moved on," Rotos said. "We don't want to still be in this spot when night falls, just in case."

Rotos pulled his hand away from Kied's and bent down and gathered up the maps. His big hands gently rolled up the parchments with great care.

"In case of what?" Kied asked him. Rotos ignored the question.

"Besides," the giant continued as if Kied hadn't spoken. "I've remembered where we need to go."

Chapter Twenty-Two

AMBASSADOR SEAPHON LEANED BACK IN HIS CHAIR AND eyed Lieutenant Adai. Zartay knew he couldn't trust the lieutenant any further than Commander Naschect could. The man was a snake. Still, he had his uses as long as one remembered which end did the biting.

"Are you sure about the description?" he asked the lieutenant.

Chalaj glanced around the tent—as if he might spot eavesdroppers among the boxes and curtains—and leaned forward over Zartay's desk. The ambassador wasn't impressed with this display. Chalaj Adai was nothing more than a temporarily useful tool. One that would have to be eliminated once the mission reached its critical stage.

"A few of the soldiers say the big one was unnatural, like he carried the blood of giants," Chalaj said in a quiet voice. Zartay expected that came from the two soldiers who had been knocked unconscious by the unknown man last night. Exaggerating the size of their attacker would alleviate some of the shame they felt at being bested so easily. They were both lucky to still be alive.

"I mean the smaller man," Zartay explained. "Are you sure about his description? Did any of the soldiers recognize him as anyone in particular?"

Chalaj shook his head.

"Not that they said to me, and most of them trust me completely."

Zartay had to stop himself from rolling his eyes.

"You know who it was, don't you?" Chalaj continued. "The smaller man—you think he's someone specific."

Zartay suppressed a sigh.

"Chalaj, there are any number of individuals who might want this mission to fail. I don't have the time nor inclination to list them all for you. Go back out there and keep digging until it looks like it's going to start drawing attention to you. Keep your ears open and report back if you find out anything important."

The lieutenant obviously wanted to know more, but Zartay had no intention of revealing anything further to the man. Chalaj hesitated, and then saluted and turned away. Just as he reached the tent entrance, Zartay spoke again.

"I mean that, lieutenant. I don't want to hear stories, or speculations, or how well those two useless soldiers are healing up. Don't come back here unless you have something I need to know. You're dismissed."

Chalaj marched out of the tent without a backward glance and Zartay turned to the curtained sleep area. As if on cue, Brother Hissiath stepped out from the shadowy alcove behind the curtains.

"Could it be him?" the priest asked.

"I don't think it could be anyone else," Zartay answered. "The message said he escaped from the prison with a huge, gray-haired companion. That matches our assailants pretty thoroughly. Though he must have traveled day and night to get here so quickly."

"He came to kill the commander?"

Zartay considered the priest's question. It was possible, though extremely unlikely. If Kied Leele had come all this way back to the very Legion that had turned its back on him, the primary target would have been Zartay himself. He had personally orchestrated Kied's downfall, once he realized the commander wasn't going to cooperate.

And yet, Kied hadn't paid a visit to Zartay's tent last night. The man had gone to find Laita Naschect. She claimed to not know who it was who had attacked her in the command tent, and Zartay hadn't pressed the issue. The ambassador had never told Laita about the message informing him of Kied's escape from prison.

But he knew she was now lying about her assailant. He knew they had served together—she should have recognized her former comrade.

"There's something more to his visit than violence," he told the priest. "Kied Leele was looking for something."

"He wants to sabotage the mission!" Brother Hissiath hissed. "That cannot be allowed to happen!"

"It won't. He doesn't know where the crypt is. He can't know where the cave is—we don't even know that yet."

"Then why was he here?"

Zartay shrugged. He had no way of knowing unless Commander Naschect suddenly decided to give it all up. Brother Hissiath would no doubt be able to get the truth out of her, but that would be rather messy. None of the other lieutenants were nearly ready to command the Contingent in her absence.

He needed her, at least for now. Which meant he couldn't tell the priest about her deceit.

"Most likely, he assumed we'd know the cave's location by now and he figured he might be able to get there before us. Maybe he thinks he can sneak past Tiath's team and find the prize first. He doesn't know anything about them, other than they exist and are out there somewhere. Regardless, he couldn't have found out anything important, and Tiath will make short work of Kied Leele should the two men ever meet."

The priest didn't seem completely satisfied by Zartay's answer, but there was little he could do at the moment. One of Zartay's personal guardsmen stepped into the doorway of the tent.

"Ambassador, I have a message for you. It came by wing."

Zartay had to stop himself from leaping out of his chair. Instead, he waved the guard forward and the man handed him the rolled-up parchment before rapidly departing. Zartay's guards wouldn't stay near Brother Hissiath any longer than they had to.

He unrolled the parchment and carefully read the message twice. Then he leaned back in his chair and turned to Brother Hissiath.

"They've found it," he said.

The priest blinked at him a couple of times.

"They retrieved the amulet and it told them where the cave is located."

Zartay grabbed his roll of maps and spread them out on his desk. He flipped through them until he found the one he thought was correct. Using coordinates to mark a location on a map was not a skill Zartay had developed. He could do it, but it would take some effort.

He continued to look between the written message and the map, making small marks as he figured out where each coordinate was located on the map. Brother Hissiath moved up behind Zartay's left shoulder, and he shuddered at the other man's proximity. The thought of the mad priest standing behind him was not a comforting one.

The ambassador focused on his task, ensuring he didn't make any errors. When he gave the commander orders to move out the support force and take control of the cave, she would need to know its precise location.

"Well? Where is the cave?"

Zartay glanced back over his shoulder at the priest.

"Don't distract me while I'm doing this. I need to be exact."

He could feel the priest's eyes boring into the back of his skull as he turned to the maps and continued his work. His skin crawled under that gaze, but he forced himself to concentrate.

After some minutes, he made the final mark on the map. He checked his work carefully, and it appeared he had not made any mistakes.

"Here," he said to Brother Hissiath, pointing at the small dot that indicated the location of the cave. The priest grabbed the map and held it up close to his face, as if he could see the cave itself through the paper.

"Are you sure?" he asked excitedly.

"I am. Those are the coordinates from Tiath."

Brother Hissiath lowered the map, and the look of joy on his face made Zartay's blood run cold.

"How soon can we get there?" he asked. Zartay considered the timelines.

"It will be a few days. I'll write the orders now and give them to the commander today. She'll need to organize the force, and then we move out. I'd say four or five days."

"Too long!" the priest snarled. "We need to go now!"

"It's not as easy as that. We need supplies. The soldiers will have to set up a camp where we can stay while we examine the cave."

Brother Hissiath glared at Zartay, and he could see the madness in the man's eyes. It was no longer lurking out of sight, but danced in his gaze to music Zartay knew he never wanted to hear.

"We are so close now," he said to the priest. "We need to do this properly. No risks, no rushing off unprepared. This is a critical junction—now is when the mistakes happen, when we feel we've already succeeded, and we hurry rather than remaining cautious."

Zartay couldn't tell if his words were having any effect on the other man.

"Let's do this right. Let's control the area around the cave, and then you can enter and examine the prize at your leisure. Think of how it will be, when the Emperor comes here in person and you present it to him yourself."

The priest stood still, glaring at Zartay, and then he blinked, and it was gone. The madness retreated back behind his eyes, and Brother Hissiath gave Zartay a small, tight-lipped smile.

"You're right, of course," he said. "Write the orders, Ambassador. We will do this correctly, but I will not accept any unnecessary delays."

The threat was implicit in the priest's voice.

"I agree completely," Zartay replied, sitting back down at his desk and grabbing his quill.

*   *   *

THE STARS WHEELED OVERHEAD WHILE KIED LAY ON HIS BACK, unable to find sleep. A few feet away Rotos snored loudly, but Kied couldn't stop thinking about what had happened earlier in the day. The image of the sky changing color—the feeling of the eye staring down at him and turning him to dust—wouldn't leave him.

He rolled over onto his side and tried to get comfortable. At least they now had bedrolls, stolen from the camp when they made their escape. It was an improvement over sleeping directly on the hard, cold ground, though it didn't seem to be helping tonight.

Kied closed his eyes and tried to relax. He needed some rest, or he'd slow them down tomorrow. Now that Rotos had figured out where they were going, it was a race to get there before the special team discovered the location of the cave. Once that happened, Laita would send out an expeditionary force to take control of the surrounding area.

Rotos and Kied had to get there before that happened.

He expected, though, that Laita would have mentioned it to them last night if she had received new orders from Ambassador Seaphon about the cave. And since two men on horseback could travel faster than the army would be able to move, Kied figured with their head start they would easily reach the cave first.

The question was the location of the special team that had been sent out to search for the cave. Kied knew they were skilled, and dangerous. If they had discovered the location, they might already be at the cave.

Rotos was powerful and dangerous, himself. But Kied had heard rumors about some of these special teams. They were trained to deal with threats like Rotos—they had skills and resources that evened the odds considerably. Might they be able to harm the big man?

Despite the turmoil in his mind, he felt himself starting to drift off. His exhaustion was catching up with him.

A light flickered on the inside of his eyelids and Kied opened his eyes to see a fire in the distance. He sat up and focused on the light—it looked like a large bonfire, with many figures moving around it. He turned to speak to Rotos, but the big man's bedroll was empty.

Kied surged to his feet and drew his sword, looking around wildly. He was alone. He turned back to the bonfire and tried to focus on the figures, but they were all backlit by the fire and were nothing but dark silhouettes.

Some of the figures appeared to caper and cavort in front of the fire, a mad dance that made Kied's blood run cold. He wondered if Rotos had gone closer to investigate. Kied sheathed his sword so the metal wouldn't reflect any light from the bonfire and began to move closer, crouched over to reduce the chance of him being spotted.

As he approached the bonfire, he began to make out some of the figures a little better. There were a handful of naked men and women dancing around the fire, their gestures strange and off-putting. At times it seemed as if they were nothing more than puppets, their movements directed by an outside intelligence.

The other figures stood evenly spaced around the fire, cloaked and hooded. They did not move, even when the dancers touched them before springing away in awkward leaps like grotesque, damaged insects. The cloaked figures radiated an aura of menace.

Kied was less than a hundred paces away when he stopped and knelt in the grass, watching the spectacle before him. He had not been spotted by anyone around the bonfire, a huge pile of branches and beams that fed the roaring flames. There was still no sign of Rotos.

Two of the dancers, a man and a woman, met in front of the flames. The woman shoved the man onto the ground and mounted him. They coupled in a frenzy of flailing limbs and discordant moans. Other dancers circled back around the fire and joined them, seeming to randomly select partners based on whoever was near when the urge took them. Gender didn't appear to matter to the dancers as they formed a writhing mass of flesh around the first couple, a multi-limbed creature connected every possible way among its component parts.

Kied found himself unable to tear his eyes away from the thrusting, undulating, moaning thing the dancers had formed in the dirt before the fire. Were these local villagers who had managed to escape the soldiers keeping them penned up inside their homes? Or had these people been hiding in the valleys all this time, sneaking through the darkness to conduct their strange rites under the stars?

The voices of the men and women in the heaving mass began to join together into a strange cadence, their tones harmonizing until it sounded like a single, alien voice singing up to the cold stars overhead. The robed and hooded figures began to chant in counterpoint to the disturbing song, and one by one they opened their dark robes and dropped them to reveal their own bodies, nude except covered in swirling tattoos of hundreds of eyes staring out from their bare skin.

Kied's mind flashed back to the eye that had looked down on him earlier in the day, and a growing sense of dread began to fill his gut. Whatever these people were doing, he was sure he didn't want to see how their ritual would end. But despite his fear, he couldn't seem to turn away.

The tattooed figures on the far side of the bonfire came around and joined the few that stood near the orgiastic group. Kied was now unable to see where one person's flesh ended and another's began, the flailing limbs no longer resembling arms or legs, but instead had become long, whip-like tentacles. The participants' heads had become a mass of dark eyeballs, spread across the surface of the creature's flesh.

In a sudden rush, the flesh-creature surged forward and grabbed the tattooed watchers, yanking them toward a vast, jagged maw that opened in the center of its grotesque body. Kied felt a howl of terror building up in him as the unnatural thing tore into the remaining figures, ripping them apart as they screamed, their tattoos flashing white as they died and leaving afterimages burned into Kied's sight.

A scream tore itself from Kied's throat as he flung himself backward, scrambling desperately to get away from that monstrous beast as it fed on the broken bodies of its worshippers. But his terrified howl drew the attention of the creature, and multiple eyes fixed on Kied, pinning him in place. He tried to pull himself along the ground, but his limbs refused to function, and he flopped helplessly in the dirt as the alien monstrosity rose up on a dozen limbs and scuttled toward him.

Kied felt a presence at his back, and he raised his head to see Rotos step out of the darkness. The giant towered over Kied and stared at the creature, which stopped a handful of paces from Kied's twitching legs.

"Help … help me," Kied begged the big man. Rotos looked down at him, and there was nothing familiar in his gaze, no spark of recognition.

A harsh, discordant screeching came from the creature and

a piercing spike drove into Kied's brain. He couldn't understand the being's alien speech, but he somehow knew that's what it was. Moaning in agony, he twisted and writhed on the ground at Rotos' feet.

The sound stopped and Kied lay on the ground, panting. Rotos stared down at him as if contemplating what he should do. Finally, the big man spoke.

"He has claimed you for his own. There is nothing I can do."

Kied had to concentrate to make sense of Rotos' words.

"Who ... who's claimed me?"

Rotos looked at the beast made of the flesh of its worshippers, and smiled.

"My father," he said.

Kied tried to reach out as Rotos turned and walked back into the darkness, but he still had no control over his own limbs. He tried to call out, but terror choked him as he realized Rotos was leaving him to this creature, this thing from beyond the reality he knew.

Rotos disappeared from his sight, and Kied turned back to see the vast bulk looming over him. He let out a final scream as that jagged maw opened once more and rushed toward his face.

Chapter Twenty-Three

ARTAY WAS ALMOST BEAMING AS LAITA ENTERED HIS TENT. He tried to hide it, but she could see his absolute pleasure. She felt her insides tighten and she fought to keep her own expression neutral. Her first thought was that Kied had been captured or killed—she could think of nothing else that would bring Zartay such happiness.

He hadn't questioned her about her "assailants" from the previous night, and that also raised her suspicions. She expected the ambassador would want to know everything that had happened. But he had not summoned her, nor had he sent anyone to ask questions on his behalf.

But now he had suddenly demanded her presence in his tent, and was obviously immensely pleased about something. Was he going to accuse her of conspiring with the enemy? Was he going to tell her Kied had been killed trying to escape from the soldiers out hunting the intruders?

"Ambassador," she said shortly, glad her voice held steady. "I assume something important has happened to require a meeting so late in the evening?"

Even her apparent annoyance at being summoned past midnight was not enough to dampen Zartay's enthusiasm.

"My apologies, commander, for the late hour. But yes, you are correct. Something important has indeed 'happened.'"

He grabbed a rolled parchment off the cluttered surface of his desk and handed it to Laita. It was not sealed, so she unrolled it and looked at the flowing script. She recognized it immediately as

Zartay's hand.

"New orders," Zartay explained. "You will arrange for a detachment of soldiers to escort me and another guest to the north end of the valley. The force will deploy and make sure we are not disturbed. Further orders will be sent by me within a few days or so."

Laita looked up at Zartay.

"A whole detachment?" she asked. "Why do you need so many Legionnaires?"

"I'm not at liberty to go into details at this time," Zartay responded with a patronizing smile.

Laita's thoughts were racing around the inside of her skull. It appeared the ambassador didn't know about Kied, after all. But these orders could only mean the special team had discovered whatever it was they were searching for, and that was ill news indeed.

Kied was rushing to the same location, but the Legion had gotten there first. And now Ambassador Seaphon would accompany an entire detachment—two hundred Legionnaires—to secure the area. If Kied was already there, he would be trapped.

"These orders are unexpected. My people are spread out in occupation and patrols. It will take some time to pull in a detachment and reassign them to this."

"You have two days," Zartay answered.

"I'm sorry, but that's not enough—"

"It's all the time you have," he said, speaking over her. "This mission is now your number one priority. Get this force ready, and then worry about moving your people around to cover the gaps."

He gave her a predatory smile.

"As you can see, I've given you explicit instructions to use whatever force is necessary to ensure the people of the villages stay put. If any of them get restless when they see the soldiers moving out, it will be your job to pacify them. You will do whatever it takes."

Laita understood how close they were to completing this mission. Zartay was no longer worried about anything except gaining control of their goal—all pretense of civility was now stripped away.

What were they looking for? What had brought Kied all the way back here, to the most dangerous place for him in the entire Empire? Why was it so important to the big man who had broken out of prison with Kied that the Legion not find what they sought?

"I'm the man who's trying to stop you from destroying everything you have."

Laita could see the man believed what he was saying. If the Ambassador got his hands on his prize, the giant clearly thought it would spell disaster for the Empire.

"There's a special unit somewhere in these valleys. They're looking for a cave. We can't let them find whatever is hidden there. It would be bad for … well, everyone."

Kied hadn't seemed to know specifically what was hidden in the cave, but the giant—Rotos—apparently did. And now Zartay had given Laita the coordinates for that cave. She had no doubt that's where the detachment was supposed to go.

The ambassador was watching Laita closely, and she knew she had hesitated a bit too long. But then, he'd be more suspicious if she didn't present some resistance to his plan.

"I'll do what I can, Ambassador. But I'm not going to 'pacify' Imperial citizens unless I have no other choice."

Zartay suddenly laughed, and there was genuine mirth in his voice.

"Of course you won't," he said, walking over to the cabinet that held his liquor stores. "You will do anything in your power to keep these people safe. As much as it inconveniences me at times, I do give you credit for sticking to your ideals."

He raised a bottle, read the label, and put it back.

"Not yet," he muttered. He selected another and grabbed two glasses.

"Join me in a drink," he said. It didn't sound like a request.

"Ambassador, I'll need to get back to my tent and get to work if I'm going to free up the detachment in a reasonable timeframe."

"Nonsense," he said in a dismissive tone. "You won't send any messages until morning, and you're far too organized to have me believe you don't already have contingency plans for the rapid redeployment of some part of your forces."

He splashed some amber liquid in each of the glasses.

"A few extra minutes won't make any difference," he told her, handing her one of the glasses.

She raised it to her nose and sniffed, smelling earth and smoke. This was, no doubt, a very expensive bottle. She was also sure it wasn't the best he had in the cabinet. He raised the glass in a toast.

"To a successful completion of this mission," he said with what appeared to be a genuine smile. Laita raised her own glass in salute and took a small sip. The liquor burned her tongue, but she held it in her mouth until she could taste the various flavors embedded in the liquid. Zartay closed his eyes and savored his own drink.

"I would like to ask a question," she said after she had swallowed down the liquor. "I notice that you haven't asked me about the assailants who came into my tent last night. I would have thought you'd be curious about the incident."

Zartay kept his eyes closed for another moment before swallowing. He looked at Laita and his smile slowly faded from his face.

"I was under the impression that it was a couple of villagers looking to cause trouble," he said.

"Might I ask where you got that idea?"

"Perhaps it was an assumption on my part. Who else could it possibly have been? I can't imagine it was some of your own soldiers. I have no doubt you're looking into it, hunting for the two men."

"Certainly," she replied. "I expect we'll find them before long."

"I have faith you will," Zartay told her.

Laita realized, at that moment, that Zartay knew it had been Kied in her tent. She wasn't sure how he had figured it out, but she was sure he was playing her. The man was well practiced at manipulating others. But Laita was an experienced commander. She understood the political game; had played them in the Legion for years.

And yet, despite the ambassador knowing about Kied's presence, he was still supremely confident. And then she realized he was enjoying all of this. She was going to give this man control of a detachment, and he was going to get his prize. And if he met up with Kied along the way, he'd use the Legionnaires to eliminate the threat.

For a moment, the thought of rebellion rose up in her mind. It would take only a few seconds to kill this man. His guards would be dead before they realized she was among them. She could take the Contingent and … what?

The truth was, she didn't know how many soldiers would choose to follow her. Most of her lieutenants were loyal to the ambassador. But where did the loyalty of the common men and women in the Contingent lie?

Rebellion? By the Abyss, what am I thinking?

Laita knew she wasn't going to take any action against Ambassador Seaphon. She would not only be throwing away her career, but her very life. She had no doubt the consequences for betraying the ambassador would be rapid and severe.

She set down the glass and clenched the new orders in her fist.

"I'm sorry, Ambassador, but I need a clear head right now, and this drink will do nothing but impair my judgement. There's still a great deal of work to be done."

Zartay looked her over before answering.

"Very well, commander. Have a lovely evening."

He knew she would now be working for most of the rest of this night. His words were a calculated taunt, a reminder of how much power he had over her.

Laita spun on her heel and marched from the tent. She tried to ignore her disappointment in herself at not drawing her blade and doing something drastic.

*   *   *

KIED FLUNG HIMSELF UPRIGHT AS THE SHADOW OF ROTOS LOOMED over him in the dark. He reached for his sword, but it was still sheathed on the ground at his feet, so he drove his knuckles at the big man's throat.

Rotos easily blocked Kied's attack and wrapped his huge hand around Kied's wrist.

"Shut up!" Rotos hissed. "You'll wake up everyone in the valley!"

Kied looked around wildly for the abomination of flesh and bone that had been about to rip him into pieces but there was nothing but darkness around them, the cold stars providing little light by which to see. He lurched forward and tried to bite Rotos' hand in a futile attempt to get free.

Rotos swung his other arm, and his open hand caught Kied on the side of his face in a resounding slap. The stinging pain blossomed across Kied's cheek and cut through his panic. He shook his head and blinked away the stars swimming in his vision.

Looking down, Kied realized his own bedroll was at his feet. There was no sign of the large bonfire that had drawn him away from their campsite. Rotos' words finally registered in Kied's brain as the mud that had filled it drained away.

None of it had been real. Kied had dreamed the entire thing.

His knees weak, Kied sank down onto the ground, gasping heavily. Rotos let go of his wrist but stood over him, watching him carefully.

"It wasn't real," Kied whispered. "It wasn't real."

He repeated this a few more times, and Rotos put his hand on Kied's shoulder, but said nothing.

Finally, after he managed to get his breathing back to normal and his heart no longer felt as if it was a caged animal trying to break out of the prison of his chest, Kied looked up at his companion.

"I'm sorry, Rotos. I … was dreaming …."

In the darkness, he could barely make out Rotos' features, but the other man seemed to give him a guilty look.

"I should apologize to you, Kied. I was the cause of your nightmare."

His words shocked Kied. He shook his head at the other man.

"How?"

Rotos sat down on the ground across from Kied.

"Tell me about your dream," he said.

Kied didn't want to think about it. The nightmare wasn't fading, the way most unpleasant dreams did upon waking. He could still remember it all, the sequence running through his head over and over.

"I'm not sure I want to talk about it."

"Kied, we are getting closer to the cave," Rotos argued. "You could experience … effects. I need to hear your dream."

He leaned closer to Kied.

"All of it, every detail."

Kied hesitated. He had the dreadful feeling that speaking the words aloud would make it real, would take those images in his mind and give them form and substance. Could whatever was in the cave bring life to his horrid visions?

"I don't think I should say anything," he replied. "It feels … wrong, somehow."

Rotos seemed to understand Kied's worry.

"Speaking your thoughts aloud does carry some danger, yes. But it's nothing close to the danger that might be lurking in your mind if you remain silent. I can protect you—to a point—but I need to know exactly what I'm facing."

Kied wasn't reassured by his companion's words. He felt he had little choice, however. Danger surrounded them on all sides. The last thing they needed was something bad lurking within Kied's inner thoughts.

He told Rotos everything, from the moment he had seen the bonfire, to Rotos himself abandoning Kied to the creature. Rotos visibly flinched when Kied said "My father."

When he finished, ending on the moment when the creature had surged forward to engulf Kied with that ragged maw, he felt as if there was an expectant hush in the air. The hair on his arms was standing up, and it seemed as if there was a faint vibration flowing through the ground.

Rotos said nothing for a long moment. Finally, he took a deep breath.

"You will never speak of this nightmare again," he said. "There is power in it, power you do not want to engage."

"What's going to happen to me?"

"Nothing. At least, not until we reach the cave. What happens then will depend on what we find."

Kied blinked at Rotos in shock.

"You don't know what we're going to find in that cave? I thought you knew what the Emperor was after!"

Rotos put up one hand.

"I do know what is in that cave. But it has been there for a very, very long time. I do not know what state it will be in."

"Who else knows about the cave? Could there be others coming to claim its prize?"

Rotos pondered Kied's question.

"There are a few others who know of the cave's existence. Your Emperor is one. But none of the others know exactly where it is. I am—I was—the last with that knowledge. I wish I knew how your Emperor discovered it was in these valleys. It was supposed to be lost forever."

"Who are you, really?" Kied asked him. "Why did you react the way you did to what I said about you claiming the creature was your father? What are you taking me to do?"

Kied could feel the panic, deep down right now but ready to bubble to the surface. He wasn't sure how much more of the strangeness he could take. It was one thing to deal with enemy soldiers, betrayal by the ambassador, the memories of the prison. But he wasn't ready to face the things from his dreams, the vision he had yesterday in broad daylight. These were far beyond his experience and his training, and he worried he would collapse under the strain if he had to interact with such things.

"I am not yet ready to answer that question," Rotos replied. "I cannot force you to come with me, but I believe you understand the importance of what we are trying to do. We must prevent anyone from finding and using what is held in that cave. The survival of the human race depends on it."

"Why did you say that creature was your father?"

Kied realized that Rotos had not, in reality, said those words. It had happened only in his mind. But he had the feeling that his nightmare contained important truths in them—that what had happened in his dream had been influenced directly by outside forces.

"You did not recognize the ritual, did you?" Rotos asked him. Kied shook his head.

"There are not many left who remember. You've heard that, long before the Emperor created the Undying Empire, there were other gods in this world?"

"Yes. The new gods and the old gods fought, and the old gods were all destroyed."

Rotos nodded once, and continued.

"That's a simplistic description of what happened, but few understand the reality of it. Humans worshipped the old gods, but that worship was different than how the Church worships the beings who live in the Great Temples across the Empire. The old gods didn't hide in the depths of their temples. They moved among the people, participated directly in their worship."

"That creature," Kied whispered. "That creature was one of the old gods?"

"Not exactly. Think of it more that a small sliver of the old god's being inhabited the flesh of its worshippers and turned it into an avatar of the god itself. In this way, worshippers could directly communicate with their gods, ask them for divine favors, and see the results immediately."

"So the ritual I saw was how the people used to worship the old gods?"

Rotos nodded once more.

"What does that have to do with our search for this cave? The old gods were all destroyed …."

Kied choked off as a realization hit him.

"They weren't all destroyed, were they?" he asked. "The cave … one of the old gods is hiding in that cave …."

The panic rose up like a wave and threatened to overwhelm him. The gods of the Empire were powerful and alien things. Their priests were all mad, because no mortal mind could interact with such beings and hold onto its sanity. But if recorded history was to be believed, the Imperial gods were an improvement over the frightful beings who had moved through the world before.

"There is no god in the cave, new or old," Rotos said reassuringly. "The old gods were … they are no longer in this world."

"Then why are we going there? What are we supposed to do?"

Rotos looked up at the stars for a moment, and then back down at Kied.

"We," he said, "are going to make sure it stays that way."

Chapter Twenty-Four

D ARK GREY CLOUDS HAD CREPT UP OVER THE RIM OF THE valley during the morning and now blanketed the sky. The sun was little more than a patch of lighter grey, now past its zenith and beginning to sink back down toward the mountain ridge. Kied knew rain was coming, and he didn't look forward to getting soaked while he rode toward their destination.

He had tried not to dwell on his dream and the information Rotos had shared with him in the night. There was little he could do about his situation. Rotos believed Kied would be able to help him protect the cave from the Emperor's grasping reach, though Kied had no idea what he could contribute besides another sword arm.

If the Legion came in force, even Rotos would be brought down and killed.

The giant rode ahead of Kied, leading the way toward the cave where Kied knew he might very well die. Still, he held onto the thought that denying the Emperor his prize would go some way toward paying back his debt to the people who had lost their lives following him into rebellion.

His thoughts drifted to Laita. What was she doing now? She had told him that she'd raise the alarm after they were gone. Once that happened, she'd have to pursue him, have to make an effort to capture the two men who had entered her tent and harmed a pair of her soldiers.

And once the cave was located, Kied knew she would have to send at least a detachment to secure the area. Were they still waiting for the special team to reach the cave? Or were the Legionnaires marching right now toward the location?

Kied wished he knew what was going on, but there was nothing he could do besides follow Rotos and hope they reached the cave before anyone else.

His thoughts in turmoil, he glanced around for any sign of pursuit.

"Rotos!" he called. The big man turned in his saddle and immediately spotted what Kied—temporarily lost in his reverie—had almost missed.

A patrol of four soldiers had spotted them. The hilly area through which they had been traveling had given the patrol a chance to get close without giving themselves away. Kied didn't know how long the patrol had been following them, but now they were only a few hundred paces away, well within galloping distance.

"Go!" Rotos ordered, and kicked his own horse forward. Kied followed suit, and the patrol immediately gave chase.

Out in the open, Kied and Rotos had little chance to escape from the patrol. The soldiers would keep pace with the two men, and the horses would likely all begin to tire at a similar rate.

But Kied knew the patrol didn't need to catch up with him and Rotos. They just needed to get within range to use their bows effectively. And once the horses were exhausted, the animals would have to be abandoned. It would give the soldiers the chance they needed to begin sending volleys of arrows at their target.

"Rotos!" Kied yelled. "We need to find some shelter, where they can't use their bows and have to come at us directly!"

Rotos glanced back at Kied and then turned his horse, angling up the side of a hill and galloping hard for the mountain ridge high above them. The ridges were lined with crevasses, caves, and other shelter. Among the rocks, the soldiers would have no direct line of sight to their quarry, making bows useless.

Of course, Kied and Rotos might also trap themselves. They'd need to abandon the horses when they reached the ridge, and if they ended up in a dead end, the patrol could wait outside and send one of their number for reinforcements.

It was going to be a gamble—they wouldn't have time to search the openings for one that would let them escape. They would have to avoid caves, and simply hope that any cut they entered didn't become a trap.

The horses scrambled up the slope and Kied glanced back to see the patrol gaining on them. At a full gallop, the soldiers wouldn't bother trying to loose any arrows, and so he didn't worry about taking a shaft in his back for the moment.

The ground leveled out for a moment, and Kied spotted a cut in the rock ahead that appeared to twist as it angled up the slope of the mountain. He called out to Rotos, who spotted the opening and drove his horse toward it.

Behind them, Kied saw the soldiers reach the level ground and spur their horses on as they seemed to realize what Kied and Rotos were attempting to do. Two of the soldiers had their bows ready, but they needed to hold onto the reins with their other hand while the horses were galloping.

But Kied and Rotos would have to stop and dismount when they reached the cut. They would also have to abandon their supplies along with the horses. In those few seconds, the soldiers would likely try to loose a few arrows at them, in the hope of at least wounding one or both men.

Kied prepared to leap from his horse as soon as they reached the opening. He used his free hand to grab a bundle of food from his saddlebag and tuck it under his arm.

And then they were at the cut, and Kied turned his horse sideways to the soldiers and flung himself down on the far side of the animal, using it as cover. He bolted toward the cut while Rotos dismounted and charged after him.

One of the horses screamed behind Kied as an arrow buried itself in the animal's side, and the creature galloped away, leaving Kied and Rotos exposed. A second arrow clattered off the rocks beside Kied's head as he dove into the cut, Rotos right behind him.

They heard one of the soldiers drive their horses away from the opening before retreating back to a safe distance. Kied raised his head and looked around. The cut was a deep groove in the rock that twisted off to his left. About twenty paces on, it curved to the right out of his sight.

Rotos drew his sword and waited just around the corner of the entrance in case the soldiers decided to follow them in. Kied signaled to his companion and moved up the cut to see around the bend. He came around the turn and found the channel continuing on, running parallel to the ridge.

Kied returned to Rotos, whispering his findings to the big man.

"It looks like we can follow the cut out of this area."

Rotos hesitated.

"I hate to leave enemies at my back. The fourth rider will bring more patrols converging on this area."

"I don't like it either," Kied agreed. "But if we go now, we could get a good distance away before reinforcements arrive. Those soldiers won't come in here until they outnumber us at least four-to-one."

Kied could almost hear Rotos grind his teeth at their predicament. The muscles of the large man's jaws bulged and flexed. Finally, he gave Kied a single nod and motioned for him to proceed.

Kied was careful to pick his steps and avoid making any noise. This patrol would stay put as long as they figured their quarry was trapped in a dead end. Rotos followed a dozen paces back, and Kied was impressed at the giant's ability to move in silence.

Glancing up at the sky, Kied hoped they could make some good time before the light faded. If they could find an exit by the time dusk had gathered, they could walk most of the night and be well away from this area by dawn. But if they were still in the cut at nightfall, they'd have to stop— the footing would be treacherous in the dark.

The two men traveled onward. They could only hope the soldiers behind them would continue to wait.

*   *   *

THE COLUMN OF SOLDIERS HAD DEPARTED BARELY AN HOUR BEFORE, the points of their spears reflecting the dull grey sky above. A sea of mud had been churned up by a combination of marching boots and a light rain that had continued to fall since late last night. Sound had seemed muffled, colors muted, as the detachment escorted Ambassador Seaphon and his unknown guest—a cloaked and hooded figure whose appearance sent chills down Laita's spine—toward their destination across the valley.

Laita stood in the doorway of her own tent, staring out at the rain. The two soldiers stationed outside her tent stood at attention, eyes constantly scanning their surroundings. The men who had been knocked unconscious by Kied's large companion—while now fully recovered from their injuries—were no longer permitted to take this duty. Their sergeant had reassigned them to the most menial tasks he could dream up, a punishment for bringing shame on their squad by failing to protect their commander.

Heaving a sigh, Laita retreated back into the Command Tent and returned to her desk. She had a long list of decisions to make regarding troop deployments, and her own lieutenants were waiting for her to summon them and delegate her orders down through the chain of command. But Laita hesitated, keeping the orders to herself for now.

The discipline she demanded from her subordinates had allowed them to pull together the detachment that was now marching with Ambassador Seaphon in a single day. He had only given her the new set of orders the night before last, and had been taken by surprise when she sent him the message at dawn this morning that the Legionnaires were prepared and ready to move out.

Laita had taken some petty pleasure in catching him unprepared. He had recovered quickly, and had then turned the tables on her by revealing his "guest." Apparently, a second man—she hadn't been introduced and still had no idea who he was—had been staying in the ambassador's tent all this time. Laita had wanted to demand information, but knew there was no point. The ambassador would reveal only what he felt necessary.

That was the problem with this entire mission. Laita knew Zartay Seaphon wasn't trustworthy, knew he would sacrifice every soldier in the entire Contingent if it meant he could accomplish his own goals. And she was stuck here, always reacting to everyone else's actions.

Perhaps it was time to take control of the situation.

There would be a cost to pay, of course. But, as Laita stood in the center of her own tent and looked around at the canvas walls, she knew she couldn't just go through the motions anymore. If she didn't take action herself, events would roll over her and drown her under their own momentum.

She stepped back to the doorway of her tent and caught the attention of one of her guards.

"Call up a runner," she told the man. The guard raised a brass whistle to his lips and blew three piercing blasts. From another tent at the bottom of a hill, a rookie soldier came running. The young man followed Laita into the command tent and waited for instructions.

"Get me a squad from … Lieutenant Friarti's detachment. Pick one that has a sergeant who understands how to follow orders without question. Get them up here on the double."

"Yes, commander," the runner said, saluting smartly before he left the tent.

While she waited for the squad to arrive, Laita buckled herself into her breastplate and greaves, and strapped on her sword.

The runner returned to find Laita waiting in full combat gear. His eyes opened wide when he saw her, and he nearly forgot to salute.

Laita stepped past him and exited the tent to find the squad standing at attention. The sergeant turned to Laita and saluted.

"My squad is ready for duty, commander!" she said to Laita, who gave her a grim smile in return.

"Good. You are all Legionnaires. That means your first loyalty is to the Legion, then to the Empire, and then to the nobles who command us."

Laita stepped up and looked at each of the soldiers, one by one, as she spoke.

"There's a threat to the Legion, right here in our camp. It's time we removed it. Follow me."

She turned and marched down the hill, and the squad fell into step behind her. Other soldiers saw her coming and stepped to one side, saluting, as Laita led the squad down the path to the right and back up the next hill.

Straight toward Ambassador Seaphon's tent.

As she neared the tent, the four soldiers stationed around the perimeter came to attention. One of the guards stepped forward and saluted her.

"Commander, Ambassador Seaphon has already left with the detachment."

Laita looked him up and down.

"I know. I am taking possession of the ambassador's tent and all its contents. All four of you are to stand down."

The guard hesitated. Despite the fact that Laita was the commander of the entire Contingent, these guards were not part of her force. They had been assigned directly by the Legion High Command and sat outside the normal hierarchy. Their duty was to maintain the security of the ambassador's camp.

Ambassadors assigned to these missions had ultimate authority. They represented the Emperor himself, and therefore the Legions were required to follow the orders of these men and women without question. There had never been a case before where a commander had attempted to take possession of an ambassador's tent and belongings. The soldier didn't know how to react to Laita's conflicting order.

"Commander …," he said, not sure what to do.

"Soldier, I am giving you an order to stand down. If you choose not to comply, you will be relieved of duty and taken into custody. Am I clear?"

The guard looked at his companions for support, and the sergeant gave a signal to her squad. As one, the ten soldiers drew their swords. The sound made the guard flinch.

"Commander, I'm under direct orders to protect—"

"Take him," Laita ordered, and the squad stepped up and grabbed the four guards, placing their blades at the four men's necks before any of the men could draw their own weapons. In moments, the four guards were relieved of their armaments and had their wrists bound behind their backs.

Laita detailed four soldiers to accompany her inside Ambassador Seaphon's tent, leaving the sergeant and the rest of the squad to make sure they weren't interrupted.

"We are going to search this tent, end-to-end and top-to-bottom. Call my attention to anything you find that may be of relevance to our mission here. Maps, orders, instructions, letters, anything."

"Yes, commander," the soldiers replied in unison. Laita herself moved over to Zartay's main trunk from which she had seen him pull papers and maps before. The trunk was locked, so Laita grabbed a short-handled axe from one of the soldiers and smashed the lock. She opened the trunk and began to search inside.

It took her less than a dozen minutes to find what she sought, a package of orders from Ythis pertaining to this mission. She flipped through them until she found what she had been searching for.

As she read the orders, a ball of lead formed in her stomach. She had hoped she was wrong, hoped she was overreacting to the supplies brought for this mission. But here it was, and there could be no denying the plan.

Once the cave was secured, everyone in the valley was to be executed without delay and without mercy.

Laita put down the sheaf of papers and noticed a pair of small parchments—the kind sent via messenger bird—tucked in among the orders. She drew them out and examined them. One of the parchments was a message that the cave had been located, and a set of coordinates.

Laita cleared off Zartay's desk by sweeping everything onto the floor. She grabbed his sheaf of maps of the local area and began searching through them for the coordinates. It took her only a moment to locate the exact spot where the cave could be found.

She looked up at the other soldiers ransacking the tent.

"Get me a rider, right away," she told one of them, who hurried from the tent.

Chapter Twenty-Five

THE SUN HUNG HIGH IN THE SKY AS KIED CREPT FORWARD toward the edge of the stone ridge. He carefully tested his weight to make sure the stone was stable—it was a long fall to the valley floor below. Rotos waited behind, near the far end of the ridge.

The two men had followed the cut in the mountainside away from the waiting soldiers and found themselves climbing the side of the mountain with no easy way back out of the stone passage. They had camped the last two nights inside the cut, with no wood to build a fire and no way to travel once darkness fell.

Now they searched for a way back down to the valley floor. Rotos was sure they were near the location of the cave, but they would not find it stuck up on the side of the mountain. And without climbing gear, they could not safely climb back down the smooth stone slope that fell away beneath them.

Kied inched his way forward toward the edge of the ridge, listening for any sound that might indicate the stone beneath him was not solid and secure. After some moments, he reached the edge and peered over at the valley below.

The rock fell away below him in an almost sheer drop of a few hundred paces before sloping out to meet the green grass that grew right up to the edge of the bare stone slope. Off to his right—a few miles away from where he lay—the rock was far less smooth, ancient rivers having cut many small channels and ridges in the stone surface.

That was where they would find the cave they were seeking.

Down below, a movement caught his eye and he turned his head back and scanned the valley, trying to pinpoint what he had seen. It took him almost a minute of searching, but then he saw it again.

There were people moving across the valley floor.

They were still some distance away, little more than specks of darker brown amongst the green grass, but now that he had spotted them directly, he could tell they were people. He squinted and stared, and then realized they were mounted riders. The figures were moving very slowly across the arc of his vision, and he figured they were mostly riding toward him, although at a very slight angle.

He continued to watch until he could be sure of the number. He counted four, though it was possible there might be another one or two behind the ones he could see. At this distance, it was hard to tell.

Still, if there were only four riders, it was most likely a patrol. If Rotos was correct, no soldiers would stumble across the cave unless they were searching for it directly and knew exactly where it was located. The two men would have to be careful to not be spotted, but there would be little danger from the soldiers once they reached the cave itself.

Kied watched the riders for another minute to confirm their direction. The figures continued to approach on an angle slightly to Kied's right. It would be some time before he might be able to get a better look at them, as it didn't seem as if they were riding at speed.

He finally pushed himself back from the edge of the ridge and squirmed his way closer to the wall of rock at his back where Rotos waited. When he was far enough from the edge, Kied regained his feet and approached his companion.

"Anything?" Rotos asked him.

"It looks like the rock is much rougher a couple of miles further on. There are cuts and channels in the rock wall—a great place to find a cave."

Rotos nodded.

"We're very close."

"There is also a patrol out there," Kied said, and Rotos narrowed his eyes. "Four riders, still quite a way off. But they're coming in this direction."

"That is no patrol," Rotos growled. "That is the group searching for the cave."

"Rotos, there are patrols all over this region, searching for us. It's far more likely a group of four riders is another patrol then it is the special team—"

"It is them," Rotos said, interrupting Kied. "They know where the cave is, and they are riding there now."

"Do you have some way of knowing this? You sense something about them?"

Rotos looked Kied in the eye but said nothing.

"Look, it doesn't matter right now. We still don't have an easy way to get down to the valley floor. But we haven't hit a dead-end yet, and those channels I mentioned might give us a passage that'll let us climb down the slope without needing rope and other climbing gear. If we can get over there, it'll be our best chance to get off this ridge."

Rotos looked at the sky and then at the passage in the rock that led farther on along the side of the mountain.

"We cannot reach the cave before they do. This changes everything."

"You don't know that," Kied replied.

"We will need to be prepared to follow them into the cave, and …."

"And what?"

Rotos hesitated, and then looked Kied in the eyes again.

"We will need to follow them wherever they go. You will have to be ready to see things you were never meant to see. You will have answers to some of your questions, answers you were not supposed to learn."

"Is that a bad thing? Knowledge is power, Rotos. You've been keeping me in the dark about a lot of things. It'll be good to finally have answers to some of my questions."

Rotos pushed himself away from the rock wall and started following the passage along the side of the rock ridge.

"There are many things mortals were not meant to know," he said over this shoulder. "Some knowledge is dangerous to the mind that holds it."

Kied opened his mouth to argue, but held his words. His mind immediately went to his dream from a few nights earlier, and what it meant. He still had trouble falling asleep each night, terrified that the dream would return, terrified that he would gain the attention of the being he knew was out there somewhere, the one that had looked down upon him from the sky.

No new dreams had come. Rotos had said he could protect Kied, at least until they reached the cave. Was he somehow blocking any further nightmares from returning? Was he hiding Kied's presence from that ancient eye that had pinned Kied in place on the hill where it had found him?

If Rotos was correct, if the riders out in the valley were not just another patrol, then Kied and Rotos would have a fight on their hands when they reached the cave. But a battle didn't frighten Kied. He had faced enemies before, opponents who wanted nothing more than to shove a spear though Kied's chest and end his life. No, he wasn't afraid of a fight.

But Rotos' words unsettled him more than he wanted to admit. What might he see in that cave? What answers would he receive, and was Kied's will strong enough to handle the truths that might be revealed? Kied was worried that he would be unable to force himself to follow Rotos to the very end.

When the time came, when they reached the cave, would Kied be able to follow Rotos inside? Or would his fear paralyze him? Would Rotos have to go in alone, to face whatever the Emperor's team had recovered in the cave?

What was waiting for them in that hole in the ground?

Kied didn't press Rotos any further. For the first time, he took comfort in his own ignorance. He simply followed the big man along the ridge, toward a future he was frightened to face.

*   *   *

ZARTAY RODE NEAR THE REAR OF THE DETACHMENT, BROTHER Hissiath at his side. The priest had been silent all day, which suited the ambassador just fine. Zartay hardly wished to spend his time in idle chatter with the madman, as much as he would have liked a diversion from the boredom of travel.

The force was moving slowly, and Zartay wished they would pick up the pace. Of course, few in the detachment were mounted, and they traveled at the speed of the foot soldiers, so there was a limit as to how much ground they could cover in a day. Still, Zartay looked forward to reaching the cave. His goal was nearly in his grasp, and he was finding it difficult to remain patient.

There was no way the force would reach the cave before nightfall. They would have to camp out on the floor of the valley tonight and resume their march tomorrow morning. Zartay didn't look forward to sleeping on a simple bedroll on the ground, but it was a sacrifice he would have to make. He was more worried about the priest—what mischief might the man get up to during the long night camped among the Legionnaires?

Zartay knew he would have to speak to the man before they made camp. Brother Hissiath would simply have to control himself tonight. They couldn't afford for him to cause trouble in the camp just to satisfy his unnatural urges.

The sound of a galloping horse intruded on Zartay's thoughts. He turned in his saddle to see a lone rider approaching the main column. Two outriders moved to intercept the horseman, and he reined in and saluted the soldiers who approached him. Zartay watched the three riders confer for a moment, and then the outriders moved back into position, and the lone horseman kicked his mount back into a gallop and rode up the length of the column toward Lieutenant Uissa, the commander of this force.

"What's happening?" Brother Hissiath asked in a low voice, moving his horse close to Zartay's mount.

"A messenger," Zartay replied. "He's in a hurry."

"Something's wrong," the priest announced. "Go find out what the problem is."

Zartay frowned at the order from the priest, but held his tongue.

Brother Hissiath obviously felt he was in charge, and Zartay was his subordinate. But the ambassador knew better. He reported directly to the Emperor himself, and as far as he was concerned the Church could go burn in the bowels of the Abyss.

Still, Zartay couldn't help but worry. There were still too many things that could go wrong. Kied Leele and his companion were still out there, somewhere, looking to cause mischief.

"Perhaps you're right," Zartay said to the priest. He flicked his reins and guided his horse into a trot up along the length of the column. His own guards began to follow automatically.

"You two, stay with Brother Hissiath," he told them, and a pair returned to ride near the priest while the other pair followed Zartay.

He would have liked to have more guards with him on this trip, but it had been necessary to leave a few behind to guard his tent. He didn't trust Laita not to stick her nose in where it didn't belong if he left his own possessions unguarded. And, of course, Kied might return to the camp and pay a visit now that Zartay was no longer there.

Up ahead, Zartay spotted Lieutenant Uissa. The messenger was speaking to her, and she glanced back and spotted Zartay, frowning at his approach.

They're talking about me, he thought.

The lieutenant had not been Zartay's choice as replacement when the original command squad was taken into custody. Uissa was a rules-follower, rigid and inflexible, a true soldier. She didn't hide her dislike of Zartay. He had suggested a different sergeant for promotion, but Uissa had an impeccable record and the respect of her superiors in the Legion.

It hadn't been worth fighting over. The rest of the lieutenants were solidly under Zartay's influence, and a lone dissenter wouldn't make any difference. Lieutenant Uissa would follow orders, and that was what Zartay needed more than anything else out of this Contingent.

He approached the lieutenant, and the messenger backed his horse off but continued to watch Zartay. He didn't like the way the messenger stared at him.

"Lieutenant, a word please."

Lieutenant Uissa looked down at a piece of parchment she held in her hands. It was obviously the message that had just been delivered.

"Ambassador Seaphon," said the lieutenant. "You may approach."

Zartay didn't like the way she gave him permission to speak to her. Didn't she realize that he gave the orders to her own commander?

"I see an urgent message has been delivered to you. I'd like to see it, please."

The lieutenant glanced at the messenger, and then at one of her sergeants. The man nodded to her.

"Ambassador Seaphon, please dismount from your horse."

Zartay looked at her in confusion. Why would she ask him to dismount? What was going on?

"Lieutenant, I'm being polite in my request. But make no mistake—I'm not asking you to show me the message. I'm giving you an order."

Zartay noticed the sergeant make a hand signal, and a squad of mounted soldiers approached, fanning out as they neared. He turned to his own guards and motioned them to move up beside him.

"Ambassador Seaphon, tell your guards to stand down, and dismount from your horse. I am taking you into custody."

The mounted soldiers began to surround Zartay and his guards. The two men put their hands on the pommels of their swords. Zartay held out one hand to signal them to hold.

"Lieutenant, you do not have the authority to take me into custody. Give me the message, and we'll straighten this out before you do something that you'll deeply regret."

Zartay put just the right amount of threat in his voice to add to his mostly reasonable tone. It was a combination he had used before, to good effect.

Lieutenant Uissa didn't appear to be impressed.

"Ambassador Seaphon, I'm placing you under arrest for treason against the Empire—"

218

Zartay's two guards drew their swords, and the mounted squad of soldiers also drew their own weapons. The sergeant barked an order, and a second squad of soldiers grabbed their bows and nocked arrows, aiming at Zartay and his guards.

"Hold!" Zartay shouted. His eyes locked on the shafts aimed at his body and he felt completely exposed. He wasn't used to weapons being pointed at him, and the experience unnerved him more than he had thought it might.

"Surrender your weapons," he said to his guards. "I will deal with this."

A shout sounded from farther back down the column.

Brother Hissiath.

"Lieutenant, you are making a vast and dangerous mistake. My companion is a priest of Iathephos. He will not permit you to place him under arrest."

The sound of swords clashing came from where he had left his other two guards to stay with the priest. Then a man screamed.

Lieutenant Uissa gathered a couple of her own soldiers and rode back toward where the fight was taking place. The sergeant stepped forward and directed his own soldiers to disarm Zartay's guards. Zartay slid down from his horse, and the soldiers bound his wrists with rope behind his back.

Commander Laita Naschect was behind this. Only she could have sent the order to arrest Zartay and Brother Hissiath and know that Lieutenant Uissa would follow orders. She must have been working with Kied Leele the entire time, counting the days until she could remove Zartay from power.

He knew what would happen. Both he and the priest would be taken by Laita's people, and they would be killed. Laita would make it look like it happened in an escape attempt, and then she would forge whatever documents she needed to "prove" Zartay was a traitor to the Empire. It's what he would do in her place.

He had to give her credit—she had outplayed him. And now she could let Kied take possession of the cave, and gain the power that waited there.

Lieutenant Uissa returned.

"Did you kill Brother Hissiath?" he asked her. She shook her head.

"One of our slingers knocked him unconscious. Unfortunately, your guards refused to surrender and attacked my soldiers. Both of your guards are dead."

Zartay had to force himself not to smile. They hadn't killed the priest. That would prove to be a mistake. As much as it might seem otherwise at the moment, Commander Naschect hadn't won yet. Zartay was still alive, and he had talked his way out of worse situations than this.

He would just have to wait for the right moment.

Chapter Twenty-Six

KIED WOKE AS THE SUN CREPT OVER THE EDGE OF THE mountains, the shaft of light shining full in his face. It had been difficult to find a comfortable place to sleep on the broken rocks, and he was on the verge of exhaustion. But he knew he would not be able to fall back asleep now.

Rotos awoke with a snort and sat up slowly, sending a shower of small stones bouncing down the twisting slope beneath them. In the light of morning, the gulley still seemed like their best bet for finding a way back down to the valley floor below.

They had found this gulley last night, just as the last light was fading. It seemed to provide a fairly safe route down the side of the mountain, though it was filled with many small, loose rocks and patches of gravel. Footing would be treacherous in places, but at least the slope was fairly shallow and there were many natural handholds.

The two men broke their fast on the last of their meagre supplies. They were now out of food and nearly out of water, though they knew they would be able to fill their water skins again once they descended into the valley. In a short time, they were ready to begin their descent.

"I will go first," Rotos said. "Take it slow and test each step before you put your full weight on it. If you slip and fall, you could break an ankle, or cause a rockslide."

Kied nodded at him and waited for him to proceed.

Rotos moved slowly and carefully down the slope. More than once, a rock shifted under the big man's boot and he was forced to take an alternate step to avoid slipping. Kied expected to have a much easier time of it. As the lighter man, he knew that any step that had held Rotos' weight would easily hold his own.

Still, Kied waited until Rotos had moved some distance down the gulley before he began his own descent. He also moved slowly, checking each step before he committed to it. At this pace, it would likely be mid-day before the two men reached the bottom. And then they would still have to find the entrance to the cave itself.

If Rotos was right, if the riders Kied had spotted yesterday were the special team that was searching for the cave, then the delay in getting back down the side of the mountain would put them well behind their enemies. What would be waiting for them in the cave when Kied and Rotos finally arrived?

Kied realized his thoughts were wandering just as he rested his weight on a jutting stone, realizing too late that he hadn't tested it first. He reached up and grabbed a handhold just in time as the stone shifted and slid away, tumbling down the slope. Kied's body slid down, stopping as he gripped the edge of another stone. He shouted to Rotos below as the loose rock bounced down the slope towards the other man's head.

Without taking time to look for the falling rock, Rotos raised his arm and protected his head. The rock bounced off his forearm and tumbled away below. He peered out underneath his arm to make sure there were no other falling rocks, and then shook his arm and grimaced.

"Are you all right?" Kied called down to him.

"Yes. Just a sting."

"Sorry about that. I let myself get distracted."

"That's the danger," Rotos called back up to him. "You cannot maintain that level of concentration at all times. Take a break if you need to let your mind wander for a few minutes. We cannot rush this, or we will both get injured and fail to reach the cave at all."

Kied swallowed down his guilt and focused on the task at hand.

Over the next hour, they made good progress down the slope. Kied took frequent breaks so that he could maintain his concentration as he descended. Rotos occasionally called up to him to make sure he was okay. The big man seemed tireless, and Kied wondered where he got his energy.

Eventually, Rotos reached a twist in the gulley as it evened out and seemed to proceed horizontally for a distance before resuming its downward journey. Rotos waited for Kied to join him.

"We have a problem," the giant rumbled. He pointed at the horizontal path ahead of them. Approximately two-thirds of the way across, the gully smoothed out and became a gentle slope for about a dozen paces. The slope was covered with loose gravel.

"That spot is going to be difficult to traverse," Rotos explained. "There is nothing to hold onto, and I expect the gravel won't stay put."

Kied eyed the spot and agreed with Rotos' estimation.

"So how do we get across?"

Rotos moved forward to the edge of the smooth area and examined it closely.

"We'll need to stretch out, spread out our weight as much as we can. I'll go first again. If I can dig my feet in, the gravel might be shallow enough that I can get a foothold under the surface."

"And if you can't?" Kied asked him. Rotos pointed down the slope to where a few stones protruded from the gravel.

"Then I will probably slide down the slope and have to grab one of those stones down there."

"What if they won't bear your weight?"

Rotos looked at Kied.

"Then I will see you at the bottom."

"There's got to be a better way," Kied argued.

"Not unless we climb all the way back up and search for another gulley."

Kied considered that, but he knew it wasn't really an option. It would take them a lot longer than an hour to climb back up to where they had started, and there was no guarantee they would find anything better.

"Okay. Be careful."

Rotos nodded and stretched out on the ground. He inched his way forward, and a steady trickle of gravel slid down from underneath him. When he had a good portion of his body out on the gravel but was still holding onto the solid rock at the close side, he jammed his boots into the loose stones, working them back and forth in an attempt to dig them in and get a solid foothold.

"There's rock here," he called back to Kied. "The gravel seems shallow enough."

The big man slowly slid himself across the gravel until his body was straight again. Then he pulled one foot from the gap he had created. The removal of his foot caused a cascade of small rocks to flow over the edge and down the steeper slope below him. Rotos slid his free foot farther out and then tried to make another foothold in the loose rocks.

Bit by bit, Rotos worked his way across the slope, and each time he removed one foot a small avalanche of stones slide away behind him.

He was just over halfway across when disaster struck.

Rotos was working his left foot back and forth into the gravel when the rock under his right foot broke free. The layer of small stones beneath his body started to flow away, and Rotos had nothing to grab, no way to stop his descent.

His body slid over the edge, and Kied yelled out to his companion.

Rotos managed to grab a protruding stone that seemed to be anchored in place as he slid over the edge. He arrested his fall and looked up at Kied. And then that rock, too, came free and Rotos tumbled backwards out of Kied's sight.

"Rotos!" Kied yelled, but he could see nothing except a haze of dust rising from where Rotos had slid away on a cascade of rocks.

Kied's heart pounded, and he looked around wildly. There had to be some way to help the other man, some way to see if he had managed to catch himself before reaching the sheer drop that lay farther down the slope.

But Kied had no rope, no equipment that might allow him to descend safely. He stood there, his fists clenched as he stared at the rising cloud of dust. He faced his own difficult decision now. He could try to cross this slope and possibly fall just as Rotos had fallen, or he could ascend and try to find another gully that might lead down to the valley below.

Either way, he had no idea if Rotos was still alive.

*　　　　*　　　　*

HE COULD FEEL IT, A DEEP VIBRATION IN HIS BONES. TIATH dismounted and dropped to the ground, his eyes fixated on the black opening in the rock. The vibration didn't increase when he stood directly on the dirt—it wasn't coming through the ground, but through the air.

The entrance to the cave had been surprisingly easy to find. Tiath wore the amulet on a chain around his neck, and it had pulled him toward this narrow channel in the rock. The channel had led them to an open gully, and they followed it around a curve to where they found the shadowed hole in the rock that was their destination.

The sunlight didn't penetrate into the cave mouth more than a few feet. Around the opening, strange designs has been carved into the stone, following the irregular outline of the passage. Tiath found it difficult to look directly at the carvings—they swam in his vision and made his stomach churn.

He turned to look at his companions. Azam had slid off his own horse, and was staring at the entrance with a frown, as if searching out any threats that might be waiting for them. Deylista had a strange, dreamy look on her face. Pasill's face was still drawn with pain, and his eyes darted nervously around the gulley.

"This is it," Tiath said to them. "This is what we've been searching for."

Deylista and Pasill dismounted, and Azam drew his sword.

"Does anyone else hear that?" Deylista asked, her gaze drifting up to the sky.

"The vibration?" Tiath asked. She slowly shook her head.

"The music," she explained. "It sounds somewhat like a flute, only … strange … like sounds I've never heard before."

"I don't like the smell," Pasill said, his voice strained. Tiath sniffed the air but only smelled dust.

"What do you smell?" he asked the other man. Pasill grimaced.

"It's like a combination of old fish and some exotic flower. One overpowers the other, and then they switch."

Tiath turned to Azam.

"What are you getting from this?"

"Nothing," Azam replied.

"Nothing strange?"

"No, nothing at all. I don't hear anything except your voices. I can't smell anything at all. There's no … sensation. It's like this place is a void, sucking all experience into itself."

"Okay," Tiath said to his team. "As usual, we're going in blind and there's obviously power here. Deylista, I want you ready with your pack. Azam and Pasill, weapons out and keep your eyes open. Pasill, you'll cover Deylista."

"I don't have much left," Deylista reminded him. "My main pack was lost in the crypt. All I've got are some backup materials."

Tiath swore under his breath. He had forgotten that all of Deylista's ritual components had been lost in the crypt some days ago. She had a few spare supplies that had been at their campsite when her pack had been taken by whatever dwelt in the darkness of the crypt, but it was limited.

"Well, be ready with whatever you've got."

He glanced back to the cave entrance before continuing.

"I'll go first. Stay within three paces of each other."

Deylista loosened the strings on her pack and shifted it onto one shoulder. When she was ready, she nodded to Tiath.

He lit his lantern and held it aloft as he stepped up to the mouth of the cave. The darkness rolled back and didn't seem to be fighting the light as it had in the crypt. These shadows seemed almost normal. The light showed him a passage leading away to the left, deeper into the side of the mountain.

One by one, the team entered the passage as Tiath pushed onwards. The tunnel was wide, allowing them to walk in twos if they had so wanted. But they remained in single file as they moved along.

The passage straightened out and continued on for a hundred paces or more before swinging sharply to the left again. As Tiath moved around the corner, the passage opened up into a large chamber. The light from his lantern glinted from bits of metal inside the open space.

He stepped into the doorway and raised the lantern. A domed ceiling rose high above the chamber, and the far walls were perhaps fifty paces away from the entrance. Off to his left, a raised dais was set against the wall and held what appeared to be a shrine of some sort. To his right, set away from the wall but not in the center of the chamber, stood a metal oval ring. Spanning five feet across at its widest point and rising perhaps ten feet in height, one end of the oval was embedded in the rock floor.

The metal of the ring was irregular, with many small protrusions and angles along its surface. The ring was the thickness of Tiath's fist, and parts of it reflected the lantern light, while other parts were dull and seemed to absorb the light.

Tiath stepped across the threshold into the room.

"By the gods," Pasill muttered. "The stench here is awful."

Tiath looked over at Deylista, and her eyes were glassy, her mouth slack.

"Deylista!" he called to her. "Snap out of it!"

She blinked a few times and then focused on him.

"Wh … what did you say?"

"Are you still hearing the music?"

"It's loud now," she replied, nodding her head to a melody only she could hear. "I think it's coming from this room."

There was a clang from behind Tiath, as of metal striking rock. He spun to see that Azam had dropped his sword and was stumbling toward the dais. Tiath lunged forward and grabbed Azam's arm.

His fingers sank into the other man's flesh, as if it was rotten meat.

Azam turned to look at Tiath, and his eyes were blank white orbs. His skin had turned an ashen grey and hung off his face in ropy tendrils, revealing his skull beneath.

Tiath yanked his hand away and spun to Deylista.

"Preservation ritual, now!"

She blinked stupidly at him and then seemed to gather her wits about her.

"I can't!" she yelled at him. "I don't have what I need!"

"Azam!" Pasill yelled, moving forward to grab the man. Tiath intercepted him.

"There's nothing we can do to stop it."

Pasill looked into Tiath's eyes, and then back at Azam. He tensed up, as if he was going to push Tiath out of the way. Tiath grabbed his shoulders.

"If you follow him, the same thing will happen to you, Pasill. You can't save him."

Tiath glanced over to see Azam stumble up the steps of the dais and stand before the shrine that crawled up the curved wall.

In a burst of light, the oval flared once and then a shimmering curtain of light filled the inside of the ring. Through the multicolored rays, Tiath could make out a desert landscape and what looked like a vast city in the far distance.

He turned back to Deylista and noticed something wrong, but it took him a moment to realize it. She had been standing in front of the tunnel that led back outside. Only now, there was no tunnel. The walls of this chamber were smooth and unbroken around its entire circumference.

They were trapped.

Deylista handed Tiath a rolled-up parchment, and she drew a black dagger with a twisted and asymmetrical blade from her pack. He realized that they could at least protect themselves from whatever was happening to Azam.

Unrolling the parchment, Tiath looked over at his compatriot. The man stood on the dais, gazing upward with his sightless eyes at the strange carvings that covered the back of the shrine. And then he opened his mouth, his jaws distending, the ropy flesh tearing as a long, glistening black appendage reached out from inside his body.

It was joined by a second, and Tiath realized the tendrils were arms. He watched helplessly, the scroll in his hands forgotten, as Azam's skull split apart and a grotesque humanoid shape drew itself from his body.

Tiath found himself unable to look at it, as his eyes kept sliding away from the creature that crouched on the dais in front of him. He got a glimpse of too many limbs, a long, distended head, glowing green eyes, and bone-white talons on thick fingers.

Pasill screamed, and Tiath tried to shake himself free from the terror that gripped him before the monstrous being on the dais attacked.

Chapter Twenty-Seven

KIED CLENCHED HIS TEETH AS HE MOVED ACROSS THE gravel slope. Rotos' earlier attempt had knocked away a good deal of the loose stones, and Kied found multiple hand- and footholds, allowing him to cross with much less danger than his companion had faced.

When he reached the point where Rotos had fallen, Kied was forced to slow his pace and proceed even more carefully. Bit by bit, he managed to move closer to the far side where the exposed stone would give him a safe place to rest.

Finally, he was able to reach out a hand and grasp solid rock. He pulled himself the rest of the way off the gravel and rolled over into the continuation of the gully. From the position of the sun, he figured at least half an hour had passed while he traversed this stretch.

If Rotos was stuck somewhere below, Kied knew he had sent more cascades of gravel down onto his companion as he slid across, but there was nothing he could do about that. Kied's only hope was that Rotos had managed to grab a ledge or rock and stop his fall before it became deadly.

After a moment's rest, Kied picked himself up and began to work his way down the gulley. Every so often, he moved over to the edge and peered over the rock to see if he could spot his companion, but the slope blocked his view.

He had traveled another hundred paces or so down the slope when he heard Rotos' voice calling to him. He raised his head and looked out at the slope to see the big man hanging by a large stone that protruded from the smooth slope.

"Rotos!" he called. The other man turned and Kied could see the relief on his face.

"I need some help."

Kied almost laughed from relief and Rotos' understatement of the situation. He moved his body up against the side of the gully and tried to see how he might lend assistance to the other man.

"I can get close to where you are," Rotos explained. "But I can't quite reach the gully. I'll have to jump, and you'll need to catch me."

Kied pondered that for a moment.

"I'm not nearly strong enough to support all your weight, Rotos. You'll pull me over the edge and we'll both fall."

"No, you won't. But you have to trust me. You have to give in to me, to my will. If you fight it, I won't be able to give you the strength you need."

Kied couldn't hide his confusion.

"I'm going to impose my will on you," Rotos explained. "Whatever you do, don't fight it. It may hurt … well, in truth, it is going to be very painful, but you'll be able to catch me and there will be no permanent damage to your body."

Rotos looked Kied in the eyes.

"But you have to give in to me, completely. If you block me, I can't help you."

Kied considered the options. He didn't like the idea of Rotos doing something to his mind. But he also couldn't save his companion with the resources he had now. If Kied did nothing, Rotos would eventually fall, and die. Without Rotos, Kied wouldn't find the cave.

Besides, there was no way he could just leave and let the other man fall to his death.

"Okay, do what you have to do," he called over to Rotos.

The big man locked eyes with Kied, and Kied immediately found himself unable to look away. A crushing weight fell on him, pushing his body into the rough stone surface and he gasped in pain. A pressure began to build in his skull, and his thoughts became sluggish and murky.

With a flash, agony speared through his mind, and he was dimly aware of the sound of his own voice, screaming. His arms and legs spasmed, the pressure of his muscles nearly snapping the bones in his limbs.

All the while, Rotos kept his gaze locked with Kied's.

Finally, when Kied was sure he was going to die, that neither his mind nor his body could take any more of the unyielding pressure, Rotos gave a great shout and shoved himself up and away from the stone ledge which he had been holding. He reached out his arm, grasping for Kied's own outstretched hand as he flung himself through the space between the two men.

Kied's fingers locked onto Rotos' wrist as the big man began to fall. Another scream tore from his throat as the giant's full weight pulled down on Kied's arm. But despite the size difference, Kied pushed back against the stone and pulled Rotos up and over the edge of the rock to fall into the gully beside him.

With a snap, the pressure inside his body and head released, and Kied clenched his eyes as the world spun around him.

Eventually, the overwhelming wave of dizziness faded, and he managed to open his eyes. Rotos lay beside him, staring at the scattered clouds drifting across the sky overhead.

"Thank you," Rotos said to him in his low rumble.

Kied rolled onto his back and gingerly touched his arm. It felt tender, but otherwise seemed unharmed. He flexed his elbow and then pushed himself up into a sitting position.

"What did you do to me?" he asked the other man.

"I lent you a portion of my strength."

Kied considered that for a moment.

"That's … well, that's a handy ability."

Rotos grunted but said nothing else.

"It's gone, though, isn't it?"

The giant looked over at Kied.

"It's not something I would have done, given the choice. Like all such actions, it has a cost. And it's not one I would willingly pay unless I had no other option."

"You mean it does something to you?"

Rotos sat up and looked down the twisting gully. Then he leaned forward and vomited without warning.

A spray of black liquid came pouring from his mouth, chunks of reddish flesh mixed in with the foul liquid. Kied recoiled as the dark stream splashed on the rocks at Rotos' boots.

Rotos pulled back his head and turned his face to the sky. A shadow fell across the two men, though no cloud obscured the sun. Eyelids fluttering, Rotos mumbled words that made bile rise in Kied's throat.

And then the shadow faded away and Rotos fell back onto the rocks. The horrid vomit steamed in the sunlight.

Rotos raised his arm and wiped away the black spittle that lined his mouth. He opened his eyes and muttered under his breath.

"What was that?" Kied asked him. "Is that because of what you did?'

Rotos muttered something again, and Kied leaned closer to him.

"I'm sorry, I can't hear y—"

"They found it," Rotos growled. "The cave. They're inside the cave."

A chill crept up Kied's spine.

"Is that why you—"

"We need to move," Rotos said, pushing himself back to his feet and carefully stepping over the pool of his vomit.

Kied stared at the big man. There was something in Rotos' eyes, a look Kied had only seen once before, when the sounds of crying children echoed across the badlands.

Rotos was afraid.

Kied stood up and faced his companion.

"Do you still want to go first?"

Rotos gave him a single nod and started to climb back down along the slope of the gully. Kied waited a moment to give him some room, and then began his own descent.

Despite all their efforts, they had run out of time.

*   *   *

ROTOS STUMBLED AS HE LED KIED INTO THE NARROW GORGE. HE caught himself on the rock wall, and then shook his head.

"Are you all right?" Kied asked him.

"I will be when we reach the cave."

Kied wasn't sure he wanted to think about that answer too much. He still remembered his dream vividly—it was never far from his thoughts.

They heard the horses before they came around the corner. Rotos held up a hand, and Kied stopped. Moving with surprising grace, Rotos approached the corner and looked around the edge of the rock wall.

"It's clear," Rotos said, and then stepped around the corner. Kied followed to find Rotos standing beside four horses. They seemed barely aware of the two men.

Kied looked up at the ridge above them, searching for any sign of a sentry.

"They're all inside," Rotos told him. Kied didn't ask how he knew.

"At least one of them is waiting for us inside," Rotos said in a low voice. "Maybe more, but I think the others went … well, you'll see in a couple of minutes."

Kied nodded, but Rotos put his large hand on Kied's shoulder.

"What's waiting for us in there is dangerous. It's no longer human, and it's strong and fast. Be careful and let me do most of the fighting. If it comes at you, just concentrate on defending yourself."

"What is it?" Kied asked.

"It's a guardian," Rotos replied. "Ancient and angry. Do what I tell you to do, and don't stop to question me. I want us both to survive this."

"Could the guardian have killed the others who came in here?"

"No. The guardian isn't there to stop the first person to enter. It's there to make sure no one follows."

Kied wondered at such a trap. This was a prize that was never meant to be shared, it appeared. He drew his sword and faced the cave mouth. Rotos drew his own blade and advanced into the tunnel.

They had no lantern, and the light from outside rapidly faded as they moved deeper into the tunnel. But just as they reached the darkest point, Kied realized there was light ahead. They rounded a corner and saw the tunnel widen out into a large chamber.

As the two men stepped up to the opening, their eyes locked on the shimmering portal, a glowing oval that sent flickering shadows dancing across the walls of the vast chamber. It faced the altar upon the dais and illuminated the ragged remains of a corpse that had been discarded there.

Rotos scanned the room, but there didn't appear to be any sign of the guardian. He motioned for Kied to remain where he was, and stepped into the chamber. The dancing light made it difficult to focus on the far walls or the ceiling, and Kied had no idea what the guardian might look like.

Rotos moved over to the dais and examined the bloody flesh piled there. He grunted and turned back to the portal. The oval frame was placed edge-on to the doorway where Kied stood, so he couldn't see through the portal to whatever lay on the other side.

He could, however, see Rotos' reaction to it.

The big man stared into the portal and froze. Rotos' face melted into a look of such longing that Kied expected tears to start running down the man's cheeks. And then Rotos shook himself out of his reverie and seemed to realize what he was seeing. His face hardened once again, and Kied could see he was resolved to do whatever was necessary to see this through.

Rotos motioned for Kied to join him. As he moved around the portal to stand at Rotos' side, Kied gazed into the world that lay on the other side of the gate.

And then the guardian struck.

Rotos shouted in pain as the creature dropped from the ceiling and hammered down onto him, driving the big man to the floor of the chamber with a bone-rattling thud. It made no sound as Kied backpedaled, trying to get enough distance to prepare himself for its next attack.

The creature's skin shimmered in time with the light emanating from the portal, making it difficult to fully see its shape in the dancing beams. Against the rough rock of the ceiling, it had been effectively invisible until it had moved into position above the two men. Kied found his eyes sliding off the creature, as if it pushed his gaze away so that he couldn't focus on it.

The guardian's glowing green eyes focused on Kied for a moment, and then returned to Rotos. At that moment, Rotos surged upward with a roar and swung his blade in a wide arc, trying to take the creature's head. But it moved too fast for the big man's wild swing, and ducked under the blade.

The alien beast flowed up against Rotos and its many limbs tore into the man's body, carving bloody swaths from his chest and sides. Rotos hammered his elbow into the side of the creature's head and knocked it sideways, following up with a quick thrust of his blade. The tip glanced off the guardian's rough skin.

With a rapid strike, the creature's claws dug into Rotos' wrist and his hand spasmed, dropping the sword to the floor of the chamber. It struck again and again at Rotos, as the giant struck back with hammering blows of his huge fists.

Kied realized he was behind the creature, and he lunged forward in an attempt to drive his own sword into the guardian's back. The point of the blade caught in the creature's skin and Kied heard a sickening crack as the flesh parted. He managed to push the sword a few inches into the creature's body before one of its arms swung back and caught him across the shoulder.

It was like being hit by a battering ram.

Kied was flung sideways, his arm nearly dislocated by the blow. He went sprawling to the ground, stunned by the impact. If the creature had come after him at that point, he would have been helpless to defend himself.

But Rotos took the opportunity Kied had given him. He wrapped his arms about the guardian's body and pulled it into a crushing hug. The talons of the creature dug into Rotos' sides and carved furrows in the man's back. But Rotos flexed his arms and squeezed tighter and the creature let out a horrific shriek that pierced Kied's eardrums.

Kied shook his head to regain his senses and tried to push himself to his feet, but he had given Rotos what he needed to defeat the guardian. The big man's hand found the hilt of the sword sticking out of the creature's back. With his arms still around the guardian, pressing it into his own chest, Rotos placed both hands on the sword's hilt and drove it through the creature's body.

Kied screamed "No!" as the sword plunged in all the way to the cross guard.

The creature writhed on the blade, no longer able to fight back. It gave a second and final shriek, and then its limbs dropped, and the creature's head fell back.

Rotos dropped to the floor, the guardian still pinned to his own chest. Kied ran over and saw that the blade had plunged right through the creature's body and then directly into Rotos' chest.

"Rotos!" Kied yelled, and the big man looked up at him weakly. Kied didn't know what to do. If he withdrew the sword, Rotos would immediately bleed out on the floor of this chamber.

"We must … go through the … portal," Rotos gasped. "We must … follow them."

"What do you need me to do? If I pull the sword, you'll—"

"Just … get me … across."

Rotos' eyes rolled back and he lost consciousness.

Kied looked at the shimmering portal and back at his companion. He had already seen Rotos recover from what should have been a fatal wound, and he knew it would be folly to question the man's instructions now.

Taking a solid grip on the sword, he slid it out of Rotos' chest. Immediately, a pool of dark red blood began to form under the man's body. Shoving the corpse of the guardian away, Kied grabbed Rotos by the arms and dragged him toward the portal.

The light danced across Kied's skin as he approached the gate, sending rippling sensations of heat and cold through his body. He looked through at the desert landscape and the vast, alien city in the far distance. He knew he wouldn't be able to carry—or even drag—Rotos all the way to the gates of those far walls.

He turned his back on the gate, lifted Rotos' arms once again, and pulled.

Chapter Twenty-Eight

As Kied backed into the portal, the shimmering light filled his vision, blinding him to anything except the kaleidoscope of colors. He felt as if he was floating, though he could still feel the solid rock beneath his boots. He held onto Rotos' forearms tightly, terrified of losing his grip on his companion during the journey to the other world.

The light dissipated as he stepped through to the other side. Rotos emerged from the portal as Kied dragged him out of the glowing oval onto the red, sandy ground of an alien landscape.

There was no strange metal frame on this side of the gate. The portal was an orb of scintillating light here, sitting on the ground and giving off a faint hum. But there was no structure to mark its spot, nothing to indicate that this was where the gate was located.

Kied's first thought was that if the orb disappeared, he'd have no way to open it again. A wave of panic rose in him, but he fought it down and forced himself to remain calm.

He rose and looked around at the vast, featureless plain that surrounded him. The ground was rough and rocky, and covered with the reddish-brown sand upon which he now stood. No mountains rose in the distance, and no clouds crept across a sky the color of polished bronze.

Kied turned to face the city, and gasped at its size and shape. A wall of what appeared to be ivory surrounded the city, which was filled with immense buildings and slender towers of unfamiliar construction.

There was something alien and deeply unsettling in the appearance of the buildings. Kied could see no rectangles or squares—rather, the shapes of the buildings were uneven and twisted. It seemed as if walls that should have been parallel somehow managed to meet up, corners were found at unexpected places, and what appeared to be straight, high bridges between spires somehow changed scale and direction as they stretched across the intervening spaces.

Kied felt his gorge rise as he stared at the alien cityscape, and he forced himself to look away. He noted that no gate had been visible in the white wall that stretched across the ground between him and those strange buildings. He had no idea how they might gain entry into the city, if that was indeed where they would need to go.

Looking down at the ground, Kied spotted three sets of tracks leading away from the shimmering orb toward the wall in the distance. He knelt down to examine them more closely, and noted that the individuals who had made these tracks were all wearing boots of a familiar type.

The Emperor's special team had already gone to find their way into the city.

Behind Kied, Rotos suddenly let out a roar of pain that thundered into the sky and echoed across the plain. Kied himself nearly screamed in surprise as the giant's voice ripped apart the near silence that had sat heavily upon the landscape.

He spun to see Rotos clutching his chest, his back arched and his legs writhing as he let out another roar, and another. A wind suddenly picked up, hot and dry and full of sand as it swept in from the unbroken landscape opposite the city.

Kied shielded his eyes from the blowing grit as the wind seemed to swirl around Rotos, obscuring his form. A strange red light rose from within the whirlwind, and Rotos let out one final shout that shook the ground and sent Kied sprawling in the sand.

The wind stopped so suddenly that the sand fell like rain.

Kied raised his head to see Rotos standing in the center of a spiral of sand. His wounds were gone, and he seemed—if anything—larger and more alive than Kied had ever seen him. There was something about his face, his skin, that radiated some kind of energy.

Rotos seemed more real than anything else around him.

Kied looked down at his own hands. They seemed leached of color, as if he had faded since he stepped through the portal.

He looked back up at Rotos, who was staring at the city in the distance, his chest heaving as he breathed in the air of this world.

"Rotos," he said to the other man.

Rotos looked down at him, and then wordlessly extended a hand and helped Kied to his feet.

"What is this place?" Kied asked him. "Where are we?"

Rotos turned back to the city. Kied saw his fists clench.

"This was built to be a home for ...."

He stopped, and Kied waited for him to continue.

"It doesn't matter," he continued finally. "It is a dead place. But there is still a residue of power here, power your Emperor wants for himself."

"There are tracks," Kied said, and then realized the wind had covered them over with blowing sand.

"I know where they are going," Rotos answered. "We must catch up with them before they reach the palace at the center of the city."

"Why? What's in the palace?"

Rotos looked down at him.

"If we succeed, you will not need to find out. If we fail, it won't matter. We will both be dead."

Kied ground his teeth. He wanted to yell at Rotos, demand some answers. He'd had enough of the mysteries, the secrets. Kied stood here, on another world, and was still being kept in the dark.

But he knew it was futile. He had accepted Rotos' word that whatever was here would be a terrible force of destruction back in their own world. He had agreed to help him stop the Emperor's minions. The two men had escaped from prison together, had traveled into the mountains together, had fought and killed side-by-side to reach this point.

Kied wouldn't give up now, and Rotos knew it.

Rotos stood there and watched Kied come to his conclusion, saying nothing else. Finally, he put his hand on Kied's shoulder.

"You have risked your life to come here with me, and for that I am grateful. I wish I could share with you everything you would like to know. But what I keep to myself I do because knowledge can be dangerous. Ideas call to other ideas, call the attention of beings to whom you are currently invisible. Your survival depends on remaining invisible."

"I thought I had already caught the attention of something."

Rotos frowned and lowered his hand from Kied's shoulder.

"You have," he said, and Kied felt a rush of fear in his gut. "I will take care of that, once all this is finished. I … I owe you that. But I cannot protect you from everything that's out there."

Kied turned to face the distant city.

"Do you think we can catch up with them? Or are we just rushing to our own deaths?"

"Distances are … flexible … here. So is time, if you know what to do. It will be unpleasant for you, but we should be able to reach them before they find the palace."

Rotos began walking toward the city, and Kied fell into step beside him.

"You can manipulate time and space?" he asked his large companion.

"In this place, anything is possible if you know the right secrets."

"Why do I get the feeling you know all the secrets?"

Rotos let out a laugh that surprised Kied.

"It must seem that way to you," he said to Kied. "But everything I know is a drop of water compared to the ocean of secrets that hide around the edges of your world."

Kied nodded but said nothing else. He chose not to call attention to Rotos' verbal slip.

*   *   *

AFTER WALKING SOME DISTANCE, ROTOS STOPPED AND TOOK KIED by the arm.

"You will want to close your eyes," he said to Kied. "When I tell you, take a single pace forward and then stop. You may hear or feel things that … just keep your eyes closed, no matter what."

Kied wanted to ask what they were going to do, but he figured it was futile. He closed his eyes.

Rotos began to mutter under his breath, and Kied suddenly smelled tilled soil. He could hear the clucking of chickens, and cows lowing in the distance. Another, sweeter smell came to him and his heart surged as he recognized the scent of the great love of his life.

"Step forward now," Rotos instructed.

Kied took a single step forward ….

He lay on his deathbed in a simple room. Dim sunlight filtered through the blanket hung over the single window. An elderly woman stood beside the bed, holding his hand. Kied looked down and saw that his own skin was wrinkled and covered in age spots. He looked up into the face of his wife, and a single tear rolled down her cheek. His chest swelled with love for this woman who had accepted him after he had decided not to join the Legion. They'd had a good, simple life together. With a last gasp, Kied's vision faded as he died.

Kied moaned as he suddenly came back to himself. He almost opened his eyes, but clapped his hand over his eyelids just in time. The solid grip of Rotos' hand on his upper arm steadied him. Now Kied could smell burning pitch. A wind came up, and distantly he could hear the sounds of battle; swords clanging against shields, people shouting, the galloping of horses. The smell of blood and sweat, hot leather armor, and dust kicked up by the booted feet of the Legion filled his head.

"Just one more," Rotos said reassuringly. "Step forward now."

Kied didn't want to take another step. He feared what he would see and feel. But he also feared what might happen if he didn't do exactly what Rotos had instructed. So Kied took another step ….

The ambush had been well-planned and flawlessly executed. Kied's forces were divided in half, and the avalanche had crushed too many of his Legionnaires on this side of the pass. The barbarian tribes charged in, howling, while Kied shouted orders at his soldiers in an attempt to get them into formation. But the attackers were too close, and the Legionnaires were forced to drop their spears and form a shield wall. A shout of alarm caught Kied's attention and he looked up at the ridge to see dozens of archers appear. The rain of shafts came down at his squad, and Kied saw the point of an arrow descend toward his face.

Kied legs were weak and he would have fallen if not for Rotos' support.

"It is done," Rotos said. "You can open your eyes."

Kied lowered his hand and blinked his eyes open to see a wall of white stretching before him. He looked around and saw that they were standing at the base of the wall that surrounded the city. He turned and looked back out at the plain, but couldn't spot the orb of light.

"How far did we ...?"

"About three miles. The orb is out there, but it will only be visible when you're actively trying to find it."

Kied raised his head to see the top of the wall far above.

"How do we get in?" he asked.

"We step over it," Rotos answered.

Kied let out a humorless laugh.

"That's got to be a hundred paces high, at least. I'm not that tall, and neither are you."

Rotos turned to face Kied.

"Look at me and ignore the wall beside you. Think back to when we were standing out there on the plain. The wall was a tiny strip in front of the city."

"But that's just perspective," Kied argued. "It's the same wall, it just looked smaller."

"Everything is perspective," Rotos growled at him. "Remember what it looked like, that little strip of white. It was the height of your index finger. Picture that in your mind."

Kied imagined the sight of the wall as he had seen it near the gate.

"Bring it into your mind and concentrate," Rotos said.

Kied found he couldn't pull his eyes away from Rotos' gaze. Something in his stomach was pulling, as if he was being dragged to the ground by his intestines. He fought that urge to vomit and focused on the image of the city from the distance.

"Now step onto the wall," Rotos said, and Kied turned to see that the wall was no higher than the top of his boot. Rotos walked over and stepped up onto the wall. Kied followed him.

The wall was at least twenty paces wide, a smooth white rock of some kind Kied had never seen before. He looked down at the rock and noticed small veins of some silvery substance through the strange stone.

When he raised his head, he gave an involuntary gasp. The two men now stood upon the wall as they had found it only minutes ago, towering over the surrounding plain. Kied could see for many miles, and the landscape was featureless as far as his eyes could make out.

He turned to face the city and nearly swooned with vertigo. The strange shapes of the buildings made him nauseous and he was forced to tear his eyes away from the alien structures.

"How … how do we get down?"

Rotos stepped over to the edge.

"Close your eyes and take a step," the other man said.

Kied couldn't help picturing himself falling to his death on the ground below.

"I don't think I can convince myself the wall isn't this high."

"Just close your eyes and step out. I will take care of the rest."

Kied stepped over to the edge and looked down. The ground below was tiled with many-sided stone slabs. Despite their uneven sides and unusual shape, they seemed to fit seamlessly together to form a solid surface. The sight of them made Kied dizzy.

He closed his eyes and reached out for Rotos. The big man grasped Kied's forearm.

"Take a step," Rotos said.

Kied stepped forward and expected to fall. As he moved forward, his foot found only empty air, and Kied nearly opened his eyes as he tumbled forward. But then he connected with solid ground and realized he had stepped down no more than the height of a typical stair. He stumbled forward and regained his balance.

Opening his eyes, Kied found himself standing on the strange tiles at the base of the wall that towered above him.

"You're right," he said to Rotos.

"About what?"

"About it being unpleasant. I don't like this place. I'm worried that if we get separated, that if anything happens to you, I'll never be able to get back out. I'll be trapped in this city for the rest of my life."

Rotos pointed to a slender tower off in the distance.

"There is a gate in the wall, but it is at the base of that tower over there. We saved some time by crossing here rather than traveling all the way around to the gate. The others had to enter the city that way—they couldn't come in the way we did. So we may well be ahead of them for now."

"Okay," Kied said. "Where do we go now?"

"We head for the palace at the center of the city. That's where the others will be going. We need to get there first."

Rotos led the way down the strange boulevard, with Kied trailing behind him.

Chapter Twenty-Nine

THE ROAD WAS BLOCKED WITH AN AVALANCHE OF TUMBLED stones from a building that had collapsed at some point in the distant past. The weight of the stones had cracked the tiles that lined the surface of the road, and the broken pattern emitted a chill that crawled across Tiath's skin like a thousand insects.

"Turn back," he told the others and led the way back to the previous intersection.

Pasill followed him resolutely, his mouth set in a grim line. He had said little since Azam had transformed into that horrid creature in the cave where they had found the gate to this world. Pasill had not wanted to leave Azam like that, but Tiath ordered them through the gate, hoping the creature would not follow.

A transformation of a different sort had come over Deylista. There was a hungry look in her eyes as she gazed at the ancient and alien buildings around them. From the moment they had stepped into this world, Deylista had seemed to realize the possibilities here. She was hunting for something, focused on finding an opportunity to gain some form of power from this place.

Tiath's goal was the palace he knew was somewhere in this city, and he could feel that building pulling him towards it. The image of the throne lay heavy in his mind. From the moment he had glimpsed it before they had entered the crypt back in the pass five days ago, he knew that this was his ultimate destination. He would find everything he wanted here in this strange city.

So far, they had avoided entering any of the buildings. The city seemed lifeless, but there was no telling what might await them inside these alien structures. And Tiath knew they were getting close to his goal.

He led his remaining companions down the wide boulevard to the next intersection, and then turned right. This street was narrow, lined on both sides by long, blocky structures many stories tall. The walls of the buildings on either side were made from a rough, dark blue stone that seemed to have swirls of other colors deep inside the surface. Tiath didn't stare into the depths of the stone—he knew better than to let himself become mesmerized by the patterns embedded into nearly every surface of this antediluvian city.

They moved down the narrow street, and Tiath felt the amulet grow heavy on its chain. He looked down to see the stone pulsing with a deep, blood-red light at its center.

"By the gods!" Deylista gasped.

From the stone tiles a dozen paces in front of them, a thick black liquid had begun to bubble up. Tiath looked back to see the same thing happening behind them. Limbs stretched up from the viscous substance—some looked like human arms, but others were many-segmented or too thick to be human, ending in ragged talons, or crab claws, or suckered tentacles.

A single, thick column of liquid rose up from the center of the mass, and a rough sphere formed at its very top. It towered over Tiath as a face pushed out from the surface of the sphere. The face had a human mouth, but above that one recognizable feature, five orbs resembling the eyes of a fly or other insect were placed haphazardly across its surface.

The mouth opened and a low rumbling sound came out, like rock sliding over rock. To his surprise, Tiath understood the meaning behind the ragged sound.

You trespass in the First City.

The amulet continued to pulse against Tiath's skin. He grabbed it in his fist and raised it up toward the horrid face at the top of the column.

"We do not trespass," Tiath stated boldly. "We have the key. This brought us here."

The dozens of limbs reared back, pulling away from Tiath and his amulet, though the face did not react.

You are not immortal. The First City is not for you.

"This is the Amulet of Queorithnuru. As I hold the amulet, so I command you to do my bidding."

Tiath didn't know where the words came from, but he knew them to be the truth even as he said them. The being that surrounded them was one of the city's guardians, but so long as Tiath had the amulet, he was in control.

The insect eyes regarded Tiath, and there was no way for him to know what the creature was thinking, or how it would react. He could only wait for it to accept the power he wielded. Finally, it spoke once more.

As you hold the amulet, so I serve you.

Tiath blinked at the creature, and then let out a breath he hadn't realized he was holding. He had no doubt that this … thing … would have been capable of slaughtering the three of them if it had not accepted the power of his command.

The others serve you as well?

The question caught Tiath off guard.

"Yes," he answered. "They are my comp—"

Their forms are not suitable for this place. They must be altered.

"No, wait!" Tiath yelled, but Deylista let out a scream of mingled terror and pain. Tiath turned to see the grotesque limbs grab hold of both her and Pasill and drag them back into the black liquid. Deylista screamed again and fought the pull of those grasping hands, claws, and talons. Pasill, however, merely closed his eyes and let himself go.

"Release them!" Tiath shouted at the insectoid face, but it ignored his order.

They must be altered.

Deylista's screams were cut off as the liquid flowed over her face, and her struggles suddenly ceased. Pasill never made a sound.

Tiath clenched his fists, the amulet digging into the flesh of his hand. He had lost people under his command before, but this was different. Their orders had been to find the cave and make sure it was secure, not to cross over to this alien world and hunt for power they could take for themselves.

Tiath knew what he had done was treason. And now he had lost all three members of his team. For a moment, he wanted to throw the amulet at the insectoid head and let himself be killed by the city's guardian. It was what he deserved for betraying his own people.

But that, he knew, would accomplish nothing. Back in the pass, when he realized what the Emperor was searching for, Tiath had decided that he was going take something for himself this time. This was his opportunity to gain power, real power. And now he had sacrificed the lives of Azam, Deylista, and Pasill for this goal.

And the goal was still within his reach. What might he do once he found the throne itself? Could he change them back, give them back their original forms, give them back their lives?

Looking at the heaving black liquid, he searched his heart and admitted the truth to himself. Once he had the power he sought, would their sacrifice really matter to him? When he found the throne, Tiath would no longer be mortal. He'd have power to rival the Emperor himself. What were three lives measured against that?

The creature in front of him drew back, leaving him room to proceed along the street once more.

You may proceed to the palace. Your servants will return to you when they are suitable.

"I told you to stop," Tiath said to the face, his anger drained out of him by the realization of what was ahead of him. "I have the amulet. You're supposed to obey my orders."

You have the amulet. Your servants were not suitable. They must be altered.

Deylista and Pasill would come back to him, in whatever forms the black liquid would give them. They would be his servants, suitable for the being he was about to become.

Without a backward glance at the churning liquid, Tiath resumed his journey toward the palace.

*   *   *

JAGGED CRACKS RAN THROUGH THE WALL, BITS OF MULTICOLORED stone having fallen to the ground and now reflecting the light from the sky in a myriad of colors.

"This city is ancient," Kied said to Rotos. The other man didn't respond.

"From a distance, it looked magnificent," Kied continued. "And it's still ... impressive. I've never seen such an immense city. Even Ythis is smaller than this."

They crossed a wide street and Rotos led the way into a vast plaza. The ground in the plaza was different from the roads they had been traveling along so far. Instead of the strangely shaped tiles, the entire plaza had a surface of smooth, unbroken stone of an off-white color. It was as if a single, enormous slab of some kind of rock had been lowered into this area, and then polished until it was perfectly smooth and unblemished.

At the center of the plaza, a wide fountain rose up. Carved in what looked like blue marble, no water flowed from the fountain anymore. At the top of the fountain, on a pedestal carved with unfamiliar flowers and geometric designs, stood a statue of ....

"Rotos," Kied said in a choked voice. "That statue. It's Laita."

Rotos looked at the statue, and Kied saw his eyes widen. He turned away, an expression of sorrow on his face.

"It's not who you think it is," the big man said.

"What is a statue of Laita doing here? That doesn't make sense."

Rotos sighed and glanced back at the fountain.

"Everyone sees someone different up there. It's always someone you love."

Kied paused, and stared at Laita's face carved on the blue marble. There was no question he loved her. He stood there and took a moment, knowing he was not likely ever to see her face again.

"We should go," Rotos said, avoiding looking directly at the fountain. Kied wanted to ask Rotos who he saw up there on the pedestal, but he knew Rotos wouldn't give him an answer. With a last look at Laita, Kied followed Rotos across the plaza and out into another street.

As they made their way around a pile of broken stones from a collapsed bridge between two buildings, Kied spoke up once more.

"This city is crumbling. How old do you think it is?"

"It is the First City," Rotos rumbled. "It is ancient beyond reckoning."

"Why was it abandoned?"

"Because it was a terrible idea in the first place. Those who built it did so for the wrong reasons. And those who dwelt here didn't deserve it. And the temptation proved to be too great for them."

"What temptation?" Kied asked.

"The temptation of power. The palace at the center of this city was off limits to those who lived here. But that edict just made them want it even more. Leaving the city entirely and hiding its location was the only way for the inhabitants to survive."

The two men walked on in silence for another moment before Rotos spoke again.

"Nothing remains hidden forever."

Kied was grateful for the answers Rotos had given him, and though he wanted to know more, he didn't want to push too hard. He knew the other man would realize he was saying too much, and then there'd be no more information at all.

"Stop," Rotos said suddenly.

Kied froze in place, looking around. They were on another long street, and in the distance Kied could make out a vast structure rising up above the surrounding buildings. The air was hazy, and Kied wasn't sure of the exact shape of the building, but he knew it was immense. It appeared to be made of some pure white stone and shone with an inner glow.

Rotos reached out and put his hand on Kied's shoulder.

"Stay close to me. Maintain contact at all times. And let me do the talking."

The still air was stirred by a slight breeze. Rotos raised his face to the sky, and Kied also looked up to see a column of green smoke descending toward them.

"What is that?" Kied asked.

"Be silent!" Rotos rumbled in a low voice. Kied snapped his own mouth shut.

The swirling column of smoke came down to land a dozen paces in front of the two men. Tendrils of smoke drifted out from the sides of the column and stretched in a wide arc around Kied and Rotos until they were encircled in bands of the greenish haze.

The sound of discordant wind chimes came to Kied on the air.

"I am not trespassing," Rotos said to the column. "Move aside and let me pass."

The wind chimes sounded again.

"I have the right to proceed."

Rotos glanced sideways at Kied before speaking again.

"You know who I am," he said to the column of smoke.

Another tendril of smoke emerged from the front of the column and drifted towards Rotos. It touched his chest, and recoiled instantly. The extrusion dissipated and the column withdrew the ring of smoke from around the two men.

"There are others in the city," Rotos said to the smoke. "Have you stopped them?"

The chimes sounded once more. Rotos swore under his breath.

"Remain silent," he said to Kied. "Let's go."

Keeping his hand on Kied's shoulder, Rotos led Kied past the column and down the street. Kied glanced back to see the column of smoke suddenly release and dissipate into the air.

"You can speak now," Rotos said. "We need to hurry."

"What was that thing?"

"One of the guardians of the city. Its purpose is to make sure no one approaches the palace unless they … have permission."

"Why did it let us pass? How did it know you? Are you … are you one of the people who once lived here?"

Rotos marched grimly on, not answering the question.

"At least tell me what you found out about the others," Kied said. "I'd like to know what we're marching into."

Rotos sighed and removed his hand from Kied's shoulder.

"The others were confronted by the guardians as well. One of those soldiers has an amulet that once belonged to someone who governed here. The bearer of the amulet will not be stopped by the guardians. At least one of them can reach the palace."

"Are they ahead of us or behind?"

"Ahead," Rotos answered. "Not by much, but we need to catch up with them before they reach the throne room of the palace. If they get there first, then all is lost."

On one side of the road, the buildings abruptly stopped, to be replaced by a stone railing looking over a steep drop. Kied stepped to the side and looked out at another section of the city on a lower level. He realized they stood at the edge of a plateau.

"The city is built on a series of different elevations," Rotos explained. He pointed ahead. "To approach the palace, we'll have to cross a number of bridges."

Kied looked where Rotos was pointing. A cluster of buildings stood atop a series of raised plateaus, almost like islands floating in the sky. Dozens of bridges spanned the intervening distances, linking the separate islands to each other.

The next hour was spent crossing one bridge after another. Some of them were fully intact, while others felt like they were ready to crumble under their feet as they crossed.

It was as they were crossing one of the last few bridges towards the district where the palace was located that disaster struck. They were on a narrow bridge, high above the ground, when a huge cracking sound filled the air. The weight of the two men was enough to shatter a section of the bridge, and the structure crumbled away from underneath them.

Rotos toppled forward, and he shoved off with all the strength in his legs, sending him across the widening gap just far enough that he managed to grab hold of the far edge. His hands scrambled for purchase, but the far side didn't crumble any further, and Rotos got a solid grip on the stone.

Kied, however, had tripped as the bridge came apart beneath him. He stumbled backward and fell. Feeling the stone crumble, Kied rolled away from the edge and barely managed to stay ahead of the cracks in the stone.

By the time the two men managed to regain their feet, they stood on opposite sides of a gap far too large to jump.

"What do we do now?" Kied called across to Rotos.

"You cannot come this way," the big man answered. "You must go back and find another route to the palace."

"What about you?"

"I will try to reach the palace as quickly as possible. If I can catch up with the last soldier, I should be able to stop him or her myself."

Kied looked around at the strange city stretching out on all sides as far as he could see. He didn't relish the thought of traveling through this landscape alone.

"What about those guardians?"

"There are no more guardians between here and the palace. You should be safe. But be careful—do not enter any buildings except the palace."

Kied nodded to Rotos. The big man turned and began to run toward the palace in the distance. Kied turned his back on his companion and started jogging in the opposite direction. He could only hope he would find another route to their destination in time.

Chapter Thirty

THE GRIM-FACED LEGIONNAIRE STOOD OVER ZARTAY AS THE rest of the soldiers took a rest break on their long march. Zartay sat on a blanket on the ground, waiting for the order to resume their progress toward the cave. Zartay's hands had been bound behind him yesterday when they took him into custody, though he had not otherwise been treated poorly. They had allowed him to ride his horse for the rest of the day, though the reins were held by one of the soldiers.

The night had not gone well. The soldier assigned to watch Zartay refused to speak with him or answer any of his questions. Zartay knew time was running out—if he was going to get out of this situation, he would need to start implementing a plan very soon.

Brother Hissiath had been bound and gagged, and placed in a wagon with two soldiers to watch over him. When he had regained consciousness, he had erupted in paroxysms of fury. It had made no difference. Without the ability to speak, he had been unable to call upon the powers of Iathephos. Now he lay off to one side during the rest break, a pair of soldiers standing guard on either side of the man.

Commander Laita Naschect had arrived last night a few hours after the force had stopped to camp. She had not come to speak with Zartay, or even acknowledge his presence. He knew it was a calculated insult, but he didn't let it bother him. The woman would get her punishment soon enough.

The one improvement in Zartay's situation was that a different soldier had been assigned to watch over him today. He could only hope this man would provide some opportunity for Zartay to gain some kind of connection with him. Once Zartay was on speaking terms with someone, he was highly skilled at getting what he wanted.

"May I have some water?" he asked the soldier standing at his side. "I'm very thirsty."

The soldier looked down at where Zartay was sitting and considered his request. The man gave a whistle and signaled to a young soldier who brought over a waterskin. Zartay's guard took the top off and put the spout to Zartay's mouth.

Zartay let the water trickle into his mouth, and then started coughing, spewing the water out onto the ground. He leaned forward, trying to make the most of his discomfort. The soldier pounded Zartay on the back a few times.

"Th-thank you," Zartay gasped, trying to clear his throat. "My apologies. It was a bit too much for me."

Zartay looked up at the soldier, putting on his most sincere face.

"Is there any way you could untie my hands? My wrists have gone numb and my arms are in pain. And I really do need some water."

The soldier looked down at Zartay suspiciously.

"My orders are that you are to remain bound."

That was the exact response Zartay had hoped for. This Legionnaire was of the type to hide behind his orders. It allowed the man to avoid the responsibility for making his own decisions, deflecting the blame to his superiors when he had to do something unpleasant.

Zartay felt his chance of escape had just increased dramatically.

"I understand the need to follow orders. Can you ask your sergeant? I'm sure you'd like to avoid having to feed me by hand. And I certainly cannot go anywhere with the entire camp spread out around us."

The guard seemed unconvinced.

"I have no way to harm you," Zartay pleaded. "I'm certainly no warrior, and I lack the special talents of our priest over there. I'd just to stretch my arms a bit. Please."

The guard turned to the younger soldier and spoke to him in a low voice—Zartay couldn't hear his words. The other man ran off.

"I'm checking with my sergeant."

"Thank you," Zartay replied, giving the man a small smile. "I'm afraid I'm not very good at being a prisoner."

They waited a short while before Zartay saw the young soldier returning.

"Sergeant says it's okay, but you have to bind his ankles first."

"That's fine with me," Zartay said, letting a note of relief into his voice. "I hardly need the use of my legs to eat and drink."

The soldier guarding Zartay took another length of rope and bound Zartay's ankles together. He finished with a complex knot that would take some effort to release. But Zartay had no intention of getting loose. Even if he could escape from the train of soldiers, he'd have no idea how to survive on his own out here.

Zartay stretched out his arms, and then rubbed some feeling back into his wrists. The truth was that his bindings hadn't been all that tight, and though his arms had gone a bit numb, he wasn't nearly as uncomfortable as he'd led them to believe. But this was the first step on getting the soldier on his side.

When Zartay was finished rubbing his arms, the soldier handed him the waterskin and he drank deeply.

"Thank you," he said again when he finished. The guard took a long pull from the skin, and then gave it back to the young soldier, who then moved off to another part of the camp.

"May I know your name?" Zartay asked his guard. "It seems you're assigned to watch over me today, and it makes things easier to be able to call each other by name."

The soldier considered the request. Zartay knew the man wouldn't have received any orders about not talking to Zartay, or answering some simple questions. He would have to make his own decision.

"Please," Zartay said to him. "I'm not used to this kind of situation. It would make me feel so much better to just know your name."

"Lisim," the soldier answered, and Zartay had to hold in a laugh. He had been right about this man after all. Lisim didn't like performing unpleasant tasks and preferred to use his orders as the excuse. But without direct orders, he would avoid being unfriendly.

"Well, Lisim, I am Ambassador Zartay Seaphon. Feel free to call me Zartay, however. I believe at this moment I have no authority as an ambassador."

"I know who you are," Lisim said to him. "You're the one who gave the commander her orders."

Zartay rejoiced at being given such an easy opening.

"Yes, I am. It's unfortunate she chose to disobey those orders and turn against the Empire. I understand how she felt about the situation—believe me, I don't like it any more than she does—but we don't get to pick and choose which orders we follow. Especially when they come straight from the Emperor himself."

Lisim looked Zartay in the eyes.

"You're the one who's been accused of treason," he said.

"Yes," Zartay sighed. "It's the most convenient excuse to take me into custody and remove me from my position. It makes sense, I suppose. Your commander may even believe that what she's doing is right. And I don't have any argument with her feelings on the matter. But her actions are what makes the difference. As a Legionnaire, you are bound to fulfill your orders, even when they are unpleasant."

Lisim looked away from Zartay, and he knew he had scored the point he wanted to make to this soldier.

"I received orders from the Emperor and passed them on to Commander Naschect. She has decided to ignore those orders and arrest me for treason. But I'm just the messenger between Ythis and this Contingent. Commander Naschect isn't disobeying me. She's disobeying the Emperor himself."

Lisim said nothing. He turned away and started pulling out some rations for their meal.

"Your commander has made a dreadful mistake," Zartay said to the other man in a low voice. "What she has done will not stand. Her predecessor tried the same thing, and look what happened to him and his entire command squad. Only this time, it's much worse."

Zartay let that hang in the air as Lisim divided his rations into two portions. Finally, the soldier looked up at Zartay.

"Why is it worse?"

"Last time, Commander Kied Leele and his command squad

were the only persons who truly committed any treasonous acts. The Legionnaires under them were not held responsible, because it didn't go that far."

Zartay put a touch of sympathy into his voice as he spoke his next words.

"This time, Commander Naschect has given contradictory orders to the soldiers under her command. Lieutenant Uissa knows it. The sergeants in this force know it. Any many individual Legionnaires know it, too. No one will be able to say they were just following orders, because those people know they are following the wrong orders. Your oath is not to your commanders. Your oath is to the Emperor."

Zartay said no more, allowing Lisim a chance to process what he had just been told. Zartay knew he had just taken away Lisim's sense of security. The soldier now knew that, if he continued to obey the chain of command that led up to Laita Naschect, he would likely still be charged with treason if what Zartay was saying proved to be correct.

And Lisim wouldn't be able to hide behind ignorance, because he had been tasked with guarding Ambassador Zartay Seaphon.

Zartay knew the seed was now well and truly planted. Now it was a matter of picking the right time to harvest what he had sown.

*   *   *

THE SUN WAS WELL PAST ITS ZENITH AND BEGINNING TO DESCEND toward the mountain peaks when the force reached their destination. Namal leaned over in his saddle and spoke to Laita in a low voice.

"What are we really looking for?"

She looked around at the sloping wall of stone stretching up into the sky and frowned.

"There's a cave," she said. "Well, it's more like a cut in the rock that leads to a gully."

She pulled out the map as Lieutenant Uissa rode over and reined in beside her. Laita examined the map and turned to the lieutenant.

"Yes, the cut is in this slope somewhere along here. Send out the scouts to see if they can find it, but tell them not to enter."

Lieutenant Uissa issued the order to her aid, who rode off to inform the scouts.

"Do you feel that?" the lieutenant asked.

"Feel what?"

"A vibration," Namal answered. "It's like the ground is shaking."

Laita looked up at the slope in concern. An avalanche was the most likely cause of such vibrations, but there was no sign of any movement from above.

Namal dismounted and knelt on the ground.

Laita handed the map to Lieutenant Uissa and rode forward, scanning the rock for some sign of the opening. She saw the scouts ride back out along the length of the rock wall.

"According to this map, it should be easily visible," Lieutenant Uissa said.

Namal stood back up.

"I don't know what's causing the vibration. It doesn't feel like anything I've experienced before."

Now that they had arrived, Laita admitted to herself that she had been hoping Kied would be here. Though, in truth, that would have complicated matters quite a bit. Her duty would be to take him into custody, and she wasn't sure how she could explain to Lieutenant Uissa why he wasn't a traitor to the Empire.

Of course, Laita was now a traitor as well. To make matters worse, the lieutenant didn't know Laita was disobeying direct orders from the Emperor. What would Uissa do when she found out? It was possible the soldiers of this detachment would split, some choosing to obey their lieutenant, some following Laita.

Before she had left camp, Laita had issued new orders to the other detachments. While Namal had accompanied Laita, she had sent Saeda, Bor, and Ellend on a special mission.

By now, the other detachments were withdrawing from the villages and returning to the original staging ground at the mouth of the first valley. But Laita's trusted companions were riding from village to village, advising the elders of each village of the danger they were in.

And passing word to those soldiers whose loyalty to the people of the Empire took precedence over following orders.

Laita knew that once the Legion High Command discovered what she had done, she would be declared a traitor to the Empire and another Contingent would be sent in to take control of this region. The Emperor's orders were that, once the cave had been secured, all the inhabitants of the villages were to be executed to remove any witnesses to the operation in these valleys.

But with enough warning, most of the villagers would have time to flee. They would leave their homes and find new lives spread out across the Empire. It would be impossible for the Legion to track down the individuals who had lived in these simple villages. The citizens who dwelt in these valleys would be safe.

Laita knew some would refuse to leave, and others would be unable to travel. There was nothing she could do for those people. But most would survive. It was the best she could accomplish in these circumstances.

Laita took the map back from Lieutenant Uissa and examined it again. They were right on top of the location marked on the map, but there was still no sign of the cut in the rock. She could see the scouts returning, and none of them appeared to have found anything.

There was a cave here, somewhere. And in that cave was something dangerous, something the Emperor should not possess. It was hidden, but Laita knew it was here. She just had to find it.

A flicker in her vision caused her to turn her head and focus on the wall of stone just to the left of where she sat on her horse. She ran her eyes over the wall, trying to figure out what she had seen in her peripheral vision.

Another flicker, right in front of her, and she gave a small shout of alarm. The very stone had seemed to disappear for an instant, revealing a passage into the rock.

"Commander, what's wrong?" Namal asked as he jogged over to her. She dismounted, keeping her eyes on the wall where she had seen it disappear.

"It's here, Namal. It's hidden, but it's here."

She approached the wall and reached out her hand. Once more it flickered, and then she touched the stone and it vanished from in front of her.

Namal, Lieutenant Uissa, and a number of nearby soldiers gasped in astonishment as the passage into the stone was suddenly revealed.

Laita stepped back and eyed the opening. It led into the rock, twisting away out of sight. According to the map, it opened back up into a gulley further on.

Namal was already assigning a couple of squads to accompany them into the passage. Laita could now feel the vibration coming up through the soles of her boots. A chill wind sprang up as a blanket of clouds began to spread across the sky. Within moments, the sunlight dimmed and the temperature dropped several degrees.

At the very edge of Laita's hearing, just above the sound of the wind in her ears, she heard a rumble. It was different from the vibration coming up from the ground, and she realized it was a host of voices yelling and screeching. As the sound rose in volume, Laita turned back to the passage in the rock.

"Form up and prepare for attack!" she yelled over the sound of the wind. She sprinted away from the opening and was relieved to see how quickly the Legionnaires formed a shield wall as the word was passed down into the ranks and everyone moved into their places. The constant training and drilling each soldier had undergone was the difference between being prepared or being slaughtered.

Laita regained her horse just as the howling and screeching reached a crescendo. And then, from the mouth of the passage burst a flood of twisted, horrific creatures from the depths of everyone's worst nightmares. Laita could only catch a handful of separate details as that wave of death crashed into the front ranks of her force. Faces with too many eyes, twisted limbs ending in ragged talons, distended jaws full of needle-sharp teeth, the terrible beings rushed at the soldiers and threw themselves into battle.

The flood of creatures didn't slow, and within seconds the soldiers were in danger of being outflanked. As squad after squad rushed toward the lines and formed up, the screams of dying Legionnaires mixed with the howls and shrieks of the horrific attackers.

Lieutenant Uissa had been unable to get far enough back, and a single squad of soldiers had formed a square around her. She dismounted and joined in the fighting, but her meager force was surrounded and overwhelmed within seconds. The horse screamed as it was ripped apart, and Laita knew Lieutenant Uissa was dead.

Laita realized she had lost track of Namal. Was he in that mess at the front of the line? Was he still alive? She didn't have time to find out. With shouted commands, Laita continued to arrange her Legionnaires to meet the threat, while more and more creatures poured from the mouth of the passage.

Chapter Thirty-One

DISTANCES WERE DECEPTIVE IN THE STRANGE CITY. AS KIED made his way along another bridge, he looked and saw that the palace had receded into the distance. Yet when he reached the end of the bridge and crossed behind a tower apparently made of solid silver, he emerged around a corner to find the palace looming over him, less than a few hundred paces away.

He stopped and stared at the vast structure in awe. Made of some kind of white stone, the palace was a collection of domes and towers of strange geometric designs. Arched bridges appeared to connect sections that were of wildly different heights, yet the bridges seemed to be level. The domes were both smooth ovals and yet also polyhedrons with faces of uneven sides.

The structure was immense, taller than any mountain Kied had ever seen. It seemed to be a city in itself, yet still a single building. Kied could only imagine the thousands of rooms that must have been inside that edifice, and what wonders he might see when he entered.

If he managed to reach it. No matter how many bridges he crossed, he was unable to find one that stretched across the final gap. Kied estimated he had been walking for at least an hour by this point. It was likely that Rotos had already reached the palace and confronted the last soldier. The danger might already be over.

He turned and looked around at the sides of the palace. It seemed as if at least three bridges spanned the distance to the plateau where the palace loomed. He had tried to reach any of those three, but he never seemed to get any closer to them.

Kied focused on the closest of the bridges and concentrated on it, fixing it in his mind's eye. He closed his eyes and thought about standing on the bridge, the same way that Rotos had instructed him when they were entering the city. He focused every ounce of his will on the thought that he was already on the bridge.

But the strange sounds never came, and Kied didn't have any unusual vision. He opened his eyes to see himself standing in the same place, the bridge off in the distance and out of his reach.

He turned away from the sight and headed off in the direction he thought might take him toward the distant span. Ahead of him was a low, dark building, with windows of mirrored glass. He could see twisted reflections of himself in the mirrors, and a chill went up his spine.

One of the windows reflected him exactly, mirroring his own movements as a normal mirror would do. But the five windows around that one had reflections that were twisted and deformed. And the figures in those reflections seemed to be moving of their own accord. As one, the twisted reflections turned toward the one true reflection of Kied.

He looked around himself and saw that he was now surrounded by those same five deformed creatures that had appeared in the mirrored windows. As one, they started to lurch toward him. Kied charged at one of the creatures, dodging to one side at the last moment as it lunged toward him with outstretched arms. He slipped between two of his attackers and took off at a run down the street.

The reflections gave chase as he ran, their lurching gait slowing them only slightly. Kied knew he wouldn't have time to stop and check his bearings, and could only hope he was heading in the right direction. He had no weapon he could use to fight these creatures, and he was sure he would tire long before they would. Desperation welled up in him as he ran.

But he turned a corner and found himself at the end of the bridge he had been searching for.

Kied knew the bridge had been quite some distance away, but now here it was, directly in front of him. He charged up onto the span, the pursuing reflections only a few dozen paces behind him.

Above him, the palace rose into the sky. He could see no entrance in the unbroken wall of white ahead of him, but a wide boulevard seemed to circle the palace. If he could keep running long enough, he might be able to find a door and block the pursuit of the creatures behind him.

In moments, he was across the bridge. His pursuers seemed to be falling back, and Kied slowed into a steady jog that he could keep up for long distances without needing to stop. He turned into the boulevard and followed it around the curve of the palace until he came to an open square.

Another, narrower bridge led out away from the palace at this point, and Kied saw Rotos running across that bridge toward him.

But was it really Rotos, or another strange reflection? Kied couldn't stop to look, as his own pursuers were still following behind.

He pushed onward across the square and spotted a wide entryway up a short flight of sprawling stairs, and angled toward it.

"Kied!" he heard Rotos shout behind him. He turned to see the twisted reflections were now almost a hundred paces behind. They had slowed as they entered the square, and Kied had time to pause a moment and take a better look.

The figure that seemed to be Rotos had scooped up a bit of broken paving stone in his hand, and he slowed as he approached the five creatures chasing Kied. Two of the reflections turned to face the big man and lunged toward him, their arms outstretched. Rotos shoved the grasping hands aside and brought the stone down on one of the reflection's heads. With the sound of shattering glass, the reflection collapsed into hundreds of shards across the ground.

The second reflection facing Rotos fared no better. But the three who had continued to pursue Kied were now getting closer. Kied couldn't understand how he had somehow managed to reach the palace ahead of Rotos. But then, Rotos had said space and time worked differently here.

Trusting that it was indeed Rotos who fought the creatures in the square, Kied sprinted around to the side of the remaining reflections and joined the big man.

"You found a way across," Rotos rumbled at him. "Good work."

Kied picked up his own chunk of broken stone. He silently cursed himself for not bringing their swords through the gate. Rocks may work against glass reflections, but they wouldn't be good enough to use against trained—and armed—soldiers.

"Careful," Rotos warned as the creatures attempted to surround them. Rotos stepped forward and heaved his stone at one of the reflections. It tried to avoid the impact but couldn't move fast enough. The rock took the creature in the chest just below its neck, and it shattered just as the others had done.

Kied waited until one of the reflections closed in, and then outmaneuvered it and hammered his own rock down onto the creature's head. He was rewarded with the satisfying sound of breaking glass. Rotos, now weaponless, demonstrated his own strength by grabbing the last creature by the arms and rending it in half.

The two men stood in the square, catching their breath.

"How did I beat you here?" Kied asked.

"You tried to use your will to cross the distance, didn't you?"

Kied nodded.

"You can't do what we did to cross the plain," Rotos explained. "But that doesn't mean you're helpless. With a strong enough will, you can still change the shape of the city for yourself, although only in minor ways. If you're desperate enough, though, there's no telling what you might do. As I've said before, there's something special about you."

Kied turned to the palace entrance.

"Is this where we need to go?"

Rotos nodded.

"This isn't the main entrance, but it will lead us to the throne room eventually."

Kied looked at the big man at his side. For the first time, he felt they might truly accomplish their goal.

And then ....

And then he'd have to return to his own world and face the consequences of his actions. If he succeeded here, and denied this place—this power—to the Emperor, would that absolve him of his guilt over the deaths of his comrades? Would that make everything they had done, the sacrifices they made, worthwhile?

And what would come next? The only way to be safe would be to for him leave the Empire entirely, and even then, there were no guarantees.

One step at a time

"Okay, he said to Rotos. "Let's finish this."

*   *   *

TWO MEN WALKED UP THE BROAD SET OF STAIRS AND APPROACHED the doors. A grotesquely decorated overhang cut off Tiath's view of them as they entered the palace. He stood on a balcony high above that looked out over the square and the bridge the larger man had crossed only moments ago.

One of the men—the smaller one—carried himself like a soldier. But Tiath knew the Ambassador wouldn't have sent any soldiers into the cave, and definitely not through the gate. Besides, the soldiers would be traveling in squads, at least. Then again, the man was being chased by a pack of some … whatever those things were. Perhaps his squad had been wiped out already and he was the last.

But what about the other man? He was huge, and definitely not a solder. Tiath was too high up to hear what they had said to each other, but despite them coming from different directions, he was sure they already knew each other. The way they had worked together, the way they approached the palace entrance, spoke to a certain familiarity between the two.

Had the Emperor sent another team to find the cave—insurance against any betrayal by Tiath and his squad? If so, how had the other men found the location? They didn't have the amulet, and Ambassador Seaphon wouldn't have had time to send these men after he received the location from Tiath's messenger bird.

Tiath considered for a moment the possibility that these men had already been here in the city before Tiath's squad arrived. From the way they acted, Tiath doubted they belonged here any more than he did. And what would bring them to the palace now, at the same time Tiath himself searched for the throne?

A soft scrape of a booted foot on stone sounded behind Tiath, and he turned to find Deylista and Pasill in the corridor behind him. He flinched back from their appearance, but was trapped by the balcony railing and the long fall to the open square below.

Deylista crouched to Tiath's left. Most of her clothing had been torn away in her transformation, and he could see her body had elongated and was now segmented, covered in chitinous plates that were a green so dark as to be almost black, and glistening in the light. Her head was now hairless, and the features of her face had melted and run together, though she was still barely recognizable as the woman who had fought at his side these last years. From her tailbone a curved scorpion-like tail curled up and over her head, a jagged barb of bone at its tip.

Pasill stood to the right, also transformed into an alien night-mare creature. He was completely naked, and nine multi-jointed legs sprouted from his hips like a deformed spider. His genitals, red and swollen, hung down from the center where the legs joined his body. Eldritch tattoos covered Pasill's torso in blood-red patterns that seemed to throb and pulse with arcane energy. His eyes had been replaced by large, white egg-like orbs, and his mouth was now a ring of puckered flesh from which a long, whip-like tongue emerged. A needle protruded from the tip of that appendage, dripping a frothy yellow liquid onto the floor that smelled of brine.

Tiath fought back the urge to retch, and a wave of dizziness swept over him. He gripped the marble railing behind him and forced himself to remain standing.

Your servants will return to you when they are suitable.

It was what the guardian had told Tiath back in that alley on the other side of the city. Tiath had believed they would not survive what was being done to them. He had already steeled himself to the idea that they were both dead, just like Azam back in the cave. But now they were here.

In the first moment, Tiath thought they might attack him, tear him apart for leading them here, for abandoning them in that alley. But they made no move, merely waiting for … something.

You have the amulet. Your servants were not suitable. They must be altered.

The guardian had believed them to be Tiath's servants. Pasill and Deylista had been made "suitable" to be servants of the bearer of the amulet.

Did that mean Tiath could now control them?

"Deylista," he said, and his voice came out as a croak. He swallowed, and tried again.

"Deylista, and Pasill. I want you to …."

Tiath thought of the two men he had seen enter the palace only moments before. Were those men also seeking the throne? What would happen if they reached it before Tiath? Might he lose everything to unknown interlopers?

He had come so far, sacrificed so much. Tiath had betrayed his Emperor, his comrades, his own oaths to reach such a source of power, and no one was going to take it away from him now.

"There are intruders in the palace—two men who search for the throne," he said to the grotesque shapes before him.

"Find them, and kill them both. Take whatever other guardians you can find who will follow you."

Deylista turned her melted face upwards and sniffed once, twice. Then she turned and loped off around a corner. Pasill turned and followed her, making no sound as his spidery legs carried him away.

Tiath waited a couple of minutes to let the two of them leave the area before he stepped back in from the balcony. He had already spent hours in the palace, searching for the throne room. He had wandered through vast galleries with ceilings of glass that showed the strange sky above. Some of them were full of lifelike statues carved from some alien substance that resembled human flesh, others teemed with unknowable plant life in a dizzying array of colors, pungent and overflowing.

Other rooms were recognizable as bedrooms or dining halls, but many had purposes of which Tiath couldn't fathom. He stumbled across puzzling devices of varying design and what he could only guess was furniture for beings whose shape differed dramatically from humans.

Artwork covered many walls, and while some had a recognizable style—paintings of great battles on alien landscapes with armies of strangely-garbed human soldiers fighting beasts whose shapes made Tiath's eyes water—most were more disturbing collections of shapes and depths and formerly unseen colors that made his head ache, and sometimes his nose bleed. He now tried to avoid looking at the artwork as he traveled, as it began to feel as if his mind was starting to untether itself inside his skull.

The architecture was maddening. He would ascend a flight of stairs to find himself emerging at ground-level into a gallery that he had seen from a balcony above only minutes before. He would follow a corridor that made four right turns, and come around the last corner to find a vast space that couldn't possibly exist in its current location. And backtracking had not once led him to the same room he had just left.

Every so often, the amulet nudged him in a particular direction. But the effect was inconsistent and Tiath wasn't sure if it was leading him toward the throne room or simply sending him through the entire palace on a tour of the alien and bizarre.

And yet, he knew, somehow, he was getting closer to the throne room. His path may have seemed erratic, but he had the feeling it was a journey he must make to reach his goal. There were no straight paths to the throne room in this place. Tiath was sure that—had it been possible to draw his path through the palace on a piece of parchment—the route would make some kind of sigil or pattern.

He was conducting a ritual on a grand scale by walking its design, step after step after step.

At the end of that ritual, he would find himself in the throne room. Before him would be the source of the power he sought.

And then everything would change.

Chapter Thirty-Two

A SPRAY OF BLOOD COVERED ZARTAY'S FACE AS ONE OF THE attacking creatures ripped apart a soldier less than a dozen paces away. More legionnaires jammed into the space and drove the beast back, hacking off its limbs as it was joined by others of its kind.

"Cut me free," Zartay pleaded with Lisim as the soldier moved to join another squad that was running toward the front lines. "Please, don't let me die like this."

Lisim paused for a second, then drew his knife and hacked through the ropes binding Zartay's wrists and ankles.

"Get to the back!" Lisim yelled as he turned and charged towards the fight.

Zartay fled away from the battle, trying to fight through his terror and gain control of his situation. For the moment he was free, and that was the first step to regaining his power. But his freedom wouldn't matter if those creatures overwhelmed the legionnaires and slaughtered everyone. Zartay would just be free and dead.

Soldiers ran past him to shore up the lines as he made his way toward the supply wagons. A few glanced at him as they ran, but most didn't seem to know who he was.

"A knife!" he yelled at one soldier as he approached. The legionnaire slowed but kept moving.

"I need a knife, anything!" Zartay called again.

The soldier drew a spare blade from the top of his boot and tossed it at Zartay's feet, and then kept going without saying a word. Zartay scooped up the knife and tucked it into his robes. It felt heavy and unfamiliar in his hands. He had used a weapon only once before in his life, and it had been against a very old man who had trusted Zartay completely. Zartay was young then, but had seen his path to power and was willing to do anything to advance—even betray the one man who had given him everything.

Zartay had found the sensation of sinking a blade into someone's chest horrid, and it was not something he ever wanted to do again. From then on, he had used words to destroy his rivals, or hired blades so that he didn't have to see the blood himself.

And Zartay really didn't relish the idea of attacking someone who might try to fight back.

But this was a desperate time. He had gotten a glimpse of the opening in the rock, and the nightmare horde pouring out of it. As much as the Legion was renowned for the combat ability of its soldiers, they weren't fighting other humans this time. It was quite possible this battle would be lost.

Zartay knew who could turn the tide, but unlike the connection Zartay had managed to develop with Lisim, that man wouldn't get any mercy from the soldiers guarding him. Brother Hissiath would have to be released, and his guards would have to be removed in order to accomplish that.

"You!" he yelled, pointing at a soldier who had lagged behind. Zartay put all his confidence, all the tone of command he could muster into his voice.

The soldier flinched slightly at Zartay's attention. The man had obviously been dragging his feet toward the fight—even the Legion had its share of cowards. And now he thought he was going to be punished for his dereliction of duty.

"Commander Naschect has given me special orders," Zartay continued. "You will accompany me to assist as needed."

Zartay wasn't sure how he might use this man, but he knew he should gather what resources he could while there was a chance. Being accompanied by a soldier would give Zartay some additional authority.

Relief was visible on the soldier's face as he realized that he wouldn't have to charge into battle just yet. And since Zartay had been moving away from the fight, the soldier probably figured he was safe for now.

The legionnaire fell into step behind Zartay, and then they spotted one last soldier running toward the front. Zartay called out to him the same way he had the first man, and the soldier slowed and came toward them.

As he approached Zartay, it became obvious that the soldier recognized the ambassador and knew Zartay had been taken prisoner. He glanced from Zartay to the other soldier and back, wariness on his face.

"Commander Naschect needs every resource she has," Zartay said before the soldier could say anything. "Demons are attacking the Legion, and we've got the only weapon that can stop them."

The soldier's face went white at Zartay's naming of demons. Even though few people in the empire would ever see a demon—even citizens who lived in cities like Ythis, where the sorcerers had their towers—stories abounded. A single demon could probably tear through most of a contingent without difficulty.

Zartay didn't know if the creatures attacking the Legion were really demons or not. But invoking their name helped his ruse.

"What are the commander's orders?" the soldier asked.

"We must bring the priest to the front before the Legion is overwhelmed. They're getting slaughtered up there."

The second soldier hesitated, obviously not ready to trust Zartay's word. Stepping forward, Zartay pinned the man with an imperious glare.

"If you wish to run to the battle lines and check with the commander, then go. I will wait here and—if you return—you can apologize to me then."

The soldier considered the situation for only a moment more, but he knew he couldn't risk the chance that Zartay was telling the truth. If demons were really attacking their force, every second would count. He nodded once to Zartay and stepped back, letting the ambassador lead the way.

As the trio neared the supply wagons, they encountered no more bodies moving towards the front lines. The only legionnaires still back here were those who were tasked with special duties that even a battle would not override. Zartay looked around and spotted the wagon where the priest was being held.

Only two soldiers watched over him. One sat in the wagon beside the priest, and the other stood on the ground a few paces away.

Zartay marched forward, his two conscripts following. The guards saw him approaching, and the one on the ground put his hand on the hilt of his sword.

"Take your hand from your weapon or I'll have it removed," Zartay said coldly to the guard. "The Legion is under attack by demonic forces, and this man is needed at the front by order of Commander Naschect."

"Horseshit," the guard replied. "The commander gave us explicit instructions to keep him here bound and gagged, no matter what."

"And now she has countermanded those orders," Zartay argued. "She obviously didn't foresee the possibility of a battle with a demonic host."

The guard looked at the two soldiers accompanying Zartay for confirmation.

"Is what he says true?"

The soldier who had not initially believed Zartay's story started to say "I don't know—" but was interrupted by the man Zartay had pegged as a coward.

"It's true," said the soldier. "Demons are attacking the Legion, and they're going to kill every last one of us."

The slight note of panic in the man's voice lent him a certain authority, as if he had seen things that would frighten even a Legionnaire. The others didn't know he hadn't, in truth, been at the front with Zartay, and was simply repeating what he had heard.

And some people think cowards are useless in the Legion, Zartay thought to himself.

"Your fellows are dying out there, right now. Only the power of Iathephos can save us, and that man is the one link we have," Zartay said, pointing at the priest in the wagon.

The two guards looked at each other, and then the one in front of the wagon stepped back.

"If you're lying to us, I'll gut you myself. And I'll do it before the priest can stop me."

Zartay gave the man a cold look and climbed up onto the wagon. He hoped Brother Hissiath would play along until he could summon the power he needed to take control of the situation. He pulled the gag away from the priest's mouth, and then used his knife on the rope binding the man's wrists behind his back.

Brother Hissiath coughed a couple of times, and then groaned as his arms were released. The guard in the wagon still stood over Zartay and the priest. Zartay helped Brother Hissiath to his feet and met the priest's eyes. What he saw there was both reassuring and terrifying at the same time.

The priest calmly took the blade from Zartay's hand and, turning, thrust it directly into the chest of the guard standing on the wagon. The blade parted the man's armor as if it was paper and plunged into his heart. Yanking the blade free, Brother Hissiath jammed his hand onto the wound, smearing blood over his palm.

The other three soldiers were shocked by the sudden death of their fellow soldier. But all three recovered quickly. The coward turned and bolted away, running for his life. The other two drew their swords, ready to vault up into the wagon and hack Zartay and Brother Hissiath down.

But the priest raised his bloody palm up to his mouth and spoke a word over it. The syllables throbbed and hummed in Zartay's ears, running together and obscuring the true sound, though he knew it would forever after echo in his nightmares until his last day.

A wave of force fanned out from Brother Hissiath's palm and shattered the bodies of the two soldiers, throwing them off their feet into a pile of splintered bone and ruptured organs. In an instant, both soldiers were dead.

"Is it true, the demons?" the priest asked Zartay in a low voice. Zartay was too shocked to answer.

"Is it true?" Brother Hissiath demanded.

Zartay nodded at him, still unable to speak.

Brother Hissiath climbed down from the wagon and grabbed the reins of a horse tethered nearby.

"Get out of the valley," the priest ordered. "Return to Ythis however you can. The Emperor must hear about what happened here. He must know how the Legion betrayed him. I will follow when I can."

He climbed into the saddle and rode towards the fighting.

Zartay slowly lowered himself from the wagon and went to find another horse. He had no idea how he would make it back to Ythis on his own. Surely the soldiers back at the main camp would take him prisoner if he returned there. Somehow, he'd have to travel by himself.

And he didn't relish the thought of returning to Ythis to explain how he had failed to complete this mission for the Emperor. It might be worse for him to go back than it would be to stay here.

No, staying would be a death sentence, of that he was sure. And perhaps Ythis would be as well. But Zartay would have plenty of time to consider his alternatives as he traveled. And as long as he had his wits, and his knowledge of how to manipulate others, he would be okay.

*   *   *

KIED LOOKED AROUND THE ROOM AND SHUDDERED. THE HUGE chamber in which they stood was covered in a greenish gray stone that absorbed the light coming from a grotesquely shaped chandelier hung over the open space in the center of the room. But it wasn't the color of the walls, or the design of the chandelier that bothered Kied.

From every wall, from the floor around the outer perimeter, from the ceiling high overhead, the surface of the chamber was carved to resemble dozens of figures emerging from the stone itself as if it was some kind of viscous liquid. Many of the figures were recognizably human, although mixed in were stranger shapes that vaguely resembled giant insects and sea-dwelling creatures in chitinous shells.

The shapes themselves would have been disturbing on their own, but each figure had been painted with delicate precision, lending them a life-like quality despite their blank eyes and frozen expressions. Kied was sure some of the human figures were wearing real clothing, though from just inside the doorway he couldn't tell how the clothing somehow merged with the stone tendrils that kept the figures attached to the surfaces from which they appeared to have emerged.

The carvings were amazing, with exquisite detail. And all were in some pose of aggression. Any beings without natural claws or fangs or stingers held some kind of weapon. Most were familiar to Kied—spears, swords, shields, daggers—but some held alien devices that resembled nothing he could imagine using in a fight.

"Why do I have the feeling these things are going to come alive as soon as we get halfway across the chamber?" he asked Rotos in a low voice.

"They won't," the big man answered, his tone flat as if he didn't want to discuss it. "There's no bringing back anything you find in this room."

"What do you mean by 'bringing back?' Were all these things once alive?"

Rotos didn't answer, but strode into the room and headed for a doorway on the far side. Kied had no choice but to follow—he had no desire to be left alone in this place.

He couldn't fight the feeling that these carvings were a hair's breadth away from suddenly waking up, or turning back into real beings. And so when he caught a glimpse of movement out of the corner of his eye, he almost yelled "I knew it!"

But there was no triumph in his mind as the creature emerged from among the carvings, its spider legs carrying the torso of a man out of the shadows. The smell of saltwater filled Kied's nose as he backpedaled away from the nightmare shape.

He glanced ahead to see Rotos turning back when another shape leaped out from among the statues and landed on his back. It was some kind of giant insect, and the creature's scorpion-like tail curved over its head and plunged a jagged stinger into Rotos' chest.

The big man roared as the barbed tail pumped venom into his body. He grabbed the tail and yanked the creature forward over his head, smashing it into the floor at his feet. It rolled away and leaped upright with frightening speed.

Kied had time to register that these things had been hiding among the statues—the other figures were not, in fact, coming back to life—before a long, whip-like tongue shot forward from the puckered mouth of the man-spider near him. He flung himself sideways and saw the bone needle at the tip pass by his face less than a hand's breadth away.

Kied rolled sideways beside a statue, gaining a moment of temporary cover as he regained his feet. He glanced over the top of the stone figure and saw the monstrous being turn to follow him. The arcane patterns carved into the flesh of the creature's torso pulsed red and Kied saw black spots at the edges of his vision.

The spider legs scuttled forward bringing the creature closer and Kied backed away, climbing over the stony tendrils that connected each statue to the wall or floor. He knew, though, that a spider could climb much faster than he could, and there was no way he would be able to keep away from his attacker.

One slender spider leg reached out and touched the stone between Kied and the creature, and there was a flash of light and a sparking sound. The creature recoiled from the statue and Kied heard an all-too human screech of pain from the horrid thing before him.

He glanced over to Rotos to see his companion struggling with the other creature. It had managed to stab him multiple times with its stinger, and he was obviously weakening from the effects of the creature's venom. Still, despite the insect's speed, Rotos had connected with a couple of blows, and his attacker was unsteady on its feet.

Kied knew he wasn't safe from his own opponent yet. His pursuer was moving around the stone statues searching for a way to reach Kied without touching any of the carvings. Kied carefully moved back further among the statues.

He knew, though, that he couldn't stay here forever. Even if Rotos managed to finish off his own opponent, he would be in no condition to fight this creature as well. In fact, it was possible that the venom coursing through his body might kill him. This was an alien world, and Kied didn't know how powerful these creatures might be compared to his big companion.

Kied reached out to steady himself and his hand touched the haft of a spear held by the statue of a man dressed in nothing but a loin-cloth. The spear came loose from the statue's grip and fell heavily into Kied's hand. He nearly dropped the spear from shock—he had been convinced the weapons were part of the stone carving.

To his right, another statue held a small, round shield of similar design to the type he had trained with as a Legionnaire. Kied grabbed the edge and pulled, and the shield came free as well. He quickly strapped it onto his arm and grabbed the spear in his other hand.

A surge of energy flowed into his limbs, and for the first time in ages, Kied felt ready to go into battle. He didn't know how dangerous this creature could be, but if he made a mistake, he was sure the bone needle on the end of the creature's tongue would plunge into his flesh, and the battle would be over.

Kied held no illusion that he would be able to resist the venom in that stinger.

But he had no choice. Rotos was obviously weakening, and they were in a race against an opponent who might very well be at the threshold of finding the throne. Kied couldn't let that happen. As much as he wanted to see the Emperor fail, Kied didn't want to let the innocent citizens of the Empire suffer for it.

He hefted the spear in his hand and stepped toward the spider creature. Those blank white orbs seemed to follow him as he emerged from among the statues. It seemed to understand that he was no longer helpless, and it didn't immediately rush to attack. Kied was disappointed—he had hoped the creature would be mindlessly aggressive and ignore its own safety.

Instead, the spider legs carried the figure back a few paces and it crouched slightly, waiting for Kied to make the first move. With the shield held at the ready, Kied carefully stepped forward.

With a whistle, the tongue darted out at Kied's face. He raised the shield and the bone needle clanged off its surface. The creature moved slightly to Kied's left and the tongue shot forward again.

Again, Kied raised the shield and protected his face.

The spider legs scuttled back a few paces and the creature raised its human arms out to either side, its palms turned to the ceiling. The red patterns on its body glowed brighter and seemed to twist and writhe over its flesh. A throbbing hum filled the air, and a wave of dizziness swept over Kied.

He felt himself swaying and tried to blink away the spots dancing in his vision, but he knew he wouldn't be able to withstand a magical assault like this. If he was going to do anything, he would have to do it now.

Kied focused every ounce of his will on controlling his limbs. He knew he'd only get one shot at this. With darkness settling over his vision, Kied lunged forward. At that moment, the creature's tongue shot out once more. Kied raised the shield without thinking and gasped as the needle-tip stabbed into his thigh.

As he lowered the shield, he drew his other arm back and flung the spear with all his failing strength at the creature's chest. With a casual swipe, the monster batted it out of the air to send it clattering to the floor among the statues to one side.

Pain exploded in Kied's leg and he collapsed to the floor. His vision cleared as the creature let its magical attack subside. He looked up to see it standing over him, and he knew he was about to die.

The pain in his leg continued to spread up into his groin, and a yellow froth was beginning to bubble up from the puncture wound.

Behind him, he could hear Rotos roaring in pain as the big man continued to fight.

Chapter Thirty-Three

THEY WERE ALL GOING TO DIE.

Laita was proud of how quickly her soldiers had formed up when the wave of monsters poured from the opening in the rock. No one had panicked, no one had run. The squads had jumped together and formed a shield wall facing their attackers, and in short order they were slaughtering the creatures almost as fast as they emerged from the rock.

But the wave was never-ending, and her own soldiers were dying one by one. Even if they killed five for every one they lost, it wouldn't be enough. The horde was beginning to surround their flanks and still more poured out from the cut in the rock.

It was only a matter of time before they would be completely surrounded. And then they would be overwhelmed and everyone would die at the claws and teeth of these fiends.

She couldn't call a retreat—the creatures were too fast, and she had no way to delay the horde long enough to get her people to any kind of safety. And there was nowhere for them to go, even if they could break away.

Laita looked back and saw the last few stragglers coming up and joining the formation. This was it, her entire fighting force of Legionnaires, minus those who were already dead. She had another five detachments spread across these valleys, but no way to bring them here in time to make a difference.

And then she spotted a man on horseback galloping up toward the battle. At first, she thought it was Ambassador Seaphon, the man's robes fluttering around him as he rode. But then she realized the robes were black, and there was only one man with black robes in the area.

The priest. He was free.

Laita was in the middle of the formation. She had abandoned her own horse when the battle started—it was of no use in this kind of fighting—and she knew she couldn't intercept the man before he reached the battle.

She watched the priest ride up and dismount, and then she lost sight of him behind the formation.

Namal made his way back to her from the front line. He had a cut over his left eye, but was otherwise unharmed.

"We don't have much time," he reported, leaning in close so that the other soldiers near them wouldn't hear his words. "The creatures are still coming out of the cut. We're going to get cut off soon."

"I know," she replied in a voice only he could hear. "Our only option is to charge forward and try to block the opening. But we'll lose cohesion if we charge and that could end us."

Namal looked at her and she knew what he was thinking. If they did nothing, they would all die anyway. It was time to act instead of react.

She was about to give the order when a shout went up from the left side of the formation. A cold wind blasted across the soldiers, bringing with it the smell of mold and rot. Something on the far side of the soldiers began to glow with a white light, but Laita couldn't see the source.

The light wasn't pure, but instead the whiteness gave a sense of alien coldness. And then the demonic creatures began to howl in pain. A rumble of thunder came from the area of the light—some kind of explosion—and blasted limbs and other demonic body parts erupted into the air above the soldiers

"The priest!" she exclaimed. "The priest is over there! He must be calling upon Iath—"

She broke off, not wanting to say the name of the god of Ythis. It was never a good idea to attract the attention of the gods.

A cheer went up from the soldiers and they redoubled their efforts.

"Charge the opening!" she ordered Namal. "Block it with their dead. Do whatever you have to, but stop that flow of creatures!"

Namal gave her a quick salute and pushed his way toward the front.

Another explosion blew apart more of the creatures.

As much as they needed the assistance of the priest at this point—he was giving them the chance to change the course of this battle—Laita couldn't shake a sense of dread at what he had done. She knew very little about the priests, but it was common knowledge that contact with their god caused all the priests to eventually go mad.

What would he do once he had finished destroying the attacking creatures?

She pushed her way toward that white light.

A third blast plowed into the massed attackers, and in that moment of relief a thunderous shout of "Charge!" erupted from the soldiers at the front. As one, the first few lines drove forward and jammed into the hole in the rock, stemming the tide of creatures.

But Laita had been correct, in that the formation loosened as it moved. There were still hundreds of the creatures, and they surged into the gaps and tore into the soldiers. If the fiends managed to drive between the soldiers plugging the cut and the rest of the formation, those Legionnaires would be torn apart in seconds.

A fourth detonation, and a fifth shattered bodies and flung them into the air. Laita saw helms and breastplates among the flying debris, and the soldiers nearest the priest began to scream. Legionnaires started to pull away from that side of the formation, and Laita had to shove her way through the press of bodies.

One of the soldiers saw her and grabbed her arm.

"It's the priest!" the man shouted. "Don't go over there, he's turned into something …."

Laita pulled her arm free.

"Plug those gaps!" she ordered, pointing at the desperate struggle going on near the opening in the rock. "Get that shield wall stabilized or it won't matter."

She shoved her way through the soldiers as they turned and pushed into the gaps in the shield wall.

Laita emerged from the side of the formation to find the priest standing a couple dozen paces away. His head was tilted back to the sky and his arms were thrown wide as if he was trying to embrace the heavens above. His skin glowed, giving off that white light, and beams of that light came from his eyes, spearing up into the sky above.

The priest's mouth opened, and he uttered a word that nearly caused Laita to vomit. Thunder rumbled forth from his body to strike into a mass of battling creatures and soldiers. The force of it ripped their bodies apart, throwing severed limbs and shattered torsos into the air.

Laita shouted in horror as she saw a half-dozen of her Legionnaires die from the blast.

The priest had saved them, had given them a chance to block the creatures from emerging onto the plain, to bottle them up in the cut. But now he was indiscriminately slaughtering her own soldiers along with the demons. The tide of battle had turned, but he was now weakening her own force as he finished off the creatures remaining out in the open.

He uttered the word again, and this time Laita did vomit. Through watery eyes, she saw more of her soldiers die in an instant as their bodies were blown apart. The few remaining creatures threw themselves at the Legion and were quickly cut down.

Drawing her sword, Laita ran at the priest. But as she got close to him, a force pushed her back and she found herself unable to reach him. She screamed in frustration as yet another explosion tore into the soldiers and more of her people died.

She turned and ran to the horse the priest had used to approach the battle. Vaulting into the saddle, she grabbed the reins and kicked the horse into a gallop at the priest's back. She wasn't strong enough to push through the force surrounding him, but perhaps a charging horse could.

Laita gripped her sword and prepared to make this attack count.

The horse stumbled as it plowed into the circle of force surrounding the priest, and Laita was nearly thrown from the saddle. But she held on and swung her sword with all her strength. The horse was deflected from its path, but Laita had just enough reach. The blade sliced through the priest's neck and severed his head from his body.

Both Laita and the horse were blasted sideways as the priest's body exploded in a shower of gore. She was flung from the saddle and barely managed to avoid being crushed by the horse as it tumbled past her.

She lay on the ground, dazed for a few seconds from the impact. The screams of the horse brought her back to her senses, and she pushed herself upright. A squad of soldiers rushed to her aid as she turned to see the horse had two shattered legs and a ragged wound in its side.

Laita slowly regained her feet and looked at what remained of the detachment as the soldiers surrounded her.

"Commander, are you all right?" the sergeant asked her.

"I'm ... I'm okay. What's the situation?"

"We've blocked the cut. All the creatures that came out onto the plain are dead. And the flood of monsters seems to have stopped."

Laita looked over at the bloody mess that had been the priest, and shuddered. She half-expected a divine attack to strike her down on the spot. She had just killed a priest while he was in the act of directly channeling his god's power.

She had the feeling she had definitely attracted the being's attention now.

"Okay," she said. "Let's go see what we need to do next."

*   *   *

KIED WAITED FOR THE SPIDER CREATURE STANDING OVER HIM TO end his life. The pain in his leg had spread up into his belly and part-way down his other leg. He was finding it increasingly difficult to breathe and he knew the poison coursing through his body was going to kill him if the creature didn't finish him off first.

The sounds of Rotos' battle behind him had ceased. Kied wondered if the other man was dead. As much as he had seen Rotos survive what should have been mortal wounds before, Kied knew the rules were different in this place.

And then Rotos roared as he charged into the man-spider and drove it backward away from Kied. The creature's tongue darted out over and over, stabbing into Rotos as he grabbed it around the torso and lifted it off the ground.

The giant heaved the creature over his head and then flung it backward to crash into the statues near the side of the room. It landed on the upraised weapons held by the statues, pierced by multiple blades of various shapes and sizes. The ring of puckered flesh that was the creature's mouth ripped open as it screamed in an all-too-human voice.

Rotos stepped forward and shoved the creature down further onto the blades, and it writhed and screamed as the edges cut through its flesh.

With a final heave, Rotos pushed the creature down until its flesh touched the stone of the statues. A low hum started up as it screamed ever more loudly. Rotos stepped back and the creature's body burst into flames, an oily black smoke boiling up as it was consumed.

Rotos came over to Kied, picked him up and flung him over his shoulder. Kied moaned in pain, unable to speak and fighting to breathe. He was carried away from the smoke and out of the room. Rotos stepped into a side chamber and lowered Kied onto a soft bench that stood against one wall.

"It got me …," was all Kied managed to say before he had to fight for another breath.

"Don't speak. You'll need your strength for this."

Rotos drew a strangely shaped knife from his belt. Kied figured he had probably taken it from one of the statues. The big man drew the blade across his palm, and his blood welled up thick and red.

Without warning, Rotos placed his palm on the puncture wound on Kied's leg.

Fire tore through Kied's insides and he screamed as his muscles spasmed uncontrollably. A thousand images crashed through his mind, places and people he did not recognize but somehow knew were part of his own world. He felt as if he would explode in heat and flame, and knew his body couldn't withstand whatever Rotos was doing to him.

Rotos withdrew his hand and it was as if Kied had been suddenly thrown out of a bonfire into a freezing cold lake. He gasped as the heat disappeared and a painful chill swept through his body.

That, too, faded and Kied wrapped his arms around himself and shuddered uncontrollably. He looked down at his leg, and the puncture wound was still there, though it was completely scabbed over. But as he regained his senses, Kied could feel the poison was no longer running through his veins.

He looked at Rotos, but there was no sign of the wounds the giant had sustained in his battle with the insectoid creature. He didn't even appear to be out of breath.

"You … you've gotten even stronger in this place, haven't you?" Kied asked him. Rotos looked down at the floor, then sighed and heaved himself up on the bench beside Kied.

"Yes, I have," he said in his low growl. "That's the danger of this city. It's why your Emperor wants to find it."

"Who are you, Rotos? How did you know about this place? What is this place?"

Rotos looked Kied in the eye and for the first time Kied saw the years that had piled up behind the big man. Rotos was far, far older than he looked. There was the sense of vast history in the man's gaze, a sense that he had seen an uncountable roll of years pass him by, one by one.

"You know something of the old gods," he said to Kied. "But most of the knowledge has been lost, or swept up into secret histories kept by the sorcerers and the priests. Many believe that, no matter how dangerous the Church is now, the worship of the old gods was much worse. In some ways they are correct."

Rotos leaned back against the wall and looked down at his hands.

"You must understand, the thing that separates the gods—old or new—from humanity is the scale of the power they wield. That's it. In the uncountable worlds that float in the Abyss, there are many powerful beings. Some are able to take the power of worship and feed on it. Others, like humanity, cannot."

Kied listened carefully. He realized that Rotos was about to answer his questions, finally giving him the knowledge he had sought all through their journey together.

"Our name for the old gods, in the language I spoke when I was young, was Ayakra, the First. The gods who replaced them are the Benakra, the Followers. They are two different races of beings, but they are both from other worlds who have invaded yours and fed off humanity's worship for eons."

Rotos looked up and down the hallway, as if hearing a noise. But whatever it was that caught his attention didn't repeat and he continued.

"As I told you before, the old gods—the Ayakra—didn't hide in the bowels of their temples and corrupt the minds of anyone who came near them. They moved among the people, they participated directly in their rites of worship, and very, very rarely … they mated with humans."

Kied gasped. This was something he had never heard, and the thought was horrific.

"Did they … impregnate …?"

Rotos gave a short nod.

"The offspring of the Ayakra looked human enough, but they weren't. They had powers beyond what mere sorcery could bring to bear, they were nearly unkillable, and they were immortal."

Kied looked at Rotos and could scarcely believe what the man was saying. The pieces suddenly fell into place and Kied felt an urge to fling himself away from his companion, to run as fast and as far as he could.

"You … you're one of the children of the old gods."

Rotos grunted in something resembling amusement.

"I think I'm well past being called a child, Kied. I'm older than you can imagine. I'm also not alone."

"The man," Kied said, realizing the truth of the matter. "The one who came to visit you in the prison …."

"Yarrian is my cousin, yes, though he prefers to call me brother because of our shared history. And there are others, spread out across the world. I no longer know if all still live—we are extremely difficult to kill, but we can still die. Back when the Ayakra were driven away—"

"You said that before," Kied interrupted. "I always thought the old gods were all destroyed when the gateways opened and the new gods came through."

Rotos shook his head.

"A couple of the Ayakra were irrevocably destroyed. The rest were driven out of your world."

"Into another world like this one?" Kied asked.

"No. Sending the Ayakra to another world would have established a link back to yours. No matter how much effort might be put into sealing it, with enough power, the Ayakra would eventually have forced such a gate open again. If they had been merely banished to another world, they would have gathered their strength and returned to continue the war. The Benakra weren't powerful enough to destroy all of the old gods, but collectively the invaders were still the stronger group."

Kied was unable to look away from Rotos' face, compelled to listen to his story to the end.

"The Benakra tore open a rift to the very edge of the Abyss. They pushed the Ayakra out into whatever it is that lies beyond the limits of the Abyss, and then sealed the rift. The Ayakra have never found a way back, as there is no permanent gate to that void. But I believe they are still out there, hunting for a way to open their own rift and return to reclaim their worlds."

"The dream I had," Kied said slowly. "The eye I saw in the sky that day when you used magic ... you said that was a sliver of one of the old gods ...."

"There are remnants of the Ayakra—residue of their power—still in your world. It's not alive, not in the sense you understand. It's more like a memory or a reflection of something that was here a long time ago. But certain actions can bring it forth, and it can easily corrupt your mind and soul. There is no intention there, but the danger is no less for that."

Rotos stood up and held out his hand once again for Kied.

"We need to keep moving. Your leg has rested long enough that the wound shouldn't break open again."

"I have one more question you haven't answered yet," Kied said as he let Rotos pull him to his feet. His leg was sore, but the pain was minor and wouldn't hamper his movement. "What is this world? Is this where the old gods originally came from?"

Rotos looked up and down the hallway once more.

"No. The Ayakra found this world and built this city as a gift."

"For who?" Kied asked, and then immediately realized the answer.

"For their children," Rotos responded. "We were supposed to abandon your world and come to live here. When the Ayakra built this city, they filled it with servants, worshippers, and guardians. But it is a dead city now. The guardians remain, along with a few groups of corrupted remnants of those who had been brought here to serve us."

Rotos began to walk down the hall, and Kied followed.

"When the Ayakra were driven away, a few of us decided to hide the location of the gateway to this world from the rest, to prevent anyone from coming here and finding the throne room."

"Couldn't you just have destroyed the gate?" Kied asked.

"We could, but we decided to keep it intact."

"Why?"

"Hubris," Rotos said shortly. "We thought we could hide it well enough, and there was always the possibility that we might need to come back here at some point in the future. We were foolish."

"I have one more question, Rotos." Kied hesitated, unsure if it was worth asking, unsure if he wanted to know the truth. "Why were you in that prison? You could have left at any time, but you chose to stay there."

"Penance."

"For what?"

"For all the lives I've destroyed over the centuries. For the wars I've started, the innocents I've slaughtered, the evil I've done. I'm not just a warrior, Kied. I'm a Warlord. And my past is littered with the bodies of the thousands slain by my own hand."

Kied considered that, considered the roll of history that lay behind Rotos' words. Few understood anything about the ancient past anymore. It was long lost in the mists of time. But Rotos had seen it all.

"What's so special about the throne? Why is the Emperor trying to find it?"

"You'll see when we get there," Rotos answered. "I only hope we're not too late."

Chapter Thirty-Four

TIATH STUMBLED AS HE TURNED A CORNER AND SAW A LONG hallway leading to a doorway sheathed in white light.

I'm here, he thought. This has to be it.

Exhaustion dragged at his feet as he lurched down the passageway. He realized the doorway was open, and the bright light filled the room beyond, obscuring whatever waited for him.

As he got closer, he was forced to close his eyes against the piercing glow. He reached out a hand and felt the edge of the doorway, smooth like marble but warm to the touch, almost like living flesh.

He tried to open his eyes just enough to squint through the light, but it was too bright to see anything.

"By the Abyss," he moaned aloud.

He covered his eyes with his hands and tried to peek between his fingers. As he did so, he took a step into the room.

Immediately, the light's intensity lessened, and he was able to see the room before him.

Tiath stood on a balcony above the throne room. The space was vast, with great white columns rising from the pale blue floor to the matching arched ceiling far above. Tiers of ornate marble seats lined the sides of the chamber, and a long golden carpet led from a wide entrance below to the base of the throne.

Tiath's gaze rested on his prize and he felt tears running down his cheeks. He had sacrificed so much to reach this point, and now here he was.

The throne rested upon a raised dais of greenish stone, with steps seemingly of diamond leading up to the platform at the top. In the center sat the throne itself, a large chair carved from some kind of blue gemstone shot through with red veins. The back of the throne was shaped like a great clawed hand rising up over the seat, the talons curved forward to point towards the hall's entrance.

The whole room thrummed with the power coming off the throne, and Tiath's bones vibrated with it. He didn't know what would happen once he ascended those steps and sat on the chair at the top—perhaps he would be utterly destroyed—but he knew he must try. This was his one chance, his one opportunity to become something more, something greater than he would ever be able to achieve on his own.

He pulled his eyes away from the throne and looked around. There was no visible way to descend to the floor from this balcony, and it was too far to jump. But the thought of retreating and trying to find another way down to the ground floor gave him doubt.

Now that he had found the throne room, he was loathe to leave it. And there was no guarantee that if he left the room, he would ever be able to find his way back here again. He might wander, lost, for the rest of his days and never find those doors below.

No, he couldn't retreat and search for another way down. There was the possibility, unlikely as it may be, that those others might have defeated Deylista and Pasill and were even now making their way here. If they reached the throne room while Tiath was still searching for a way down ....

He had no rope, but he could still reduce the distance he would need to drop from the balcony. Quickly, he stripped off his clothing and tied them together into a crude rope. It wasn't much, but every bit counted—it was a long drop to the floor below.

Tiath secured his makeshift rope to the balcony's railing and gave it a few experimental tugs. He wasn't entirely sure it would hold his weight, but he had little choice. He would have to trust the fabric would hold together long enough for him to climb down to the end.

His skin tingled with the power pouring off the throne like a thousand tiny needles pricking into his flesh. It wasn't painful, yet neither was it pleasant. There was something off about the sensation, as if his body wanted to recoil from it rather than embrace it.

He forced himself to concentrate on the task at hand as he eased himself over the balcony's railing and took hold of his line of clothing. Carefully, he lowered himself down until his full weight was off the balcony and hanging above the solid floor below.

Hand over hand, Tiath lowered himself down until he reached the end of his makeshift rope. He looked down and saw that he was still at least two stories above the floor of the throne room. There was nothing to break his fall, yet he had no other choice. He would simply have to try to roll with the impact when he landed and hope that he didn't break a bone or knock himself unconscious.

Taking a deep breath, he steeled himself for the jump and then let go. The floor rushed up toward him and he wrapped his arms over his head to protect his neck and skull.

And then his feet slammed into the hard surface of the floor and he heard a sharp crack as pain lightninged up his left leg. He shouted as he rolled sideways and the impact of his body hitting the floor knocked the wind out of him. His body rolled a second time and then he sprawled out on the pale blue floor of the throne room.

Gasping for breath, Tiath pulled himself into a fetal position as fire tore through his left leg. He looked down and saw his left foot was twisted away at an angle and a bone from his ankle protruded from his flesh. His blood dripped onto the blue tiles and sizzled as it hit, though the tiles felt cold to the touch.

Clenching his teeth, he held back the scream that wanted to tear itself from his throat.

So close. So close and now he couldn't walk.

Tiath turned his head and saw the raised dais a few dozen paces away, the diamond stairs leading up to the source of the power he so desperately craved.

Snarling curses under his breath, he gingerly moved his leg and a fresh wave of agony flowed up into his chest. It wasn't just the protruding bone—he had damaged his left leg in other places as well.

But he was so close. He couldn't just give up, not now when he had almost reached his goal.

Rolling onto his stomach, Tiath gasped again at the pain in his left leg. He pushed himself up onto his right knee, and the movement in his left leg was nearly unbearable.

Gritting his teeth, he tried to crawl onto the golden carpet that led to the base of the throne. Nausea rose in his stomach as the torture of his injured leg made him dizzy. He paused for a moment, and then tried to push himself up so that he was standing on his uninjured leg.

Once he was upright, he gave himself another moment of rest. Knowing that what he was about to do would cause more pain to blossom in his wounded leg, he set his jaw and focused his eyes on the throne at the top of the dais.

With a lurch, he hopped forward on his good leg. The sudden movement sent an explosion of agony through his body and he nearly toppled over. But he forced himself to hop forward again, and again, and again.

On the third landing the pain became unbearable and he lost his balance and fell back to the floor. He had just enough presence of mind to twist and land on his right side, but the impact blinded him with the pain that had become a living thing inside his body.

He blinked his eyes open and realized that he must have lost consciousness for a few seconds—or perhaps it was minutes, he couldn't tell. He wanted to scream in frustration but he swallowed it down.

There was no way he would be able to hop on one leg. His only option was to crawl toward the dais and up those stairs to the throne that loomed above him.

He turned onto his right side, resting his left leg on his right. Then, trying to keep his legs as still as possible, he used his arms to drag himself forward. The movement sent fresh spasms up his injured leg, but he managed to avoid the worst of it by using only his arms to pull himself along.

The fabric of the golden carpet felt like the most expensive silk under his body, and he thanked his fortune that it was smooth and soft and wasn't tearing up his skin as he dragged himself toward the dais.

Tiath didn't know how long it took him to reach the stairs leading up to the throne, but he didn't care. As long as he reached his goal, everything would be okay.

Finally, he found himself at the bottom of the diamond steps. He looked up and counted thirteen steps to the top. There was no way for him to drag himself up those stairs without using his good leg, and he knew the pain would be nearly unbearable. But it was his only option at this point.

He would do this, no matter the cost.

Pushing himself up, a cry escaped his throat as he lifted himself up onto the first step. Tears dripped off his face, and the trail of blood along the carpet behind him continued to sizzle. He felt himself getting weaker and weaker and he pushed himself up another step. He let himself cry out this time, not wasting any energy to fight it any longer.

Step by step, he dragged himself up the dais, blood pouring from his shattered ankle, waves of agony sweeping through his body, his throat raw from his cries and moans. Time seemed to stretch, every second taking days to pass until he could no longer remember anything but this climb and the constant, unending pain.

And then, he reached out for the next step and there wasn't one there. In a daze, he raised his head and looked up at the throne looming above him.

Tiath had reached the top.

With a final, defiant scream, he pushed himself up onto his good leg.

"Stop!" a deep, booming voice shouted from behind him. "On your life, do not sit in that chair!"

Tiath twisted his head to look back down the length of the chamber. Standing in the doorway at the end of the golden carpet were the two men he had seen earlier.

The giant and the soldier were here.

Pasill and Deylista had failed.

The huge man took a step toward the throne and raised one hand.

"You cannot survive this," he said, an almost pleading tone in his deep voice. "It was not meant for humans, and it will destroy you."

Tiath looked back at the ornate chair before him. It waited, patiently. He could feel the power of this throne, the waves passing through his body like ghosts, chilling his blood.

The giant could very well be right. Tiath might be killed by the power flowing through the throne. It might be far too much for his mortal frame to handle.

But then again, the big man might be lying. Tiath didn't know who these two men were, didn't know how they had found the cave and followed him here. But they had fought their way through multiple guardians to reach this place. It seemed to him that their purpose here might really be to stop him from sitting in this chair.

If the throne would simply destroy Tiath, then why were these two men trying so hard?

He spun on his heel and flung himself backward into the seat.

His naked flesh made contact with the throne and the power in this place became aware of him, as if it was a vast mind that had only just noticed his presence.

He heard the giant yell one last time, but the man's words were drowned out by the thrum that rose in Tiath's ears.

And then he heard his own scream begin as his flesh erupted.

$$* \qquad * \qquad *$$

KIED WAS PICKED UP AND FLUNG BACK TOWARDS THE DOORWAY from the pulse of light, sound, and force that burst outward from the throne. He caught a glimpse of Rotos stumbling backwards but he lost sight of his companion as he hit the floor and rolled into the side of a pillar. A terrible human scream rose to fill the room like a banshee's howl, full of fear and agony.

Gasping for breath, Kied shook his head and tried to regain his senses. He looked around for Rotos and found the big man leaning on a marble bench and staring up at the throne.

The naked man who had been standing on the dais as he and Rotos entered the throne room was being slowly torn apart by the power of the seat upon which he sprawled. Blood boiling, his flesh was splitting open with the pressure inside. His muscles were engorged and seemed to be growing larger with each passing second.

Two large bulges arose on either side of the man's head, and then the skin split apart to reveal nubs of bone that rapidly grew outward in jagged spikes. The man's screams were taking on a lower, thicker tone, and were becoming bellows of rage instead of howls of agony.

"KIED!" Rotos yelled at him, and he turned back to his companion, who was now limping over to him.

Kied pushed himself to his feet and grabbed Rotos' arm.

"What's happening to him?" Kied asked.

"We're too late! You must leave here. Get back to the gate and across to your world."

Kied looked back at the throne. The man's body was getting larger and Kied could feel the thrum of power flowing through the room toward the figure on the throne. Rotos grabbed Kied's shoulders and shook him.

"Listen to me! I can't stop what's happening to him. He wasn't meant for this—no mortals are."

"If he's dying …," Kied mumbled, confused.

"He's not dying, he's changing. He's formed a connection to one of the old gods. He's going to become its servant, and he'll try to make it back to your world. He'll be a conduit, a way back for the old gods. You have to make sure that doesn't happen."

The sounds of flesh and bones popping, tearing and breaking were growing louder. The man on the throne bellowed again, and it sounded like some ancient beast, vast and powerful. Kied turned back to the throne to see the figure rise up from the seat.

He was huge, easily half again as tall as Rotos. His flesh had transformed into a red, chitinous covering that glistened in the light of the room. His head was a strange mixture of a bull and a snake, wickedly barbed horns rising up from a long snout covered in dark green scales.

Whoever the man had been before, his humanity was stripped away, and his flesh shaped into something alien and monstrous.

Kied felt disconnected from his own body. He was still disoriented from getting knocked across the room, and couldn't quite understand the urgency in Rotos' voice.

The big man spun Kied around and slapped him hard across the face.

"Kied! You have to concentrate! I don't know how long I can delay him. He'll take a bit of time to get used to his new body, but that won't last for very long. You must get back and destroy the gate!"

The ringing blow brought some clarity back to Kied's thoughts.

"I can't do it myself. I can't get across this city without you …."

"You can! Fix the gate in your mind. You need to see it, feel its presence."

The beast on the dais stretched out its arms and focused its reptilian eyes on the two men.

"Rotos," the creature said in a deep and resounding voice. Kied felt his gorge rise and he vomited onto the stones of the floor. Blood dripped from his nose and ears.

"Run!" Rotos shouted one last time and walked toward the great beast.

"I know your thoughts," the creature rumbled. "You cannot stop me from returning."

Kied's stomach twisted at the sound of that alien voice but he was already moving. As he passed through the doorway, he took one last glance back.

Rotos stood at the bottom of the steps. The beast on the throne loomed over him, great and wicked claws extended from its hands. Black cloven hooves nearly as thick as Rotos' thighs stomped on the diamond steps, shattering them like glass.

Kied flung himself out of the throne room and raced down a wide hall back toward the gallery with its strange statues.

There was no way he was going to get out of the city in time. It would take hours to return to the gate, and Kied had no doubt that creature would be able to traverse that same distance in a fraction of the time.

Distances are … flexible … here. So is time, if you know what to do.

Those were Rotos' words. But Kied didn't know what to do. He couldn't just collapse distance and reach the gate in a few minutes. Rotos might have been able to do that, but Kied didn't know anything about this place.

A great shout rose up from behind Kied and he realized that Rotos was yelling.

No, he was screaming.

That creature was going to kill Rotos. It didn't matter how powerful the big man was, Rotos had obviously expected to die trying to give Kied time to get back to the gate. Kied didn't want to die here, in this alien world. He needed to reach the gate and find some way to close it. Desperation lent him speed as he raced through the hallways.

He turned a corner and expected to see the bench on which Rotos had healed him, and the gallery beyond. But instead he pulled up short in front of a pair of large double doors.

He had taken a wrong turn and was lost.

Kied wanted to scream out his own frustration. He considered backtracking, but knew there would be little point. He shoved at the doors and found himself ... outside? Looking up, he realized that he had just emerged from the palace onto one of the streets that ran along its outside edge.

Somewhere around here was the bridge that he had used to reach the palace grounds. But the place was so large, it might take hours to make his way around the outside and find it. He took off running in the direction in which he thought it might lie.

Rounding a corner, he found another bridge. It wasn't the one he had originally crossed, but that didn't matter. It led back out into the city, and that was good enough for him.

Kied took off running, constantly scanning ahead for any signs of danger that might be waiting for him. He reached the far side of the bridge and picked a direction that he believed would lead him back to where he and Rotos had first entered the city.

A cry came to him in the still air, across the chasm that separated the palace from the rest of the city. A thousand voices mingled in rage and hunger. The sound nearly caused Kied to lose control of his bowels.

The creature was no longer in the palace. That meant Rotos was probably dead.

Kied didn't have time to mourn his companion. A second howl went up, and Kied understood the threat implicit in that sound.

The creature had begun to hunt.

It wasn't going to race him to the gate. It didn't need to. It wanted to find Kied and end his life before it turned its attention to the next world.

It was coming for him, and he hadn't even reached the edge of the city yet.

He threw himself forward and tore down a wide boulevard lined with ancient statues of beings who looked human but had a subtle wrongness to them that lent them an otherworldly air.

The street ahead was blocked by a vast wall, and Kied turned down a side street to move along parallel to the barrier. He had gone almost two blocks when he saw an archway up ahead, an immense stone gateway through the wall.

Kied slowed to look through the archway to see whether more of this endless city lay beyond. But on the other side, it was bare sand, broken by clusters of rocky ground.

He stood there for a moment, not understanding what he was seeing. And then his brain registered where he was. The city ended here. The wall was the outer wall, and this gate led out into the flat plain where the portal had originally brought them over from Kied's own world.

Kied had somehow found his way to the edge of the city in minutes, not hours.

Another howl went up behind him, much closer than the last had been. The beast was closing in.

Kied flung himself under the archway and out of the city. Somewhere out here was the gateway to his own world. As he ran, he pictured it in his mind and focused all of his will on reaching it before the beast caught up with him.

Chapter Thirty-Five

LUNGS BURNING, LEGS ACHING, KIED KNEW HE COULDN'T GIVE up. He didn't know how long he had been running—five minutes or five hours. There was no sense of time passing here, and the landscape in front of him was nearly featureless, each patch of rocky ground protruding from the dark red sand looking much like another.

He continued to run and tried to keep his mind focused on the gate. He didn't dare look back now. The beast was behind him somewhere, though he didn't know how close. Kied couldn't risk looking behind for fear of tripping.

Or perhaps because he didn't want to see how close his death was at his back.

The ground passed beneath his boots, too fast for the pace at which he ran. He tried not to think about it too much in case he lost his concentration and the effect disappeared.

With a strong enough will, you can still change the shape of the city for yourself, although only in minor ways. If you're desperate enough, though, there's no telling what you might do. As I've said before, there's something special about you.

Rotos had said that to him when they entered the city. Well, Kied was certainly desperate now. He was in a life-or-death race and the beast was hunting him, assuming it couldn't just catch him whenever it wanted and wasn't just toying with him for sport—don't think about that!

The gate, he needed to find the gate. Time was running out and he hadn't found it yet.

Jump!

The thought came to him unbidden and Kied leaped sideways, flinging himself through the air as something hit the ground where he would have been had he kept on the same course. He tumbled across the ground, time and space snapping back into place with a jarring twist as he lost his concentration.

Kied rolled to his feet and found himself standing before the beast. It had smashed its great claw down where Kied had almost been, but had missed.

Kied couldn't read emotion in the alien creature's face, but he was sure the beast was as surprised as he was himself. How had he known to jump at that precise moment?

I told you once there is more to you than I understand. She is the same. There's something greater happening here, but I can't see where it's leading.

Rotos had been confused by Kied's resilience, and had seen something similar in Laita. But that didn't matter now. The beast had caught up with him, and Kied knew he was going to die.

The beast raised its head and bellowed in rage rather than attacking again immediately, and Kied took that instant's respite to sprint away. He could hear the beast's hooves pounding into the sand behind him as it gave chase. Whatever game it may have been playing before, it was obvious the game was now over.

He'll take a bit of time to get used to his new body, but that won't last for very long.

Could it be that the creature hadn't been toying with him at all, but was still confused by its transformation? If so, did Kied have a chance to find the portal if he kept his concentration?

Jump!

He leaped sideways again as the monstrosity pounced. This time, he felt the wind of the claws passing perhaps a hand's span away from his body as he fell. He pushed himself into a roll, regained his feet, and came up running.

The beast bellowed again, and Kied could hear the urgency in it. Was the creature getting worried? The gate! It had to be near. It was the one thing the beast wouldn't want him to find ….

It came easier this time—the image of the gate appeared in Kied's mind and he felt the ground flowing under him, faster than he could ever hope to run. The huge beast was close behind him, grunting with the effort of catching its prey.

Kied could hear the monster gaining on him, eating up the distance between them with every stride. He couldn't outrun it, but twice he had managed to outmaneuver it ….

He turned suddenly to his right, but didn't throw himself down. Instead, he ducked his head and tried to put on a burst of speed. The creature nearly caught him, but it stumbled past him as he regained some distance before it could turn and lumber after him.

If the actual distance didn't matter, if Kied could find the gate if he concentrated hard enough and his need was strong enough, then direction probably didn't matter either. If this was true, he could run in circles and still end up at the gate eventually.

As the beast gained on him again, he made another rapid turn and once more the distance increased. Kied started to feel confident he might keep out of the reach of the abomination long enough to find the gate ….

He stumbled as his focus dissipated like smoke in a strong wind—time and space suddenly snapping back into reality—and the beast hammered into him from behind. Kied was flung sideways through the air and landed in a heap on the sandy surface. The creature lumbered to a halt and looked around, seemingly unsure what had just happened.

Kied had lost his need, his desperation for a moment, and that had neatly severed his connection to the gate. Groaning, he pushed himself back to his feet.

The monstrosity was suddenly in front of him, appearing to move without crossing the distance between them. Kied threw himself to one side as the sabre-like claws sliced through the air at his torso. He felt a sharp pain down the length of his arm as the tip of one claw opened his flesh from shoulder to elbow.

Crying out in pain and terror, Kied rolled to his feet and tried to race off away from the creature. With an all-consuming desperation, he looked for the gate, seeking it with every ounce of need and suddenly it was right there in front of him.

This time, when the blow came, Kied was unable to leap aside in time. Though he managed to avoid the claws, the beast's huge fist hammered into his side and lifted him into the air. He heard and felt his ribs break and then shimmering colors surrounded him. He felt as if he was floating rather than flying, and for an instant he thought he might be dead.

Realization that he was passing through the gate hit him just as the colors dissipated and he came flying out of the portal. His body hit the stone floor and he rolled over twice, screaming from the impact on his ribs, blood pouring from his wounded arm.

He was home, back in his own world once more. The agony in his chest and arm muddied his thoughts, but he knew he had made it back.

But his feeling of victory was short-lived.

He raised his head, and through the portal he could see the creature looking around, seeking him out. And then it turned toward the portal and its blood-red eyes focused on him.

It raised its head and let out a bone-rattling roar. This time, Kied could hear the triumph in its voice.

*   *   *

KIED HAD FAILED.

He knew it even before he tried to move. Rolling over onto his stomach, he tried to push himself up. The piercing pain in his chest took his breath away, and he didn't have the strength in his injured arm to raise himself off the floor.

Collapsing, he managed to turn his head to see the massive beast striding towards the portal.

Rotos had died for nothing. He had given his life so that Kied might close the gateway between the two worlds, and it was all for naught. He had been a son of the old gods, ancient and powerful in his own way, a man of honor and strength.

And now, everything he had been was so much dust in the wind. Meaningless.

Kied wanted to weep in despair. He had come so far, only to fail at the end, when the entire world hung in the balance.

The creature would come through the portal and create a link back to this world from wherever the old gods were trapped. They would return with a vengeance, attacking the gods of the Empire with surprise. The battles would consume the Empire, and mortals would die by the thousands.

The gods of the Empire fed on the worship of humans, so Kied had heard. The old gods would no doubt scour the great cities in an attempt to remove that source of power. Everyone in those cities would die. Titanic energies would be unleashed once again, and perhaps this time the mortal races would be wiped away entirely from the face of the world.

And then there was Laita.

Kied didn't want to die, but he was a soldier and had faced the possibility of death many times already. He knew that it was inevitable, and could face it without flinching.

But he couldn't bear the thought of Laita being cut down by this creature. She was close—he could feel it. This beast would tear into her soldiers and slay them all. Kied knew Laita, knew she would be in the thick of the fighting. He knew she would die on the claws of the beast.

And there was nothing he could do to stop it.

He watched the beast step up to the portal and peer through. It seemed too large to fit through the opening, and for an instant Kied thought it might not be able to come across.

But his hope drained away as the creature stepped forward. His eyes ached at the sight as the portal seemed to stretch wider, while at the same time the beast seemed to shrink down, until it crossed the threshold and stood here in this world.

The image of both the portal and the beast snapped back into place and a searing ache strobed through Kied's skull.

This was it. Kied's failure was complete.

He had failed to save his own squad. He had failed to avenge them as well. He had failed to save the people who lived in these valleys among the mountaintops. He had failed to save Laita. He had failed

Rotos.

He had even failed his father, who expected nothing more from him than to become a loyal officer in the Legion.

That loyalty had crumbled in the face of the reality of what he was being ordered to do.

And now, Kied had failed his race and his world.

Despite the enormity of the doom facing him, his thoughts returned once more to Laita. He could feel her, as if she was by his side. He knew now how much he loved her, and yet it was all for nothing.

The beast looked down at Kied. It stepped forward and raised its massive hoofed foot above his head.

With the face of Laita filling his final thoughts, Kied closed his eyes and prepared to die.

Chapter Thirty-Six

THE GREAT BEAST ROARED, AND KIED HEARD THE HOOF HIT the floor beside his head. He opened his eyes and looked up.

Three spears protruded from the chest of the creature.

With a swipe of its muscled arm, it tore the spears from its chest, and they clattered away on the stone floor, shattered into pieces.

But a shout rose up from behind Kied, and his heart nearly burst with joy at the sound.

"For the Empire!"

A dozen Legionnaires charged forward and drove more spears into the creature's chest, forcing it back a few paces before it regained its balance. Kied watched the men and women maintain a tight formation as they pushed at the creature.

Two more soldiers grabbed Kied and lifted him. The pain in his chest was overwhelming, and he screamed as his broken ribs shifted. The men laid him back down on a stretcher and rapidly pulled him away from the fight in front of the portal.

More soldiers streamed into the room and then Laita's face was looking down at him and Kied couldn't speak.

"Get him out of here and have the medics see to him immediately," Laita ordered.

But the beast, which had been taken by surprise by the sudden attack, had now collected itself.

Its great claws sheared through the spears and it lunged forward, tearing into the soldiers surrounding it. In an instant, at least a dozen men and women were dead, and the wounds inflicted by the spears didn't seem to have any effect on the creature's body.

Laita turned to the fight and began to bark orders, and the men carrying the stretcher started to move toward the tunnel entrance.

Kied reached out with his good arm and grabbed Laita's wrist. Something snapped open inside him and it was as if his whole body had suddenly been plunged into icy water. Laita spun around, gasping at the shocking contact.

"Kied, what …," she managed to say, and then recovered her wits. "You need to get out of here. We'll take care of this."

She tried to pull her wrist away, but Kied clung on with all his remaining strength.

"You can't," he said to her though gasping breaths. "We can't kill this thing."

The pain in his chest and arm were distant things. All he could feel was Laita's skin under his hand, every cell connected to his with some force, some charge that froze his blood and brought the entire world into sharp focus.

Laita stared into his eyes and he saw everything, her entire life laid out before him from the moment she had taken her first breath to this moment right now. He knew every thought, every feeling, every sensation she had ever experienced. And he could feel her in his soul, seeing his entire life in her own eyes.

They were special. He couldn't quite see what it was, what connected them to each other, but it was there, a thread that bound them together and gave them a power that was far, far more than the sum of their parts.

It seemed as if the experience of seeing her whole life took years, but he knew it was barely a heartbeat.

And as they stared at each other, lives ended on the claws of the beast that had invaded their world.

And he knew, just as he could tell she knew as well, that nothing the soldiers could do would harm the beast. They had no weapon that could kill it. It was from another world, and contained power that was beyond anything the Legion could handle.

But together, Kied and Laita had a chance.

They snapped back to themselves as another soldier died.

Laita grasped Kied's wrist and helped him to sit up. He could feel his broken ribs moving in his chest, doing more damage inside of him, but the pain was held back by his contact with Laita. He knew he was going to die when this was over, but he had one last thing to do.

"Commander ...," said one of the soldiers holding the stretcher.

"Change of plans," she replied. "Get us both spears."

The soldier blinked at her stupidly as Kied regained his feet.

"Now!" she barked at him, and he dropped his end of the stretcher and ran off to find her the weapons they needed.

Laita turned to Kied.

"Is this really going to work?"

"I don't know. It's the only chance we have, though."

He paused for a moment, and then blurted it out.

"I love you."

"I know," she said, and it was the truth. And he had seen the truth in her own heart, that she loved him as much as he did her, and that she wasn't yet ready to say it.

But that didn't matter. He knew it, felt it, and also knew that even if they succeeded, there was no way he would survive his wounds. He would spend the rest of his life with her, and though that might only be a matter of moments, Kied would cherish what time they had.

The shaft of a spear was thrust into Kied's hand. The Legionnaires in the chamber were fighting desperately, defensively, trying to hold back the creature that ignored their spears and swords. It ripped shields from arms, sliced through armor, and the bodies piled up as the creature fought its way forward.

"Ready?" Kied asked.

Laita nodded once and gripped his wrist tighter, lifting her own spear in her other hand.

"Don't let go," he told her. "If we break contact, it's all over."

"I won't," she said, and he knew it was true.

He raised his spear with his bloody arm, its strength having returned if only temporarily.

Laita signaled the soldier beside her, and he raised a trumpet to his lips and blew the signal for a rapid withdrawal.

Despite the desperate battle being waged, despite the mounting dead, the soldiers responded with precision and discipline. A gap parted down the center of the force, leaving an opening as the soldiers suddenly pulled back and away. The creature's talons carved through air where soldiers had been a moment before.

Kied and Laita charged.

Despite his injuries, Kied was able to keep up with her as they ran toward the creature. He raised his spear high, knowing that Laita was doing the same with her own.

The beast turned to face them just as they stepped into range. With all his strength, Kied thrust the spear forward. His aim was true, and the point plunged into the creature's chest just below its right collarbone.

Laita's spear impaled the creature in the same spot on the left side.

The scream that tore from the creature's throat was almost human, and Kied knew that these weapons had somehow managed to wound the beast.

Shifting his grip on the spear, Kied shoved on the haft with everything he had. Laita did likewise and the beast was driven back, pace after pace, toward the portal.

Despite its size and strength, it seemed unable to get purchase on the stone floor and regain its balance. Though it had taken a dozen soldiers to drive the creature back from Kied's body a few moments earlier, this time just the two of them continued to shove the beast across the room.

Its great hands grabbed the shafts of the spears and tried to pull them from its chest, but it merely stumbled backwards.

And then the portal was shifting in size as the creature was driven into its opening. The beast's body contorted to fit through the aperture, and with a last surge, Kied and Laita shoved forward until Kied slipped across the threshold of the shimmering curtain.

Immediately, he was weightless and flying through the tunnel between the worlds. Laita stopped herself from being pulled in and kept a tight grip on Kied's wrist.

But in the weightlessness of the tunnel, the beast yanked itself off the end of the spears and, reaching out, grabbed Kied's other wrist.

Kied felt the pressure building as he was pulled between worlds, Laita on one side and the creature on the other. The pain in his chest was returning, too much even for his connection with Laita to overcome. If the creature didn't release him, he would either die here in this non-space, or Laita would lose her grip.

And if the connection between Laita and Kied was broken, he knew that would be the end of them both. The creature would return through the portal and slaughter everyone in the chamber.

Kied felt himself screaming from the pain, though he couldn't hear any sound. He couldn't take much more of this. He felt himself losing his grip on consciousness, just as he felt his hand beginning to slip out Laita's grasp.

Behind the creature, a figure rose up into view, carrying a huge sword in one hand. Kied couldn't believe what he was seeing.

Rotos was a mess. One of his arms had been severed at the elbow, and half of his skull was stripped of flesh. Blood poured from huge gashes across his chest.

But his one remaining eye focused on Kied for an instant.

And then the giant raised his sword and he leaped onto the back of the creature, plunging the blade through its body to emerge from its chest.

The beast's great fist spasmed and it lost its grip on Kied's wrist. It tumbled out of the portal into the alien world, wrenching the sword from Rotos' hand. Kied was pulled back across the threshold to land at Laita's feet.

Across the shimmering curtain, Rotos regained his feet a moment before the beast. He raised his good hand in a final farewell, and then made a chopping motion. Kied knew he was signaling them to destroy the gate once and for all.

The beast rose up in front of Rotos and grabbed him by the throat, lifting the giant off his feet.

"No!" Kied screamed, as the beast pulled back its other arm.

With a single swipe, Rotos' head was separated from his body to go tumbling into the dust.

The sound of Laita's sword clearing her scabbard brought his attention back to his immediate surroundings. He still held her hand, though he could no longer regain his feet. It didn't matter, though. She was more than capable of ending the threat.

With a wide swing, her sword hammered into the edge of the ring surrounding the portal. There was a great cracking sound, and the portal flickered.

But it didn't disappear.

The beast contemptuously tossed Rotos' body away and charged toward the portal.

Laita swung again, and the portal flickered a second time, but then came back. There was a great dent in the ring around the portal, but it wasn't broken.

The strange effect began to form as the beast started to enter the portal. It began to shift and grow to accommodate the creature's immense size.

Laita tightened her grip on Kied's wrist and, twisting her body, pulled the sword back. She swung her arm around, untwisting her body to add momentum to the blade. The creature's torso began to emerge from the portal, but the edge of the sword connected perfectly with the same spot she had struck twice before.

There was no crack this time.

This time, the world exploded.

Chapter Thirty-Seven

LAITA DISMOUNTED FROM HER HORSE AND HANDED THE reins to the waiting soldier. She pulled off her gloves and stopped in front of the small tent, breathing slowly.

She knew they were all watching her. This was not a time to show weakness.

Squaring her shoulders, she took a deep breath. Then she ducked down and stepped into the tent.

A small lantern sat on one side, and a simple camp stool was set up in the middle. On the other side, opposite the lantern, was Kied's body, wrapped in a shroud.

Laita sat on the stool and dropped her gloves to the ground.

"You bastard," she whispered.

She could feel the tears coming, and she wasn't ready to deal with that yet. So she closed her eyes and took another deep breath.

"You really have no idea what you've done, do you?" she asked in a low voice. "You started something…something I can't just ignore. And then you left me to deal with it on my own."

She felt a tear run down her face and resisted the urge to wipe it away.

"You fucking bastard."

That last swing of her sword had shattered the ring around the portal. The backlash of energy had picked up everyone in the room and thrown them to the far edges of the chamber. The closing portal had cut the creature in half, and the explosion had torn its head and torso to pieces.

Laita, standing directly in front of the backlash, had lost consciousness. By the time she woke up, Kied was gone.

He hadn't even had the decency to say goodbye.

"This is *your* mess, you know. I was fine being a good soldier, a loyal member of the Legion. A successful Commander. And you had to go and destroy it all for me."

She clenched her teeth to prevent the sob from escaping. Her cheeks were completely wet now.

"And I can't even go back. I disobeyed orders. I killed a priest. I…I know too much."

She could still remember everything she had seen in Kied's soul. She remembered his life as she had lived it herself. Some parts were fading, but the important parts were vivid. She understood Kied as no person had ever understood another in the history of the world.

"You could at least have survived. I never got to tell you…"

It was too much. And there was no point to this. Kied couldn't hear her anymore. He was gone. And she had responsibilities to her soldiers. Those who had come with her were in almost as much trouble as she was. Some would no doubt end up in prison. Some would be kicked out of the Legion.

She and her squad would be executed as traitors.

"You saved the world. And no one will ever know except me. I can't even tell people the truth, not without making an enemy of the Emperor. I'm going to have to run, to hide, for the rest of my life."

That wasn't exactly true, and she knew it. Laita took another deep breath and wiped the tears from her face.

"Why couldn't you be doing all this with me?"

Laita picked up her gloves and pulled them on. She closed her eyes and took a moment to compose herself. She was a leader, and she needed to lead. It would be easy for her to just disappear, but she had an obligation to those who served under her. There would be time to disappear once everything was in place.

She stood up and stepped over to the tent entrance. She didn't want to look back at Kied's body. So she lowered her head and whispered to him.

"I love you, you fucking, *fucking* bastard."

Then she stepped out of the tent and went to take care of her people.

*　　　　*　　　　*

AMBASSADOR ZARTAY SEAPHON WAS BARELY CONSCIOUS AS HE rode, his body and mind exhausted beyond anything he had ever experienced before. One of the legionnaires rode close to him, ready with a steadying hand whenever Zartay threatened to slip out of the saddle.

They had ridden throughout the remains of the day and all through the night. It was pure chance that Zartay had managed to find these four men so far back from the fighting. He knew as soon as he saw them that they were attempting to desert.

It had come down to a single moment, when he saw in their eyes that they were about to pull knives and cut his throat. But their knives were nothing compared to Zartay Seaphon's own weapons—his words. In that moment, he had outlined the rewards that awaited the soldiers who would return the Ambassador to the base camp so that he could alert the Empire to the traitors in the Legion.

The men had seen the opportunity before them. They had gone from deserters to loyalists in an instant, the rewards for helping Zartay far greater than anything waiting for them if they killed him and ran.

By now, either the monsters had overrun the Legion and slain everyone—including the priest—or the tide had been turned and the danger contained. Either way, it was not safe for Zartay to be anywhere near the area.

Struggling to keep his eyes open, he silently cursed the woman once again. Dawn was less than an hour away, and Zartay expected to reach the camp by the time the sun was up. He would hastily compose messages and get them on their way, and then organize a proper escort for his trip back to Ythis.

There was no way Zartay would wait around for either the creatures or Laita Nashect.

The Empire's response would be swift and merciless. It would take some time to get the regiments of the Twelfth Legion into the area, but once they were there, the tide would soon turn. If Laita was still alive, if she had succeeded in overcoming the monstrous hosts attacking her forces, she would face the rest of her Legion arrayed against her. They would waste no time in eliminating the traitor in their ranks.

It would be a matter of honor.

Zartay gripped the reins tighter and fought the exhaustion that was trying to drag him down into unconsciousness. He had much to do before he could rest.

But it was only a matter of time before he would be back in Ythis again.

*   *   *

NAMAL STEPPED DOWN FROM THE RIDGE AND RETURNED TO HIS horse. He pulled himself up and met Laita's gaze.

"There's no one else coming," he told her.

She nodded once and turned her horse to face the soldiers who had abandoned the Legion. Over the last couple of days, word had gone out to those who were loyal, who could be trusted. In ones and twos, in small groups, they had left the camp outside that cursed cave, had snuck away from the rest of the forces spread across this region, and headed toward the west end of the valley. Now they had gathered here and awaited their orders from the woman they had chosen to follow.

Approximately two hundred legionnaires stood before her. They had formed ranks and stood to attention, their discipline and commitment nearly taking Laita's breath away. These men and women were her responsibility now.

Her instinct was to lead them away, to the edges of the Empire and out into the world. To save them from those who would surely hunt them. Two hundred soldiers—two hundred former legionnaires—would make a fine mercenary company.

But she couldn't do that. She had sworn an oath to protect the people of the Empire. And the greatest threat to their safety was the man at the very top, the Emperor himself. She couldn't just abandon her duty.

"As of dawn today, we are all traitors to the Emperor," she told

the assembled soldiers. "There is no going back, no forgiveness for us, no mercy from our former comrades. They will think to hunt us down, to slay every one of us. They will see themselves as the predator and us as their prey."

Laita's eyes scanned along the rows of legionnaires. No one flinched at her words. No one shifted in discomfort at the thought. These were the men and women she needed to accomplish what must be done.

"They are wrong. *We* are the hunters. We must be careful, for our enemies are more numerous, they have resources we do not have, and the whole of the Empire stands behind them. But they do not understand. They think we will scatter. They think we will flee."

She raised her voice as she drew her sword from its scabbard.

"They are *wrong*! We do not run from our enemies. We use our brains, we fight the battles worth fighting. We use the right tactics for the situation. Sometimes we must face our enemies straight on, and sometimes we must use stealth, subterfuge, and trickery. But we do not give up on our mission!"

She raised the sword above her head.

"We are not just the Legion! We are the only *true* Legion! We do not fight for the Emperor. We fight for the *Empire*, for its very survival."

She could see the effect her words were having on the men and women arrayed before her. They were committed, they were ready, and she had only to give them the word.

"Today we will split up into individual squads, to better travel to our destination without being found by our enemies. Bit by bit, we will gather inside the heart of the Empire. And then, when we are ready, we will cut out the cancer that grows inside it."

She cast a quick glance at Namal at her side. He sat impassively, knowing what was coming. Her pretty words and impassioned speeches wouldn't move him. No, Namal had seen too much to be impressed with this kind of show.

And yet, he was still here. He had decided to follow Laita into the dangers of the unknown. It wasn't her words that had impressed him. It was her actions.

I'll follow you into the heart of the abyss itself, he had told her last night. *I may be an old fool, and maybe it'll be my death. But I believe in you.*

His words had nearly broken her tight control over her emotions, and she had fought to keep the tears at bay. Her thoughts had turned once again to Kied, and she felt the desperate ache for him to still be at her side.

But he was gone and she was here. He couldn't do what needed to be done now. The rest of the duty was hers.

"Today," she called out in a clear voice, "we march for the heart of the Empire. We march for Ythis!"

~ End ~

The Undying Empire: Rebellion *story continues in book 2,*
The Traitor and the Thief.

Thank you for reading The Soldier and the Slave. *If you enjoyed this book, please tell others about it. Honest reviews are also greatly appreciated and are the best way to help other readers discover new authors.*

About Andrew J. Luther

Andrew J. Luther lives in Burlington, Ontario with his wife and son. He currently works as a communications professional in his day-job, but spends his spare time playing tabletop roleplaying games and writing.

You can keep up-to-date with Andew by joining his mailing list at www.andrewjluther.com or on Twitter @andrewjluther.